MW00737178

How I Became a
Fisherman Named
Pete

by

David Spencer

BASKERVILLE
PUBLISHERS

Baskerville Publishers, Inc.
2711 Park Hill Drive
Fort Worth, Texas 76109

Library of Congress Cataloging-in-Publication Data

Spencer, David, 1976–
  How I became a fisherman named Pete / by David Spencer.
      p. cm.
  ISBN 1-880909-65-0 (hard cover : alk.paper)
  I. Title

PS3619.P6443 H69 2003
813'.6--dc21

                                        2002014002

Manufactured in the United States of America
First Printing, 2003

For Tom Streett
1947-2000

How I Became a Fisherman Named Pete

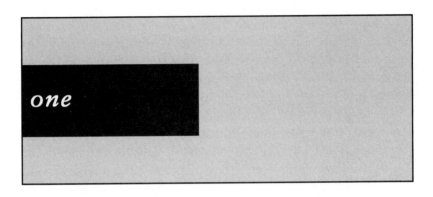

one

IT WAS THE FIRST TIME we had been on the roof since last summer. You couldn't come up here in the winter because of the aching cold and because of the strong wind that came off across the bay—you could easily get swept off the roof in a sudden gust. It was a sixty-foot drop onto nothing but concrete. On the warmer days, we usually came up here to watch the speedboats in the harbor while we ate our lunches.

Today we were hiding. Instead of eating peacefully, listening to Conrad tell stories of his criminal days, we sat almost speechless, listening for the clanking sound of footsteps—someone coming up the ladder. I had my hiding place picked out, behind a large pea-green air conditioner.

We'd been watching some drunken boaters getting ticketed. Conrad was mumbling in protest—something about how they weren't being subjected to embarrassing sobriety tests.

"Do you suppose it's safe to go back?" I asked.

Conrad thought for a second but didn't say anything. When he didn't have a solution to something, which wasn't often, he'd remind me that I was the dock manager and wash his hands of the problem. I didn't mind most times, but if we'd been caught up on the roof, we both would have been fired. With Conrad's thuggish background, I thought him more experienced with handling our boss. After all, I was his boss, and he rolled me over everyday.

But he wouldn't budge. After a couple of seconds, I offered to go down and look for Steve.

Steve was RHP residential shipping's general manager and the reason we were hiding on the roof. Every other month, RHP held an orientation for new employees. Young kids, probably freshmen in college, had to take an extensive tour of RHP's shipping area, the offices on the ground floor, and other places like the break room and bathrooms before they could start work.

Before the last orientation, Steve had rounded up Conrad and me to scour the whole building. We found out later that they picked us to do this because RHP didn't want to pay for the cleaning crew this year—they'd always hired a crew before. I was given the job of cleaning the windows and vacuuming the carpeted floor around the operators' and secretaries' cubicles. Conrad had to pick the parking lot free of soda cans and trash, which he did so slowly and poorly that Steve told him to stop.

"I'd like for you to speak to Steve about all this," Conrad was saying.

I had a habit of never looking people in the eyes and usually looked at my feet when they talked to me, but Conrad looked up to my face to show me that he was being serious.

"Tom, I'm not doing this every time there's an orientation." This was one of the rare moments that made me remember that Conrad was twelve years older than I was. He could be weighty when he wanted to be, making the thin lines around his eyes and lips as dark and pronounced as black twine.

"Well, what would you like me to say?" I squinted in the sun.

"Just tell him that he's slowing production down. He'll understand that."

"He's not, really. It'll be slowed down either way because we'd either be cleaning up or hiding. I'd rather hide."

Conrad, who had been sitting, stood up and sighed. "I don't think you understand me. We shouldn't have to do *either*. We should just ship boxes, Tom."

"But that's stupid. Production shouldn't have been slowed down because we were *supposed* to be working. What do I tell him? I can't say we had to miss work because we were *hiding*. He'll know I'm lying."

"You don't get it," he said more to himself than to me. "I'll talk to him, I guess." Conrad pulled open the gray hatch that led down to the shipping area and waited long enough, sighing and moaning, for me to stop him.

"Oh, Christ, I'll do it."

STEVE SAT IN HIS CUBICLE, talking on the phone. When I knocked on his cubicle opening, he motioned for me to sit in one of the two blue steel folding chairs in front of his desk. Steve was on a personal call, which surprised me greatly. The only person I ever saw Steve speak to personally was a teen-aged shipper named Terry—who, at this time, was drinking a soda and talking to an elderly woman at her cubicle; Terry had taken off her glasses and was now wearing them himself.

Steve told the person on the phone that he needed to buy some pants at the mall before they could get together. I assumed that he was either speaking to his mother or a guy. It was no secret around the office and dock that Steve had never been on a date in all his life. However, it was never rumored that he was a homosexual, which he wasn't. He said that people only marry because they either feel they have to, or they fear growing old alone, or they always need someone around because they simply can't stand themselves. To this, Conrad said—to Steve's face—"It's always the guys who don't get laid that say shit like that."

Steve was exhaustingly strange, and the target of countless rumors. He had coal-black hair that was always wet, which darkened the collar at the back of his neck. Among the rumors about Steve was that after every time he used the bathroom, he'd run his head under the faucet and pat his hair dry with a paper towel. Nobody ever caught him doing this because Steve locked the bathroom whenever he used it. Steve still lived at home and referred to his parents' basement as his apartment. He lived on Clinton Avenue and walked to work, carrying an imitation tortoise-shell briefcase, which contained nothing more than his lunch in a brown paper bag.

"I'll be home before seven, at the latest," Steve said to the person on the other end of the phone.

I still couldn't get over hearing him talk on the phone to someone outside of work. To me, Steve didn't even exist outside of RHP. He was like some specter that vanished like steam the second he walked out the two glass doors and into the parking lot. Steve's head, it seemed, had no room for the outside world, just as it made no room for women or men. There was only the sound of humming computers, screeching fax machines, and the deadpan chatter of tele-operators taking orders. He smelled only of printer toner and wet cardboard, and his eyes had capacity for nothing more than pink and white invoices, computers, desks, and policy manuals.

But, looking at these things like the invoices and the fax machine that was personally for him and file cabinets filled with employee documents and actual important papers, made me think about my own work area. My desk had only one telephone on it and a small black lamp. The only papers I kept on it were the weekly invoices, which were given to Steve every Friday. To compare his desk and mine was absurd. Steve was the boss. I was only the dock manager, a job given to me because I was the only one on the dock—including Conrad—who had a college degree, though it was only from a junior college. Steve had control over the entire building, whereas I had control over people like Terry and Conrad—one of whom was now flirting with an old woman, and the other had bullied me up to this office to fight with Steve. I was out of my league, and I was going to hang myself.

It was too bad that I hadn't remembered how important Steve was until it was too late. He was off the phone and asking me what I wanted. He placed both elbows on the table and rested his chin in the palms of his hands.

I had a lie ready about why I'd come to his cubicle, but Steve spoke first.

"I was looking for you this morning, you know." His face was scrunched up and bitter when he said this, and his voice set off a pang in my neck.

"I was on a box run," I said, and Steve let his face show he didn't believe me. But I said nothing more. My father once told me that if I had to lie, "Say as little as possible—keep it vague—and play dumb, dumb, dumb."

"Box run?" he mocked, as if he'd never heard the words *box* or *run* before. "Well, I need you to help out tomorrow, then. I need you to clean the break room before the tour gets here. Throw out any rotten food in the fridge, mop the floors, and see if you can get that orange stuff off the microwave door."

I agreed only by nodding my head. While Steve spoke, I always held my breath.

"I *wanted* you to do this today . . . but you weren't around." There was a pointlessness to the way he said that. He sounded almost sad, as if he could at least manage to make me feel guilty about not helping him when he needed me.

"Anything else?"

He thought for a moment, more intensely than he probably should have, then smiled and said, "No. I think that will do it. Just get that break room clean. It's embarrassing, you know."

I really did want to say something about making the shippers clean the building before I left, but I couldn't come up with the words. He wasn't drumming his fingers on the desk, so he was listening. He was sitting still, his left hand curled around his cheekbone, looking at me with the emotionless eyes of a snake.

Instead of saying what I had wanted, I told him that I'd get on the break room first thing in the morning. I backed away from him silently not once looking him in the eye.

Back on the dock, Conrad exploded. "You didn't say anything, did you?"

"He knew I was lying."

"Did he say he knew you were lying?"

"No."

Conrad rubbed his hand over his bald head. His scalp shone bright pink, as if his brain was boiling and about to pop out of his skull. "I could have said something . . . but instead. . . "

On the wall next to his desk Conrad had a calendar with girls washing cars in their bathing suits. He used to have a Playboy calendar until a shipper stole it. He was now using a cheap calendar I'd found for him in a dumpster behind a bookstore, with its front cover ripped off. After he hung it, he threatened that if *any*body took it, he'd urinate on *all* our lunches. Naturally, we took turns hiding the calendar everyday, and Conrad would threaten and cuss until he'd announce that he was going into the fridge in the break room to relieve himself, then we'd bring out the calendar from its semi-obvious hiding place (if we hid it too well and couldn't find it, he, no doubt, *would* have pissed on our lunches).

"Conrad," I said, my stomach swimming, "let's just please stack boxes before the trucks come."

"You do it. I'm going to have at it with Steve."

"*Don't.* Just leave it alone."

"I'm sorry, Tom, but you have to admit that you've choked on this. You're too afraid of him."

"I'm not *afraid* of him."

"Then let's just say you can't handle the situation. You're still a kid."

"I'm twenty-five!"

He laughed paternally at that. "Twenty-five isn't shit, I hate to tell you."

"Well, if I'm not shit, how come I'm *your* boss?" I said defensively. "Steve's only twenty-nine, and he's your boss, too. So be careful calling the people who sign your checks and keep you employed 'shit,' Conrad."

"You're both kids, is all, not *shit,*" the thirty-seven-year-old said. "If you go up there to talk business, it's just two kids trying to act like grown-ups. But if *I* go up there, things will get done. I'm not playing, Tom. If that's what it takes, I can bully someone like Steve."

Conrad could have kept arguing with me until my teeth rotted and my body turned to dust. He possessed a rare talent for penetrating any tiny hole in an argument, the way termites find ways into houses. Worse than his ability to dissect a debate was his unyielding patience. Conrad would let you talk yourself in circles before he'd finish you off. He could have finished me off easily, but I got lucky.

Conrad stopped when the first of the afternoon trucks

backed into the dock. We could tell the truck was coming before we saw it because of the wave of diesel fumes clinging to the smell of low tide that came into the dock.

We scattered around as the driver complained that his boxes weren't ready to go. The drivers always complained. That was nothing new. But this time (which was a first), the driver had reason to complain. He said he had to pick up his son from school at three-fifteen. Conrad told the guy to take it up with Steve. Then he said to me, "You're not just letting us down; you're letting this guy *and* his kid down."

More trucks backed up into the dock. The first driver sat in his cab, scowling at me and kneading a banana in his lap.

The sun was swallowed up by the rain-filled sky. It got so dark that the yellow sensor lights behind the dock came on. Gnats and mosquitoes swarmed around the yellow-orange bulbs.

I was putting some boxes from Scottsdale, Arizona into a pile going to Hunt Valley when Conrad asked me, if I didn't ask Steve to leave us alone, what did I talk about?

"He said he wants you to clean the break room."

It took us all about two and a half hours to load all the trucks. The man who had to pick up his son called his wife to ask her to pick up their kid instead. She must not have been too happy about it, to judge from the look on the driver's face while he was talking to her.

Terry came down to help only after the last truck was closing its door. Then he grabbed his jacket, punched out, and left.

I avoided Conrad before I left. I didn't want to say goodnight to him because he would have wanted to apologize to me about our argument. I wanted to leave quietly and undetected.

Although I was able to slip out of the dock without any shipper seeing me (I didn't even bother to punch out because everybody had gathered by the punch clock), there was one person who spotted me. As I put the key into my car door, the last RHP truck drove past. The driver—the man whose kid I'd supposedly let down—slowed down and threw the pummeled, bruised-brown banana at me through his open passenger side door. It exploded at my feet and speckled my shoes and jeans with dots of banana guts. I didn't even look up to see him give me the finger.

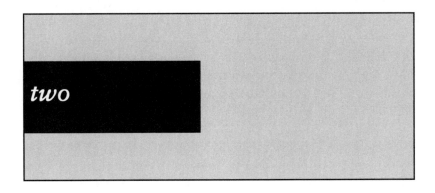

two

WHENEVER I HAD BEEN DISAPPOINTED IN MYSELF, I thought of my father.

On the day I was hit by banana shrapnel, I drove home in the rain to my one-room apartment on St. Paul street and slept immediately. I did not make myself supper, nor did I undress when I got in bed—I even kept my work boots on. Traffic was subdued on my drive home; I parked only a block away from my building. The rain that had fallen on my clothes and hair was drying as I lay awake in bed. My ribs fluttered when I thought of telling Steve to clean the break room himself and to leave the shippers alone. I *was* scared of Steve.

My father had died before I had a chance to impress him, so I made up for it by doing things that he would be proud of, had he been with me. Today was a setback. Every time I had volunteered to work extra hours and was able to load a truck faster than anybody else, I always wondered if my dad would have been impressed. He, no doubt, would not have been impressed with RHP—or with Steve and Terry, and especially not with Conrad—lugging boxes onto trucks would not have impressed Leo Banner. But he would have respected the fact that I was a manager. He always had commended hard work. When I was a child, I never saw my father too much. He passed away before I was able to do any hard work of my own.

My father had died the best death a cancer victim could hope for—a quick one. He went to his physician in the morning after being woken in the night by stabbing pains in his hip. For my father to complain openly about pain, and for that pain to be strong enough to force him to go to a doctor, was a terrible sign; it made my mother cry in nervous spasms throughout the day. My brother recalls her hiding in the basement, crying for an hour while she waited for my dad to get back from the doctor. I never remembered anything like that. "Of course, you don't," my brother told me later. "She cried in the basement so you couldn't see her."

My father came home and told my mother that he would have to go to an oncologist in Towson to run some more tests. The doctor's name was Martin Wen. I remember seeing his name signed with uncharacteristically neat penmanship on a prescription slip for pain pills that my dad had had to take. Doctor Wen, my dad had told us, was a short man with a deep voice who had his own suspiciously cancerous-looking black mole over his left eyebrow. My dad had said Dr. Wen couldn't stop rubbing his index finger over the mole as he diagnosed him with prostate cancer. Two weeks later, my dad died while taking a bath.

I was ten years old when I lost my father. It was late in the fall, when brittle leaves were in a clutter under the bushes and the sun going down was dark red in our back yard. When I learned of my father's death, I was listening to my teacher read us *Little Women* while we sat at our desks and she rocked gently on a rocking chair that creaked whenever her tiny feet touched the floor.

The school's principal and guidance counselor were the ones who came to get me out of class to send me home. They knocked sheepishly on the door and asked my teacher if they could see me. They stood so close to each other that it looked like their sleeves had been sewn together.

My teacher, a frail women whose skin was the same pearl color as her hair, had read *Little Women* so many times—every year to the fifth-graders for the last sixty-two years—that she barely had to look down at the pages as she recited the story.

Sometimes, when she recited from memory for an especially long time, looking down at the printed words only threw her off and she'd lose her place. She was a veteran teacher who should have retired before I was born, but she was deceptively smart. She knew the mannerisms and moods the administration employed on children. So my teacher knew what her visitors wanted. She knew I was about to be given news of a death in the family. She read the administrators' faces as carelessly and easily as she read *Little Women*.

When the two adults asked if I might be excused, my teacher smiled and motioned for me to stand. As I got up and pushed in my chair, she added, "Thomas, I think they want you to take your books, too, honey." I shrugged, grabbed my things, and walked down the dark hall while the two adults stood on either side of me, not saying a word to me or to each other. Above the gray lockers in the hallway were tempera paintings from my art class that my teacher had just hung. I looked for mine, one of a brown dog, but it hadn't been selected.

I *thought* I knew why I was being taken to the office, but I didn't know why Mrs. Hartly, our guidance counselor, was there. She was a tall woman—striking to a fifth grader—and I grew ashamed of what I had done as we walked down the hall. The echoes of her high-heels bouncing around in the cold hall made me nervous and sick; the porridge I had eaten for breakfast was burbling in my stomach.

I didn't want her there. She had only been at the school for a couple of months. On her first day, a pre-school girl asked her if she was Barbie. Mrs. Hartly was younger than I am now when she walked me to the principal's office. She came to us fresh out of a private college somewhere in western Maryland, and she had little hands-on experience with children and often became flustered by situations she couldn't help or control. Her first name was Shelly, but it would always sound foreign to me. Twenty-three-year-old women might as well have been forty, and they had no first names. She made me feel horrible about myself because I'd always be just a little boy to her—at best, a sweet one.

In the principal's office, I was asked to take a seat at a round conference desk at the rear of the room. Mrs. Hartly sat next to me and held my hand. I would have been the envy of all the fifth grade boys who made appointments with her with phony problems just to see her make-up and high-heels and her figure that looked nothing like their mothers'. One boy told her that he was contemplating suicide—before he knew what the definition of "suicide" or "contemplating" was—and he got the police sent to his house. Apparently, he thought "contemplating suicide" was a term for turning over a new leaf and not getting into so much trouble. He told her he was "contemplating suicide" with the casualness of someone declaring that they'd be getting a haircut. When he said, "You know, I think I should start contemplating suicide one of these days," she broke down and wept over the boy's cheerfulness about killing himself.

Mrs. Hartly rubbed her thumb across the back of my hand; the blood-red painted nail of her thumb scratched softly on the white of my middle knuckle. Because she was touching me so tenderly, I felt more ashamed for what I had done earlier that day. I almost began to cry. What I *thought* I had been in trouble for was what I had done in the bathroom after art class: I'd urinated into a trash can because there were too many boys in the bathroom, and I couldn't get to a toilet. I thought one of the boys had turned me in, which little boys loved to do. But my principal said nothing about me peeing into a trash can, and Mrs. Hartly kept holding my hand, even though it was uncomfortably sweaty.

"Tom, we need to send you home today to be with your mother," said the principal after he took off his navy blue sports jacket. His powder-blue vest was tight against his let-go-with-age stomach, and held a gold watch with a chain that had been broken but fixed with a paper clip. "Your mother called us earlier today and told me that she would like for you to go home."

"Why?" I said, still holding onto the suspicion that a boy had turned me in. "Am I in trouble?" I remember thinking, tell them you'll buy them a new trash can, or tell them you will at least clean out the old one.

"No, of course not," Mrs. Hartly said cautiously. "You're

not in any trouble. Your mom needs you right now, and she wants me to drive you home. Is that OK with you, Tom?"

I nodded, and the principal told me to stand and shake his hand. Mrs. Hartly went with me to get my coat from my locker, supporting me nervously and unnecessarily the whole way. When I opened my locker, she offered me a hearty, "Very good." She even congratulated me when I successfully buttoned my coat. Mrs. Hartly complimented my every step and breath on the way to her car. She was so beautiful that I loved every word she said. I didn't notice that every time she spoke, her voice was strained by stifled tears. She had cried for the boy who was going to turn over a new leaf by contemplating suicide, and she was going to cry for me.

Her car had velvety red upholstery. She had a cassette sticking out of the tape deck, which I wanted to see. I was curious about the music that a guidance counselor listened to. In the back seat of her gray station wagon was something that took my by surprise (and would have crushed the other boys in my class)—a white plastic baby car seat, which I found more depressing than the constant build-up of tears clouding her painted eyes. Mrs. Hartly was a mom. *Not* being a mom was what we found most attractive about her. She was, for most of us, the only beautiful woman in our lives. All the ugly secretaries and lunch ladies could have been wives and mothers, and we couldn't have cared less. Mrs. Hartly was a mother at twenty-three. I wouldn't understand how young that was to have a child until I was that age.

As a boy, I assumed everything—because everything was done for me. Mrs. Hartly was neurotically cautious about everything. She didn't want to pressure a child or give him false hopes about asking for directions to his house, as if saying: "You'll have to show me the way back to your place," would either embarrass them because most of the kids did not know directions or the street names back to their houses, or because they might think the attractive guidance counselor wanted to make men out of them. I didn't think of either. I just assumed she knew where I lived, because when she turned left out of the school parking lot, it happened to be the right way to go. She did OK for a mile, but when she drove past my road, I just assumed she knew a better way. She finally asked me if she was heading in the right direction. "You just tell me where to turn, sweetie."

"Oh," I said, "I think it'll be faster if you just turn around. My house is back that way."

She was too kind to get mad—as she very well should have been.

I had been distracted by Mrs. Hartly's foot on the gas pedal. She had taken off her right high-heel shoe to drive. Her toenails were painted the same painful red color as her fingernails. I hardly noticed that she was trying to keep from crying. She held her trembling mouth still by biting her upper lip. If she had blinked, tears would have streamed down her cheeks.

My mother sat at our kitchen table, still in her nightgown. I was embarrassed when I saw her. Mrs. Hartly walked in, introduced herself as the person my mom had spoken with on the phone, and stood in front of the sink; she didn't want to ask for a chair. Her arms were folded under her breasts, and she looked down at the floor. In the light coming through the kitchen window above the sink, I could completely see Mrs. Hartly's white bra under her pillowy blouse.

"Your father is gone," was all my mother could say. I knew that "gone" meant that he was dead. I had heard people referred to as "gone" in movies before. But this was nothing like a movie, so I was unaffected by it. My mother was in her ugly nightgown—I hadn't seen that in a movie, nor had I ever seen a movie with a beautiful but disheveled guidance counselor standing aloof by the sink and blubbering.

Mrs. Hartly exploded when my mother said "gone." She gripped the space between her eyes, as if she were trying to pull the front of her face off. Mrs. Hartly's crying, like her smile, was contagious. My mother *had* managed to compose herself enough to tell me that my dad was dead, but she crumbled when she heard Mrs. Hartly start to sob. I stood in the doorway and watched my mother get up and hug the poor girl. My mom was only momentarily distracted to see that Mrs. Hartly wasn't wearing her right high-heel pump. She'd been so nervous getting out of the car that she had forgotten to put her shoe back on. How she didn't notice, my mother and I did not know; we talked about the incident fondly many times since. My mother said, "Her heels were like *six* inches! She walked like a hunchback. How could she forget?"

I was glad that my mother was too preoccupied by Mrs. Hartly's wailing to notice that I didn't cry the whole day after I learned of my father's death. Mrs. Hartly, after she had collected herself and assured my mother (who thought she was a pretty girl who was too young for her job) that she was all right, bent down, put a hand on the top of my head and looked me in the eye. "When you feel like returning to school, you make an appointment to see me, OK?"

"I'll probably see you tomorrow, then," I said. Both my mother and Mrs. Hartly exchanged pitying glances.

"Tommy," my mother spoke up with a quivering voice, "I'll need you here for a few days. There's a lot I'll need your help with."

I stayed home for a week before returning to school. When I went back, I never did make an appointment to see Mrs. Hartly. She would only last another two years at my elementary school; the same principal who accompanied her to get me from the classroom refused to renew her three-year contract, and she moved back to western Maryland. During my rest from school, my older brother, Shawn, stayed with us, and I mostly watched television and played in the woods. My brother and mother would sit at the kitchen table covered in funeral home bills and brochures all day, crying and exchanging stories about my dad (which all took place before I was born).

Later it shamed my mother that I didn't cry once when I was told that my father was dead. I was ashamed of myself when I couldn't cry at his funeral, so I pretended. The faint smell of incense and dead flowers irritated my eyes enough to make them water. To bring the small tears out of my eyes efficiently enough to be noticed by my mother, I dug my fingernails into my septum.

I sat in a wooden pew between Shawn and my mother, in a too-big black suit. I stared at the venerable crucifixes on the walls and felt detached from everything. The funeral was not sad. My father lay in a silver coffin that looked like a big cigar tube, while relatives who sat around me wouldn't look me in the eye. The priest, who had never met my father, spoke of him fondly but mechanically. His speech was routine and bland, delivered with forced cheerfulness and littered with such theatrically dramatic pauses that his eulogy actually gave everybody a break from crying. The priest said anonymous things about my father, that he was a good man, that he sought strength and happiness from people, and that he loved God. My father was a good man, but he preferred to be alone, and the only time he had ever been in a church, except for his own funeral, was at his wedding. Then the priest read off a list of my father's hobbies and interests, which sounded more like a personal ad than a eulogy. After the priest was done, my brother was asked to say a few words, which he did clumsily. His speech was too long and directionless, and it ended with him crying so hard that an aunt of mine, whom I had never met, had to collect him off the podium before he embarrassed himself any further. If she hadn't got him, my brother would have stood there forever, frozen and weeping. People were coughing politely to tell him to wrap it up, but he couldn't move. I sat in the hard pew and covered my face in my hands until the whole mess was over. My nose was bleeding.

My father and I never had the chance to become close. My brother and my father were work partners and best friends. At fifteen, my brother became my father's apprentice at his contracting company. My brother hung drywall and roofing shingles and took over the business after my father had died. When I was fifteen, and Shawn was twenty-five, he turned me down when I asked to be his apprentice. I didn't have the right build, nor the coordination Shawn inherited from my father and demonstrated so effortlessly. My brother inherited my dad's handiness and strength, and other useful genes. I was handed down my mother's frailty and inability to comprehend math. I sometimes doubted that my father was really my biological father, except that we had the same green eyes. But however much Shawn inherited from my dad, my father's wit and charm did not go to him. Shawn was a talented and skilled laborer with an excellent trade, yet he was stiff, awkward, and charmless. If my brother had had my dad's charm, then his speech wouldn't have been so painful to sit through, or he would have thought it wiser to skip the speech altogether.

That my father and I were not close wasn't my fault or his. The problem was age. I was too young, and my dad was too old. My brother would tease me that I was an unwanted pregnancy, which I was—and so was he, I found out years later. Shawn would joke mean-spiritedly that I was a let's-sleep-on-it decision away from becoming an abortion. He said this to me when I was only six years old and he was sixteen. At the time, I didn't know what an abortion was, but when I found out a couple of years later, I was haunted by it.

The baby years of my life, the years I cannot remember, were great, I'm told. My father played with me endlessly. My mother had said, "He was always fussing over you or picking you up. He was never like that with your brother. I used to have to say 'Leo, put that boy down before he grows up hating to be touched.'" My mother told me that during my restless nights my dad would sometimes sleep in a rocking chair next to my crib and hook an arm over the cage door to hold onto one of my chubby baby legs. "You never walked or crawled," my mother recalled. "If your father was home, he'd carry you everywhere like you were a small pet."

As I grew older, my father developed serious back pains, from hanging drywall since he was twelve years old. So I never remember my father picking me up. The problem with his back was caused by the joints in his spine swelling after he'd been working all day. When he would rest at home on a leather La-Z-Boy, the tendons and muscles around his vertebrae would balloon up and keep him from moving. He would be fine as long as he kept moving, but as soon as he stopped, he'd lock up. My brother was lucky to have my dad in his prime, to wrestle with him until dinnertime—then wrestle again before bed. My mother described my dad holding my brother upside down by his ankle and swinging him like a pendulum until Shawn begged him to stop. This was when my brother was seven or eight, before I was even born. When I was seven or eight, my dad had to ice his back down or he wouldn't be able to walk the next day. And he usually went to sleep two hours before I went to bed. I saw him less than four hours a night, and during that time, he watched television and I stayed in my room.

The most I saw of my father was at my relatives' barbecues. It was always summer, and the warmth would help his back a little. I used to stand next to my dad as he played horseshoes, and he'd let me have the warm backwash of his beers. I loved standing next to my dad at these things because everybody wanted a chance to speak to him. Some cousin or in-law would wander up to my dad and make small-talk. They'd ask how the business was, or how our garden was doing, then, when they thought they had stretched out the small talk for an appropriate amount of time, they'd ask something like: "Leo, what's it mean when a radiator makes a *rat-a-tat-tat* sound just before it shuts off," or another would ask, "It's got oil and gas, and I just put a new battery in it last week, but the damn thing just won't turn over," or "Do you know anything about refrigerators?" To all their questions, my dad would just stare at the incoming horseshoes splashing into the sandbox and say, "I'll stop by after work sometime this week and take a look at it." Then they'd leave, and I'd wait for the next uncle or cousin to come by. When they approached my dad, I'd grab the back of his jeans pocket and pull myself close to him. This way, they couldn't push me out of the way (which some would), or, if they were able to pry my dad away from a horseshoe game, I'd have to be dragged along behind him.

Since my dad was less operable than he was during my brother's childhood, we had to find something in common that didn't involve wrestling or swinging me like a pendulum. What we found my mother hated: we were both fascinated with ghosts. On rare weekends when my dad stayed up past his seven o'clock bedtime, he'd tell me ghost stories and bloody war tales in the same rocking chair that he had used when he held onto my baby leg as I slept, always with a blue ice pack on the small of his back. Macabre and eerie stories—he enjoyed telling them as much as I liked getting scared by them.

Every so often, I could convince my dad to stay awake on a Saturday night to watch Hammer horror movies with me on *Ghost Host*. He never lasted to the end of a single movie because he always fell asleep. I would watch the movie in the dark, and the glow from the TV would make it hard for me to tell if my dad was sleeping, because his closed eyelids looked as if he was staring at me with white, zombie eyes. Like my dad's stories, I watched the movies to see my dad's reaction to them more than I watched the movies themselves. If my dad got startled, I'd smile, watching him in my periphery. If he admitted that a movie was scary, I would feel proud, as if I had made the movie myself. But my dad had said that he didn't like watching movies too much. He grew up in the days of radio and would rather *hear* a ghost story than see one. Stories about ghosts that were supposed to be real he loved most of all. He had an entire bookcase of so-called real ghost stories, and twice he read them to me outside at night with a small campfire. He read me stories of ghost trains that can still be heard from abandoned stations. Side by side hoofprints in England that stretched for miles and miles and seemed to go through walls and through trees. Figures of people who had died seen floating in the houses they had once lived in.

My dad's voice, deep and craggy, was perfect for ghost stories. He was an excellent out-loud reader, never stumbling, and better, never trying to be too dramatic. He just read the story the way it was written and let the tale itself frighten me. "Because it is *real*, is what makes it scary," he would tell me. "These things actually happened, and they could happen to us. *That* is what frightens me."

More than the books that he read to me, I liked to hear him tell his own stories or his adaptation of an already existing story. I never remember him telling me a story that seemed made up as it went along. But my mother proclaimed that every single story—except for the favorites that I had him tell me again and again—was made up off the top of his head. They were all excellent tales—for a seven or eight-year-old. And although I liked the ghost stories very much, they disturbed me when it was time to go to sleep. Every nerve in my body was alert to any moan, creak, or rattle to come out of the dark. As scared as I ever got, the only person who could calm me down was my father. But because he slept before the sun went down, he would be unwakeable by the time my mind started playing tricks on me. Once, as I was getting under my covers, I swore I saw a shadow dart across the opening of my closet. Earlier that night, as my dad sat paralyzed on his La-Z-Boy with his ice pack, he told me all about Bigfoot. Usually, before I fell asleep, I would just *hear* the house settling, and I could just put my head under the covers and sleep, but I actually *saw* this—or truly believed that I had. This was the only time I had to wake my father. "I saw Bigfoot, Dad," I whispered to him in the darkness of my parents' room. I begged my dad to come into my room to look in my closet.

"You shouldn't be afraid of a shadow, Tom," my dad yawned. After he said this, my mom spoke up in the dark room— nearly filling it with her horrible breath—and told me that if I was going to have trouble sleeping, then my dad would have to stop telling me stories. But I knew the stories were the only thing my dad and I had, so I left the room and slept on the rug under the kitchen table.

Ghosts were an interest of my father's and mine alone. I kept my brother out of it as much as I could. I had always tried my best to keep Shawn from having everything. My brother was able to have my father when he needed him. My brother had a father growing up—someone to learn from, depend on, and look up to. I had only myself.

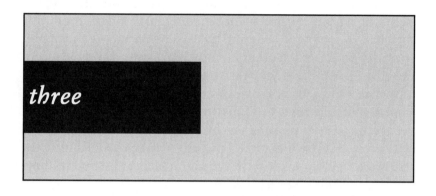

three

WHEN IT WAS TIME TO WORK ON THE BREAK ROOM, Conrad never bothered asking me to help him. He just grabbed me by the arm and said, "Let's get on that break room." To Conrad, every job was a two-person job. He always had to have someone there to talk to.

Conrad designated the chores for us. I was told to clean out the fridge, while he mopped the floor and scoured the microwave.

Everything cooked in the microwave exploded. No one ever bothered to cover their food with a paper towel or wax paper, and no one ever cleaned up the splattered bits of TV dinners that over-boiled and spat dabs of meat sauce on the white walls inside.

"Mother of Christ!" Conrad slammed the microwave door shut so hard that it popped open again. "These people are pigs, you know that? Goddamn pigs!"

I nodded but said nothing.

Conrad was volatile with his emotions. I had known the man for about four years and had seen him cry too many times to remember. It never surprised any of the shippers anymore when Conrad would sob. We all knew he had a lot to cry about.

Conrad lived in a row home which was an acting halfway house in Patterson Park. He lived with eight other men, all searching (under duress or otherwise) for sobriety. He shared a bunk bed in an eight-by-eight foot room with a former Pentagon employee who was addicted to cocaine. When I met him, he shook my hand and told me that if I ever wanted to fake my death, he'd teach me how—for fifty dollars. Conrad's room was big enough for bunk beds and a dresser that the two men had to share. To pass each other in the room, Conrad and his roommate had to shuffle sideways. Conrad slept in the bottom bunk, which was littered with pictures of his two sons—some of the photos he had copies of in his wallet, and he showed them to me all the time. If he began to brag or to tell me a story about one of his kids, he'd dig out a picture of the boy, aged to when the story was supposed to have taken place, and hand it to me to look at while he talked.

Conrad wasn't allowed to see his wife until he completed his treatment—at her request. This decision came after Conrad had dropped his two boys off at the movies, while he went to a bar until the movie was over. When Conrad returned to the theater three hours later to pick his boys up, he had seven Budweisers in his bloodstream. Seven beers is a lot of alcohol, but to a chemically dependent alcoholic—whose liver and tolerance had dwindled down to nothing over the years—seven beers was pure poison in his system. Conrad had made it about a quarter of the way home before he fell asleep behind the wheel and crashed his truck into a cottonwood tree that stood on the outskirts of a large fenced-in farm. His children weren't harmed because they were both wearing their seat belts (and Conrad had only been driving eighteen miles an hour). But Conrad, who *wasn't* wearing his seat belt, split his head open on the windshield and bruised two of his lower ribs on the steering wheel. The officer that came onto the scene of the accident said Conrad wouldn't have been hurt if he hadn't been leaning so far forward to see the road.

When the cop pulled up alongside Conrad's truck on the secluded road, the two boys were crying, and Conrad was trying to bandage his head with a handful of spade-shaped leaves from the marred cottonwood tree. With blood streaming down his cheeks and wearing a green wig of leaves, Conrad's first words to the dumbfounded cop were, "Please don't call my wife." Of course the cop *did* call Conrad's wife, and poor Conrad was committed to the halfway house in Patterson Park only minutes after the warm numbness of the Novocain around his eleven stitches wore off.

That had been six years ago. He had tried four times to complete the two-year program at the house in Patterson Park. He only saw his kids on every other weekend, and his wife would speak to him only once every two months until he could actually finish his treatment. "I'm not leaving you," Conrad told me she had said to him. "But I'm not staying with you. I won't sleep with any other men as long as you can prove to me that you're trying. *Please* keep trying, Connie."

But Conrad had been *trying* to get sober for as long as he'd been drinking. He'd been a member of Alcoholics Anonymous several times and had been to dozens of halfway houses from his home state of Ohio to here. His journey of sobriety made a Z-shape on a map, from house to house in Bath, Ohio; Pittsburgh, Pennsylvania; Charleston, West Virginia; and now, Baltimore, Maryland. In each state, he had been in about five AA programs and about three halfway houses, while his tired wife and children followed close behind, promising to stay loyal. His stint in the house in Patterson Park had been his longest. He had only a couple of weeks to go before completing the program.

Conrad's last setback was partially my fault. For his birthday, I invited him to my apartment for dinner. His wife didn't see him on his birthdays because it was supposed to give him an extra incentive to get sober; but all it did was make him cry more. It was awkward at my apartment because we both knew he wanted to be somewhere else, so I tried to keep him from thinking about it by talking constantly.

Another incentive Conrad's wife gave him to clean himself up were nude Polaroids she took of herself—which he would tastelessly show me as readily and proudly as he would the pictures of his sons. In each picture, his wife tried to look as seductive as possible, but she always looked disapproving. On the night I made him his birthday dinner, he showed me the latest snapshot of his naked wife—in that picture she looked especially hurried, as if the patter of the children's feet were coming down the hall and ready to burst into the room. She was kneeling on their bed and had managed to take off everything except for her blouse, which she left unbuttoned and open. "Look at what I'm missing," he said, forcing the picture in my face. I hadn't the heart to tell him that the first thing I noticed in the photo was that his wife had taken off her wedding ring. Her left hand was clearly displayed, resting on her bare hips.

"You want your present now?" I said, knowing that that would put the picture of his wife away. "It's nothing big," I said, "but I think you'll like it."

I had bought him a shaving set from Rite Aid. The set included a mustache trimmer, a box of foam disks, a mug for the disks, a bottle of after-shave, a box of razors, and two blade handles that were plastic but looked like jade. Conrad thanked me, told me he wanted a nice shaving set to have at the house. He then opened the box and laid out everything like a little kid about to assemble a toy model. He opened the box of disks, put his nose in, and breathed deeply.

"The men in the house will be jealous of this," he said as he counted the razors. He placed the small bottle of after-shave in front of him, twisted off the plastic gold cap and smelled it, too. "Smells like limes," he said. Then he dug out the plastic plug that only let out a drop at a time with his thumbnail. I wasn't sure what he was doing. Then, as sure as someone would dab a few drops behind his ear, he drank the green liquid in one gulp. Fat green bubbles rapidly rose to the top of the over-turned bottle. He packed up the set hurriedly and left my apartment without saying another word.

When he returned to his house, he couldn't cover up his breath. He tried eating Oreo cookies and potato chips, but they didn't help. He then made things worse by eating a red onion the way normal people would eat an apple. The combination of drugstore-quality cologne, the belch smell of potato chips, and the armpit smell of a red onion was making the other men in the house sick. His breath actually shocked some of the men out of their sleep. His roommate, the reforming coke addict, refused to sleep in the same room. The house manager was one of the men who had been awakened by the stench of Conrad's breath. He knew Conrad had consumed the after-shave for its alcohol, and he called me up to complain about it—but only after Conrad was safely outside, airing out his mouth, as the house manager put it.

The manager phoned me after it was decided that Conrad would sleep in the bathtub. "How could you give *him* pure alcohol?" he asked. "I've been so careful with the other men, but I've been *extra* careful with Conrad. You need to wise up, buddy. You need to be a better friend."

"I didn't think he'd *drink* it," I said. "Who in their right mind would drink goddamn after-shave?"

"Wake up, buddy," he warned me. "These poor bastards would eat a stick of deodorant if they thought they'd get a good buzz from it."

I looked at Conrad with pity as he wiped the face of the microwave clean. The scar on his head from where his head slammed into the windshield of his truck was like a thin crack in dried mud. His children were growing up without him, and all he had of a marriage were some nude snapshots of his disapproving wife—snapshots that came less and less often as he neared the end of his rehabilitation.

At my RHP employee orientation, there had been thirty people; the orientation today had seven. A folding table had been set up in the corner of the building which held doughnuts and coffee. The unimpressed seven new employees watched a video all about the history and expected future of RHP residential shipping. Steve stood at the back of the group, wearing a black suit that was too small for him. His arms were crossed at his chest and the sleeves bunched up around the middle of his forearms.

When I had to get the suit for my dad's funeral, my mom had me do what she called the "Frankenstein test." When I tried the suit on, I'd put out my arms as if I were Frankenstein. If they jutted from the sleeves, exposing half my arm the way Boris Karloff's arms did in his Frankenstein costume, I'd try on another one. The suit we bought was two sizes too big. "You need a suit you can grow into," my mom had said. Steve's suit looked as if it had been bought to grow into, but he'd grown too big for it.

The orientation was conducted by the head of Personnel. He wore a suit the same color as Steve's, and it looked as natural on him as a second layer of skin. He worked out of RHP's headquarters in Glen Burnie and only came around to give the orientations. He had nice, trimmed hair, and a nice tan. He looked out of place in the sun-faded add-on building of RHP.

The orientation was held at a pre-planned and misleading time of day: three o'clock. The sun was safely hidden over the building and all the operators had their sunglasses tucked away in their desks. The poor, bored people on the tour had no idea that from nine until noon, the place where they sat and ate doughnuts and sipped coffee would be as bright as the surface of the sun. They didn't seem to notice the sun-faded calendars and pictures on the cubicles' walls.

The video they were watching was almost over. It was a morale booster to get the new employees excited about joining RHP. For the first ten minutes they were just given a rundown of policy and procedure. Then the video bragged about what an up and coming business RHP was. The video stressed that RHP would not be in only Maryland for very long. It showed a yellow map of the United States with each individual state outlined in red. A cartoon RHP truck sat over the outline of Maryland. The deep-voiced narrator said that you shouldn't be surprised to see more and more RHP trucks on the road. Then cartoon trucks popped up over New Jersey, Pennsylvania, and Virginia. Every time a truck popped on the screen, it made the sound of a stone being dropped in deep water—*ploomp*. "RHP is one of the fastest growing parcel delivery businesses on the Atlantic seaboard," the narrator said. "And we keep expanding. We keep providing our customers with the most efficient and prompt delivery services possible. And our goal is to keep expanding and reaching out to meet the needs and demands of every person out there who is depending on fast, reliable delivery of his or her private parcel." As the narrator kept speaking, more and more trucks popped on the screen. "Our operations will soon be spreading to the west coast: in Arizona, Nevada, and California,"—*ploomp, ploomp, ploomp*. Soon, there were so many cartoon RHP trucks ploomping up on the yellow map of America, crawling over each other like vicious insects, that it looked like RHP was taking over the world.

I couldn't help but smile about the video. It was the same video I had watched for my employee orientation, four years earlier. RHP hadn't expanded; it was just treading water in Maryland, where the miserable company was about to drown in the black water of Chesapeake Bay. It would never take over the world.

Steve looked up at me as I stood, watching the tour watch the video with their uninterested, deadpan faces. I held up the putty knife I'd borrowed from him to clean with and mouthed, "All done," to him. He nodded, and I went to return the knife to his desk.

When the video was over, the tour people were talking with each other, eating doughnuts. The Personnel guy from Glen Burnie talked to two teen-aged boys, pointing to them with his C-shaped doughnut. Steve stood strangely aloof in the corner with his arms still folded like a pouting Frankenstein. He was told to be on hand in case a question was asked that the Personnel guy didn't know the answer to—but the current group didn't look like question-askers. Steve wasn't normally allowed to speak, so the people in the tour might think the well-dressed handsome man from Glen Burnie was going to be their boss. They wouldn't find out until their first day on the job that not only would the building be blindingly bright, but that the charming person who served them coffee would never be seen again. They had no idea that the gloomy figure in the ill-fitting suit would be in charge of them.

On my tour, I had decided to be nice to Steve. I felt as if he were being ignored. When we had our coffee and doughnuts, I saw him standing in the corner, looking as he did now. "So," I said with half a plain doughnut in my hand. "What's RHP stand for?"

He looked at me tiredly. "It doesn't *stand* for anything. The owner of the company just liked the way those letters look placed next to each other."

"Oh." I couldn't quite hide how puzzling I found that, nor could I successfully hide how rude I thought Steve was. Why bother hiding it, I thought, the other guy's going to be my boss.

I wrote Steve a list of what Conrad and I had cleaned and put it on his desk with the putty knife.

Something written on a folder caught my eye. My name was typewritten on the tab—Banner, Thomas—along with my social security number. It was my employee file.

Questions quickly surfaced. Should this just be sitting out in the open like this? Are they updating the files? Where are everybody else's files? Why is this file so thick? Why are there so many papers in it? The normal employee folder had no more than your job application, your resume, your W-2's and W-4's, and a card that listed anything you were allergic to. I'd seen the employee files before; the average file had maybe six to seven pieces of paper in it, but mine had around *fifty*.

I craned my head over the partition of Steve's cubicle to see if anybody was coming. The Personnel guy was talking to a girl now, still gesturing with the doughnut, which was down to a nub. I flipped open the file with one finger, and the first piece of paper I saw was a Xerox copy of the back of one of my old paychecks. The check was placed crookedly in the middle on the white paper and traced with black toner. The photocopied check was signed by me and had my bank's account number. A stamp was under my signature, canceling the check on the date I must have cashed it—sometime in late November.

I looked back at the tour. They were filing out over the cubicles. The Personnel guy was walking backward as he spoke. Steve never moved from his spot in the corner. He was staring at me. I shut the folder and walked to the dock, trying to keep myself from running.

LATER I APPROACHED Conrad about it.

"Let me ask you something." I lowered my voice and turned my back to the shippers. "Is it strange to see your employee file sitting out on Steve's desk?"

"No, I guess not," Conrad said confusedly. "Who else would

have it? Why?"

"Well, when I went to put the knife back on his desk, my file was there. Just sitting out in the open."

"So . . .?"

"*So*, what's it doing there? Why is he looking through it?"

"Well, I wouldn't say he was looking through it as if it were a newspaper or anything. Maybe he had to get some tax information on you, or maybe he had to put something in it. Why does it bother you so much?"

"I guess what's bothering me more than the fact that he's got it out, is just how *big* my file is. It was something like fifty pages."

"Is that a lot?" he asked.

"I think so. I mean, how big is *your* folder?"

Conrad sat up on one of the benches. He looked bored. "Actually," he said looking around the dock, "where's my calendar?"

"Forget your calendar! How many pages does your file have in it?"

"Well, I'd say it's only—" he paused. "Wait, you know what, I don't think I've ever seen my file before. Maybe fifty pages is a good thing." Conrad hopped down from the bench and slapped me on the back. "He probably pulled your file to look something up, and now he's going to put it back."

"Still, I hate the fact that he's looking through it . . ."

"Well, I don't think it's anything. I bet he was just looking something up for payroll."

"He can't," we heard a voice say. Neither Conrad nor myself had noticed Terry standing behind us. "Steve doesn't have access. Those files are kept in Glen Burnie."

"Jesus," I said, "the Personnel guy must have brought it with him."

Conrad admitted it was possible. I'd heard enough.

THAT AFTERNOON Conrad put a mousetrap on the seat of a forklift and Terry sat on it. Terry came to me walking as if he were holding an egg between his knees.

"I've been kicked in the nuts before, but it ain't ever felt like this. Something's *wrong*. I think something might be busted."

"I'd go to the hospital if it's that bad."

"You think I should?"

I shrugged. "Well, it wouldn't hurt. I mean, you wouldn't want to find out in ten years that you can't have kids because of this."

Conrad came over and watched Terry waddle away. He was trying to hide a smile, but I caught him. At least he had enough respect for me to wipe it off his face.

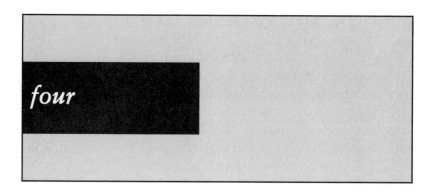

four

WHEN I PULLED INTO WORK ON MONDAY MORNING, I was ten minutes early. A few shippers and tele-operators stood in front of
the double doors of RHP, waiting to be let in. The shippers
huddled with each other; two of them shared coffee out of a
pea-green thermos with a silver cap. The operators talked with
their backs to them.

I sat on the trunk of my car and looked out over the harbor.
Fog bled off the black Chesapeake water, and the sky was pewter, threatening rain. The buildings across the bay—past the
harbor market and shops—looked rotten on sunless mornings.
The Domino Sugar factory sign sat unlit—its burgundy
crossbeams and thick frame looked like the rusted remains of
an abandoned Ferris wheel. Near the factory was a three-story
brick building that had been eaten to nothing by sea spray and
humidity; its roof had collapsed in on itself. Fog vapors came
out of its smashed-out windows like smoke coming out of the
eyes of a skull, something I must have seen in a horror movie
long ago. I wished I was in that building, buried under the
wrecked roof that lay inside, smashed down to the bottom floor.
I wanted to be nestled like a baby in soft, rotted wood of the
old roofless building, safe from Steve and my employee file.

Conrad wasn't in line with the rest of the shippers. He was
usually late, because the house manager preferred to bring him

to and from work. After I'd given Conrad the shaving set, and Conrad's release from the house was pushed back six months, the house manager told me that he would be keeping a closer eye on him. And now that Conrad was nearing the end of his treatment, he had become a personal mission to the house manager. "*This* one's not going to fail," the manager told me. "Until he's out of here, I'm on him like stink on shit."

Steve came walking up to the building, carrying the tortoise-shell briefcase, his hair glistening wet. The crowd of people out front parted for him to unlock the doors. I stayed on my car until everybody was inside. Then I walked around the building and pounded on one of the delivery doors to be let in. I intended to keep away from Steve for the rest of the day, just to be safe.

When Conrad had finally been dropped off by his house manager, he seemed genuinely worried that Terry hadn't come to work. We were slicing open a skid that had been over-wrapped in cellophane when he asked me why Terry hadn't showed up. I had to explain to him that Terry had taken himself to the emergency room after he tried urinating, and it felt like, as Terry described it, pissing a river of cactus needles and gasoline.

"Oh, Jesus," Conrad mumbled. "Will he be all right?"

"I think so."

Terry had called me at home on Saturday to tell me the horror story of his doctor's visit. His terminology made the story more painful still.

"They stuck a eight inch Q-tip down my piss hole!" he said excitedly.

"Your urethra, Terry."

"Yeah, they stuffed almost the whole thing down there to see if there was any infection. It looked like they were loading a musket!" Terry had been instructed to take pills that turned his urine the color of a traffic cone, and some muscle relaxants, because his damaged groin was causing him terrible cramps. "I was told to ice it down, on and off, every twenty minutes for a couple of days. I think I'll miss Monday." Then he said suddenly, "My mom and dad want me to sue, and I think I should. We're going to sue Conrad *and* RHP."

"Well," I said, "I'll be in some trouble, too. Why don't you wait until Sunday night to make that decision—for my sake, not theirs."

"Forget it, Tom! I'll leave you out of this, but Conrad's going to pay."

"Conrad *will* pay for your doctor's bill and a little extra, but don't *sue*."

Terry sounded disappointed that I wasn't showing him the sympathy his mother and father no doubt were. "I got tennis balls down here!" he shouted. "You know what that feels like? I'm suing!"

"Wow!" Conrad said as we gutted the skid, "as big as tennis balls?"

I told him I doubted they were *that* big. "Only people with testicular cancer swell that badly," I said.

I cautioned myself about telling Conrad about the suing. I didn't want to upset him, so I suggested that he call Terry before he returned to work and offer to pay the hospital bill. Conrad didn't bother denying that he was the one who had put the trap on Terry's forklift seat.

We took all the smaller boxes off the skid and placed them in their designated spot for pick-up. I was putting some small padded envelopes in a pile going to Baldwin, when Steve came through the two metal doors and onto the dock. From where we stood, Conrad and I watched him as he timidly made his way over to us. He stopped about thirty feet away from where I stood at the Baldwin pile and looked around the shipping dock, neither disapproving nor dissatisfied. I think it had just occurred to him that he didn't know what to say to me. He stalled by picking up a small package from off the top of a small hand truck, putting it up to his ear and shaking it as if he were trying to guess what was in a birthday present. Conrad moved closer to me as we watched him.

Steve then looked over and me and pursed his lips and said, "Tom—" He placed the package back on the handcart. "I'd like a word please."

AS EXPECTED, the new employees from Friday's orientation didn't wear any sunglasses. Where they sat at their bare desks they were squinting like moles at their computer screens. (RHP made all of us who worked on the dock wear sunglasses to protect our eyes.) One guy—whom I did not recognize from the tour but knew was a new employee—wore an empty manila folder on top of his head and typed freely. The folder helmet made him look like a Spanish soldier.

Steve asked me to sit in one of the aluminum chairs in front of his desk. He sat down and put on his sunglasses—more to avoid eye contact than for protection from the sky. He had my employee file sitting on the desk in front of him. He cleared his throat before he spoke.

"Tom," he began, "you didn't work this Thanksgiving, did you?"

"No. I never work on Thanksgiving—or on Christmas or Easter."

He opened my file and shuffled through some pages. He breathed in deeply as he scanned the papers, from top to bottom with his eyes, and his nose made a whistling sound when he exhaled. "That's what I have here." He lay a computer print-out from the punch clock on the desk. It showed all the times I had punched in and out of work for the two week pay period that Thanksgiving fell upon. "Yeah, I don't have a record of you working on Thanksgiving," he said. "And you're *sure* you didn't work that day? You didn't come in and forget to record on the punch clock or anything, did you?"

"Steve," I said, straightening up in my chair, "I thought you told me that I didn't have to work on Thanksgiving."

"No, no—it's not that," he said, still looking up and down the pages. Steve spent a considerable amount of time on each piece of paper. He slid the computer print-out from the punch clock in front of him. "You definitely did not work on Thanksgiving, that we're sure of." He wrote something down on the print-out. Then he was quiet again, looking over the pages, following over the printed words with his finger as if he were reading Braille. I was soothed by his even, deep breaths and the soft, whispering sound of his fingertip tracing sentences on the paper. He picked up his pen again and wrote something down.

My palms began to sweat as I sat motionless and quiet, listening to the constant, obstructed whistling of his breathing and the soft scratching of his pen on the paper.

We were silent for two minutes.

"OK," Steve said and put down his pen. "There's a problem that was brought to my attention about one of your paychecks." He placed the Xerox of my canceled paycheck in front of him, the one I had seen when I had peeked into the folder. "OK, did you sign this? Do you recognize this as *your* signature, not a forgery?"

I leaned forward and looked at the Xeroxed check. "Yes— I signed that. That's my handwriting."

Steve jotted something else down on a piece of paper, saying the words as he wrote them, "has . . . signed . . .check."

He was quiet again, putting all less important pieces of paper back into the folder. Now there was only the punch clock print-out and the Xeroxed check in his hands. He sat the two papers neatly in front of him and drummed all fingers of both hands on the desk. "Well," he said, breathing out strongly, "we have quite a problem."

"Which is?"

"Well, after talking with you and reviewing your paperwork, it seems that you didn't work on Thanksgiving. *However*, you have been paid for it."

I was relieved when I heard that it was only a payroll error. "Oh, well then," I said. "I didn't know I got paid for it. I'm sorry."

"You were paid about *eighty* extra dollars on this paycheck. You didn't notice?"

"No, sorry, I didn't," I said. "I never noticed. But I'm more than willing to pay the money back. I have eighty dollars at home right now. I could run and get it at lunch."

Steve sat still and looked the check over again. "If it were up to me," he said slowly, "I'd say fine and let you pay the money back. But, you see, this was discovered by someone over my head. Unfortunately, they found this mistake in Glen Burnie."

"Yes," I said, "a *mistake* that I didn't even make. This is payroll's fault, isn't it?"

Steve sighed. "You're right: it *was* payroll's fault when the check was issued. But it became *your* mistake when you cashed the check. And when you didn't pay the money back, it was considered theft."

"I didn't *steal* anything, Steve. This was just a mistake. I swear I never noticed that money. Let me call them and explain. I'll pay the money back." I tried to laugh it off, hoping Steve would join in, but he just sat there, transfixed by the Xerox as if he were trying to finding extra words in the dark trace of the toner around my canceled check. "Steve," I said desperately, "I'll pay the money back. I didn't know."

And when Steve didn't respond, I knew that I was going to be fired. My throat felt as if I tried to swallow a child's building block, sharp wooden edges digging into the soft membrane of my esophagus. I felt embarrassed for how irresponsible I had been with my money. How easy it would have been to just double-check the goddamn pay stubs. Forty hours multiplied by ten dollars an hour. I could have done it in my goddamned empty head!

"I know you want to pay the money back, Tom," Steve said. "I know you didn't *intentionally* do anything wrong. But it's their decision, not mine."

"And what's their decision?" I asked miserably.

He sighed and took off his sunglasses. His eyes were filled with sincere remorse. I'd had never seen Steve look that way, and it forced my gaze down, as if magnetically, into my lap. "They've decided to end your employment with RHP, effective immediately."

"What can I do?" I said, looking at my lap. "That can't be it—almost four years of work and then nothing. What can I do to change their minds? Tell me. I'll do anything, Steve. You know I work hard; I never call in sick; I never complain."

"I'm sorry but it's already been decided," Steve said, a painful permanence in his voice. "It's final. I have absolutely no say in the matter. If I did, I'd keep you on—and let you keep the damn money."

I sat still for an age. I couldn't swallow. It was as if my

throat was solid concrete, and my brain couldn't communicate with the nerves in my neck.

"I'm really sorry," Steve offered, with surprising tenderness.

"I'm sorry, too." I smiled at him and he, for the first time, smiled back. His teeth were white and straight.

I stood up and shook Steve's hand. "Listen," Steve said, "I'm not completely helpless on the matter. I may not be able to get you your job back, but I'd like to help out." I watched Steve dig a form out of a black file cabinet behind him. "Sign this and say you found another job." He slid the paper over to me and set a pen on top of it. "This way, it'll look like you quit, and weren't fired. You can still leave me as a reference if you need to, and I won't mention any of this."

I signed the paper, then Steve ran it through his fax machine and gave me a copy.

He shook my hand again and apologized again.

I walked out into the bright parking lot in shock. My body felt as if it were going to fall apart, bone by bone, muscle by muscle, nerve by nerve. As I walked, I had a thought: if my dad thought loading boxes onto trucks was a job for mindless dim-wits, how would he have felt about his son getting fired from such a job?

I WALKED OUT OF RHP IN A DAZE, with nowhere to go and nothing to do. My knees were jelly and my skin felt like it hung too loose on my body. I was sickened by my stupidity. The only thing I felt was hollowness, and all I had the strength to do was sit on a large flat rock behind the parking lot, a few feet out in the water. I sat Indian-fashion and watched the moored boats in the harbor. The rock was shaded by trees and moss grew on it. The trees had thin, blade-like leaves like silk-oaks.

It was very humid and hard to breathe on the water. I watched a two-liter Mountain Dew bottle drift past me, covered in bay slime. The bottle struggled against some jutting rocks in the water, but it kept drifting along the edge of the bay.

The water was oil-black and laced with rainbow pools of oil on its surface. The water seemed bottomless to me—like a black bog, consuming and devouring. I felt that if I ever fell in,

I couldn't swim my way out. I wouldn't even be able to float. The blackness of the water would drag me under; my body's physiological structure would change as soon as I was submerged in it, bones turning to steel, blood hardening into granite. I would sink forever. Drifting. Lost. Blind.

I sat, motionless, on the rock before going back to the dock to say goodbye to Conrad.

The operators instinctively detected that I had just been fired. I guessed I had an aura about me, because they couldn't help but awkwardly stare. Some smiled apologetically, while others examined the ground or their fingernails as I walked past them on my way to the dock. Seeing the tele-operators didn't bother me too much because I didn't know them very well.

It was the shippers I'd miss. The smell of oil from the train compartments that had been assembled in the ugly building a century ago filled my lungs. The seafood smell of the musty cardboard boxes cracked a smile on my face. I scanned the room and let everything soak into my eyes, like an image burning onto film.

Everything looked the same, but one part of the shipping area looked different. Conrad's desk was bare. His jar of pens was gone and his calendar was gone (it couldn't have been hidden because I hid it on Mondays and Wednesdays). Instead, the calendar and jar of pens had been relocated to my old desk. The calendar hung on the wall above my telephone, surrounded by snapshots of Conrad's children.

"I never asked for the job," Conrad said to me, standing defensively as if he expected me to hit him. "I was just next in line. That's the only reason they picked me. I swear I didn't ask for it."

I told him I didn't care. He was my assistant, and I understood that he would take over after I was gone.

"Steve just came down today and asked me if I would take over running the dock."

"Conrad, it's all right." I collected some things out of my desk, and he stayed on my heels, apologizing and gushing. He almost cried, as he did about everything else.

He hugged me before I left, and I promised to keep in touch

with him—even after he got out of the halfway house. I didn't say goodbye to any of the other shippers because I would have been there all day. I told Conrad to say goodbye for me.

I didn't go home after I left the dock. I stayed at a pizza place until about five-thirty, drinking cola after cola. They had sweet fountain sodas with soft, crushed ice. I sat in the corner and cleared my head. I stared at the uncountable copper bubbles that studded the inside of my glass. If I had thought of anything, I would have worried about money and having to move. The owner of the place played old songs from the forties, most of which I had never heard before. The only song I recognized was *True Love,* sung by a lady with a French accent. I listened to the song, grinning, with a mouthful of crushed ice that I let melt on my tongue.

When the dinner rush came in, I was asked to leave because of the shortage of tables and chairs. Suited twenty-somethings from downtown computer software companies came in herds. These guys piled in and unfastened their ties and unbuttoned the top button of their dress shirts. Their suits looked like they still had to be grown into. Some of the guys looked awkward and uncomfortable in the stiff dress shirts and creased trousers. Girls came in with them, wearing tennis shoes with their pantsuits. As soon as they all had ordered their pitchers of beer and pizza, they talked viciously about their coworkers and bosses. I hated them all. I hated them because I was sure not one of them would have missed being paid eighty extra dollars on a check. And if he had, I was also sure he would have had the courage to fight and get his job back.

THE FIRST DROPS OF RAIN touched my shoulders as I unlocked the front door into my building. It was raining in buckets once I was safely in my apartment.

I was sitting by the window at my kitchen table, eating two poached eggs with toast and watching the prostitutes outside my apartment run for safety from the violent storm. From the yellow street lights, the rain drummed on St. Paul street, looking like gold coins glimmering in a sifter pan.

Cars crawled outside my window and exploded through

oil-filled potholes. One car U-turned in front of my building and parked on the other side of the street. The man who got out was my upstairs neighbor, who sold handguns out of his apartment. He was dark and lean, with hollowed-out eyes and a long nose. I thought he was Persian, but he had no accent. His body was shaded with hair, which seemed contagious to me, as if shaking his hand would have caused tiny black hairs to grow in between my fingers.

When I first moved into the building, he'd invited me up to his apartment for spearmint tea and sugar rolls filled with peach jam. He spoke very politely and showed me some of his guns. I thought he was trying to sell me one. "This is a Glock," he explained, and held up an unloaded handgun. "It has less recoil than most guns because the gas from the spent bullets comes out of these vents here," he said, tapping on the top of the gun. "You can shoot it very rapidly without having the gun going everywhere on you."

He let me hold the gun briefly, just letting me weigh it in my hand. I was nervous with the gun because I was convinced that he wanted to sell it to me. I was also convinced he wouldn't allow me to say no.

"It is lightweight. It is reliable," he rambled on, holding the gun in his open hands as if it were a King's crown. Then he added matter-of-factly, "It used to belong to a cop, so it can't be traced." I gulped a mouthful of peach jam. "Now, I must be alone. It was nice to meet you."

He helped me up with his left hand, Glock in his right. I still held the teacup in my hand as he hurried me out of his apartment. As I stood, facing him in the hallway, he displayed the gun again for me to see, in one hand this time, with his index finger on the trigger.

"Now," he said, "if I ever catch you stealing my mail or my paper, this will be the gun I use on you, OK?" As he shut the door, he snatched the half-full teacup from my hand without my feeling it.

Now the gun-seller was zigzagging across the street as if he were trying to dodge the pelting rain. He was bundled up inside a bright yellow raincoat, and he waved to me as he ran to the stoop.

Crossing the street he was nearly hit by a white mini-van that stopped to let a prostitute out in front of my building. I recognized her as a thirteen-year-old girl that spent a lot of time on my street but lived nowhere near the area. I used to give the girl my newspapers when I had finished them. She had been stealing the gun-seller's paper until I caught her one morning when I was going to work.

"I need to know what time movies are playing," she complained. "I never know the movie times, so I just guess, and I always show up too early."

"I understand," I told her. "Just don't take *his* paper, OK." I omitted the fact that she could be shot if he caught her. "Tell you what, I'll just start leaving my movie section out on the stoop for you." Since then, she'd thank me whenever we happened to run into each other, and she'd tell me new things she was finding to do with my newspaper. She used it as a shoe insert, as long underwear, and sometimes, rolled tightly around her fist, as a knuckle-duster.

Apparently, my newspaper made a terrible umbrella. As she hopped out of the van and held the folded paper over her head, it disintegrated like the roof of the rotting building across the harbor from RHP. As she ran to join the other prostitutes on the stoop across the street, the paper was reduced to tatters in her hands.

I watched her as she talked with the other prostitutes. Her hair was cut too short, almost shaved, and she had a very boyish face, although at night, she slathered make-up on to look older. She wore red tennis shoes that were too big (but filled with newspaper, so it didn't matter), and a raggedy fur coat. Her coat looked like the material that Teddy bears were made from—but only after the fur was old and in dry clumps, from being slept with and cried on too much. Under the coat, I suspected that she didn't wear anything at all. She always had the collar pulled tightly up to her jaw line, and the tail of the coat went to the backs of her knees. At most, she probably wore underwear and a bra under there—assuming she was old enough to wear a bra.

I had lived in that one-room apartment on St. Paul street since I was twenty-one. My mother had become difficult to live with after my father had died. While she grieved, I loved and cared for my mother very much. She went into a depression after my father died, trudging through healthy bouts of crying and wandering through scrapbooks, being pulled into memories of fishing trips and Christmases and then repelled back to the reality of grief. My mom was sweet and kind going into the depression, but when she came out, she was a bitter, God-fearing woman.

When I still lived at home, my mom would ask me nightly why I hadn't started a relationship with God. I never gave her an answer because it would have led to an argument. My mother had become a spirited debater after her grief had subsided. Something always depressed me about the new view she had on religion. She no longer told me about a God who would forgive my sins as long as I knew what I did was wrong and truly felt sorry about it. My mom used to say, "God forgives all," or "God will listen," or "God understands." But now she never used the name God—it had changed to Jesus Christ, and he only loved a few, and he only let the selected into heaven, and he was to be feared. I, according to my mean-spirited brother, had once been a possible abortion. He claimed that my parents contemplated it very seriously and thoroughly. But now, at the mention of the word, my mother would wince in apparent discomfort.

My mother's change in attitude had cast a consuming black cloud over our friendship. Our relationship had declined into debates and pity. She pitied my spiritual state and I pitied her loss of identity. We still talked occasionally, but only when we had agreed to keep religion out of the conversation.

The day I moved into my apartment, she resembled her old self again. She walked around my tiny apartment and asked me if it was a safe neighborhood and if I had plenty of parking.

My dwarf apartment amused her. She was especially tickled by a piece of paper my landlord had taped over my sink. It read: ACCORDING TO MARYLAND LAW, IT IS ILLEGAL FOR ANY BALTIMORE CITY RESIDENT TO SCRUB OR

CLEAN HIS OR HER SINK—FOR ANY REASON WHAT-
SOEVER.

"I guess you better not, then," she said seriously.

When I had moved in, my mom gave me the kitchen table I
sat at now, and an old telephone that had once caught fire when
it rang. It was an item that she couldn't throw away because
she had used it when she worked as a secretary at an insurance
office. She had stolen that phone on her last day of work. "That
monstrous phone is the only thing I have ever stolen, and I
cannot seem to throw it away."

The problem with the phone (which caused it to catch fire
the one time) was that the ringer got stuck and rang for hours.
The friction of the little hammer hitting the bell caused a small
fire in the casing of the phone. My father had since fixed a
loose wire inside, but I couldn't help but get nervous when it
rang. I wasn't yet born when the phone caught fire but, from
my mother's exaggerated description of it, I had always expected
the phone to burst into flames upon ringing. However dangerous the phone was supposed to be, I couldn't bring myself to
throw it away, either. I felt sorry for it. Each day when I would
come home from work, I'd place my hand over the dial pad to
feel it for warmth, judging whether the phone had behaved itself while I was away.

My mom had helped me move into the apartment much
more than she should have. She helped me move my mattress
and dresser, and it pained me to watch her tiny frame struggle
with the other hulking pieces of furniture as we brought them
into my building. Although I lived on the first floor, the work
was exhausting for her. All Shawn did to help was lend me a
spare truck of his. Even then, when I went to pick the truck up,
he wasn't home, and his wife gave me the keys, apologizing for
Shawn not being there. His wife, Lisa, had always liked me and
was mad at Shawn because he clearly did not care one way or
the other.

I had lived on St. Paul Street for four years—Shawn had not
once visited me.

A truck slowed down to look at the prostitutes across the
street, and the driver apparently yelled something degrading at

them, because one lady threw an apple core at his bumper. A lot of people slowed down to look at the prostitutes. Some people gawked at them because they were the sick kind of people who loved watching car wrecks and tragedy. Some were curious tourists lost from Pratt Street and the Inner Harbor. And some pompous busybodies coasted by, desperately wanting the hookers to see the disappointed looks on their faces. But the only people who mattered to the prostitutes were the ones who were going to pick them up, and give them money.

A silver Volvo with a purple bumper sticker on the back windshield slowed down and stopped across the street; the sticker said MY CHILD IS AN HONOR STUDENT AT SOUTH HAMPTON ELEMENTARY. The thirteen-year-old girl threw down the wet inky remnants of my newspaper and climbed in. The car drove off, and I followed it between the fat trails of rain coming down my front window. Then my phone rang.

"Where have you *been*?" It was Conrad. "I've been calling you!" His voice was hushed, but piercing. Conrad had a habit of holding the phone too close to his mouth, which made his whispering physically painful to hear. He had to whisper on the phone, because there was only one phone in the house, in the television room. When he called me, he was sandwiched between guys watching a sitcom on a television that was mounted to the wall the way a TV is mounted over rows of liquor bottles in a bar.

"I was out," I said. "What's wrong with you? You sound panicked."

He didn't answer or explain his urgency. "Well . . .? What happened?"

I wasn't sure whether he wanted to know what happened while I was at the pizza place, or wanted more information about what happened between Steve and me. He sounded so manic I wondered if he'd been drinking. "I left work and had a soda. Why?"

"No!" he hissed. "What happened with the *police*?" This outburst caused a wave of shushes to erupt from the men around him.

"The *who*?" I brought the clunky phone over to the kitchen table and sat down. I braced myself for a drunken rant like the one I'd heard after knowing him for a week, when he'd dropped LSD and chewed on his fingers so badly he'd worn them raw. He had called me up with bloody hands, crying because he would have to start the program over again.

"Were you home around five or six?"

"No, I told you—I went to have a soda at a pizza place near here. I stayed there for a few hours."

Conrad exhaled loudly; it sounded as if half the receiver was in his mouth. I pulled the phone from my ear. "You must've missed them, then?"

"Who?"

"The *police*!" There was a loud *SHH!* "Don't you know they were looking for you?"

"Conrad—have you been drinking?"

"Listen, after you left, Steve called the *cops* on you. I'm being deadly serious, and I have *not* been drinking."

"What the hell for?"

"Steve claims that you stole $240 from payroll."

"It was *eighty*!" I snapped. "And I didn't steal it! It was a goddamn clerical error on payroll's part—and I got fired for it."

"No, no, you're right—It *was* eighty," he said softly. "You got paid for a Thanksgiving that you didn't work." Conrad explained this to me as if I had forgotten why I'd been fired. "You were paid extra on a check and you kept the money. That there is eighty dollars, OK."

"I know what happened, Conrad. Now why is it $240?"

He sighed "Two-hundred and forty is eighty three times. It turned out—and Steve didn't catch this until you left—you were paid for *three* Thanksgivings that you didn't work. So he called the cops. I was just calling to see what happened."

My body turned cold as I sat there. The hand holding the phone began to shake. "Are you being totally straight with me? The *police*?"

"Yeah, afraid so."

"Do you know if they're coming back?"

"Well, I'm sure they might, since they didn't get you the first time."

"How do you know all this?"

"Terry."

"But Terry didn't work today. He called in sick because of the mousetrap thing."

"No, he came in after you left. He told me all this after he was done hanging out with Steve." Then Conrad asked me, "So how come you didn't spot eighty extra dollars on your paychecks?

"I just didn't, OK?"

"Don't you look at your stubs? Don't you know how much you usually make?"

"*Conrad*," I said tiredly, "what does Steve want me to do about this? I have the damn money here. It was for June's rent, but I can give it to him. I can give it back first thing tomorrow."

"You damn well better give the money back. Terry says Steve's pissed—not so much at you for taking it, but more at himself for missing it. We're talking almost two-hundred and fifty bucks taken from under his nose. He's going to have to do some explaining."

"It wasn't *taken*, all right!" I said, offended. "At least, I didn't know I took it."

"I know, I know—don't get pissed at me. Just write out a check and get it in the mail." Conrad's whispering had turned to regular speaking and someone immediately told him to "stuff it."

"I can't write a check. You know I don't have a checking account. I'll just bring the cash in tomorrow."

"*Don't*," he burst in an odd whisper-shout, which received a few shushes and shut-ups. "Steve wants to put *your* balls in a mousetrap. If you show up at work, he'll definitely call the cops on you."

"That's stupid," I said. "What's he care as long as he gets his money?"

"He cares, believe me. Terry was up there for an hour today, trying to calm him down. Terry said Steve said that he even tried being nice to you, that he bent the rules and let you quit so the record wouldn't show you were fired. Steve's all business now."

"You think if I mailed the money Steve would drop the charges?"

"Well," Conrad said, "that definitely wouldn't hurt, but don't mail it. Never mail cash. Someone will steal it—especially if one of our guys gets it before Steve."

"Well, I guess I could drive it over and slip it under the door with an apology taped to it. You think I should pay interest?"

"No, don't pay interest. This was their mistake, so I think they'll be happy with what they get."

"Well, should I put it under the front door? Steve opens up in the morning—he'll be the only one who'll see it."

"I know," he said hesitantly. "But $240 is a lot of money to slip under the door. So many things could go wrong. Try sneaking it in while Steve's on lunch."

"Well, what if I just gave it to you," I suggested. "I'll give it to you and *you* put it on his desk. I could drop it off tonight."

"Don't get me involved. This is your mess, Tom."

"Well, Christ, Conrad, how the hell am I going to give it to him? You say I can't give it to him face-to-face, because the cops will get me. You say I can't put it under the door! You say I can't mail it! Goddamnit, what *can* I do?"

"OK, shut up," he interrupted. "Bring it over tonight, and I'll do it. *Jesus.*"

"Hey, thanks. I don't have to tell you what it's like to have the police after you."

"You know," he said, "this just might not get you in the clear."

"What do you mean?"

"Well, just to be safe, I'd stay with your mom for a week." Conrad knew me well enough to not mention staying with Shawn. Shawn would have driven me to the cops himself.

"You think that's necessary? Won't that be like evading?"

"No, I don't think it's that serious." he said. "You can only get in trouble for something like that if you *know* the police are looking for you. But you haven't seen them yet, so I'm sure if you pay the money back, everything will be fine. But just to make sure, I'd disappear for a bit."

"Well, I'm not staying with my mom. No way."

"Why not take a vacation or something? Go out west for a couple of weeks. Make the most out of this."

"Two weeks? Really, that long?"

Conrad was quiet for a second, thinking. "Yeah. Scratch the one week idea. Make it two. Definitely two."

"Where will I go?" I asked him as much as I asked myself.

"West. That's where I'd go."

I began to consider going west, but someone told Conrad to get off the phone. Actually, it was a male chorus: "Off the phone, asshole!" at the same time. Someone actually wrestled the phone away from him and hung it up on me.

I didn't see Conrad until I drove to the house to give him the money. The rain had stopped, and he was waiting outside on the steps with his roommate, the ex-Pentagon employee whose knowledge of faking one's death now intrigued me for the first time. Conrad's roommate was sitting on the top step wearing slippers and a robe, smoking a cigarette. His face was hidden in the shadows. Conrad was standing on the sidewalk as I double-parked outside the row home. When I was at my apartment and putting the money into an envelope, I was going to write Conrad's name on it when I briefly forgot his last name. It came to me after I remembered a homemade certificate the house manager's wife made for him, saying: FOR ONE YEAR'S SOBRIETY, WE HONOR CONRAD BEGG. He had this displayed with the many pictures of his two boys on his bunk bed. I gave the envelope to Conrad and thanked him, and he assured me that everything was going to clear up by the time I got back.

"Is this the one who's in trouble?" the roommate asked. Silver trails of smoke wafted above his silhouetted head.

"This is him," Conrad said, smiling at me.

The roommate stood up and stepped into the light. His face looked drained of blood, and his eyes were as dark as river stones. "And now," Conrad's roommate said, opening the front door, taking one last drag of his cigarette, "he goes away." Then he flicked his cigarette into the street, and I watched its sparks vanish on the cold, wet ground.

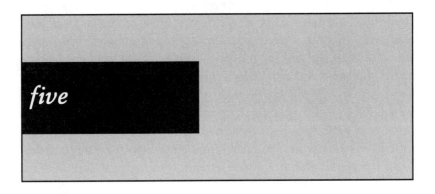

five

OUT OF THE MANY BOOKS that adorned his library on ghost encounters and famous haunted places in America, my father was particularly fond of a book by a man who had no legs. The 700-page paperback was entitled _They Are Still Among Us,_ by Dr. George W. Regal. Although Dr. Regal spent a considerable amount of time telling ghost stories and relating folklore of particular places in America and Europe, it was chiefly a book about how to find ghosts, not unlike a manual for game trappers or birdwatchers. My father lived by this book: it provided the bones for many of his own stories and he constantly read sections of it to me.

The home for the clunky volume was in the wire magazine rack next to my father's La-Z-Boy—my dad always needed it within reach. Its pages were yellow, its spine concave and cracked, and its cover nearly torn in half. My father must have read it (if not just his favorite passages) a half-dozen times. The only flaw my father found was the author's constant mention that he had been born without any legs below the knees. "He'll be talking about a tower in Scotland," my father had complained, "then he'll bring up how he never liked the artificial legs his parents bought him when he was a kid. It's very distracting."

Maybe the only reason the author made so many allusions

to his handicap was to guilt the reader into sticking out all seven-hundred pages plus (not including acknowledgments, bibliography, or index) of his dubious book.

"I bet he isn't even handicapped," I said once, upon looking at the author's photo, which was placed on the front of the book. Dr. Regal was wearing a navy blue suit with a red and white striped tie and sitting in a high-back leather chair. His beard was streaked with white hair around the chin. He had a conceited and bored expression on his face. He didn't *look* like he had no legs. The picture stopped at about his waist, the way Roosevelt had been photographed.

But my father respected the book, even though its premise was far-fetched. What was far-fetched was the fact that George Regal truly and passionately believed in the existence of ghosts, and worse was that he believed they were scarce and near extinction. He believed that nowadays we have to *hunt* and *search* for a ghost.

The book explained where to go to find a ghost, what time of night to go, and what season. "Despite the burdening handicap of being born without my lower appendages, I quite enjoy fishing," wrote Dr. Regal. "And, when I fish, I am selective of where to fish. I am careful to fish only where I know there are many fish to be caught. This is no different from searching for apparitions. One must simply go where there are the most ghosts. If I want to fish where I know I am bound to catch something, then I go to a trout hatchery. The same can be done with phantasms. And, it is well-noted that Gettysburg, Pennsylvania is the most haunted place in America. It is the world's only ghost hatchery." These were the opening lines to the only chapter I bothered to read.

WHEN CONRAD ORDERED ME TO GO WEST, Gettysburg was the only place I could think of to go. It was the only place I had ever really been.

After my father's first reading of George Regal's book, he took me to "the most haunted place in America." He didn't take me because he wanted to *see* a ghost or because we were going to *hunt* for one—he just wanted me to appreciate the settings for some of the ghost stories he had told me. There were many "haunted tours" available in downtown Gettysburg that would take groups of people onto the battlefields and to the outside of some of the suspected haunted houses in the area. All of these "haunted tours" were private businesses—the historical society of Gettysburg hated them.

My dad and I hiked the black battlefields on a windless night. The moon was very high and as small as an egg, but it was piercingly bright. As my father and I hiked, the toes of our shoes were drinking the dew of the grass. While we walked, he told me ghost stories and some true things about war that were horrible to me. Walking down a long aisle of a peach orchard just after season, he explained to me how German Hessians during the revolutionary war used to hold their bayonets at shoulder-height and aim for the throats of American soldiers. He ripped a branch off one of the ramulose peach trees and tapped my Adam's apple with it, saying, "They'd get you right here. Hessians didn't bother stabbing you in the guts. They had to know that you were dead."

My dad told me other things about war, like how some musket balls had collided in mid-air and formed together, how soldiers used to put nails and glass along with grapeshot into cannons, and how some flustered soldiers would forget to take the ramrod out of their muskets before firing, and they'd either blast the rod out of their guns, or else the guns would blow up in their faces. "I don't know what would be worse," my dad said, "being hit with a minie ball or a ramrod."

On the black fields, I could imagine thousands of ghostly soldiers fighting in white tattered uniforms. I could almost hear the sounds of their powder flasks clinking on the brass buttons of their uniforms and the frantic thudding of their boots on the ground as they charged one another. On a clear night, I wondered if I would be able to smell the ignited gunpowder and drying blood. I imagined the dead soldiers fought until dusk, when they'd slowly disappear into the fog that blanketed the fields in the pre-morning hours. Their bodies would vanish down into the tall grass and into the honeysuckle that devoured the stone fences.

The split rail fences that straddled the stone walls terrified me. The jutting black posts looked as forbidding as the crown of thorns on the Lord's head, displayed on many of my mother's crucifixes. I could almost see impaled officers on the posts of the fences, flung off by startled horses.

My father and I hiked miles through fields, Confederate graveyards, Devil's Den, and the thick woods. In both the woods and the fields, facing the same direction they did during the war, were cannons—turned aqua green from age. Every one we passed I slapped, and my hand would sting and go numb. The entire time we walked, my father was telling a story. It was the most I had ever heard him talk, and I wondered if that was the most he had ever spoken in his entire life. The only time he stopped the storytelling was when we hiked through the woods and had to concentrate to keep from tripping over the fallen trees. My dad didn't bring any flashlights to "ruin the mood." The soldiers in his stories didn't have flashlights, so neither would we.

As my father and I emerged from the dark woods, we came to a large field, marred with tall dead grass. We had entered the west side of Gettysburg National Military Park from out of Pitzer woods. The monuments in the field were hidden by the darkness. All but one. In the distance, sitting in the field just before a fenced-in grazing pasture, sat the Pennsylvania memorial. It was the height of a small cathedral, marble and granite. The hulking shape glowed in the moonlight. My father and I walked up to it, picking prickly burrs and twigs out of our hair. I stared up at the peak of the building and my knees felt numb. The dome of the monument had the radish shape of a mosque, and jutting from it was a statue of Winged Victory. With sword raised it looked like murderous bird ready to swoop down and snatch me.

But Winged Victory was perched so high, it was the least of my worries. There were other things on the memorial which were much closer and more threatening. On each of the four corners of the memorial, stood two ten-foot tall bronze sculptures of Union leaders. My father read their names out to me, his voice echoing as we walked around the gloomy building.

Our footsteps sounded like marbles being dropped on thick glass. "Curtin, Hancock, Birney," he read. "There's Gregg, Pleasonton, Reynolds, Meade. Then there's Abe."

I couldn't see any of the statue's eyes; the moonlight shadowed them deeply in the men's skulls. But I believed that if I could have seen their eyes, I would have found them all scowling at me. The faces were like death masks, and they moved; I was sure of it. In my peripheral vision, I could see the heads turn to watch me as I walked around and around the building and my echoing footsteps masking their muttering. I was sure that Commander Meade had turned so far from his perch that, if I turned around fast enough, I could catch him snapping back to his balanced pose.

It didn't take long for the bronze statues of the northern leaders to force my eyes toward the ground and away from them. Their bearded faces (except for Lincoln, he was clean-shaven) looked savage, their mouths appeared to be moaning as if they had been dipped into a cauldron of boiling bronze while they were still alive. I couldn't bring myself to look at them, which was hard since there were eight of them watching me like vicious gargoyles; one always made sure that he was dominant and threatening in my peripheral vision.

My father and I settled on the monument's parapet, and, by the moonlight, he read to me from *They Are Still Among Us*.

"Because I was born with a disability," my dad read, "I am denied the spiritual pleasure of exploring the battlefields of Gettysburg. With the use of my wheelchair, I can only sit, alone and uninvolved, and watch the haunted fields from Sickles Avenue, Wheatfield Road, Hancock Avenue, and so on. But the ones who voyage out onto the vast, rolling green fields can experience what I am denied. And if one is fortunate, when they explore the fields, they might just get treated with a truly glorious surprise. Don't be afraid of what you might find. If you see a figure, go to it. Embrace it."

I HADN'T THE PATIENCE REQUIRED to drive for a long distance. I just cannot sit still in a car for longer than a half hour. I squirmed in my seat as I followed Conrad's advice. I headed west—for

Gettysburg. I had no interest nor energy to commit myself to a two-week-long trip, but Gettysburg, I was sure, would keep me happy for three days at least. Maybe I could stay on if I earned some pocket money by washing dishes. Wherever I settled I could do odd jobs for two weeks.

Money was low starting out. When I packed, I pocketed all the cash I could find—a fistful of ones and fives, equaling a little over thirty dollars.

After driving for about an hour and a half, just outside of Frederick on route 70, I pulled into a truck stop to get directions and to rest.

The parking lot was overrun with Mack trucks. They parked in angled rows outside the diner. When I got out of my car, the sky was threatening rain and the smell of diesel rested sourly in my lungs.

I watched prostitutes climbing up to the cabs of Mack trucks and peeking into the windows. One trucker unrolled his window and a skinny blond girl climbed inside. The other prostitutes were being shooed away from truckers trying to get some sleep. One trucker was being harassed by a hooker while disposing of three two-liter milk jugs that were filled with urine.

I noticed that the hookers here were a lot different from the ones around my apartment. These girls looked a little more healthy, but they were dirtier. One girl, wearing a red sleeveless western shirt and turquoise spandex shorts stood in front of the truck stop's diner doors. She smiled at me, baring a mouthful of wrecked, rotten teeth. Her front tooth was as black as soot and she had gaps between her other teeth as wide as a pencil. She wore no shoes, and the bottoms of her feet were black from road tar and dirt.

She was blocking the way to the door of the diner, so I had to brush by her as I walked in. As I excused myself, she pushed herself against me, like a cat spreading its smell. I could smell her oily hair and the cigarettes on her breath. I reached behind me and hooked my thumb over my wallet as I slid through the door.

The diner wasn't as busy as I had judged from the number of trucks outside. I took a seat at the counter next to a guy who was talking to a pretty waitress and spinning a cellular phone on the countertop.

The waitress had dark brown hair in a ponytail. Her face looked pretty despite tired eyes and some lines from age and too much tanning. Her face was familiar, like that of a boyhood friend's pretty older sister after she had grown up. She slouched, but she was tall, and her baby-blue uniform was unbuttoned too far at the front, showing the freckles on her chest. I sat next to the guy with the phone and smiled at her.

When she said hello, I knew. It was Mrs. Hartly, my pretty but frantic elementary school guidance counselor. I didn't say anything in case she didn't remember me, which would make saying hello and having to identify myself embarrassing. I was sure she would remember me, but only as a ten-year-old-boy. I had aged and changed. Just as I was sure I would remember one of the monuments my father and I had visited fifteen years ago as being much larger and more threatening, she would remember me as being much smaller and more coy.

Mrs. Hartly and I had only one encounter with each other before my father's death. Surprisingly, our first encounter was more memorable than the second.

One morning on the bus ride to school, I vomited all over myself. I had become so sick so suddenly, I hadn't any time to turn my head or cover my mouth. I upchucked right down my chest and into my lap. When the bus pulled in front of the school, I sat frozen and horrified in my seat, covered in a hot, rank liquid that looked like beef vegetable soup and pooled in the crotch of my blue shorts.

Our bus driver was a farmer who drove the bus part-time and always wore a Cat Bulldozer baseball cap. We called him Zombie because he never changed expressions or yelled at us when we acted like barbarians. Some of us acted like absolute savages for the pure challenge of getting Zombie to yell at us. One kid even ricocheted a tennis ball off the back of Zombie's head to see him move, but we all saw in the rear view mirror that he didn't even blink. Zombie was a man who possessed the patience of a lunatic. A man hellbent for revenge always disturbed me more if he had a capacity for exhibiting bottomless patience. We could have easily laughed and had fun with a bus driver who would turn around violently while driving and scream at us through clenched teeth. But Zombie never exploded and never yelled at us; he coolly sought revenge when the chance presented itself by tripping a kid who was trying to get off the bus, or spilling a snotty girl out of her seat with a sharp turn, or perhaps by causing a kid to miss the bus on a rainy morning and have to chase after it in the blue trail of exhaust fumes.

But I'm sure Zombie never knew he would be fortunate enough to have one of his little terrorists puke all over himself minutes before first bell. I asked him if he would drive me home. I even said *please* and *sir*. But Zombie, displaying a frighteningly unrestrained smile, told me I had to go to the nurse to call one of my parents to pick me up. I thought Zombie was smiling simply because I had vomited on myself, but he was smiling because he knew that the nurse's office was in the heart of the building; any route you took meant parading yourself in front of countless classrooms and children. He even managed a little chuckle, maybe because the bastard knew very well that I had to see the principal, *not* the nurse, which meant that I would have to trudge back the entire way through a hail of insults from horrified girls and cruel boys.

The principal was busy delivering the morning announcements as I walked into the office. The secretaries all gasped at me as I came in. One lady in a pink sweater with a kitten printed on it pinched her nose and dry-heaved over her red typewriter. The secretary who was able to feign being sick at the sight *or* the smell of me told me to wait until the principal was free—in the furthest corner of the room possible and with my back to them. I stood, humiliated, like a cigar store Indian in the corner of the room, with drying vomit and bile crawling down my bare legs and dripping into my tennis shoes.

When the principal came out of his office, he told me to call my mother to pick me up. He even gave me a quarter to use the pay phone by the gymnasium, claiming half-heartily that the phones in the office were broken—phones that I heard ringing as I stood in the corner. Luckily for me, the pay phones were in a part of the building that was empty that time of day. After I called my mom to pick me up, I went back to the office and the secretaries told me to wait in the hall for my mom. I sat in the hall on display to anyone who came in or out of the office. This was when Mrs. Hartly offered to let me wait in her office. "So the *insensitive* people don't have to make him feel ashamed of himself," the counselor said bitterly to the principal (which may have contributed to her tenure being denied). I waited in her office, and she gave me a green trash bag to wear, with two holes cut out for my arms. We played checkers to pass the time until my mom came.

Although our two encounters were pretty memorable, she didn't recognize me when she asked me what I wanted to drink.

"Water, please," I said.

She set down the glass and went back to talking to the guy with the phone, but she seemed distracted and kept glancing over at me. I looked at the menu and pretended not to notice. She was listening to the guy next to me talk, but she couldn't help but look at me, suspiciously.

It wasn't until she gave me my late dinner, a bowl of clam chowder, that she asked me why I was so familiar to her.

"I *know* I know you," Mrs. Hartly said. "I just can't put my finger on it."

I pretended I didn't know her either.

She looked to the guy next to me and said, as if I weren't there, "I know this guy, and I can't think why or from where." Then she looked at me: "And it's killing me."

She still looked pretty, though not as pretty as I had remembered, and there was something very different that I couldn't figure out. Still, it wasn't enough to make her a stranger to me or to make her eerily foreign in my memory. The only thing that bothered me about seeing her was her name tag with SHELLY written on it in blue ink. It seemed wrong to me; it should have read MRS. HARTLY.

She shook a finger at me playfully and said, "I'll figure it out." Then she walked into the kitchen.

The diner seemed as if it hadn't been redecorated since the mid-sixties. The countertop was trimmed in silver chrome. The walls of the diner were sky blue tile, broken up with mustard yellow bull-nosed trim at the top. Above the swinging silver door to the kitchen was a wooden wall sculpture of two knights standing back-to-back, as if they were preparing to duel.

As I looked around the diner, I noticed again how empty it was; and then it occurred to me that I was sitting unnecessarily close to the man beside me. He sat to my right, and we were the only two people sitting at the counter. I wanted to move, but I didn't want to be rude. I know I would have been offended if he slid over to the stool to his right.

The man next to me was painfully good-looking—that is, his handsomeness made me feel terrible about how I looked. Worse was the fact that he *knew* that he was handsome. He knew that he was the best-looking person in the diner, and he didn't even have to bother to look over to make sure that he was better looking than I was.

But he did have his imperfections. For instance, he looked, much like the diner itself, trapped in time. He wore his hair like a greaser, dark and slicked back with *Groom and Clean* in a duck tail at the back of his neck. A few weighted-down strands of hair hung in his face down to the tip of his tiny, sloped nose. He was around forty, though the only aspect of his appearance that gave his age away was the silver hair at his temples. Both his arms were sleeved in tattoos, which a lot of people would have considered unattractive, or at least a wasteful shame to be displayed on such an otherwise good-looking man. He had a mishmash of large, intricate tattoos of seductive-looking female angels and, strangely, of homely weed-like flowers, interweaving around his wrists and elbows. All the tattoos were black and gray, which made his arms look like two post-like grave markers. On the face of his right forearm, he had a portrait of a little girl missing her front baby teeth. The light-haired girl looked about three years old. Under her picture, which was circled in poison ivy vines, the name SANDY was tattooed in Roman lettering.

Just then, the cellphone that he had been twiddling with his pinkie went off. Simultaneously, Mrs. Hartly burst out of the kitchen, remembering me. The man next to me answered his phone and walked off.

"I knew you when you were smaller," Mrs. Hartly said. She placed both hands on the counter in front of me and squinted in my face. "What's your name?"

"Tom Banner," I answered.

"Oh my God!" she shouted and put both hands on my shoulders. "Tom Banner. I remember you! I'm Shelly Hartly, remember me?"

I couldn't help but grin. Although my memory had embellished her good looks, she could still split a smile on my face. "You were my guidance counselor."

"That's right! I never would have dreamed that I'd run into you *here*!"

The man next to me came back. He sat down two stools away from me and slid his coffee over to his new seat. "That's it," he said to Mrs. Hartly, "that shit order was canceled! I'm free tonight." He smiled at her.

"Fritz!" Mrs. Hartly snapped at him. "Stop *cussing*. We're trying to turn this into a family place. With you truckers, all we here is F this and F that. Kids don't need to come here for that language."

He looked around the diner. "You have hookers out front breaking into trucks and shooting up behind the dumpsters and I can't say shit, piss, or bastard?" He sipped his coffee and snorted a little laugh. "Kids don't come in here, Shelly."

"This is one." She pointed to me. "Well, he was when I knew him."

I smiled, stupidly, and sipped my soup.

"I knew this guy when I used to work in Baltimore County."

"When you were a counselor?"

"Yeah," she said. "This is Tom Banner. He used to be the sweetest little boy in the whole school."

My ears burned and I sank toward my white soup. Then she fired off a round of questions: how was my mother, where did I go to high school, was I married, did I still talk to anybody from elementary school. The only question I tried to answer in detail was "What are you doing all the way out here?"

Though she was a waitress now, I still saw lots of counselor in her. There was always something warm and welcoming, so I told her everything (except about the police looking for me). I told her I'd lost my job, to which she responded with an "Aww," and patted my hand. I told her about the unfairness of why I got fired, and she pumped my hand three times, turning her knuckles white. I was going to say something about going to Gettysburg, but Fritz cut me off.

"I just told you I can spend the night here and you haven't said shit about it," he said, sulking.

She simply kissed her right index finger and put it to his lips, then turned back to me. "Now, tell me, Tom, what is RHP?" she asked. "What do they do?"

Before I could answer, Fritz cut me off again. "They're a poor man's UPS." Then he gave me a look that seemed to say: "Sorry, but it is."

"And they fired you because you were paid too much?" she asked confusedly.

Fritz took a cigarette out of his breast pocket. "That's bullshit."

I looked over at him and scowled. "What's bullshit? I'm not *lying*."

"No, I'm not saying you're lying. I just never heard of someone getting canned because they were paid too much." The unlit cigarette bounced in his moving lips.

"Why not?" I asked. "What's so unbelievable about it?"

"How long did you work for the company?"

"A little under four years, why?"

"That's it. They wanted to get rid of you."

"What the hell is that supposed to mean?" I said, offended.

Mrs. Hartly cleared her throat as a way of telling me to calm down. "Fritz, now I'm sure he doesn't have to prove to us why he was fired. Leave it alone."

"It's not bullshit." I said.

"Sure it is!" he said, which prompted him to get his own throat-clearing by Mrs. Hartly, but he ignored her. "RHP *finds* reasons to fire employees. That way they don't have to give them raises each year."

"It's not bullshit," I repeated.

"Boys," Mrs. Hartly said sweetly, "you need to calm down."

"No, I won't calm down, Shelly!" Fritz cried. "I told you twice now that my order was canceled and that I can stay the night here, and you haven't said a damn thing about it. All you've been doing is talking to numb-nuts over here about his shit job with a shit company!" He waved an arm at me, and I rolled an undercooked piece of potato, too hot to swallow, on my tongue.

"First off," she said firmly, "I've told you to watch your mouth. Second, I *know* you're staying here tonight; I was going to talk to you about it after I was finished speaking to my friend here."

Fritz threw his unlit cigarette down on the counter, and it bounced into my lap. "Well, I don't know this guy. I was just hoping for a little reaction from you, is all." He reached over and took the cigarette from my lap and sat in the stool next to me. "Jesus, Shelly," he mumbled, "It's not like I see you every day or anything."

"I know," she said. "But don't be rude. I get off in twenty minutes. You can wait." She was about to turn back to me, but something sent her off on a tangent. "What am I supposed to do, Fritz, jump up and down and scream? We never *do* anything when you stay over. We just go back to my place and watch TV."

"We don't go anywhere because you can't stay awake past one o'clock. Every time I take you to a bar, you complain about the smoke and the noise and all the *goddamn* cussing!"

"Oh, a *bar*!" She rolled her eyes. "I want to go somewhere, Fritz!"

"Where? I don't know this area too well. I just know the bars in Frederick."

"I don't care *where* we go. I just don't want to go to a bar." She reached across the counter, collected his hands and kissed them. "Fritz, Amanda's at her father's; I don't have to be home early—we can stay out late and do something *new* for once."

He smiled and shook his head tiredly. "Honey, I don't know any place *new* around here."

"You both could come with me," I said. I didn't see the point in visiting haunted battlefields all by myself.

"Well, where are you going, sweetie?" Mrs. Hartly asked.
"Gettysburg."

She smiled and clicked her tongue a couple of times. "I'm sorry, sweetie, but I'm sure everything's closed this time of night."

"That's the whole point. I was going to hike the fields while the place is closed. The fields are supposed to be haunted, you know? I read a book about it."

Fritz turned to me with a mixture of disgust and puzzlement. "What?" The word fell like a glob of mud from his mouth.

I cleared my throat. "The battlefields are supposed to be haunted. It's supposed to be the most haunted place in America. It's just for fun."

The look on Fritz's face didn't change.

I blinked at him a few times. The diner was so quiet I could hear the clanking sound of a man in a booth spooning his soup. Mrs. Hartly laughed nervously to lighten Fritz up, but he just looked at me indignantly without saying a word.

I knew what would make him stop. I looked up at Mrs. Hartly and said, "You see, my dad took me there just before he died." And that set the former guidance counselor into motion. She could smell the tempera paint drying on pictures in the hall, and the squeaking footsteps from children echoed in her head. She took control. We would go to Gettysburg. Fritz would stop cussing. And we would have fun—all because a former student needed her.

FRITZ HAD AGREED TO COME under two conditions: one, Mrs. Hartly had to bring a case of beer from the diner, and two, one of us had to drink with him. I was finishing my fifth beer as we all lay on our backs in the belly of the Pennsylvania memorial. Fritz had drunk seven beers, and was still pretty much sober; the only effect the alcohol had on him was that it dispelled his coolness a little. He lay on his back with a beer balancing on his chest and Mrs. Hartly's head on his right shoulder. She had fallen asleep at exactly twelve-thirty. The five beers swimming in my bloodstream blunted the concern I had as to how I would get back to my car. Mrs. Hartly had insisted on driving. "If you boys are going to be drinking, I think we should take my car."

It was the same gray station wagon she had when she drove me home the day my dad died. I sat in the back where the baby car seat had once been. Fritz sat up front and smoked. Mrs. Hartly drove with her hand in his lap, and I made a point of peeking to see if she took off her right shoe to drive; she didn't. Although it was my suggestion that they come along, I was uneasy as I sat in the back seat. The drive was thirty minutes, and I never said a word. I just watched Mrs. Hartly's face in the rear view mirror and looked away when she glanced back at me.

When we got to the memorial, I gave Fritz and Mrs. Hartly a chance to be alone. I walked along the auto tour road with a beer as they kissed and cuddled on the parapet. The winds on the fields were strong and the black-orange sky, just over the horizon, shone gold where the University of Gettysburg was. As I walked on the road, I was disappointed that neither the fields nor the memorial evoked any strong emotions in me. I hadn't expected to be swept away in a flood of visions of my father—because I hadn't that many. I did expect to feel at least *something*, happiness or sadness.

But I didn't.

I even tried to force it, like I had when I couldn't cry at my dad's funeral. I forced myself to picture my father's face as he told me a story. But I couldn't feel anything.

When I walked back to the memorial, I cleared my throat to give Fritz and Mrs. Hartly a warning that I was coming. When they saw me they disengaged quickly. Mrs. Hartly pulled her skirt back down. I started to leave, but Fritz assured me— much to Mrs. Hartly's embarrassment—that they were done doing whatever it was they had been doing.

After she had fallen asleep, Fritz and I started to talk to each other, side by side, his feet at my head and my feet at his head. I had a hard time finishing my sentences because I was drunk, but Fritz chatted calmly. Seven beers was the same amount Conrad had consumed the night he wrecked the car with his boys inside. If Fritz had been driving, the boys would have been fine. And if I had been driving, with only my five beers, those kids would have been dead.

But through the lovely fog brought by alcohol, I noticed two things I couldn't pick up on when I was sober. First—as pretty as Mrs. Hartly was, she looked mismatched with Fritz. Seeing them together had made me realize that Fritz was slightly too handsome for her. And as she mumbled nonsense in her sleep, using the tattooed trucker's upper thigh as a pillow, I noticed something else that had been bothering me since the diner. It wasn't just age that had changed her, there was something in the way she talked and in the way she carried herself. Mrs. Hartly was happy. She might have been a waitress in a dingy diner, but she had found a cleansing focus.

"So," Fritz whispered after his seventh beer was gone, "what'll you do now? For money, I mean?"

"Fritz, the police were looking for me."

He propped himself up on his elbows. "The police?"

"Yeah," I said, "the money I was overpaid was reported stolen."

"So what are you going to do?"

I sat up too; my head felt as if it was filled with marbles. "I paid the money back, now I'm going to hang out here for a couple of weeks."

"Doing what? You just going to hike the fields, looking for ghosts?"

"No, no—I don't believe in any of that; it's just something I was into when I was a kid. I thought it'd still be fun, but I guess not. I'm going to hang around here for a couple of weeks, then I'll go back, and, hopefully everything will blow over."

"Yeah, but what are you going to do *here*? Where're you going to stay?"

My body weight became too much and I slumped over on my side, my forehead rested on the hard marble and my mouth hung open. "I'll stay in my car; I don't know," I said irritably. "I'll make some pocket money washing dishes or painting fences or cutting grass. I'll do *something*."

"You're just going to knock on doors and ask if you can paint somebody's fence or cut their grass. You got paint or a lawn mower?"

I groaned. "I'm just saying…" My body felt as if it had just been pushed down a steep hill, spinning upside-down and sideways.

"Anybody going to miss you? You got a girlfriend back home?"

I moaned again, talking was making me nauseous. My jaw muscles tightened and my stomach bubbled every time I formed a word with my lips. "No. No, I don't have a girlfriend. I only have a thirty-something-year-old alcoholic who drinks aftershave. Now shut up and leave me alone. I feel sick."

Fritz sat up, and I heard Mrs. Hartly's head thud on the marble. "*Hey*, the fucking hell, Fritz?" she mumbled.

"Sorry, sorry," he whispered. Fritz scooted over and knelt above me. He took off his western shirt, I could hear the pearl-colored buttons pop undone. He settled the shirt over me like a blanket and sat down near my head.

"Forget this place, you hear me? You ain't going to find shit to do around here. You'll stay here for two days and run out of money, or worse, you'll be picked up for loitering." I tried to nod in agreement but my forehead was mashed into the marble floor. Fritz lit a cigarette; the light cracked my skull. "A place like this, I hate to tell you because you think it's neat because of ghosts or something, isn't meant for a man trying to make some spending cash. This is a tourist trap. They don't want you around here, and they won't be shy about telling you." He paused. "You listening to me? I'm telling you what to do."

"Yeah, I hear you," I mumbled.

"Good. Do you know where Dewey Beach is?" I didn't answer, so he slapped me on the back of the head. "Do you know where Dewey Beach is?" he repeated.

"Godamnit, yes," I moaned.

"I grew up there. I used to sell beach umbrellas all day, then me and my buddies would pick up girls, get some beer, and sleep all night on blankets on the beach. Every night I'd get a new girl. They'd be in their twenties and I was only fifteen."

"Good for you. I don't care. I told you I feel sick."

He slapped my head again. "Just listen, numb-nuts! OK, so, that job selling umbrellas was under-the-table and temporary—me and my buddies would do shit like sell beach umbrellas, fiberglass boats, shuck oysters in bars. Everyday we had a new job. That's just the way it is. There are a lot of people there who have odd jobs for someone to do. But even though we'd work all day, we'd still go out looking for girls. What do you think about that?"

"I don't know."

"Jesus," he moaned. "It's perfect for you. You can make some money, have some fun, sleep on the beach—you can do whatever you want. Hell, that's what I did all through high school. I don't think during the summer I even saw my parents."

"What would I do there? I don't know who needs help."

"Go there and see my niece, Leah. She can find you a job—guaranteed. I'll give you directions and her number. She works at a bar called Paradise. My brother owns the place."

". . . I don't know."

"What do you mean, you don't know? Do what I tell you. I'm trying to help you out. I'm not asking you what you want to do."

Fritz kept talking about adventurous things he did growing up as I tried to stop my head from spinning. He told me about all the jobs he had been fired from. His voice was being pinched from sleep; the words sounded like they were coming to me under water.

"You should be thankful that RHP let you go," I remember him saying. "Why does it bother you so much?"

With my left ear creating suction against the hard marble, I could hear my heartbeat and the blood pulsing around inside my head. Fritz's voice and Mrs. Hartly's snoring and the sound of my rushing blood melted into the distant sound of waves. My heartbeat slowed. The marble became warm and forgiving like sand as I was carried off into a dream.

I was on a beach. The sky was boiling with dark gray clouds. The water was pine green and crashed in unison with my heart as it pulled in and pushed out blood.

In the distance, a solitary figure sat in a wheelchair on the beach. He wore a navy blue suit with a red and white striped tie. Nobody else was around, no seagulls were swooping down to collect hermit crabs from the sand. There was just one man. I was about a hundred yards away, and the figure waved to me. The wind was spraying sand into my eyes. Everything was quiet. I walked on the warm sand and stopped about eighty yards away when I saw the invalid's face.

It was my father.

And I went to him.

six

I WOKE WITHOUT THE SLIGHTEST TINGE OF A HANGOVER, yet I woke in pain.

The first thing I saw that morning was a fat trail of rain trickling down the window of my back seat passenger door. It looked like a crystal furrow running down a slab of pewter. The rain was fine and warm, and sounded like sizzling bacon on my roof.

It took me a few minutes to realize where I was. My back ached from the cold air and from a safety buckle that had imbedded itself between my shoulder blades. My jacket had been pulled out of my duffel bag and stuffed under my head, but nothing covered my body, which trembled from the cold. As my brain focused through the dull haze of sleep, I felt a stinging burn under my chin.

When I sat up in the seat, I noticed that I had a map stapled to the front of my shirt. The edges of the paper had rubbed against the skin under my chin all night, and I was bleeding. It was a map of Maryland, torn from an ADC road atlas. Frederick had been circled in pink highlighter, and so had Dewey Beach. Fritz had highlighted the entire route. Written on the map (in the light blue gap of the Chesapeake Bay) was a note, which read: HERE'S HOW TO GET TO DEWEY BEACH. GO TO PARADISE BAR AND GRILL ON ROUTE ONE AND ASK

FOR LEAH GREENE. SHE WILL FIND YOU WORK. FRITZ.

His note bothered me for many reasons. At first, I thought the message was the shortest thing he could have possibly written. He didn't wish me well, didn't say he had fun last night, nor did he mention how I got to my car. Fritz had been ordering me around so much last night that I was disappointed to see how little he cared that I went to Dewey Beach to hide from the police.

As I became more awake and blood began to saturate my brain, it occurred to me that Fritz cared a little too much. He cared so much that it was exhilarating. There was much more to the letter than just the writing.

Nobody I knew carried a stapler on him. A pen, sure; a paper clip, maybe. But not a stapler. After Fritz (or Mrs. Hartly) put me in my car, one of them must have either gone to his truck or inside the diner to get a stapler. Then one of them had to find a road atlas from which to tear out a page. Fritz could have easily written me a note on a napkin with an eyebrow pencil from Mrs. Hartly's purse. Why bother getting a map? And why *staple* it to my shirt, why not just put it in my pocket or rest it on my chest? It was clear that Fritz wanted to make sure that I had to see the map. It must have been after two or three in the morning when he or Mrs. Hartly drove me back to the truck stop. I didn't understand why anybody would put me in the car, then go find a map of Maryland, mark the route with a highlighter, then walk back to where I lay and staple it to my shirt.

As I sat up, yawning, the map was snatched from my hand by the static on the door's glass. The cling suspended the paper on my car door like a crooked X-ray.

When I got out of the car and stood up completely, I knew I wasn't rid of all the alcohol in my system. I looked at my watch, and it was only two minutes past seven in the morning. I wasn't due for a hangover for a couple of hours.

The traffic on Route 70 was light; I watched it from where I stood on the slick pavement. The morning rush wouldn't start for an hour. The truck stop was more crowded than last night. The diner looked very busy with truckers getting coffee and breakfast. At the edge of the parking lot, a possum had his entire head in a can of beans, pushing it across the pavement, trying to eat whatever was left inside. I had never seen a possum during the daytime before.

From the glow of the white sky, the spilled gasoline and oil on the pavement gave the parking lot a sheen like ice.

When I sat back down in the back seat of my car with my legs on the wet pavement, I read the note again as it was suctioned to the glass of the door. Fritz had used a black ballpoint pen to write the message. I could see where the point of the pen had indented the paper, displaying the strokes he used to make each letter. There was something strange about his handwriting; the letters looked funny. I squinted at the note. I followed the curve of each letter with my eyes. That's when I noticed that Fritz had written each letter twice, one on top of the other. I pulled the map from the car door and held it up against the sky; the squiggly lines of roads from Massachusetts bled through from the other side. I followed each letter with the tip of my index finger as if I were reading Braille. The note Fritz had written was done first in pencil, then traced over with ink, which was how we had written our book reports and essays in elementary school. First we'd write a rough draft in pencil. Then, when we were sure there were no spelling mistakes or grammar errors, we'd trace over the pencil in ink. Fritz not only took the time to find a stapler and a road atlas, he also was careful enough to write the note *twice*—a rough copy in pencil and another committed in pen.

The possum slid the can of beans to a concrete parking divider, which kept the can stationary enough so the possum could get to the beans at the bottom.

I closed the door and walked around to the driver's side. The misting, warm rain felt good on my skin. It caught in the hair on the backs of my forearms in hundreds of silver beads. I put the map on my dashboard and studied it for a moment before starting the car. It was a good thing Fritz had stapled the map to my shirt and taken the time to write me the note twice. If he hadn't, I still would have stayed in western Maryland and followed Conrad's plan. But I wanted to see what Fritz found so important in Dewey Beach. There was more than just work there.

As I was pulling out of the parking lot, a few miles away, Mrs. Hartly and Fritz were probably sleeping in bed. Steve was probably wetting down his hair, getting ready for work. Conrad would be waiting impatiently for his house manager to drive him to RHP. I knew my brother would already be at work. And, undoubtedly, my mother would be praying. I felt a remarkable freedom from them—none of them knew what I was doing. No one, especially the police, knew where I was. It was a wonderful feeling.

As I hit route 70 east, I glanced back at the parking lot and smiled.

Two Mack trucks started up, burnt diesel belching from their exhaust pipes. Their motors growled and scared the little possum—who was running blindly for cover with the can of beans stuck on his head.

It took me almost four hours to get to Dewey Beach.

I made only one stop on my way to see Fritz's niece. I stopped in at an empty family restaurant for some lunch. A man wearing a brown sweatshirt took my order; he wrote it down in a red spiral notebook. I ordered a grilled cheese sandwich, the cheapest thing on the menu (which was hand-written on a three-by-five index card and thumb-tacked to the wall next to my seat). The sandwich was two dollars and came with a pickle and potato chips. The man in the sweatshirt also cooked the sandwich; he seemed to be the only employee. Before he grilled the sandwich, I asked him if he had any work for me to do.

"Doing what? What looks like it needs work?" he asked. He seemed a little offended, as if I didn't think he could handle the restaurant all by himself.

"Well, if you're the only guy working here, there might be something I could do."

"Like what?" he asked, rolling the spiral notebook in a tube and wringing it in his sweaty hands.

"I don't know, I could wash dishes, clean your windows, cook stuff…"

He looked at the front entrance. "My windows are dirty?" He stuck out his tongue, which wagged across his bottom lip like the tail of a cow.

"No, your windows are fine. I'm just trying to make some pocket money. Is there a job around here that you don't want to do and would rather pay somebody to do it for you?" The man didn't answer; he was still staring at the windows, searching for the smudges and streaks on the glass that only I could see. He still hadn't pulled his tongue back in his mouth. It was as if he needed his tongue out to concentrate.

"Forget it," I said.

He seemed relieved that I stopped asking for work. He went behind the counter and started the grill. Before he started to cook, he put on a Redskins baseball cap and turned it backward. He faced away from me as he worked, shifting his weight from foot to foot as if he were dancing to a song that echoed around in his skull. A woman walked through the kitchen and patted his back. She looked out over the tables and chairs of the restaurant with a grim face. Her hair was stringy, the color of dishwater. I could see her skull through the skin of her face. Her eyes were like white marbles pushed into clay. She was startled when she saw me sitting in a booth.

"Is that for *him*?" she asked the man at the grill.

"He wanted a sandwich, right?" he asked her. Questions seemed to confuse the man. He yelled to me, "You still want this sandwich?"

I nodded and tried to smile.

The woman looked back at me and grinned. Then she caught a glimpse of herself in the reflection on a stainless steel refrigerator and gasped. She combed her hair with her fingers and laughed to herself. I didn't think she was expecting to see any customers.

When my sandwich was done, both the man and woman presented it to me as if it were a birthday cake.

"Here you are," he said. The woman was quiet; she just stared at me and smiled. They both stood next to me, hovering like vultures the entire time I ate. Each time I'd take a bite, I'd turn to them and smile with a mouthful of bread and melted

cheese. They watched me eat with an uneasy mixture of aston-
ishment and pride. They acted like this was the first time anybody had been willing to eat something they had prepared. The
man even took off his hat and held it to his chest, as if the
National Anthem was now playing in his head.

The sandwich was cut in two. I ate the first half politely.
But when I realized that they were going to linger around for
me to finish the whole thing, I stuffed the entire second half of
the sandwich in my mouth. After that, I nearly ran out of place.
The man and woman watched me leave through the front window.

I promised myself no more stops until I reached the Paradise Bar and Grill, and no more trying to find myself work. I
would leave that to Leah.

The sun came out when I pulled into the Paradise's parking
lot. The sky was dirty blue from all the humidity. Here near the
water the air was warm and dense.

It was easy to find the restaurant; Dewey Beach was barely
three miles long. The Paradise was in a strip mall on Route
One, sandwiched in between a tanning salon and a dog groom-
ing academy. Some of the cars in the parking lot had tarps pulled
over them for protection from seagulls that bombed the parking lot; the unprotected cars were speckled with globs of white
droppings.

On the Paradise's sign, the letters were written in orange,
and at the bottom, there was a cartoon drawing of a bearded
fat guy lying on a hammock that was stretched between two
palm trees. Behind the lounging fat man, a surfboard was stuck
into the sand. This sign was a little misleading; palm trees are
not native to Maryland, and nobody surfs in Dewey Beach.

The first thing I saw when I went into the restaurant was a
chalkboard that had all the beers they kept on draft written in
pink and baby blue chalk. Under the board was a bowl of peppermints that sat on a little ledge. Before I went in to talk to
Leah, I filled my pockets with the mints.

A short blond woman wearing a pink Polo shirt was vacuuming the cardinal-red carpet when I went inside. Everything
inside the Paradise was red: the upholstery was red vinyl, the

walls were stained mahogany, and every table had a candle in a red globe. The woman was struggling with the vacuum; its left wheel was bent and wouldn't move. As she shoved the vacuum forward and wrestled it back, she held her breath, which made her face as red as the walls. Her scalp shone pink through her straw-colored hair.

She shut off the machine and wiped her forehead with the back of her hand. She stood, panting and dizzy, when she saw me and could barely speak. "Not open," she managed to say. "Open...one o'clock."

"Actually," I said, "I'm here to see Leah. Is she around?"

The woman teetered on her feet trying to catch her breath. She plopped down in a booth and held her right hand across her chest.

"Are you Tom?" she asked.

"Yes."

Her breathing simmered down, but her face still glowed from the blood that was trapped in her cheeks. "Fritz called us this morning, but it was too late. Leah will be in Ocean City for the summer."

"Oh." I wasn't sure what else to say. I thanked her and started to walk out.

"Hold on," she said. "Let me get Mike. Maybe he knows where she is down there."

I didn't really want to go looking for this girl in Ocean City, but the lady had already walked off, dragging the immobile vacuum cleaner behind her.

Mike came out, wearing a filthy apron and a white towel over his shoulder. He was probably six years older than Fritz, but instantly I saw the resemblance. Mike was a little over-weight, but it was evident from the fleshy slackness of his jowls that he had just shed a lot of pounds. His eyes were pretty, like Fritz's, and he had a nice smile with bone-white teeth. His hair was thinning, but he wore it down to his shoulders.

"Tom!" he said as if he knew me. "I'm Mike Greene. Fritz called me from Shelly's place this morning and told me you'd be by." Before he extended his hand for me to shake, he pulled the dish towel from off his shoulder and rubbed his hands in it.

Mike was a big guy, but his grip was strangely weak, as if he had lost some of his strength along with his fat.

"What can I do for you?" he asked.

The woman who had been wrestling with the vacuum came back. She pulled a chair from off a table and sat down. The red vinyl cushion rumbled when she settled her weight.

"I'm only going to be in town for a week or two, and I was looking for some work."

Mike shook his head and sucked his teeth. "Sorry, kid. You're a little ahead of the ball. It's still the off-season around here. Nobody I know will be hiring for at least two weeks."

"But after that," the red-faced woman said, "*every*body's hiring."

Mike smiled at me and shrugged. "She's right."

"Is there anything I could do around here?" As I talked, my eyes shifted from stain to stain on his apron.

"Sorry, kid," he took the towel of his shoulder again and rubbed his hands in it. "I'd like to help you out, but I just don't have anything open right now."

I nodded and sighed.

"Yeah, I feel bad. I don't know what Fritz was thinking telling you to come here for work." Mike reached over and slapped me on the shoulder.

"He told me to come here to find Leah, though." I said.

"Oh! Are you going to work with Ron, too?"

I shrugged. "I guess. Fritz just told me that Leah could find me a job."

"So she's going to get you a job with her at the Sunset?"

"I don't know, what's the Sunset?"

"It's a bar in Ocean City," he said. "Her boyfriend Ron's the assistant manager. He gave her a job tending bar while she's house-sitting."

I shook my head. "Maybe that's what Fritz meant. He wasn't real clear about it. How far am I from Ocean City?"

Mike pointed to the front door of the restaurant. "That road out there is Route One—stay on that until it becomes Coastal Highway. When it turns into Coastal Highway, you'll be in Ocean City. It'll take you about half an hour."

"That's it, just go south and I won't get lost."

He laughed. "If you go left, you'll drive into the ocean, if you turn right, you'll go in the bay." He slapped me on the shoulder again and bared his gleaming teeth. "Fritz told me you were a funny guy." He turned to the woman on the chair. "Did you know this guy took my brother and Shelly Hartly to a cemetery last night?"

The woman screwed up her face. "A cemetery?"

"Yeah, Fritz said this kid was looking for ghosts!"

I groaned. "It wasn't a cemetery, and I wasn't looking for ghosts." I wanted to explain what I was doing there, but I didn't have the energy. The alcohol from last night was turning sour in my body. My legs had started to ache and my head felt like a melting glob of wax.

Mike saw that I wasn't smiling, so he tousled my hair and punched me in the arm. "Don't worry—Fritz said you were a good shit. Just a little queer is all."

"Honey," the woman said to Mike, "don't say *queer*—that means something else these days." It seemed as if both Mike and Fritz had found women who were keen to clean up their language.

Mike looked back at her and laughed. "He knows I don't mean nothing by it. Fritz just said this kid was a little goofy."

"Then call him goofy—if you *have* to."

They were talking as if I weren't standing there, so I cleared my throat.

"Actually," Mike said, "if you're desperate for cash, I have something for you to do."

Before I left, Mike paid me twenty dollars to clean his bathrooms. I scrubbed the toilets and sinks with a washcloth and a canister of Comet. I poured the white-green powder on the pink porcelain of the toilet and marveled that Conrad's roommate (the man from the Pentagon who wanted to tell me how to fake my own death) once snorted this stuff, thinking it was cocaine. The cleanser had completely devoured his nasal cavity. The guy had to wear a scarf over his nose and mouth in the winter because breathing in crisp, cold air dropped him to his knees in pain and tears.

Mike sent me on my way with a day-old bag of potato rolls and directions to get to the bar called the Sunset.

"I'd tell you where Leah's staying if I knew," Mike said as I was leaving. He walked me out to the front entrance. "She left two days ago and she didn't tell her mother or me anything—just said she was house-sitting for a friend." He shook his head and squinted in the sun. "How do you like that?"

I smiled with forced sympathy.

"Well, you tell her that her dad wants a phone call when you see her. Got that?"

I nodded. "I'll tell her."

Mike wished me well and thanked me for cleaning his bathroom. As the door was closing, I heard him shout, "Where're all my goddamn mints?"

ON THE MAP, Ocean City resembled a coccyx (that tiny bone at the end of the human spine that hugs the outside of the colon). I found the shape fitting, because I thought Ocean City was a shit-hole.

I parked on a side street behind the Sunset but walked along the boardwalk for a couple of hours before going in.

The shops along the boardwalk were closed. Large green wire garbage cans were set outside of every fourth store. They were so full that trash was spilling onto the ground.

The sun slipped back under the cover of the one luminous gray cloud that covered the sky. The rain had stopped long ago, and the air was warm, which eased some of my soreness from last night.

DOWN THE SIDE STREETS bits of trash blew in the wind and slipped into the gutters. The salt from the sea breeze ate away at the buildings, dissolving wood and rusting trim. On some of the buildings' foundations, the cracks in the cement were as thick as my thumb. The planks of wood on the boardwalk were deeply grooved and splintered.

I peered into some of the stores that sold T-shirts and posters and sunglasses. None of them had doors; instead they had large plastic partitions that covered the openings, like the stores in a shopping mall. Only one man had his shop open. He sat in front of it in a lawn chair while eating cantaloupe with a plastic fork. He sat next to a spin-rack filled with postcards that were curling into C-shapes from the humidity. He didn't look at me when I walked into his store. He sold useless crap: Budweiser beach towels, hippie T-shirts, drug paraphernalia, and cheap silver jewelry. Above his cash register were designs of things that he could air-brush onto a T-shirt or a license plate for you. Everything in the store was tourist shit; and almost every single store along the boardwalk was the same as his, a caravan selling beer T-shirts and flip-flops.

A huge Ferris wheel was at the end of the boardwalk. In the gray light, it reminded me of the Domino Sugar factory's sign— a big, ignored, skeletal hulk. It sat motionless in the gray air, surrounded by other unused carnival rides and game stands. I walked along the empty stands, where people would get ripped off trying to knock down lead bottles with a baseball or throw blunted darts at under-inflated balloons. Everything was deserted. I only saw one other person, one guy sitting on a stool reading a car magazine outside a fun-house. He was the ticket-taker. When he saw me, he disappeared into the fun-house and left his magazine on the padded seat of the stool.

As empty as the boardwalk was, the Sunset was pretty crowded. Most of the customers were wealthy-looking elderly men. They were drinking imported lager and good brandy. Their faces glowed red from the alcohol as they played cards and cackled to one another. One man—wearing white pants, navy jacket, and a white captain's hat—had a nose so purple it looked as if it might fall off, like a cigar ash, into his scotch.

The walls of the bar were darkened from the smoke that roiled around the pine green, stained-glass chandeliers. The shutters had been drawn to block out all the light from the front windows. The interior was so dark, it was hard to see your own feet as you walked.

Two men stood behind the bar. One guy was unloading bottles of liquor from a cardboard box, and the other was watching a soap opera on television. They wore crisp white shirts, black vests, and black bow ties. The man watching television was a heavy-set black guy. He watched the soap opera with a mixture of disgust and curiosity.

I went up to the counter and asked the guy emptying the boxes if Leah was around.

He looked at me suspiciously. "No," he said with enough finality and rudeness that it made the black guy look over at us. The man I was talking to looked about thirty. He was an inch shorter than me but had a thick frame and tan skin. His hair was short and combed back.

"Well," I said, "can you tell me when she works next?"

He pulled a bottle of Seagram's lime-twisted gin from the box and volleyed it from hand to hand. "I don't know when she works next," he said flatly.

"Can you find out?"

He slammed the bottle down on the bar a little harder than I think he intended to; he immediately checked to see if he'd cracked it. "Hold on." Without saying anything more, he walked through two silver doors and into the kitchen.

The black guy turned the soap opera off and turned to a golf match. The men at the tables cheered. I sat at the bar, and he asked me if I wanted anything to drink. I said no, but he set a coaster in front of me anyway. The bottles of alcohol sat in front of a large mirror that had been dulled from age and smoke. I looked at my face and saw dark rings around my eyes. I was as shocked to see the harshness of my face as the woman in the family restaurant had been to see hers.

I waited about ten minutes for the other guy to come back out. The black guy started to wash some glasses in soapy water in front of me.

"Is he coming back?" I asked him. "Do you think he's really checking to find out when Leah's working next?"

"Ron?" he said. "I guess so."

"That's Leah's boyfriend?" I asked and pointed to the door from which he left.

"Who's Leah?" he said, then he asked me again if I wanted anything to drink.

An elderly woman came out of the kitchen and yelled at the black guy. "Who turned off my stories?" She reached up and turned the channel; the geezers in the tables jeered. She looked at me then slapped the guy on the arm. "Have you waited on that kid yet?"

"He doesn't want anything," the man said defensively.

"Excuse me, ma'am?" I said. "Can you tell me when Leah's working?"

She came over and pulled a piece of paper that was in a plastic sleeve out from under the bar; it was dotted with spilled beer.

"I have her down to work tomorrow from noon until five," she said. I asked her if she was hiring, but she frowned at me and said, "If I come back out here and you're not drinking, out you go." Then she walked back into the kitchen.

The black guy gave her the finger behind her back and turned the channel again.

I looked towards the kitchen, and saw no sign of Leah's boyfriend. I could understand being a little cautious about a stranger asking for your girlfriend, but he had been so short with me that I felt pissed off.

As I left, I took the bottle of gin that he had unpacked from the box and tucked it under my jacket. One of the men in the bar saw me steal it. He smiled at me and nodded approvingly.

Out in the rear parking lot, Ron was pacing, smoking a cigarette. He stopped when he saw me and dragged deeply. I thought he was out there to fight me. He glowered at me from the parking lot, and I just blinked at him. If he had attacked me, I would have thrown the bottle of gin at him and run. I had never been in a fight before. Hitting him with the bottle would have been the only thing I knew how to do. But it was unnecessary. Ron only spat on the ground and went back in through the rear entrance.

I DIDN'T REALLY REMEMBER having the dream until I was on the beach that night.

One hundred yards in front of the Sunset, I lay on my back and tried to go to sleep on the sand. For dinner, I had eaten a handful of peppermints and three of the rolls Mike had given me. To get rid of the spongy staleness, I toasted the bread in a little fire I had made in an empty beer can. I had tried hard to go to sleep, but my head was welling over with worries.

The moon was low in the sky, the color of dark urine. Its light shone down on the crashing waves and made the sea foam spilling onto the sand glow yellow like sulfur.

I lay on my back and stared at the black sky, unable to blink. I wished the dream I had about my father meant something. I wished I could have talked to him. In the dream, I walked to him on the sand, then everything around me dissolved into another dream. One second I was approaching my father, the next I was in a parking garage somewhere being told by a gang of fifties greasers that I could join their gang if I was willing to eat a candy bar in a haunted covered bridge.

I mostly couldn't sleep because I was worried about the police. I worried that RHP still wanted to press charges even though Conrad had paid back the money for me. It made my head ache to think of cops pounding on my door, disturbing my neighbors and making them think I was some kind of criminal. I wondered if my gun-selling neighbor had panicked when he saw the cops pull up to the front of our building. Maybe he thought he was lucky because they'd knocked on my door by mistake.

I sat up and took the bottle of gin from my duffel bag. I took a deep drink of it and gagged. The liquid burned like a gas in the center of my chest. I wondered if drinking after-shave could have tasted much worse. Stealing the bottle was my petty revenge for how much of an asshole Leah's boyfriend had been to me. I capped the bottle, grabbed it by its neck and heaved it into the ocean. It cartwheeled in the yellow moonlight, but I couldn't see where it smacked down in the water.

I lay back down on the sand and tried to close my eyes, but my mind just kept rolling things over in my head. Two days ago, I had a life. I slept in a warm bed and I ate hot food. I had my friend. Now, I slept in the cold and ate stale bread. The police wanted me for a crime I was too stupid to realize I had committed. I was a hundred miles away from my home, but everything seemed to be waiting for me just over the wall of buildings on the boardwalk; the copper glow from the street lights was where the police were waiting for me. With every wave that spilled out onto the wet sand, I could hear them plotting when to grab me.

A large wave unfurled to about five feet from where I lay. I scooted myself back.

I was far away from home, but the black water outside RHP was still following me. It had trapped me at the end of the world. I listened to the water fizzing out on the sand; it sounded like laughing. There was nothing at the line of the horizon, just black. Each wave that broke was reaching out to snatch me up and take me out to sea, carry me on the crests of black water until I was treading and bobbing in complete darkness in the middle of the ocean. Every direction I'd swim would lead me further out into nothing.

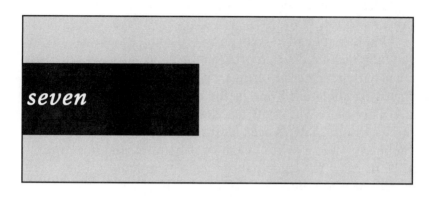

seven

FOR TWO MONTHS AFTER MY BROTHER MARRIED, his wife was convinced that I hated her. Lisa admitted that she had even been a little scared of me.

"The first time I met you I panicked when Shawn left us alone in the same room together," she had said. "You just sat there and wouldn't even look at me."

But Shawn's wife and I became friends pretty quickly. In time, I liked her much more than my brother.

Because she'd get lonely, Lisa liked to call me on the phone or have me over to the house when Shawn was out. I didn't mind talking to her on the phone, but I usually wouldn't see her in person. She liked to gossip about Shawn more than I was comfortable with. I never felt qualified to say anything about my brother. I just smiled and nodded, understanding nothing she was talking about.

She'd say something like, "Don't you hate how critical Shawn gets when he watches hockey?"

Then I'd say, "Shawn likes hockey?"

One Friday night, about two years ago, Lisa called me up to play board games with her. Lisa used to call them "bored" games. Shawn was at a bar, and Lisa suspected that he had been having an affair. She was in an intense Shawn-bashing mood that night. It was around eight at night when she called, and I had been staring out my window.

When I told Lisa I didn't feel like coming over, there was a long pause on her end of the phone.

"Please, Tom," she said. "Just come over. I don't want to be alone right now."

I knew that I had to go over. So far, being friends had meant playfully picking on each other and teasing. This was the first time I had heard her be serious with me. So I went over, and we played Scrabble until one in the morning. She seemed better after I got there. She made us celery and peanut butter snacks, and we drank Shawn's beer. At some point—drunk—I thought "hobberly" was a word. I vaguely remember thinking it meant to be miserly. We argued about it for ten minutes. I had connected the word onto the Y of Lisa's misspelled "truley."

"Hobberly?" she said. "What is that?"

"You know," I said, "*hobberly*—it means to be tight with your money."

"Honey, *hobber* is not a word, so how can somebody be *hobberly*?"

"It *is* a word!" I slurred, crunching on a piece of celery. "Ebeneezer Scrooge was a hobberly old man."

Lisa started laughing so hard she had to spit a glob of peanut butter onto a drink coaster.

"My mother is a hobber with her money!" I said, taking a big swig of beer.

"And Shawn is a hobber in bed!" Lisa cried (but I pretended not to hear her).

The more I heard it spoken, the more I realized it wasn't a real word.

"OK, Hobberboy," Lisa said, "it's time for the dictionary." She got up and stumbled into the living room and thumbed through a blue paperback dictionary.

I followed and looked over her shoulder. I saw it wasn't a word before she did. I looked in the space between *hob* and *hobbism* and didn't see it, so I wrestled the dictionary away from her. We rolled around on the living room floor, trying to get to the book as if it were a fumbled football. Lisa jumped on top of my chest and tickled me until I almost pissed myself.

"OK, OK," I cried. "It's not a word! I made it up!"

She let go, and we lay side by side on the living room floor panting and dizzy, our laughter still spluttering. When Lisa finally caught her breath she propped herself on her elbows and said, "You know, you can be so much fun sometimes."

I smiled.

"Still, you make the worst first impression of anybody I ever met."

"Really?" I sat up and wrapped my arms around my knees. "What do I do?"

"Well, for starters, when we were introduced and you shook my hand, you didn't look me in the eye—you looked at my *belt*."

"I was nervous."

She sat up and crossed her legs. "I know, but when you're meeting someone for the first time, you *have* to look them in the eye."

"OK, I'll start looking people in the eye."

"That's not all. You have to be friendlier. When I first met you, you said maybe two words to me the whole time. I remember sitting in your mom's living room thinking: 'God, Shawn's brother *hates* me.'"

"I didn't know you," I said.

"That doesn't matter. You have to learn how to make small talk. When you make small talk with people, they figure you're at least *trying* to get to know them."

"OK."

"Remember: eye contact and small talk."

I would always remember that advice. Before my interview for RHP, I called Lisa and she told me over and over, "Eye contact and small talk, Tom. Eye contact and small talk."

This was how I prepared myself for meeting Leah, by chanting, "Eye contact small talk, eye contact small talk," to myself over and over.

I washed up in a gas station that sat next to a miniature golf course before meeting her. The man who had given me the key was an auto mechanic who must have cut his hand badly. He sat on a stool behind the cash register; his right hand bandaged up so much that it looked like he was wearing a white boxing glove.

The gas station's bathroom was speckled with drying blood. When I hit the light switch, the fluorescent bars flickered on, displaying the blood on the dirty tile floor. I looked at my hand; my right index finger, which I had used to turn on the light, was dabbed red-black with engine grease and blood. The light switch looked as if someone had hit it with a sponge dipped in red paint. The door to a navy-blue first aid kit that hung on the wall was wide open. Bandages had spilled from it onto the floor.

The blood on the sink ran down the sides; only oil and grease stained the basin, dark streaks running down from the knobs as black as India ink.

I brushed my teeth, shaved, and washed out all the sand that had been sprayed into my hair overnight. I washed under my arms with an olive-green bar of Lava soap. Water and suds spilled onto the floor and broke up the pools of blood in the tile joints.

When I returned the key to the wounded attendant, I checked myself for bloodstains. On the way back to the Sunset, I stopped to look at the back of my shirt in case I had accidentally bumped into the wall.

At four o'clock when I arrived at the Sunset, the same old buzzards from yesterday were there. It was as if they were as permanent to the bar as the support posts and walls. When I went in, I spotted Leah standing on a chair, writing lunch specials onto a green chalkboard that had been mounted to the wall over a broken jukebox. I knew it was her even before being introduced.

I walked over and switched my duffel bag to my left hand, ready for a handshake. I made myself look her in the eye. "Excuse me . . ." She looked down. "Are you Leah?"

She stopped writing and hopped down from the chair. Her lips were pursed, and her eyes blinked like they were dripping water.

"Are *you* the guy who came looking for me yesterday?" Her tone was accusing, and she looked like she was going to slap me. I kept my eyes locked on her anyway.

"Yes. My name's Tom. I was wondering if you might be able to find me a job."

"Ask Belle," she said and pointed to the old woman behind the bar who watched soap operas. "She owns the place, not me."

"Well," I began and paused to think of what I was going to say, "I was told that you were the person who could find me a job."

"Well, who *are* you?" she snapped suddenly. "How do I know you?"

"I'm a friend of your uncle's."

"Yeah, which one?"

"Fritz. He told me to come down here to find you."

Leah blinked in disbelief and disgust. I couldn't look away from her. Then her boyfriend came over and stood next to her with his hands on his hips.

"Who *is* this guy?" he asked her.

She threw her hands up. "I don't know!" she said. "I've never seen him before in my life!" The men at the tables looked over and snorted with laughter. The man who had seen me steal the bottle of gin smiled at me and raised his glass.

"Well he knows *you* . . ." the boyfriend said.

Leah grabbed me by my left forearm, and I dropped my bag. She headed me for the front door. Then she spun around (still clutching my arm) and pointed to Ron. "You! You butt out because I can't even stand the *sight* of you right now! You have no right to question who I talk to." Then she opened the door and shoved me out. I tripped on the door jamb and stumbled onto the boardwalk. She stabbed a finger at me. "And *you*, whoever you are, wait out there, and I'll get to you in a minute." Then she slammed the door shut, and I could hear the old bastards inside explode with laughter.

The sky was pale blue, no clouds. Sunbathers on towels were scattered about the beach. A little girl in a purple bathing suit stood just out of reach of the waves and assaulted a disabled jellyfish with fistfuls of wet sand. I sat on a bench and waited for Leah.

She came out of the Sunset and crossed the boardwalk to

meet me. Leah was a few inches shorter than me, deeply tan with short blond hair parted to the right. She wore black pants, a white shirt, and a burgundy vest with matching bow tie. There was a strong resemblance to Mike in the softness and round-ness of her features.

Leah came over and sat down next to me. I didn't look over at her; eye contact had gotten me nowhere. We both just stared straight ahead.

"We broke up yesterday," she said, and I kept quiet. "I don't know how much longer I can work with him." She sighed and lowered her head.

"Are you OK?" I asked flatly.

Leah shook her head but didn't respond. "I *know* I seem mean, and please don't get mad . . . but you are the last thing in the world I have time for right now."

I nodded and said nothing. I just stared at the amber and violet stained glass on the Sunset's door.

"I don't know why my uncle told you I can find you a job," she said. "And I'm very sorry he lied to you." She turned to face me, but I didn't bother to look over.

"Was he having fun with me?"

"Uncle Fritz? Yeah, probably."

I nodded and gritted my teeth. Should have just listened to Conrad, I told myself.

"I'd like to help you out—I would," she said. "But I'm go-ing through a difficult time right now with the boyfriend and everything."

"I'm sorry."

She laughed. "Me, too."

I stood up and turned to face her. "Sorry I bothered you."

Leah gave me another apology, and I walked back to my car.

I got to my car and sat inside. What now? I sat silent and stared at the flies buzzing around the trash cans outside the Sunset. The shiny green flies sucked at a brown slime that ran down the side of the plastic trash cans. Then I looked down the side of the building to the people walking on the boardwalk. One person turned the corner and ran to the parking lot.

It was Leah. She was running towards me with my duffel bag in her hand. She tried to lift it up in the air to show me, but she couldn't raise it higher than her shoulder.

"Oh, God, thank you," I said, getting out of the car. "Everything I own is in here practically."

Leah wasn't the slightest bit out of breath. She handed the bag over and frowned at it. "So you don't live in the area?"

"No, I'm from Baltimore."

"Baltimore? How do you know Uncle Fritz?"

"I met him through Shelly Hartly in Frederick."

"Oh, you know Shelly, too; she's great, isn't she?" Leah smiled and sat on the hood of my car.

"She was my guidance counselor when I was a little kid."

"*Really*? I remember her saying something about working for a school once." Leah shook her head and laughed. "How long ago was that?"

"A good while," I said.

"That's hilarious."

"I met your uncle a couple of nights ago, and he told me to go to Dewey Beach to find you. But your dad's the one who told me to come here."

"Oh, you met my dad, huh?" she said quietly. "Did he seem mad?"

"I don't think so. He was really nice. But he told me to tell you to call him, though."

Leah looked up at the sky and scrunched her face. Her eyes were not like her father's; they were dark green like pine.

"You drove all the way from Frederick?" she asked.

"Yes I did," I said seriously.

Leah sighed and stood up. She scratched the back of her short cropped hair. "Listen," she sighed, "I'll make a call or two tonight and see what I can do. Where can I reach you?"

"I've been sleeping in my car."

"No car phone or anything?"

I shook my head.

"OK. Meet me at the corner of 88th and Coastal, ocean side, at eight o'clock tonight."

"OK."

"I'm not promising you anything. I'm going to try, that's all. So don't get mad if I can't find you anything."

"I won't."

We shook hands before she walked away; her grip was stronger than her father's. In the sun, the hairs on the back of her arm looked like white needles.

I got in my car and started the engine. Her boyfriend came out of the back door and stamped to my car like a rhino. When I put the car in drive, I saw him in my rear view mirror, starting to sprint towards me. I pulled onto Fifth Street and drove off with him chasing behind me.

I DIDN'T HAVE MUCH HOPE THAT LEAH COULD FIND ME A JOB while I hid from the police. I was sure that I had to start making money on my own.

I went back to the gas station I had washed up in earlier. The same injured mechanic waited on me; his bandage was starting to leak. I bought a bottle of Windex. Before I left, I stole a squeegee from a pan filled with soapy water that hung next to a gas pump.

For four hours, I went up and down Coastal Highway, asking store owners if they would pay me to wash their store's windows.

I had learned pretty quickly to stay away from chain stores. The employees (I only asked to speak with managers or supervisors) either didn't have access to the petty cash, or they thought I was homeless and shooed me off. I went into a Dunkin' Donuts and asked the manager if I could wash his front windows for five dollars. He said nothing, turned around and plopped a telephone down on the counter, picked up the receiver and dialed three numbers—9-1-1. Then he stared at me and sucked his teeth.

Privately owned surf shops and restaurants had pretty nice owners. They'd stand outside and chat with me while they smoked cigarettes and I scraped their front windows clean.

After cleaning only a few stores' windows, I learned that it was stupid to charge a flat price; I had been asking for five dollars. I made more money when I asked for a tip. Tips were especially generous at strip malls. I'd go to a strip mall, start at one end and would work my way down the line, washing the windows without anybody's permission. When an employee would come out and ask me what I was doing, I'd say, "I'm cleaning your windows. I'm not charging anything, but if you could offer a tip, I'd appreciate it." Sometimes this worked, sometimes it did not. But when it did work, I always got more than five dollars. A manager at a Food Lion on the bay side of Coastal highway gave me fifty dollars for cleaning the entire front of the store. The people who chose *not* to tip me weren't rude about it. They just went back inside after I had told them what I was doing, and they didn't come back out. A fat lady who owned a liquor store came running out after I finished with her windows, screaming at me that I had left streaks. "Look what you did," she shouted. "It looks worse now!" I cleaned it again to her liking, but she didn't pay me.

I had made almost one hundred and eighty dollars by the time I was to meet Leah. My right shoulder ached from squeegeeing and my legs were turning to marmalade. I had walked from Fifth Street to Sixtieth Street and back down again—up the bay side then down the ocean side—washing giant windows. Three times I had to dip into my profits and buy more Windex. I almost fell asleep behind the wheel when I drove to meet Leah.

I saw her as I pulled into a deli on 88th street. She sat at a bus stop still in her work uniform, drinking a glass of what looked like vegetable juice. Leah stared at the traffic as if her mind was miles away. Her eyes looked like glass. Her lips were parted and frozen, as if they'd been fixed in time while she was in the middle of a sentence.

I walked up to her and she didn't blink.

"Leah?" I said, waving a hand in front of her eyes, and she bolted up, blinking and confused. She dropped the glass from her hand. Thick red juice splattered on the sidewalk. The glass rolled slowly in a half circle but didn't break.

"Hi." She managed a smile for me and sat down again.

I sat next to her looked at her worn-out face. "Are you OK?"

She dropped the smile and looked into her lap. "I'm fine," she said.

I could smell alcohol fumes wafting up from the spilled glass of vegetable juice. "You look tired," I said cautiously.

She shook her head and breathed in; her nose whistled sharply. "I'm cold. Let's go inside."

Leah was staying at a condo that sat between a deli and a motel. She stayed on the second floor of a pale yellow building with white trim around all the windows and doors. We walked up the steps that were in the front of the building. The condo's address was nailed above the door on a plaque with black, burned-in numbers.

Leah offered me a seat on the couch, and sat on a wooden rocking chair in front of me. She took a large gray blanket off the back of the chair and wrapped herself in it.

The condo was decorated with crappy seashells-glued-to-driftwood art. The walls were painted peach and punctuated with paintings of sailboats riding on rough, choppy waters. A tin of crayons sat on the coffee table, on top of a stack of children's place mats from a Denny's. All the crayons were reduced to nubs, and none of them had their wrappings.

"I talked to my dad today," Leah said, collecting her bare feet under her legs. "He told me you were nice."

I smiled and looked around the room.

"He brought good news. He found you a job," she said.

"Really? Where?"

"He knows a lady who owns a crab house on 42nd street. She told him to send you there tomorrow. She has some chores for you."

"What time?"

"Nine," she said, staring into the bin of crayons. "Her name is Betty something…" We sat in silence for three long minutes. The loudest thing in the apartment was the whirl of the refrigerator coming on.

My body felt heavy. My eyelids dipped down. Last night on the beach, I'd slept less than two hours straight. Every stiff wind spat stinging sand into my face. Sand mites gnawed at my bare arms, and every time I'd start to drift off, a mosquito would come by and scream into my ear. On Leah's couch, I could almost feel my body falling forward, crashing through the tin of crayons.

"You look sleepy," she said finally, her voice breaking the silence like shattering glass. "Where are you staying tonight?"

"My car."

"You can stay here; you're more than welcome. There's a spare bedroom."

I thanked her with a gentle smile. "The car is fine. I think I should get going. Can't hardly keep my eyes open."

Leah stood, dropping the thick blanket back onto the chair. The bow tie of her uniform was still a tight little knot at her throat. "You can stay. Honestly. It won't be any trouble, I swear."

"Oh, I'm sure," I said. "I'd just prefer to stay in the car is all."

Leah smiled and shook her head. "You have no idea how insulting it is to hear someone say they'd rather sleep in their car than to stay with you."

"I don't mean to offend you, but I just don't think it's a great idea."

Leah sat down. "Listen, I just don't want to be alone tonight, OK? Just stay with me *tonight*. Then you can go."

She used the same tone Lisa had to get me to drive to her house while Shawn was gone, and I caved in. "Well, as long as whoever owns this place wouldn't mind."

"No, no—they wouldn't. Trust me."

I thanked her and went out to my car and got my bag. When I came back in, Leah was in the kitchen (that was to the right of the living room), making some sandwiches. A waist-high counter was the only partition between the two rooms.

"Just take your stuff to the last door on the right," she said over her shoulder. "You hungry? I'm making us some cheese sandwiches."

"Thank you," I said and walked down a long dark hallway. Old tin signs for motor oil and tobacco hung on the veneered walls. The bedroom was painted sky blue and had pink frilly curtains on the windows. It had two twin beds separated by a nightstand that had a lamp and a brass alarm clock on it. The lamp's base was a wood-carving of a white-bearded fisherman in a yellow slicker. Between the fisherman's pinched lips was a hole with some wood glue residue crusted around it. I imagined the fisherman had a missing pipe. It looked as if the pipe had been broken, glued and re-glued so often that somebody just threw the damn thing away the last time it snapped off.

I flopped face first down onto the bed. My legs hung off the sides. The ticking of the alarm clock thudded into my chest, and my body felt as if it were being washed over with warm bathwater. My breathing slowed, and my eyelids had sealed shut so tightly that I couldn't imagine a power on earth that could open them again.

I fell asleep almost instantly.

Sometime later, the door creaked open and woke me. I lay still and opened my eyes just enough to look out through my lashes. Leah came in with a sandwich on a plate and a glass of milk.

She stopped on the side of the bed and stared at me. I pretended to sleep. I even kept my mouth open and let the drool keep spilling out. I could hear her sigh with disappointment that I had fallen asleep. She set the plate down on the nightstand. The china met the wood with such a crack that it sent a shock down my spine. Leah picked up my legs and rested them on the bed. I made an appropriate mumbling sound. Then she walked to the door and turned out the light.

But she didn't leave.

In the blackness, I could feel her in the room, could feel her staring at me. It felt like a needle being pushed slowly into my neck. My whole body tingled. I lay there not breathing and could hear her swallow. The floorboards under her squealed as she shifted her weight from foot to foot.

Leah watched me in the pitch black room for over twenty minutes. She never made a sound louder than her slow, calm breathing. Then, without a word or a huff, she turned and left. As the door opened, the dim light from the hallway flooded the room. She closed the door slowly, turning the knob so that the latch wouldn't strike the jamb.

I stared into nothing, listening to her walk aimlessly about the apartment. She seemed to wander from room to room in a clumsy figure eight. Finally she settled into a room at the beginning of the hallway. When I heard her light click off, I exhaled in a rush.

Then I ate the sandwich and drank the milk in the dark.

I WOKE TO THE SOUND OF CARS on Coastal Highway. It was ten after eight. I lay in bed for a few minutes, staring up at the spiderwebs of light and shadows on the ceiling.

I heard the shower shut off down the hall in three quick screeches of the knobs. The curtain was pulled back, and I heard Leah's bare feet thud on the floor. I waited until I heard her door close before I got up.

The bathroom was filled with damp air. Steam clung to the walls in tiny beads, and the mirror over the sink was gray. It felt good to shower. I could feel the oil and grit peel from my body, exposing warm pink skin. My head was crooked back, and I let the water fill my mouth. If I had looked at my feet, I thought I would've seen the filth that had collected on my body pool and swirl above the tiny holes in the drain.

Leah hadn't left a towel for me, so I dried off like a dog. The only thing that hung from the towel rack was a white bra that I was sure Leah must have forgotten was there. I changed while sitting on a sky blue toilet, after drying my hair and chest with a tiny wash cloth I found on the floor.

Leah was sitting on her kitchen counter, eating an apple, when I came out. She wore a white bathrobe and a white towel over her hair in that Indian wrap that only women seem to know how to do.

"Sleep well?" she asked. She seemed a little brighter this morning. Her eyes were focused and clear.

"Yes." I walked into the living room and sat down on the coffee table.

Leah looked at the duffel bag that was by my feet and offered a distant smile. "I'd like to apologize for last night," she said and set the apple down on the counter. "I know how I must have seemed."

I said nothing. The crashing sound of the ocean was carried

in through the open windows of the condo. I looked down at my feet.

"I feel better today," she assured me then hopped down off the counter. "And I'll understand if you don't want to stay with me, but you are more than welcome."

I shook my head. Lines of water from the shower ran down my forehead, and I wiped them away with my palm before they could go into my eyes. "Thank you," I said.

Leah walked over to me, handing over directions to Betty's crab house. "If you're done before I get home from work, you can wait on the porch."

I took the paper from her and smiled. "Leah," I said, but the words caught in my throat. "It's nice of you to let me stay here and all, but I'm not sure it's a good idea."

Her face didn't change; she sat on the rocker and took the towel from her head.

"I think you and your boyfriend have some things to work out. Me being here will only make things worse. I mean, you still have to work with the guy."

"Ron and I have been breaking up for over a year. Things were finally sealed a couple of days ago." Before I could ask what happened, she said, "That's all you need to know, and that's all I feel like saying about it. You can go if you want—if you don't feel comfortable with me. Or if you're scared of Ron. But *I'd* prefer it if you stayed."

"OK. If that's how it is, I'll stick around until I have to go back to Baltimore."

Leah asked why I left in the first place, and I told her I wasn't going to talk about it. I didn't feel like telling anybody how stupid I was for getting myself fired that way. And I certainly didn't want to tell her that the police were looking for me.

I left when Leah was changing for work and went to this woman Betty's place.

The crab house sat on the bay side of Coastal Highway. When I pulled into the driveway, a stocky woman and a slender man were waiting for me.

When I got out of my car, the woman, Betty, came over and

shook my hand. She was a round little woman who looked about sixty. She wore thick bifocals that made her eyes look like black marbles just under the surface of clear water.

"Are you the boy Mr. Greene has sent me?" she asked. She looked up into my face and smiled, keeping her lips pressed tightly together.

"Yes," I said. "My name's Tom."

"Good," she said. "My name is Betty, and this is my husband Earl."

She pointed to the man standing uncomfortably close to her. The outside of Earl's left foot was touching her right. He had two green and clear plastic tubes running out of his nose that connected just below his nostrils to a solid cylinder that ran parallel with his lips. The tubes looped around the backs of his ears, down his back, and into a green tank by his feet on a little wire cart.

"Can you paint?" Betty asked. "I need my place painted."

"I can do it," I said.

"I want to get the place looking good for crab season. My husband was going to do it, but I don't need him climbing ladders and breathing in paint fumes."

I looked over at her husband, who was glaring at me disapprovingly. The oxygen in his tank made a soft hissing sound. She didn't need him up on a ladder; I was getting nervous just watching him standing on the ground. He was a walking skeleton. The wrinkles on his face and neck looked like wire sunk into dough.

Betty and her husband walked me around back to a small shed.

"First," Betty said, "you have to fill in all the cracks in the concrete." She pointed to a bag of concrete mix that lay in a blue wheelbarrow. "Then, scrape off all the old paint, don't just paint over it. Brushes and paint are in the shed."

"OK," I said and looked at her husband. He was still frowning at me.

"Now," Betty said and slapped her hands together, "this is how it's going to work. You'll get paid if I like your work. If I like it, I'll give you a hundred bucks for painting the place. If I don't like it, you go home broke. Sound fair?"

"Yes."

"Good. Get started." She patted me on the arm and walked off. Her husband didn't move.

I smiled at him, but his face was still. The only sound from him was the hissing of his breathing tubes.

I mixed the concrete with water from a faucet that was attached to back of the building, stirring the gray powder and rocks and water together with a flat-head shovel. The concrete mixture they had bought was for making walls or pathways; it was hard to fit into the tiny cracks in the building. Earl stayed behind me and watched without saying a word.

The crab house was falling apart. The salty air had turned the mortar in the brick joints into sand almost. The old paint boiled off the walls like the skin of a fish. I could pick off flecks as big as maple leaves.

The front of the building, where you ordered crabs, had two concrete pillars that held up a seven-foot lip of the red Mexican-tiled roof. Around the sides of the building, ivy grew like green veins into every crack. Painted-over cables ran down the back of the building, held in place together by rusty nails bent into L-shapes that stained the walls.

Betty didn't have a trowel or a putty knife in her shed, so I had to put all the concrete into the cracks with my fingers. My hands were stained gray from the drying concrete, which drank the moisture from my hands. The tips of my fingers were rubbed raw as I pushed the wet mixture into rough cracks between the bricks and in the foundation.

I scraped the loose chips of paint off the walls with the hobnailed sole of a shoe I found in the shed. Flecks of dry paint showered down into my hair and eyes. I had asked Earl for a knife or a spade, but he didn't answer, just stared at me and sucked in his air.

I started to paint a little after eleven. Earl watched me the whole time. He stayed in my vision like a crow in a distant corn field. Whenever I'd round the corner and start on a new section, I'd hear the squeak from the oxygen tank cart, and the crow would be perched on a new post.

After an hour of painting, I was switching arms. Betty didn't have a roller. She only had one five-inch brush, which frayed against the coarse concrete walls. I stopped and massaged my arm with my knuckles, and the scarecrow behind me cleared his throat.

After the first coat, Betty came out and gave me a sandwich and iced tea.

Orange sherbet-colored cloud streaks marred the turquoise sky as the sun came down.

Earl went inside and decided to keep an eye on me from the window. After he had left, working became a lot easier.

I liked working out in the hot sun. My muscles ached and I was tired, but I seemed removed from the pain. After a while, my arm just went numb, and daydreams took over the work. My mind was carried far out into the bay while hours passed like minutes. I never noticed the street lights come on from Coastal Highway. The cars blended in with the sound of the television Betty was watching as I dragged the wet brush down and up the now shiny white building. Time dissolved my thoughts, and I listened to everything as if I were under water.

I finished the job at around eight in the evening. Betty came out and circled the crab house four times, looking for missed spots. Earl stayed inside. I guessed he had tuckered himself out frowning all day.

"Not bad," Betty said.

"Thank you."

"I told you I'd pay you if I liked it," she said, "and I like it." She slapped five twenty-dollar bills into my hand. Then she told me to clean out her brush and to put everything away.

I washed the brush in a gray galvanized pail. The paint turned the water milky and swirled like clouds in a gray sky. The warm water washed away all the concrete that had formed in my hand, revealing the raw and cracked skin. I knelt down on the ground next to where the bucket had spilled over. The wet earth bled through my jeans. Crickets sang all around me. I was too tired to move.

I held up my bloody hands to my face and smiled. A fat trail of bright blood ran out from the side of my index finger. It filled every crevice of my sucked-dry hand, spreading out like the vines that I had pulled from the building.

I knelt in the mud behind the dingy crab house with bloody hands and laughed. I had never been happier.

As the chips of paint fell from my hair and from my shoulders down into the diluted white paint and mud, I knew that something was happening to me. With every white chip that touched the wet ground, I felt pieces of my old self disappear. I was falling apart muscle by muscle, bone by bone. Soon I would be put back together into something new.

eight

I WAS SITTING ON LEAH'S COUCH before the first sign of daylight dusted the room. It was a quarter past four in the morning. I stared off into the blue-black nothing of the dark room. It was quiet. The only sound was the whirl of the refrigerator and distant tumbling of waves in the ocean. Occasionally, a car on Coastal Highway would shush through the quiet, headlights projecting yellow on the ceiling.

I was too excited to sleep. My nerves vibrated as if I had a million honey bees crawling under the skin of my chest. I was excited because I had worked, not RHP kind of work but important work. I liked how I felt as I covered the rust stains on Betty's crab house with a new coat of white paint. I liked stirring the concrete mix in the barrow, feeling my shoulders ache as I spread the gravelly mix around with the shovel.

For a brief moment, I wanted to call Shawn. I knew that he would be awake, sitting at his kitchen table eating porridge or pancakes and drinking his coffee. I wanted to tell him that I had painted an entire two-story building by myself. I had even repaired the foundation. Maybe he would reconsider letting me work for him. But I hadn't talked to Shawn in months. The gap in our relationship needed to be bridged by more than painting a crab shack. The last time we had spoken to one another was when Lisa and I were playing a game of backgammon.

Shawn walked into the kitchen, patted Lisa's shoulder and went into the living room to watch television. Our eyes never met. I rubbed an ivory game piece between my fingers and kept my eyes on the blue and white checkered tablecloth.

When it was time for me to leave, Lisa stood up and called into the living room. "Tom's leaving, Shawn," she said. "Come say goodbye."

Shawn didn't move; I just heard him holler, "See you," as I walked out their back door.

A smile split across my face like stress on glass. I leaned forward, elbows on knees, and rubbed my sore hands together, like a fly. The skin around my fingernails was raw and dry, with many pink hangnails. The sweat spread into the cracked skin and hurt my palms like sparks. I picked at the cuts to make them bleed again. The slick feeling of blood dabbed my fingernails, and I wiped it away on my jeans. I knew the more damaged my hands were, the tougher and more callused the skin would heal. My dad used to cut off the bean-sized calluses on his palms with a pen knife.

"When they grow back," he said, "they'll be tougher than leather." My dad's hands had been so tough that you could stab a pin in his palm and it would stick without him feeling a thing.

I stopped playing with my hands and let them rest on my lap, stinging and pulsing.

As morning approached, dull yellow light cracked into the room, highlighting the edges of the rocker, the kitchen counter, and the refrigerator. I decided to sit there a little longer before sneaking back to bed, careful not to wake Leah. I swung my legs up on the couch and lay on my side. I had already dressed in my room. I never turned on the fisherman lamp, thinking the mustard-colored light that would border my door in the black hallway might pull Leah out of her sleep. I just knelt on the floor, groping around for my duffel bag, and dressed between the two twin beds.

I watched the blurry-edged shapes of a large bouquet of plastic and polyester flowers sitting in a cream-colored vase come into focus and wondered what I was going to do with myself today. There was no more work. I had asked Betty if she needed me to come back, but she told me that wasn't necessary. I figured while Leah was at the bar, I would try and wash more windows. I had made *some* money while I was here, but I still needed more. I felt the front of my jeans for the thick knot of cash in my pocket. I had two hundred and eighty dollars. The rent for my apartment was covered, but I still had to pay the phone and electric and gas bill; they would be crammed along with junk mail into my mailbox when I got back. And I would need more money for groceries.

Dawn came suddenly. Within an hour, light poured into the room. I was slightly above eye-level with the coffee table. I watched the sunlight glow on the carpet, heat registers, and the bottom curls of the curtains that touched the floor. The shiny, pole-like legs from the dining table chairs gleamed like ice in the dull light. I wasn't sure which legs belonged to which chair.

When the room was fully lit by daylight, I noticed another pair of legs at the dining table. They came into focus like a Polaroid, one thin tan leg reached the floor; the other leg was across the seat of the chair.

Hidden behind the large bouquet of fake flowers on the dining table, was Leah. I got up and walked over to her.

She was asleep, her head resting on her crossed arms. Sprawled out in front of here were several sheets of paper. A pen jutted from her right fist. She had been trying to write a letter to Ron, without any success. Several crumpled up pieces of paper were scattered on the glass-top table. I looked at the letter under which her arms were resting. All I could read was: DEAR RON, HOW CAN I TELL— After that I could read only the first word of every line going down the page because her arm was in the way.

I tapped her on her shoulder. "Leah?"

Her body didn't wince under my hand, but her eyes flickered open. She sat up and looked around the room. "I hate it here," she said, rubbing her hands through her short hair. "I can't ever sleep."

"Me neither," I said.

Leah got up and walked over to the rocker, gathering up

and crumpling her letter as she did so. She wore a white tank-top and a light blue checkered pair of men's boxer shorts. She sat on the rocker, brought both her knees to her chest and wrapped her arms around both legs. Her face was red and creased from sleep.

"How long have you been here?" I asked.

She yawned and rubbed her face. "All night." She held the crumpled remains of the letter in her left hand.

Leah had been in a good mood last night, eyes clear and bright. When I came home from painting Betty's place, we had watched a movie on television until I fell asleep on the couch. She had told me to stay up as late as I wanted because Mike hadn't found me any more work. "We can sleep in tomorrow."

I made us breakfast while Leah showered. She took her crumpled-up letter with her, and as soon as the bathroom door closed behind her, I heard the toilet flush.

When she was finished getting ready, Leah came out of her bedroom with her wet hair showing dark roots that ran along her part. She walked down the hall barefoot and adjusted the knot of the bow tie at her throat.

I made us scrambled eggs with diced pieces of green pepper. I wanted to use ham, but Leah didn't have any. The only thing in her fridge was an open can of soda, carrots in a plastic bag, a few eggs, a green pepper, baking soda, and milk. When we ate, Leah picked all the green peppers out of her eggs, piled them on the side of her plate, then ate them separately.

"Do you want to stay here while I'm at work?" she asked after finishing her eggs.

"You don't mind?"

"What do I care? It's not my house." She stuffed a few things into a black canvas bag, saying their names as if checking them off some list in her head.

I put her plate in the sink.

"I only have one key," she said then, "so if you're staying you can't leave, OK?"

"Sure."

"If you get hungry, the deli across the way will deliver. The number is on a sticker on the side of the phone."

"OK."

She smiled and looked around as if there was something else she wanted to say, but she just shrugged. "Have fun, I guess. I'll be home around six or seven."

I nodded and leaned back on the kitchen counter.

She turned back when she was almost out the door. "Don't answer the phone, OK?" She looked around the room again. Suddenly it seemed as if she wasn't sure if she could leave me alone.

"I won't," I said. "Don't worry; nobody will know I'm here."

Turning back again, she added, "Don't even answer the door." She shut the door behind her. Through the curtains and glass, I could see her standing on the balcony. She hesitated a second, then finally hurried away, her feet making a soft padding sound on each step going down.

WHILE LEAH WAS AT WORK, I cleaned the condo. I needed to keep busy with polishing and scouring and straightening.

I tried to go back to sleep after she left, but the worry about the police kept me from even closing my eyes. I lay as stiff as a pole under the white sheets of the guest room bed. I worried that the police had called my mother to ask her if she might know where I was. I was sure they had already talked to my neighbors, giving them cards with numbers to call when they saw me next.

First, I straightened the magazines on the coffee table, then I washed the breakfast dishes. These chores couldn't block the worry from my mind. Panic was expanding to the brink of an explosion between my lungs, constricting my air.

I needed to stop thinking about it. I needed to push the fear into a black chasm in my mind, which was where I seemed to put everything. The best way to stop the worrying was to dissect Leah's condo and scour every inch.

I took all the furniture out of the living room and piled it high in the long hallway, stacking end tables, lamps, and the coffee table on the sofa. When the room was bare, I vacuumed it, going in slow even strokes along the tan carpet as if I were mowing a lawn. Then I put everything back into the room and polished the coffee and end tables with a bottle of Old English.

Next I scoured every inch of Leah's bathroom, getting on my hands and knees and scrubbing the rust off the shut-off valve and the two silver bolts that held the toilet to the floor. My head was clear while I cleaned. I watched the orange rust and gray dirt stir together and dissolve in the frothy purple lather of Naval Jelly, and I couldn't even think of where I was or why. Years of steam had blurred the mirrors' silver trim and the pole legs of the sink. I scrubbed the boiled grayness of condensation with ammonia and vinegar with no effect. Then I sat in the bathtub and picked all the mildew out of the joints with a pen cap. As the black flecks of mildew rained down, worries about police and money went away like the ticking of a clock you just don't hear anymore.

After I'd cleaned all the rooms, I did the detailing. I unscrewed all the outlet and switch plate covers with a bone-handled letter opener that sat on a stack of bills on the kitchen counter. I took all the tan plastic covers and soaked them in bleach to get the finger smudges and bits of paint off them, careful to keep all the tiny screws together, in a Dixie cup with a Charlie Brown cartoon on it. The bleach crept into the cuts on my hand; the sting went straight to the bone and fizzed up my arm like carbonation. I put all the plates back and washed my hands. The cracks in the dry skin were purple-red lines circled by pink infection. I squeezed at the cuts and watery pus welled up between my pinched fingers, burning like acid.

I had vacuumed, scoured, washed, and disinfected every room, and it was only three in the afternoon. I wished I had more to do to distract myself, so I walked around the apartment and searched for other things to scrub and disinfect.

The only room I avoided cleaning was Leah's. At first, I thought she trusted me too much, leaving me, a stranger, alone in the apartment she had been house-sitting. But when I polished her doorknob with a tea-colored dab of Brasso on yellow chamois leather, I noticed that she had placed a six inch long red thread a foot down from the doorknob. If I had opened the door and the thread fell, she would have known I had rummaged through her things.

Leah came home early, around five-thirty. When she opened the door, I had all the burners off the electric stove into a pink plastic tub filled with ammonia and water.

Leah stopped a few feet from the door and sniffed the air. Her face was screwed up like she was about to sneeze. I could tell that she didn't like that I had cleaned.

"Did you move anything?" she said before greeting me.

"Well, if I did," I said shaking the suds off my hands into the soapy tub, "I put it back where I found it."

She nodded, still searching the room with her eyes. "Good."

I turned around and washed my hands in the sink. "I thought you'd like it," I said over my shoulder. "I had to keep busy, you know, so I thought I'd pay you back for letting me stay here."

"Oh, I like it," she said. "I was just worried that you moved things."

I shut off the water and dried my numb hands in a pink dish towel.

"Did anybody call?" she asked. "Nobody came to the door, did they?"

"No."

She exhaled through her nose and put a hand over her heart. "Thank God." She put her bag down on the kitchen counter and sat in the rocker. I stood there kneading the towel.

Leah craned her head towards me. "It's nice out. Want to go swimming?"

"Not really."

"Me neither," she said. "Want to see a movie?"

"No." I walked over and sat on the couch, making a trail of indentations on the puffy, vacuumed carpet.

"Well, I'm not staying another minute in this apartment. Go for a walk with me. We can walk on the beach."

I was tired and didn't really feel like it, but I said I would anyway.

LEAH AND I SAT ON A RED BLANKET on the beach just out of reach of the waves that fizzled out on the sand. The water was brown-green in the sun, and the crest of each unfurling wave had a white web of salt.

We had been walking for a while, parallel to the water, but I had to sit because the uneven surface of the sand hurt my ankles. We spread the blanket out and sat without saying much.

I picked up a tiny seashell, the size of a thumbnail, and crushed it into tiny shards between my fingers. Leah stared out over the water and squinted in the wind. She still wore her work uniform and had taken off her shoes. She buried her feet in the sand, looking like she grew out of the ground. Sand dusted her black pants with every breeze and she just wiped it away without thinking.

The sand was cream-colored and speckled white with pieces of sun-bleached oyster shells so bright that they looked like chips of broken china. Behind us was a wall of sand dunes spiked with long jutting blades of grass and outlined with rotting snow fences. A wave rumbled onto the sand and vomited out a pile of seaweed that looked like some kind of funny sea creature.

"I never come out here," Leah said softly. Her voice was like static under the loud waves. The wind sounded like the rushing blood in my temples.

"Why?" I asked, picking up a handful of sand and letting it sift through my fingers and fly away in a breeze.

"I can't let the neighbors see me." She turned around and looked back at all the condos and apartments at the edge of the beach. "But today, they can all eat shit."

I turned to face her. "So, you're not house-sitting." I said this as if she wasn't sure what she was doing and needed to be reminded of what she was *not* doing.

"No, I'm not," she admitted. "This is my grandmother's place, and nobody knows I'm here except Ron."

"This is your dad's mom's place?"

"No, my mom's mother. This is her summer place, but she's not using it this year." Leah stopped watching the water and pitched her head forward. Worry spread across her face like old age. I thought she was going to cry. "Listen," she said to the ground, "I had a lot of time to think today. I know *I'm* the one that told you to stay here, but I think I've been being too nice to you." She looked up at me. "I can appreciate you not wanting me to know why you're down here. But if you're in any kind of trouble that might get *me* in trouble, I'd like for you to leave."

I nodded.

"Do you want to tell me why you've come here?"

"No."

"*Are* you in trouble?"

"Are *you*?" I asked.

Leah snorted a little laugh. "My trouble doesn't affect you. What I'm really asking is: am I breaking the law by having you here?"

I stood up and brushed the sand off my jeans. "If you want me to go, I'll go."

Leah remained where she was. She tilted her head up at me and squinted. The skin around her nose scrunched up, pulling her lip up like she was going to spit. "I want you to stay," she said. "I really like you being here; I almost need you here. But I can't get in any trouble right now."

I walked a few paces away to the water. Seagulls swarmed around something down the beach; their calls slashed the air.

"Talk to me!" she shouted. "Please—"

"I'm not a criminal," I said, spinning around, my heels burying in the sand. "And that's all I'm going to tell you. If that's not good enough, then I'll go. You're the one who wanted me here. I don't care one way or the other."

Leah came over and stood in front of me with her back to the violent jade water. She stood on the wet, packed sand that the waves flattened into dark tan cement. Only her heels could dent the sand, pushing up a bubble of air around her feet.

"What's wrong with you? Why won't you just tell me what's going on?"

"Because I don't *know* what's going on," I said. "Leah, I think I'm in trouble, but I don't know for sure."

"With whom?" she asked. "Cops?"

I slumped. "It's a possibility."

"Oh, Tom," she said, pitying me. "You should have told me something like that!"

I stared at my feet, and Leah bit her thumbnail. The awkwardness between us was as thick as tar. If it hadn't been so windy, the quiet would have gnawed at me.

"Listen, I don't know for sure if the police are looking for me." I sat down on the edge of the sand where the water couldn't yet reach, and Leah walked over and sat next to me. "I was fired a couple of days ago for accidentally taking some money. The police were notified, and I'm down here until everything blows over."

"How did you accidentally take money?" she asked.

"I was overpaid on some checks and I never gave the money back. I didn't even know I had been paid extra. But my boss said it's theft and he called the cops on me. I paid the money back, and I'm down here just waiting and seeing."

"Waiting and seeing about what? How long will it take for you to know?"

I smiled, embarrassed not to know anything about the money or the police—as if everything had been decided for me, while I drifted along. "I don't know. I have a friend back home who's been keeping an eye on things."

Leah stood up and offered me a hand. "When we get back, you go and call your friend."

I stood and nodded, lips pressed tightly together.

"If he says things are cool, you can stay. If not—you go."

"Fair enough."

Leah stepped forward and hugged me. Cigar smoke and liquor reeked in her hair. She let me go and gave me a strange look. I realized that when she embraced me, my arms had been hanging by my side.

THE PHONE OUTSIDE THE DELI was busted (there was only a silver cord), so I walked up the block and used a phone in a booth outside a hot dog stand. The black phone was dressed in stickers for surf shops and tattoo studios in the area. I couldn't call Conrad collect (the men couldn't accept collect calls), so I emptied all the change out of my pockets onto a stainless steel ledge under the flat bottom of the phone. Someone had marked up the little ledge with the pencil cross-hatching of a game of tic-tac-toe.

The men who answered the phone at the halfway house always seemed to be pissed off that you'd called. I always seemed to be calling when they were sitting down to dinner or taking a nap. There was one man named Bill who used to answer the phone by just saying "What?" When I'd ask for Conrad, he'd put the phone down on the table without telling me to hold on, then I'd hear him scream, "Connie, get the goddamn phone!" Usually the men just answered the phone by saying, "Yes . . ." as if they had been waiting for the answer to a question you never heard.

I had a hard time dialing the number—and keeping the phone still against my ear, because I was shaking so badly. All morning I'd been closing off thoughts of the police.

A new kid answered the phone. He seemed unsure how to address me, as if he were working in a department store and had answered the phone before memorizing the store's little speech. "Hello . . .? May I help you?" he said. Someone else was in the room and mocked the way he answered the phone. The boy took the phone away from his ear and hissed for the other guy to shut up.

"Is Conrad in?" I said.

The kid paused for a second then told me to hold on. I heard him ask the guy who had mocked him who Conrad was.

The person replied, "*I'm* Conrad. Jesus Christ! Give me that phone."

"Connie Begg."

"Hey, it's Tom."

"Tom—how goes it?" Conrad said. Then he told the kid to piss off while he was on the phone. "Where are you?" he asked.

"I'm in Ocean City right now. How is everything?"

He immediately plowed into a story about the dock. "You should have been there," he said laughing. "We wrapped this new guy's arms to his chest with plastic wrap and kicked him out on the dock and closed the doors. The kid waddles around to the front of the building and knocks on the front door with his head to be let in."

"Steve didn't see any of this, did he?" The words popped out of my mouth as if I were still in charge.

"No. We did it at lunch."

"Well, how is everything else—with the police, I mean?"

Conrad lowered his voice. "Oh, *that*. Terry tells me that Steve's still pissed but things are simmering down."

"Did you give him the money?"

"Yeah, I put it on his desk while he was taking a piss. When Terry talked to him today, he said Steve didn't mention your name once."

I breathed out. "Well, that's a start, right?"

"Terry says things are cooling off, but I'd stay where you are. Give this at least another week and a half. He *may* have dropped the charges already, but I'm not really sure."

"Is that something Terry could find out?"

Conrad sucked his teeth. "I don't know—that's pushing it, don't you think? I mean, if Terry keeps asking these questions, Steve's going to get suspicious. What do you think?"

"I guess."

An electronic voice told me to deposit another twenty-five cents.

"Sounds like you got to go," Conrad said, "so I'll make this quick. Stay put and call me in a couple of days for an update. Call me on the dock, not here. Use the third line."

The third line was to the phone on my old desk. "OK."

"Tom, listen to me." He spoke slowly. "I know you're scared, but don't worry. I swear to God nothing bad will happen to you, OK? Just stay there for another week and a half, and you'll be fine. I promise." The authority in his voice held me like a vise, slowed my breathing, stopped my hand from shaking, and my blood ran warm.

I wanted to tell Conrad how much I appreciated everything he was doing for me, but the phone cut off. It was just as well. If I had told him how much I liked him, he would have held it over my head.

Before I left, I stuck my finger into the coin return to see if there might be some change, and I felt something soft and warm. It was a flamingo-pink piece of used chewing gum, stringing from the coin slot to my finger like a piece of stretched cheese.

THE SIGHT OF LEAH sitting on a man's lap on the couch and weeping sucked all the air from my lungs as if cold water had been poured down my back, and I wanted to run away. I thought it was Ron. Leah had her head pressed in the man's neck; the back of her head blocked his face. Her shoulders heaved up and down as she hyperventilated from crying. She sucked in air in quick gasps and let it out in a long, quivering wail.

"Oh, I'm sorry," I said, backing out the door.

Leah looked up and rubbed her bloodshot eyes with the back of her hand. The man holding her was Fritz.

He wore light blue jeans and a white dress shirt with snap-together pearl buttons. His shoulder was splotched wet from where Leah's face had been. When I walked in on them, Leah stood up and went to her room, embarrassed. She just rolled her pink eyes and took off down the hall. Fritz pursed his lips and stared straight out in front of him. I still hadn't moved; the door was open behind me and the salty air was coming in.

"You staying here?" He didn't bother to say hello or ask me how I was doing. He stood and combed a few strands of hair out of his eyes with his fingers.

"Just for a few days," I said. "It was her idea. I wanted to stay in my car." I inched my way to the open door. Then Fritz walked over and around me and pulled the door closed. I winced when it slammed.

"You been nice to her?" he asked.

"Of course."

"Good," he said, nodding. Then he walked over to the sofa and sat down. He looked up at me and pointed to the rocker, snapping his fingers. "Sit."

I walked over and eased onto the seat, never taking my eyes off him. The rocker creaked as I sat back. "If she's not allowed to have anybody here, I didn't know."

Fritz looked at Leah's closed door and listened for a second. "How long are you going to be in town?"

"Another week," I said.

"Good. I need you to do me a favor. Promise me you'll stay here and watch her. You're going to owe me one."

"Owe you for what?"

"I'll tell you later," he said then narrowed his eyes. "Will you stay with her?"

"If you want me to."

"I do," he said. "I need you to keep an eye on her."

"Sure," I said uneasily. "I'll try."

"Tell me," he said, gritting his teeth. "Has that Ron guy been to see her?"

"Not when I've been here."

Fritz screwed up his face and kneaded his right fist into his left palm. "I swear," he said, "when I see that piece of shit, he's spitting teeth." He was scowling at the tin of crayons, and I pictured him smashing it against the wall.

"Why do you want to beat up Ron?" I asked, swallowing hard after I said it.

Fritz's eyes snapped over. They were no longer pretty. "Don't worry about it."

Just then Leah came out of the bedroom, rubbing her eyes as if she had just woken up. The mean look on Fritz's face changed to one of sadness.

"Honey," Fritz said, "I want you to take a nap."

Leah shook her head and sat back down on his lap. She hooked her arm around his neck, and she rested her forehead against his temple. Leah still wore her work uniform, but the sleeves were rolled up and her bow tie and vest were gone.

I sat there in the rocker wondering if I should leave them alone.

"What did your friend say?" Leah asked me, without moving her head from where it rested. "Is everything all right?"

I looked at Fritz before answering. His eyes were closed. "Everything is fine."

Leah didn't react to what I said. My voice was as far away as the faint sound of the crashing waves. It was as if she couldn't hear me and was still waiting for an answer. Her eyes were raw pink, drained from crying, and her lashes were dark and clumped together. She stared straight out at nothing.

Fritz picked her up, turned around and put her down on the sofa. He grimaced with her cradled in his arms. His face was flushed when he stood back up. "Honey, I'm going to get us some dinner."

Leah nodded then rolled over with her back to us. I still

hadn't moved.

Fritz walked around the coffee table and pulled me to my feet by my left arm pit. "Let's go to that deli over there," he said pointing with his chin.

We walked to the deli across the parking lot. Inside, a man with light brown hair pulled back into a pony tail with a green rubber band stood behind the counter, under a sign with vinyl letters that said: YOUR DELLY. The sign was white and lit up, with the listings of food and prices written with red and black block letters. The edges of the glowing sign were turning yellow from age, and it buzzed louder than the tiny radio that was broadcasting a ball game.

"What does Leah like on her pizza?" Fritz asked me.

I was sitting in a orange plastic chair next to a dusty gumball machine that dispensed jawbreakers so old that I crushed the one I bought between my fingers. "How should I know?" I said, rubbing off the candy grit.

Fritz told the guy to put nothing on it, then he looked over at me and held out his hand. "You owe me five bucks."

The cashier told us it would be ten minutes, so Fritz and I went outside and sat on the curb to wait.

The street lights came on and the wind picked up in high-pitch whistles as the sky darkened. Fritz pulled out a crushed pack of cigarettes from the breast pocket of his dress shirt. The tattoos under the white sleeves were a dirty gray blur. He picked a cigarette from the pack with his lips, and lit it with a yellow Bic lighter. Then he rattled the pack around to see if any were left. He shook one cigarette from the pack and offered it to me. I took it by the tan filter without thinking. Then he gave me the lighter, and I just held it and the cigarette in one hand.

"You said back there that I owe you. What did you mean?"

"Found you a job," Fritz said, blowing smoke streams from his nose.

"Where?" I slid the cigarette behind my left ear.

"On a fishing boat up near Salisbury."

"How far is that?"

"About fifty minutes." Fritz turned and faced me. Smoke curled around his fingers and twisted up in the air. "But you'll stay here."

"What would I do on a boat?"

"Crabbing mostly. Ever done that?"

"No," I said. "I've never even been on a boat before."

Fritz lowered his head. "Jesus," he mumbled.

"I can do it, though," I said.

"You damn well better," he said. "And do a good job, too. My buddy Joe's doing me a favor by letting you work there. He just lost his main helper two days ago and has a spot for you." He sucked deeply on the cigarette. "A lot of boys want this job. You understand, he's doing me a favor by letting a kid he don't know work for him."

"I'll do OK," I said.

"Good. I'm holding you to that. You're not chartering a boat to fish with your buddies. This isn't *RHP* monkey work— Joe'll expect you to sweat. Tell me now if you can't handle that."

"I can do it, Fritz," I said again. "Trust me."

Fritz held up a hand and nodded. "I know. But my ass is on the line. I spent an hour last night talking Joe into giving you a chance. I told him you were Shelly's cousin, and dreamed of working on a fishing boat—full-time."

"But I can't go full-time," I said. "I'll give him a week, then I'm gone. He knows that, doesn't he?"

Fritz shrugged. "You can jump off that bridge when you get there."

I sighed. "Is this guy OK? I mean, will I get along with him?"

"Who—Joe? He's OK. Kinda quiet. Nobody I'd be an asshole around. Just shut your mouth and do as he says, and he won't break your jaw." Fritz nodded as if he was pleased with his thoughts about his friend, but I sat there feeling anxious. He saw the look on my face and reached over and squeezed my knee. "Relax. I wouldn't have set this up if I didn't think you could do it."

A long quiet swept between us as Fritz smoked and looked off at the traffic.

Suddenly, I turned and shoved him. "Why'd you *lie*?" I shoved him pretty hard, but he just lolled to the side like a tree in the wind and swayed back upright.

"About what?"

"About Leah," I said and turned to face him. He didn't look over at me; he just showed me his perfect profile and smoked away. "She doesn't know anybody who can find me a job. God, she thought I was a big pest when I first got down here."

Fritz ignored me. A smile worked its way across his face. "So, what do you think of her now?" he said.

"Leah?" His question tripped me up. "I don't know, she's OK, I guess."

Fritz looked over at me and flicked his cigarette, which was carried away by a stiff wind. "*OK*? What do you mean only *OK*?"

"What? She's nice."

"*Nice*? That's it. She's *OK* and *nice*? Don't you think she's pretty?"

"She's all right, I guess."

Fritz stood up and blinked in amazement. "Holy shit! You think she's just *all right*. What the hell's wrong with you? You should be thanking your goddamn lucky stars this girl's taking you in, box boy."

I stood and threw my hands up. "OK, fine—she's pretty, so what?"

"You bet your ass she's pretty!"

"What? Did you send me down here so you could play little miss matchmaker or something?"

"I sent you down here because you two are the most miserable people I've ever met in my life. I thought you'd get along." Fritz stepped down off the curb. "How can you not like her?"

"Because I'm not available," I said.

"You told me the other night you don't have a girlfriend."

"I live in *Baltimore*. That's three hours away."

Fritz made a sour face. "What the hell's in Baltimore? RHP? Move here. You got water and sun. Baltimore's got shit."

The cashier leaned his head out the door and told us our food was ready.

"You know, you're lucky to even be under the same roof as

Leah. You're no box of chocolates, you know."

Compared to Fritz, nobody was a box of chocolates, or so I thought.

"I'm not talking about this anymore," I said and chopped the air with my hand as if I were marking the exact place where I wanted to end the conversation. "I'm here for a week and half, and then I'm gone. That's it. End of discussion."

"Fine!" Fritz said and held the glass door open for me. "When I get back home, I got to remind myself to have a word with Shelly. If she thought *you* were the sweetest boy in the school, now I know why they fired her ass."

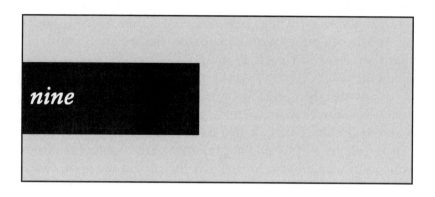

nine

WHEN I WAS FIVE YEARS OLD, one of my mother's friends had an in-ground pool and charged to give swimming lessons to the neighborhood kids. The lady's name was Barbara Crothers. She owned a lighting business (she had set up all the overhead lights in my elementary school). Her house was always overcrowded with cardboard boxes of light bulbs and fluorescent bars. Mrs. Crothers conducted the lessons with her son, Randy—who was a bully and friend of my brother.

When I went for my first lesson, Mrs. Crothers told me and six other boys to line up down one side of the pool. She hopped into the deep end of the pool and bobbed in the water like a buoy wrapped in pink and purple spandex. Her son came down the row of us boys and handed out pieces of Styrofoam the size of gravestones. It was early May, and we hugged the white boards as soon as we got them, gritting our teeth with every stiff breeze that shot up our bare backs.

Then the lady told us to jump in. None of us budged; we just stood there and looked at each other uncertainly. I put my own foot in the water and a gripping cold pain shot up my leg; goosebumps welled up on my arms. More boys tested the water, then laughed at Mrs. Crothers as if she was crazy. Most of the other moms had stayed to watch their sons. Now I wanted to leave, and I looked around for my own mother.

When nobody was willing to jump into the water, the lady's bully son came down the line and started pushing us in one by one. The boys in the pool were trying to scream with mouths full of chlorinated water, and their Styrofoam gravestones disintegrated into fat white chips. We (and our mothers) thought the Styrofoam pieces were kickboards, but we later found out that they were just packing material from a box of infrared light bulbs.

Once the boys surfaced, they immediately sank back down again, because they were trying to hug themselves and tread water at the same time. When Randy Crothers came to me, I ran to find my mother and beg her to take me home. I ran from woman to woman who sat in lawn chairs near the pool, to see if one of them was my mom. The bully son chased me the whole way. Eventually, I made it to the road and ran home, my bare feet slapping and stinging on the hard pavement.

When my dad got home from work that night, he called me into the living room.

"Your mother tells me you refused to swim today," he said as he adjusted the blue rubber ice pack to the sore spot on his back.

"It was too cold," I said.

"I understand that, but your mother and I have to pay for your lesson—whether you get in the pool or not."

I looked down at my feet. I wasn't sure what he wanted me to say.

"Thomas," my dad said, "we don't always do what we feel like doing. Sometimes we just have to shut our mouths and do it."

Shawn walked into the room and snorted a laugh at me. "Crothers told me he had to chase your stupid ass all over his yard because you didn't want to *swim*?"

My mother called from where she sat at the kitchen table. "You're not helping, Shawn." She felt bad because she had gone shopping instead of staying, like the other moms. She was ashamed when she found out I had been chased all over the yard by Randy Crothers.

Shawn laughed again and punched me on my upper arm

and went to his room. "I'll never understand you, Tommy."

"Ignore him," my dad said to me. "Listen. You'll go back next week, and you'll get in the water." I started to say something, but he raised his index finger to tell me to wait. "Thomas, when your back's against the wall, you'll be surprised what you're capable of doing."

He was right. I found that when I was pushed against the wall, I could lie, very easily and without shame. On the drive to Joe's house, I told myself not to mention anything about RHP or the police. If he asks why I'm here for only a week and a half, I thought, tell him whatever will get him to leave you alone.

I ARRIVED AT JOE'S ten minutes late—7:10. Fritz had given me directions on the same map of Maryland that he'd stapled to my shirt back in Frederick. He told me it would take fifty minutes to drive to Joe's, but it actually took me over an hour.

Joe's farm was surrounded by a gray stone fence, fuzzed with moss on the north side. The dark joints in the mortar were an inch and a half deep. His three-story brick house sat almost a mile back from the road. Ivy grew up one of the front chimneys. My dad would have disapproved; he said the worst thing you could do to your house was let ivy grow on it. The tiny fingers of the plant work into cracks in brick and wood, loosening the mortar joints and pulling boards from the house (a good entrance for snakes). To the left of the house, the jade surface of a large pond rippled with slivers of sunlight. A new-looking barn, the size of a airplane hangar, with beige corrugated walls and no windows, sat to the right of the house. Past the barn, the horizon was blanketed with chest-high stalks of corn.

I drove down the pebbled driveway so fast I thought my car was going to shake apart, dust kicking up as if it were on fire. I passed an apple orchard on the right. On the left were fields ribbed with furrows of potato, green bean, squash, and tomato plants stretching out of view into a black-brown wall of elm and oak trees.

Around the back of the house, about fifteen teenage boys rasped at each other like seagulls. Most of them stood over bikes without kick-stands that lay in the dirt; a few sat on the hoods of their cars, smoking cigarettes and hugging themselves in the cold morning air. A redheaded kid with a buzz cut was loading a wet saw into the bed of a large red Ford pick-up. The rear of the truck had been backed up to the side door of the barn. He secured the saw with bungee chords, then playfully shouted something to the crowd of boys, and they puttered with nervous laughter.

I got out of my car and walked over to where the kid was loading the truck. He moved with the jerky movements of a bird building a nest. It made me uneasy to watch him. His forehead and cheeks were studded with pimples. His face seemed to be boiling right in front of my eyes. The zits on his face were swollen white, ready to pop like firecrackers if he tensed his face. When I got to the truck, he zipped back into the barn before I could say anything to him.

Most of the boys looked sixteen or seventeen—Terry's age. They wore dirty jeans and kept checking each other out. One boy, wearing a long-sleeve undershirt with a pack of Winstons stuck in the breast pocket, walked by me.

"Hey," I said and stopped him by placing my hand on his shoulder. He looked down at my hand as if it might leave a stain. "Are all these kids here for the job?"

The boy looked up at me suspiciously. He'd been trying to grow a mustache, but only had a little fuzz. From a distance, it looked like he had been eating chocolate. "Yeah, but only one of us is getting it," he said.

"Why are there so many people here?"

The kid made a disgusted face. "You don't *know*?" He rolled his eyes. "Greg, the guy who used to help Joe, is in jail." He pointed to where the redheaded kid had disappeared into the barn. "For years it's been Greg and Doug." Then the boy looked around and lowered his voice. "I hear he pays a shit-load."

That made sense to judge from the size of the house, which blocked out most of the sky from where I stood. I nodded to the kid as a way to tell him I was done talking. He walked off and sat on an oil drum next to a diesel pump with GULF written on its candy-orange belly in fat white letters. He pulled an

E-Z-out Gerber knife from his front pocket and sharpened it on a whetstone the size of a pack of chewing gum.

The kid named Doug came out of the barn, hugging a wrecking bar, a sledge hammer, and a six-foot level in his arms. He waddled over to the truck and let the stuff drop into the bed.

"Has Joe been out yet?" I asked him, raising my voice over the clatter of tools.

"No. He's inside somewhere. He'll be out in a second to pick somebody."

"You work here, right?"

"Yeah, I do." He tried to smile shyly, but a bright grin split across his face. I could tell he was proud to work for Joe. "I'm Doug," he said and held out a hand, which I accepted. I was surprised by the firmness of his grip; he was a foot shorter than me and probably forty pounds lighter, but my knuckles popped when he pumped my hand.

I smiled at him and walked away, massaging the blood back into my fingers and hiding the pained expression on my face. I walked over to the back porch and sat on the first step. Doug climbed into the back of the truck and counted the tools, mouthing the name of each one as he pointed to it as if he were taking roll call. I looked over at the boy on the oil drum. He tested the sharpness of his knife by rubbing his thumb across the blade a few times, then nodded, satisfied.

The screen door behind me opened and clacked shut. Joe came out, carrying two green trash bags, which he dumped into a gray dumpster at the end of the long porch. He walked past junk that was bunched up against the house—the propeller from an outboard motor, a welding mask, a push-mower's engine, spare boots, and three oil-stained wooden boxes filled with tiny motors for things like weed-eaters and chain saws. Joe stopped at the dumpster, his feet scraping on the gray chipped paint of the porch.

I stood like the rest of the boys and faced him. He looked out over us and scratched the back of his gray buzzed hair. His eyes were like two balls of ice, peering out between slits in old leather. As Joe looked the boys over, each held still as if his picture were being taken. Then Joe looked down at me and frowned.

"You the one who called me last night?"

I wasn't sure what to say.

"Well, you still want the job or are you going to Florida?" he asked.

"No," I said. "I've decided to stay here." I didn't even blink when I said the lie.

Joe shook his head. "Good." The deepness of his voice boomed the word like a fist into my chest. Then he turned and started to go inside.

I looked out over the boys. They already knew they wouldn't be getting the job. Some slumped their shoulders and others spat on the ground.

"Pete," he said, snapping a finger at me, "come on."

I walked up on the dusty porch and pulled back the wooden screen door. Before I slipped inside, I saw Doug walking through the crowd of disappointed kids.

"OK, guys," he shouted to them. "Better luck next time. Let's clear it out now."

I walked in the house through a mud room with coats hung on the wall and into a messy kitchen. Joe stood with his back to me and finished the rest of his coffee at a table strewn with junk mail and newspapers. His upper back was as wide as a bear's. He turned and walked over to me, his footsteps thudding on the floorboards and vibrating up my legs. When he stood in front of me, my eyes were level with the knot in his throat.

"How old are you?" The words were a quick spurt.

"Twenty-five, sir."

He nodded. "Good. I was afraid I was only going to get kids." At the sink he balanced his empty mug on a pile of dirty dishes. "What made you change your mind?"

I shrugged, remembering what my dad said about lying. If Joe thought I was somebody else, then I was going to shut my mouth and let him keep believing it.

"I'm still tiling that place in Salisbury. I'll be there tomorrow, too, so I'm not going out on the boat."

I nodded but didn't know why.

"So instead, you're going to clean this place up." Joe stepped past me and opened the pantry door. "Come here."

I went into the small room; the peppery smell of spices burned my eyes. In front of me was a small window with a screen. I could see Doug sitting on the hood of the red Ford. He was eating something and it took me a few seconds to see what it was; the screen distorted my vision. Doug was sucking the catsup out of one of those little packets that you get from fast food restaurants. My stomach went queasy, and I looked away to the pantry shelves that went up to the ceiling.

Joe pulled four white boxes off a shelf that was level to his waist, sweeping dust in the air which writhed in the blades of sunlight that came through the window. Each box had DOMINO: BALTIMORE, MARYLAND stamped on it in black letters. He cracked one open and showed me hundreds of white sugar packets. "I want you to open all these and pour them in here." He set an empty large pickle jar on the floor and tapped his gold wedding band on its lip twice, which made a hollow clinking sound. I must have made a face because Joe said, "It's cheaper this way."

I nodded again, as if I understood. I looked out the window, and Doug caught my eye again. Now he tipped his head back and let a line of red catsup fall from the packet that he held two feet above his open mouth. Then I looked at the shelves and saw a box that had HEINZ stamped on it. I pointed to the box of catsup packets. "You want me to put those in a jar, too?"

Joe shook his head. "No. It's better to take them on the boat as is." Then he squinted out the window at Doug. "Besides, he likes them out of the packet."

Joe stepped past and out of the pantry, which flattened me to the wall. It wasn't that he was fat, he was just large. His arms were corded with muscle and his hands were like the paws of a great beast. It wasn't a bodybuilder's physique; Joe's could have been carved from slabs of granite. He was also handsome—but not in the pretty way Fritz was. Joe had a masculine seriousness about him, focused eyes and a pleasant smile that tugged on the side of his mouth sometimes when he talked. His hair was mostly gray and cut into a short bristle on top of his head.

"When you finish all that," Joe said, "do the dishes, mop

the floor, and straighten up. You got all that, or you want it written down?"

"Dishes, mop, straighten," I said, nodding on each word.

"Good. You'll be alone here for most of the day. I'll be back around noon, then you're free to go. Any questions?" When I said no, he left without saying goodbye.

I watched him walk out to the truck through the small pantry window. Doug hopped down off the hood and opened the rusty door and climbed inside. The truck rolled away, crunching on the pebbled driveway, and I started to work. I sat on the dusty floor and set the empty pickle jar in my lap and pinched four white packets of sugar between my fingers, shook twice, tore, and poured.

It took me two hours to fill the pickle jar. My back cramped and my hands were warped into claws from all the tearing. When I finished, I put the jar onto the shelf and flattened the white boxes like I used to do at RHP.

One key to Joe's wealth must have been self-sufficiency. Almost nothing in the pantry looked as if it had been purchased from a supermarket. The shelves were stocked with jars of homemade tomato paste, red plum jelly, soups, and honey that was starting to crystallize. On one of the bottom shelves, there was a huge supply of cured ham in saltwater, stored in about a hundred old baby food jars. The commercial products were purchased in bulk quantities. On the floor, there were burlap sacks of rice and oat meal that all had NOT FOR RESALE stamped in red on the front of the bags. The only items in the pantry that seemed to have been bought from a normal store were on the very top shelf. Bottles and jars sat under a glaze of dust and spider webs. He had several imported jars of Polish jam, unopened bottles of scotch and whiskey, and Canadian maple syrup that came in the same kind of can as rubber cement and had a picture on the label of a family sitting in a sleigh in front of a log cabin. I reached up and ran my finger down a fat-bottomed bottle of cognac, making a trail of gold on its gray-copper hide. The dust collected on my finger in the shape of a horseshoe, and I wiped it away on the front of my jeans.

Washing the dishes made me sick. As soon as I touched the

first dirty plate, a dozen fruit flies fizzled around my face and went into my ears. They seemed to be propelled upward by the smell of food that had never been cleaned off the plates. The dull odor of rotten, wet meat and clumpy spoiled milk wafted into the room. As soon as the smell of the decaying food darted up my nose, I held my stomach, bent over and dry-heaved over the sink. Then I moved the trash can close by in case I threw up while I washed. I had to scrape the food on the plates with a knife. The green and gray pieces of beef that had been lying in old dish water came off easily. When I scraped them over the trash can, the smell made me gag bile up in the back of my throat.

There was one plate at the bottom of the sink that had a Sunday flyer for paint supplies mashed into dried spaghetti sauce that had petrified into orange-brown woodworker glue. I took this plate, went outside to the side of the house, and threw it like a Frisbee into the green pond next to the house. It smacked down into the calm surface, and I waited until it sank away out of sight into the dark green water.

Then I cleared all the old newspapers and junk mail off the kitchen table. Under the paper were some more dishes and an array of stray bullets. The shiny brass casings looked like metallic pills scattered onto the dark pine tabletop. I found an empty shoe box next to the refrigerator and filled it with the bullets, letting the .22s, red shotgun shells, and Winchester .30-06s fall from my palm one by one. Then I put the box on top of the fridge, next to a thirteen-inch black and white TV with flags of aluminum foil as an antenna.

If there are so many bullets, I thought, where are all the guns? Then, as if their camouflage were dissolving, I noticed about fifteen rifles and shotguns leaning on the veneered walls of the kitchen. I walked over and picked up a double-barreled shotgun and cracked it open to see if it was loaded. It was. The owl's eyes of two brass twelve-gauge primers stared back at me.

Conrad had once told me about an eighteen year old member of his house in Ohio who tried to kill himself with a gun just like the one in my hands. The kid was from Turkey and had only lived in America for two years. Conrad thought the kid was insane because he never talked to anybody and ate toothpaste like candy. The kid's father put him in the halfway house after he was kicked out of college for sneaking a flask of Southern Comfort into class. After half a year in the house, the kid, Conrad said, sat the butt of the gun (which he had stolen from the house next door) on the floor between his legs and balanced a butter knife over the trigger. He was going to step down on the knife with both feet like a pedal. Somehow, he lost his balance and the gun lurched to the left and went off. He blew off his jaw, his left ear, and seventy-five percent of the skin on his face. The force of the buckshot sinking into his skull shattered his nose and both his cheekbones into jagged pieces. Conrad and most of the guys from the house were at church when this happened, but he said an elderly neighbor (whose gun the kid had stolen) heard the shot and drove the kid to the hospital. A week after the poor guy got out of the hospital, he sat down on some railroad tracks and finished the job. I closed the gun and set it back against the wall.

I finished cleaning more quickly than I had at Leah's. I hadn't the energy to pick apart Joe's house and polish it piece by piece.

For lunch, I ate a bag of oyster crackers that I had taken from Leah's; it was the only thing she had in the house to eat, and Fritz had told me Joe wouldn't feed me. I ate on the front porch, sitting next to an orange milk crate filled with different-colored telephone receivers. I shoved the crackers into my mouth by the handful and looked at the junked cars and trucks that were next to the barn. A small blue Toyota sat in a field where grass had grown higher than its wheels. Next to that was a tan Mercedes station-wagon with all its doors missing and no hood. There was also an old golf cart that was missing a motor; tall blond-tipped grass jutted from the rear of the machine where the small hood had been left open. More cars and trucks were in the field with flattened tires and missing doors and wind-shields. All the vehicles were scattered randomly, as if they had all fallen from the sky and Joe never bothered to have them hauled away.

When I went back inside, I roamed around the first floor of

the house. I went through an awning to the left of the kitchen and into the dining room. A long dark-stained oak table sat on a dusty Persian rug in the center. Two tall white candles sat in the center of the table in crystal holders, placed on a long white doily that ran down the middle of the tabletop. The sunlight hit the prisms of the crystal holders and spread razor-thin green and red and purple lines across the room. There were six high-backed, leather-padded chairs at the table but only two places were set. The dishes were Sango china and the knifes and forks sterling silver. Both places at the table had their own thimble-sized salt and pepper shakers. Everything on the table lay under a veil of dust.

My hand left a print on one of the chairs. I wiped the print away with the side of my palm. All along the wood-paneled walls were hutches filled with dinner plates and champagne glasses with stems as thin as pencils. Everything in the room seemed to be decaying. Large bay windows filled the room with light, and I could see the dust particles spiral in the air and convulse in front of my eyes when I breathed out. Above the fireplace was a stuffed marlin whose brilliant indigo and turquoise skin had been dulled under the gray film of dust. The fish's gaping mouth had spider webs stringing from the top to bottom jaw, looking like lines of saliva.

I walked out of the dining room into an open space with a large spiral staircase going up the third floor. The newel post was chest high and as thick as a squared-off telephone pole. On top was a lead cherub looking like he wanted to swim up to heaven, but his right arm had been busted off. I could see inside its hollow chest from the opening of the amputated arm. I stood in the center of the room and looked up and to the ceiling three stories above. There was a bronze box-shaped chandelier with sepia-toned stained glass in it. On the second and third floors white rails with cranberry-red banisters encompassed the opening in the floor.

Past the foot of the red-carpeted steps was a dark, windowless parlor. I slid back a heavy door by a brass ring. The door slid into the wall on aluminum rails. It was the only room in the house that looked as if it was lived in. Across the dimly-lit room were two body-molded leather chairs with brass buttons punched into the backrests. The dark leather looked sectioned, like rolls of bread. The chairs were on either side of a fireplace with an iron rail going around the front with chafed mustard-yellow padding on the top. On the mantel was a row of crystal decanters, filled with different colors of liquor. Some of the bottles were box-shaped, molded with the cross-hatching texture of a handgun's grip, and the others were the shapes of bowling pins.

I walked across the room and plopped down in one of the chairs. The only light in the room came from the hallway. When I looked up, I could make out the shapes of twenty or thirty stuffed animals, surrounding the parlor's entrance. Joe appeared to be an accomplished taxidermist. He had a gray screech owl, a red-headed woodpecker, a buck's head, a few hawks, and above the door was the head of a black bear on a tan wood plaque. I got up from the chair and flipped on a light switch. The lights were mounted to the walls and looked like torches with honey-colored glass globes. The yellow light flickered across the room and made the bear's glass eyes blink to life. Air escaped from my body, and I didn't know how to pull any in again as I stared at the glassy yellow fangs in the dead bear's violent mouth. It was as if the bear had been letting out one last defiant roar before his head was lopped off, and the snarling look never left his face. It scowled at me like the dead faces of the Union leaders on the Pennsylvania memorial. I had to look away.

Bookcases surrounded the parlor walls. The shelves were filled with books which seemed to have been read a dozen times, their spines cracked and darkened with palm sweat. Joe had the books that I expected to see; things about saltwater fish and safaris and wilderness survival and several versions of *The Shooter's Bible*. He had every edition of *Audel's Carpenters and Buyers Guide* ever published. He also had some investing, real estate, and day-trading manuals with titles like *Become a Millionaire Without Even Trying* or *Born Poor, Die Rich* or *101 Tips to Becoming a Millionaire—Fast*. Joe didn't have any fiction on his shelves; instead, he had dozens of memoirs of sailors at sea. Some were reprints of books written around the 15th century by Portuguese sailors trapped in the dead calm of the equator and unable to get home; others were by sailors traveling around the world, describing what they had seen or discovered or felt. I pulled a thin trade paperback off the shelf. It was a memoir of an officer in the Royal Navy who got knocked off a small personnel carrier leaving Swaziland heading for southern Zanzibar sometime before the first World War. According to the book synopsis, when the author, Bradford Waltz, struck the water from the fast-moving boat, he pulled a groin muscle and separated his left shoulder. Then the author swam for two days to the coast of Majunga.

I sat back down in the worn leather chair and read part of the book. Bradford Waltz spent two chapters discussing the survivalist stroke he used to swim eleven miles to land, using only one arm. But what interested me most was his description of the one night he spent floating half-asleep in the water.

"I have seen death, and I know what awaits us all," wrote Waltz. "A universe of mindless floating in the tar-black water of the Indian Ocean at night."

I took the book and stuffed it down the back of my jeans. After I had a chance to read it more closely, I would return it.

Then I went back into the kitchen and waited to go home.

I could see Leah through the lacy white curtains of her front door. She was sitting in the rocker, wrapped in the gray blanket.

I knocked on the door. She opened it for me, hugging herself in the blanket, then walked back to her chair. We exchanged awkward smiles.

"Is it all right if I go lie down?" I asked.

Leah shook her head, annoyed. "You don't have to ask. Just go."

"Oh." I smiled an apology and walked down the hall.

Fritz was asleep in the bed next to mine. He lay face down, his head stuck in the crack between the wall and the edge of the mattress. The air in the room was thick and gray with the smell of old cigarette smoke. A whiskey-colored glass ashtray sat in front of the fisherman lamp, filled with mashed cigarette butts.

I closed the door quietly and sat on my bed, careful not to make the springs creak. Fritz still had all his clothes on, and he lay on top of the blankets. I watched his side expand and contract as he breathed. The warmth of sleep washed over me as I watched him. I lay on my back and closed my eyes.

Joe had told me to come back tomorrow at seven. I would have to work there for at least a week more before he'd pay me. When Joe had come back from his tiling job, he and Doug came into the house covered in a tan dust. Doug's fiery red hair was dulled under the powder. They both sat at the kitchen table; their dirty hands left trails on the dark wood. Joe didn't tell me if he liked my cleaning job or not. He just rubbed the back of his neck and said in a low groan, "Be here tomorrow at seven."

Doug got up from the table, stretched, and said that he was going home. Joe looked up and nodded. As Doug walked past me, he gave me an army salute and walked out of the kitchen. I watched Doug go outside from the doorway. He went into the barn and came out pushing a yellow Honda moped with a gray milk crate fastened to the back. RUTTER'S DAIRY was written on it in thin white letters. Doug reached in the crate and stuck a red baseball cap on his head, then twisted it backward. He got on the bike and pedaled for about fifty feet to start the motor, wobbling from the effort. The motor gurgled while he pedaled, then he hit the choke, and the moped raspberried to life.

I waited a few minutes for Joe to say something to me. The only sound I could hear was the buzz from Doug's moped tailing off down the dusty driveway. Joe took a small notebook out of the breast pocket of his flannel shirt and wrote in it with a tiny golf pencil. Then I realized that he wasn't going to say anything else, so I backed out of the kitchen and went outside.

I rolled over in bed to face the wall like Fritz, and I heard a crinkling noise under my pillow. I lifted up the pillow and there was a note for me, written on hotel stationery. It had been folded neatly in half with my name written on it. I opened the letter and two twenty dollar bills fell from it and pinwheeled to the mattress. The note said: TOM, TAKE LEAH OUT TONIGHT.

SHE HASN'T BEEN FEELING WELL. USE THIS MONEY. FRITZ. I crumpled the note and lobbed it over to where Fritz lay. It bounced twice on the bed beside him, but he didn't move.

I didn't feel like taking Leah out. All I wanted to do was sleep. But if Fritz was paying, I couldn't say no. I swung out of bed, not caring how much noise I made, and went to the door. I looked down at Fritz. The wax he used in his hair made a dark stain on the pillowcase. The slick strands looked like the grooves in an old record.

"I know you're not sleeping," I said. His body didn't move, but I saw his ears raise with a smile. I sighed and went out of the room.

I walked up behind Leah in the living room and placed the forty dollars on top of her head and sat down on the couch. She crossed her eyes to look up at the bills and shook her head and let them fall into her lap.

"Your uncle's paying for us to go out," I said.

Leah placed the two bills together and folded them in half. "He is?"

"Yes. So what do you want to do?"

Leah frowned at the money in her hand as if she wanted to ask it a question. "I don't want to do anything."

"Oh," I said. I started to get up, but I let my weight collapse down onto the couch. "Why not?"

"I don't know. Don't have the energy right now."

I waited a minute. "Well . . . he *is* paying. I don't like turning down free food."

Leah nodded, but her face was still blank. "We could eat, I guess."

"Good," I said. "Where?"

"Do you want to go down to the boardwalk?"

"Whatever you want," I said.

Leah stood up and dropped the blanket back on the chair. She hadn't dressed today. She was wearing a pair of boxer shorts and a white tank top.

"I guess I should shower," she said, looking down the front of herself. Then she ran a hand through her hair and rubbed her fingertips together. "How does my hair get so greasy in one day?"

"I don't know."

Leah took the blanket and draped it over the back of the chair. Deep impressions from the blanket ran up her tan legs like scars. She tried to rub them away like she was trying to get wrinkles out of a pair of pants. "God, I look horrible," she said.

I clapped my hands together playfully. "Let's go. I'm starved."

She smiled and told me to give her twenty minutes to get ready. Then she walked down the hallway and stopped in front of her door. She stood there for a moment, frozen, as if there were a snake in the carpet and she was about to step on it. Hunger made my stomach feel as if it had collapsed on itself. Then Leah turned around and said, "You know what my uncle is doing, right?"

I nodded.

"And you know it's not going to work, right?"

I nodded again.

LEAH AND I TOOK THE BUS down to the boardwalk and ate at a restaurant that had volleyball nets strewn all over the walls with plastic crabs and lobsters and starfish in them. All the walls were speckled with gimmicky nautical crap: bamboo fishing poles, brass portholes (which you could not see out of because they were just stuck to the walls), anchors, and paintings of sailboats just likes the ones at Leah's. All the tables had yellow or red or green citronella candles on them, which filled the room with the burnt waxy smell of a blown-out birthday cake. There was only one other couple in the place.

Tonight was the first time I had seen Leah wearing anything besides her work uniform, a robe, or her sleep clothes. She wore a pale yellow T-shirt, faded jeans, and a pair of white canvas dock shoes. The yellow of her shirt made her skin appear more tan than it really was. She wore some kind of gel in her hair, which made it look wet. All through dinner, I wanted to reach across the table and feel the slick strands of her blond hair. She didn't wear any make-up except for a tiny bit of mascara.

Before dinner, Leah ordered us a shrimp cocktail. I only ate one shrimp and gave the rest to her. Leah ordered steamed shrimp for her meal. A few times during dinner Leah blew on her fingertips because the Old Bay on the shrimp was getting into her hangnails. She had painted her nails a pretty burgundy color.

Leah and I didn't talk much during dinner. A few times I had asked her how her food was, and she just said it was good, and we were quiet again.

Leah was now sitting with both elbows on the table and a white mug of coffee in her hands. Her silver bracelets bunched up around her forearms. She blew on the surface of the coffee, then took a sip.

"You work tomorrow?" she asked, jolting me out of my blank stare.

"Yeah—have to be there at seven."

"Good," she said. "My uncle was worried that Joe would turn you down."

I couldn't help but smile.

"What?" Leah set her coffee down. Her eyes were suddenly clear.

"Joe thinks I'm some guy named Pete."

"Why does he think that?"

"Joe was expecting somebody and thought I was him. So I never bothered to tell him who I really was." Leah gave me a disapproving look, so I tried to calm her down. "I'll be gone in a week and a half. If he finds out, then I'll just leave."

Leah pursed her lips and thought for a second. "Just as long as it doesn't come back on my uncle."

"You and Fritz are pretty close, huh?"

"Yes, I suppose we are."

"You seem to get along well."

"It's funny you say that," she said. "Because I've only really known him for about three years."

"Fritz wasn't around when you were a kid?"

Leah sipped on her coffee. "I remember bits and pieces of him from when I was a little girl. I remember things like him showing up for a birthday party here and there or dropping by to see my dad." Leah smiled, remembering something. "Now, every time he comes around, my girlfriends all want to come over to look at him."

"Did you know he was your uncle when you'd see him as a kid?"

"No," she said. "I just remember thinking he was a friend of my dad's. My parents never talked about him, and I never asked who he was."

"So how did you become so close?"

"He came back as soon as he started dating Shelly. I think she's the one who told him to. Before he met her, nobody even knew where he was."

"He disappeared?"

Leah nodded and picked up her cup again but didn't drink from it. "I think I may have been six when he went away for good. He came back the day I graduated high school. When me and my parents got back to the house, Uncle Fritz was sitting on our front steps with a white teddy bear for me. The bear wore a graduation cap and it had a felt diploma in its hand—I think I still have it. He handed it to me and told me he was my uncle. Then we spent the whole night talking."

"Did he say where he'd been?"

"It was weird . . .we talked about my dad, and we talked about where I wanted to go to college. He even asked my advice about Shelly. But the whole time he never told me a thing about himself. I'd try to ask him something, and he'd just dance around the question." She stared into the black mirror of her coffee, then shook her head. "Ever since, we talk all the time—which is hard. My mother won't let him in our house."

"Why?"

"Oh, God, she *hates* him. She just thinks he's just the biggest troublemaker."

"Is he?" I asked.

"No! God, no. I love him to death." Leah sulked for a second. "I just wish he'd get rid of his nickname. I hate it."

"What's his real name?"

"Robert. I like that name. It's better than *Fritz*." She made a sour face.

"Where'd he get that name?"

Leah waved a hand in the air. "Don't ask me. He's been called Fritz for so long I'm sure he doesn't even know where it came from."

We were quiet again. Leah finished her coffee, and I picked at my fingernails.

"You about ready?" I asked.

"You want to go back?"

"Kind of."

"Well . . ." she said, as if admitting a secret. "I'm sort of enjoying myself."

"OK. We can stay—for a little longer. I can't be out too late, though."

She leaned across the table and touched my hand. "I know something we can do."

"What?" I said.

She shook her head. "Come on—I'll show you."

We walked on the boardwalk toward the carnival rides. The air was sweet with the smell of spilled cola and funnel cakes. Yellow jackets flew in figure-eights around the wire trash cans. More people walked on the boardwalk than when I first came here. Most of the shops were open. Their lights spread a mustard yellow glow on the dark beach. In the distance, I could see the white crests of the waves exploding onto the sand. We passed the public showers and stands that rented bicycles. Near one of the showers was a sand sculpture of a crucified Christ. The artist had set up green and orange lights to illuminate the figure in the dark. In front of the sand Jesus was an empty water jug filled with coins and a few dollar bills.

Leah walked to my side, and I kept my hands in my pockets. She stopped outside a ride and hooked onto my arm. "Look." She was pointing to the ride. It was a haunted house. "I figured you'd like this one. My uncle told me you like ghosts."

"Your uncle tells everybody that I like ghosts."

The sign said THE HAUNTED HOUSE in fluorescent orange letters under a giant, plaster black bat which had a crazed look on its face. Tickets were a dollar and the woman who took them sat in a booth behind a Plexiglas window with holes drilled in a circular pattern so she could hear us. She was eating a messy sandwich. Grease and mayonnaise trailed down her hand and forearm. The lady took our money and sucked the grease off each of her fingers one by one. She handed me two red tickets that were still connected together and told us to sit in the first available car.

The cars looked like purple midget coffins. In front of them was a headless motorized mannequin. Leah and I sat in a car and pulled a steel bar over our knees and into our guts. We waited a few minutes as the woman warmed up the ride. Above us, *The Monster Mash* played on a static-filled loudspeaker. We waited for so long that I thought the woman was going to come out of the booth and tell us the ride was busted. Then our little coffin jerked forward, snapping our heads back.

We went through two double doors, and everything was black inside. The squeaks from our wheels echoed inside the building. As we rounded a corner, wax figures of monsters on hydraulics were set up to jump out at us. The sharp hiss of the oxygen in the hydraulic poles startled me more than the monsters themselves.

Most of the ride was broken. A rubber man on an electric chair convulsed as we went by, but the lights around him were burned out so we couldn't really see what he was doing.

Leah laughed and shook her head. "This is terrible," she shouted over the squeaks and moans of the ride. Just then a big spider with googly eyes rappelled from the ceiling and splatted down on the front of our coffin. As the thing wound back up, Leah batted it with her hand as if it were a piñata.

We went up a steep incline and passed through another set of doors which led outside. We squeaked along in our little coffin above where the ride started, and everybody on the board-walk looked up at us. We both covered our faces and laughed. Then we went through another set of doors, which was studded with discarded pieces of chewing gum. The first thing we came to was a small cemetery with cardboard headstones with fluorescent orange names and dates on them. Everything glowed from a black light overhead. A coffin sat in the middle of the graveyard. The door sprang open and nothing was inside except the gears that worked the hydraulics. There was no zombie or vampire.

Before the ride ended, I saw someone sitting behind a thin black curtain near an emergency exit. I thought it was somebody dressed up like a monster who was going to run up and scare us. I tapped Leah on the knee and pointed to him.

But as we came to the figure, I saw it was a teenager eating a slice of pizza, sitting on a green transformer. It was the boy I'd seen outside the fun-house the first day I came here. He saw us and raised his half-eaten slice of pizza as if he were proposing a toast.

After that, Leah and I went on every haunted house ride and fun-house we could find, trying to determine which was the lousiest of them all. We came out of one fun-house which had a giant plaster Indian on top with glowing, hypnotic eyes. He wore a white turban that glistened from its enamel paint, and both his arms moved back and forth as if he were motioning for us to come inside.

"That one," Leah said, "was pretty crappy. You have to admit."

I was holding my knee, which I had twisted when we walked up some stairs inside that shook from side to side, trying to disorientate you. "That was just painful," I said. The only thing in that fun-house that didn't try to trip you was a long hallway with mirrors that made you fat or thin or gave you a big forehead. Leah made me stand in front of every mirror and look at myself.

There was only one haunted house that was scary. It was a house at the beginning of the boardwalk that you walked through, called *Morbid Manor,* where people in costumes jumped about and tried to scare you. The outside looked like an old weather-beaten mansion. All the windows were shuttered, and the outside of the house was decorated with plaster sculptures of skeletons, monsters, and giant insects. The tail end of an old German World War I plane jutted from the side of the second floor as if it had crash landed. A teenage girl dressed up like the grim reaper tore our tickets at the door. I asked her if you walked through the house or rode on something, and she just glowered at me, deep in character. The actors at this attraction took their jobs seriously.

Leah and I couldn't make fun of *Morbid Manor*, because the people inside scared the shit out of us. Leah had screamed so loudly when a skinny bald man in blood-stained overalls jumped out at us, wielding a yellow chainsaw (with no chain blade), that she thought she had torn something in her throat. The bald guy swung the chainsaw wildly and the sweet fumes of gasoline filled the room and made me dizzy. The sound of the screaming motor bounced around on the plywood walls and slammed back into our ears. Leah put both her hands over her ears and screamed, and I grabbed her arm and buried my face in her shoulder. When we left, we laughed nervously together and had to sit on a park bench to calm down.

"Let's not do that again," Leah said.

I nodded, the high-pitched whine from the saw's motor still buzzing in my head.

"I thought that guy with the chain saw was going to hurt somebody swinging it around like that. I kept thinking he was going to lose his grip and hit me."

"Yeah . . ."

I was quiet for a moment and looked at Leah. I was starting to feel very comfortable around her. "I'm not tired anymore," I said.

Leah smiled at me. "Me neither. You want to play some games?"

I shrugged. "I don't care; I just don't feel like going back yet."

Leah and I went to an arcade and separated for a bit. She played skeeball, and I arm-wrestled a machine. The arm-wrestling game had a human-looking arm on a stand which you stood in front of. The arm was attached to a backdrop of a three-dimensional picture of a cartoonishly-evil looking cowboy. There were different levels of strength, and I started down low and worked my way up. I could only get through two levels, then it became so tough that I thought the machine locked up on purpose. A guy with his kid came by and saw me struggling with the arm, so they stood back and watched. When I still couldn't push the arm down (I was using all my weight and dangling from the thing), the man stepped up and pushed down on the arm, too.

"What a rip-off," the man groaned through clenched teeth.

I let go, and the machine arm almost lifted the guy off the ground. "I don't think you're supposed to win," I said to the guy and walked off. But he put a quarter in the machine, and tried again.

The arcade was getting pretty crowded. It was hard to move around without bumping into somebody. I went over and stood next to Leah as she pitched the little wooden balls up the skeeball ramp. Every time she hit the fifty point pocket, blue tickets would eject from a slot by her right knee.

"I'm bad at this," she said. She rolled another wooden ball up the ramp and it landed in the zero point pocket. "But I have enough tickets to buy a toy. I saw a Spider-man pencil over there that I think I have enough tickets for."

"How many tickets is that?"

She stopped and looked over at me with a grin. "Like a hundred, I think."

"For a pencil?" I said.

Leah rolled another ball up the ramp and hit the fifty point pocket again. "Last ball. Want to see what I can win?"

"No. Go ahead. I'm just going to wander around."

Leah walked to the booth where they sold the toys you could buy for tickets. I leaned up against a video game and waited for her.

The guy behind the booth said something to Leah and she laughed. I wasn't used to seeing her smile. She had a pretty smile. Around the apartment, she had a grim blankness to her face. The corners of her mouth were always bent down in a frown. Her eyes always had circles around them from lack of sleep and worry.

As I watched Leah at the booth and saw her compared to other people, I realized something—Fritz was right: she *was* very pretty. When Leah smiled, her dreariness washed away and it was difficult to ever imagine her sad. As much as I tried, I couldn't see her moping around the house, bundled in the gray blanket and still in her food-stained work uniform. Now her face was bright and healthy. As she smiled, I bit my fingernail to keep from laughing. I was proud of her, but didn't know why and didn't want it to show on my face.

Leah came from the stand waving the Spider-man pencil in one hand and two plastic spider rings in the other, one black and one orange. I wiped the grin off my face.

"Give me your hand," she said, coming up.

I reached out my left hand, and Leah took the orange spider ring and stuck it from finger to finger, trying to find the right fit. When the spider was on my little finger, Leah looked up into my face and smiled.

Suddenly, sadness pressed down on me, and I couldn't return a kind expression. I looked at the ring on my finger.

"What's the matter," Leah asked, still holding my hand.

I didn't answer, just offered a slight smile. I knew then that I would miss Leah very much after I was gone.

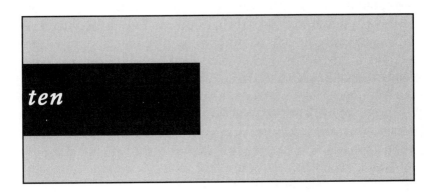

ten

JOE WAS WAITING FOR ME when I pulled around the back of his house. He sat on his porch, wearing blue jeans which were worn at the knees and a red flannel shirt with the sleeves rolled up. He was jamming his foot into a tan leather work boot, the toe curled up and chafed. I watched his lips as he did up his raw-hide laces; he was mumbling to himself out of frustration. For a second I thought he was upset that I was so early; he might have wanted to relax alone before work. But because I had been late when I came to apply, I'd forced myself to be on time today. I was a half hour early.

I'd tried to get some decent sleep after I had been out with Leah the night before. We got back to the condo around eleven, and I went straight to bed. When I opened my bedroom door, Fritz was sitting up in his bed, drinking a bottle of *Red Rose* wine.

"How'd it go?" He set the bottle between his legs and motioned for me to sit on the bed across from him.

I slumped on the unmade bed, took off my boots, then pulled the covers over me. "It was fun," I said. "But she doesn't like what you're doing."

"She'll thank me, one day," Fritz said.

I rolled over and looked at him with the covers bunched up around my ears. "She will?"

He nodded and said, "You will, too," then reached over and turned out the light.

Fritz and I lay awake talking to each other for hours in the dark, passing the bottle of wine back and forth. Our conversation was punctuated with the sloshing sound of the thick liquid. The bitter wine made my jaw muscles ache and my stomach burn. Fritz mostly asked me to tell him everything I could remember about Mrs. Hartly.

"What did her hair look like then?" he asked.

I took a drink and waited for the awful taste to fade before I could answer. "She used to dye it blonde. It went down to about the middle of her back." I heard Fritz laugh. "It didn't look bad, though."

"What did she used to wear to work?"

I handed over the bottle. "I remember her always wearing a gray skirt with a white shirt." Through the wall I could hear Leah pacing up and down the hallway. She went from room to room, walking in a fluid motion, never stopping or sitting. I heard Fritz sigh as she passed our door. "All the boys had crushes on Mrs. Hartly," I said.

"Yeah, all boys seem to like her," he said, yawning.

It was quiet for a minute. I wasn't sure if he had fallen asleep.

"How did you meet Mrs. Hartly?" I whispered. Leah passed by our door again; her feet slashed the tiny light coming out from the bottom of the door.

Fritz tapped on the wall. "Get some sleep, honey," he called to her.

"Fritz?" I said, "how did you meet Shelly?"

He yawned and set the bottle on the end table. The bed springs creaked as he rolled over to face the wall. "You get some sleep, too."

After that, I couldn't sleep at all. Around four in the morning, I groped around in the dark for the bottle of wine and finished it off, to help me sleep. It didn't work. I stayed awake all night listening to Fritz's heavy breathing and the waves in the ocean. By the time I got to Joe's, I was dead.

"You know anything about tiling?" Joe hollered to me as I stepped out of my car. My legs felt weak, as if my bones were thinning to glass.

"Not really," I said.

Joe took a deep breath, set both his hands on his knees, and stood up. "You can hammer a nail, can't you?" The raspiness of his voice made it sound as if he needed to hawk phlegm out of his throat.

"Yes, sir."

"Good enough. Help me load the truck."

We filled the back of the truck with ten pieces of drywall that were taped together in pairs. On top of that, we placed six sheets of concreteboard, two plastic buckets, and two paint-speckled aluminum sawhorses. Joe looked at them and made sure he had everything.

"Where's Doug?" I asked.

"Sick." Joe touched the items in the bed and mouthed their names and purpose. "'Greenboard'—for tub. Trowel—for adhesive. Mesh tape—for joints." Whenever he said the name of a tool, I repeated the word quietly to myself.

Once I got into the truck, I saw that my side of the seat had been cracked and fixed with hunter-green electrical tape. Three boxes of glazed tile had been placed between us.

On the drive to the tiling job, Joe drank coffee out of a silver thermos and smoked a tiny cigar the size of the last digit of my thumb. He let the thick white tobacco smoke leak from his mouth slowly, then, after a second, blew it away from his face. The sun poured in through the driver's side window, making his skin glow red; when he turned his head, I could see the tiny purple veins in the translucent funnel of his ear. His fist gripped the top of the steering wheel, knuckles yellow-white. The back of his hand was scarred and his thumbnail was blue-black. Joe didn't speak on the drive. He didn't play the radio. I sat in my seat and listened to the wind slash into my open window.

The silence caused a tension in the truck. I talked to relieve the pressure. I talked too much. Joe made me so nervous that I mispronounced a lot of words and stammered. I commented on the weather, asked him about his truck, and cleared my throat when I couldn't think of anything to say. Trying to get him to talk back was like extracting a tooth with chopsticks. I knew I was talking too much, but I couldn't stop myself. At one point, I said something about the amount of trees on the road we were on.

Joe looked over at me and raised an eyebrow. "Too many trees?"

Just shut up. Please shut up.

But I couldn't. "What's wrong with Doug?" I asked.

Joe cleared his throat. "Don't know. Said his stomach hurt."

"From what?"

Joe took the steaming thermos from its holder and took a long drink. He winced as the hot liquid slid down his throat. "Said he swallowed a ketchup packet."

I frowned and looked out at the road ahead. "How did he do that?"

"Well," Joe said and took one last drag from his cigar before flicking it out the window, "he's always got one of those packs in his mouth. He bites them, then sucks out all the ketchup. I guess one just slipped down his throat."

"He's lucky he didn't choke to death."

Joe frowned. "You're right," he said, as if he hadn't thought about it before.

"Well, not if he swallowed it like a duck," I said stupidly, in Doug's defense. Joe looked over at me and raised an eyebrow. "Well, you know," I tried to explain, "ducks don't chew their food—they just swallow it." Joe sighed, and we were quiet until we reached the house we were going to tile.

The house was in a middle-class neighborhood. A man was cutting the grass on a yellow lawnmower around the side of the garage. The smell of gasoline and dew soaked into my hair and skin. A small boy with brown hair sat in a sandbox, playing with action figures. He wore a pair of olive-green army pants cut off below the knee, and no shirt. His skin was the color of weak tea. Two bands of pale flesh went down his shoulders and chest to the front of his pants as if he had worn suspenders the day before without a shirt. When he turned to pitch an army guy out of the sandbox, I saw the tan-lines crisscross between his shoulder blades.

A woman in a yellow summer dress stood in the open garage, pouring water from a garden hose into a ceramic dog dish; a golden retriever at her side tried to bite the water as it came out of the hose. The woman scooted the animal back with her leg, and the dog's slobber made a stain on the flower pattern of her dress.

When we parked in the driveway, Joe exploded from the truck to get away from me.

The woman waved to Joe and let the dog go. The animal lapped up the water so frantically it made the water look like it was boiling. Joe nodded hello to the woman and grabbed his leather tool belt from the back of the truck.

"Come on," he said to me and jerked his head towards the house.

"You need me to bring anything?" I asked.

"Not yet. Want to look inside first."

The sun was rising just above the brown-shingled rooftop. The air was clear, and the heat burned on my face. The woman walked back into the garage, past a row of rakes and shovels suspended from the ceiling by a row of rubber-coated hooks, and went into a side door to the kitchen.

The bathroom we needed to tile was on the second floor, and it looked like the inside of a whale, studs like ribs and pink insulation. The bathtub and sink had been covered in clear sheets of plastic, secured with tabs of duct tape. The toilet had been removed; an egg-shaped residue of caulk on the floor traced where it had been. Joe sat on the edge of the bathtub and looked around the room.

"First things first." Joe's voice boomed in the empty room. "Hanging drywall."

The woman came up behind me and squeezed into the room. Her curly brown hair smelled of apple-scented shampoo. She looked from Joe to me and smiled, wanting to be introduced. "Last day, Joe?" she asked him, still looking at me.

Joe stood up and walked out of the room. "If all goes well."

The woman and I stood there for a second, and I smiled at her like an idiot. "I'm new," I explained. Joe called to me from halfway down the stairs, and I excused myself.

Outside, Joe pulled four pieces of drywall off the truck. He heaved the gray boards up on top of his head, then he started walking towards me, boards bowing ready to crack in half.

"Get the concreteboard," he said. "Bring it up to the bathroom."

The concreteboards were heavier than they looked. They were half the size of the drywall, but when I tried to pull three pieces off the back of the truck, I couldn't budge them. Concreteboard is exactly what it sounds like: thin sheets of concrete, held together with mesh. It keeps moisture from rotting the studs in walls and is hung around showers and sinks. The edges of the boards were rough and they scratched open the cuts on my hand. The little boy saw me struggling with the sheets and started laughing. The wet-faced dog walked over to him, licked his face and knocked him out of the sandbox. The boy rolled backward on the freshly-cut wet grass. He sat there for a second and checked himself for injuries. When he realized he was OK, he started laughing at me again.

Joe and I carried all the drywall and concreteboard up to the bathroom. It was my job to cut the boards with a utility knife, following Joe's marks. He made all the marks with a level and a carpenter's pencil with a flat, broad lead tip, which he had sharpened with his pocketknife. I'd score the board Joe needed with the razor, then I'd crack my knee into its other side, and the board would snap along the cut. Then Joe held the board in place with his knee and hammered it to the studs. It amazed me that he could hold the boards and nail them at the same time. He only used just enough nails to hold the board in place. He wanted to finish the room before securing all the drywall to the studs.

Joe gave me a spare hammer with a yellow fiberglass handle. He reached into a brown paper bag full of drywall nails and stuck them into the front of his nail apron, then he kicked the bag over to me.

"Start nailing," he said. "Space them a foot apart on every board. If you miss the stud, pull the nail out and do it over."

The drywall nails were ribbed and coated with a grease that stained my fingertips black. I had a hard time getting the nails to go in straight. I'd start hammering, then the nail would bend into a L-shape and I'd have to pry it out, marring the clean sheet of drywall. The nails I hammered in straight missed the studs, and I pulled them out with my fingers. I watched Joe tack up his boards. First, he'd push the nail through the outer paper of the drywall with his callused thumb to make it stick, then he hit the head twice and the nail disappeared. At most, Joe had to hit a nail three or four times before it sank into the studs—it took me eight to ten hits to get the nail in.

The concreteboard was difficult to nail, so Joe didn't even let me try. If a nail went in crooked, the concrete around the bent nail would crumble and weaken the strength of the entire board.

Joe had gone around the entire room before I finished my third board. He looked at the drywall that I had nailed up and shook his head in disbelief.

"What is this?" he said, rubbing his thumb over the nail heads. "You didn't hammer them in all the way." Then he looked around all the edges of the board and made a low groaning sound in his throat. He touched his finger to the dents in the drywall from where I had missed the nails. "Look at all these donkey tracks! What is this?" Joe punched a hole in the board and ripped it from the wall. The crooked nails stayed in the studs. He ripped all three of the boards I had nailed off the walls. I kept quiet. Ripping through the drywall, the stationary nails sounded like loud coughing.

Joe took the notebook from the breast pocket of his flannel and wrote something down. Then he re-measured the bare spaces on the walls and cut new boards.

"So far," Joe grumbled to me, "you're not getting paid."

He nailed up the new boards with me standing behind him, my face burning from shame.

When the last board was tacked up, he put his hammer in his tool belt and faced me. "On the phone, I asked you if you had apprentice experience, and you said yes."

I looked down at the chalk dust on the floor and said nothing.

"You lied."

"I'm just bad at drywall," I said. But he ignored me.

"I'm not paying you a dime for your work today, so let me know now if you want a lift back to your car."

I rubbed my hands through my hair. "If I improve, will you pay me?"

"You'd have to improve *a lot*."

"But would you pay me?"

"I don't know. . . "

"I can do better than this, I swear. Just let me show you what I can do."

Joe lowered his head and thought for a minute. "Oh, hell," he mumbled, lowering his eyes. "You'll cut tiles for the rest of the day. If you do a good job, I'll pay you a *third* of what you would have gotten."

"Sounds fair," I said.

BEFORE I STARTED CUTTING THE TILES, I sat outside the house next to the dog and cursed myself. Shawn did this kind of work at fifteen, I said to myself. You're ten years older than he was and you can't hammer a goddamn nail into the wall.

I looked down at the cuts and blisters on my hand. I didn't deserve them. The pride I had felt while painting Betty's crab house had been dashed from my body and ground into the pavement like a cigarette.

You have to get better, I told myself. I repeated this out loud to myself over and over. "You have to get better; you *must* get better . . ." The dog beside me raised an eyebrow when I started to chant. I looked down at him and said it again as if I were talking to him. "*You* have to get better." Then the dog blinked his black marble eyes and stared straight out in front of him. The little boy laughed at me while I talked to myself.

"Crazy person!" he shouted, and scooped up two handfuls of sand and threw them up into the air. He gritted his teeth and closed his eyes as the sand rained down on him. "Crazy, crazy, crazy!"

Joe set the wet saw up on the two aluminum sawhorses and showed me how to use it. The blade was circular with a flat, diamond-encrusted tip, which didn't cut the tile—it ate away at it. Water dripped down from a chamber above the spinning blade to keep it from overheating. The dirty water was collected in a plastic pan.

Joe went back upstairs and slathered tile adhesive on a section of the wall with a notched trowel, and measured the tiles that he needed me to cut. He marked the tiles with a red grease pencil and put a big X on the part of tile he didn't want. I'd run outside with tiles he'd marked, cut them with the saw, then run back up to him. My calves burned and swelled after only a few trips up and down the stairs.

The little boy watched me cut the tiles and inched his way over. He walked from bush to bush pretending to inspect them. The dog took off and hid under a car in the garage as soon as I turned on the saw.

As I pulled the whirling blade through, the scream of the ripping tile stabbed my ears. Fine dust spread over my left hand, and the trickling water on the blade spit tan specks onto the white tile. I gritted my teeth so hard, I thought they were going to crack in half.

When I hit the red stop button, the little boy was standing right behind me.

"Is that thing sharp?" he asked.

"Very," I said. "Don't touch it." My teeth felt like pencil erasers in my mouth.

"Is it sharp enough to cut off my arm?"

"Sure."

The boy pressed his finger to his lips, as if he suddenly wanted to try. "Will it cut this?" He held up an action figure. I wasn't sure what it was a figure of because the boy had melted the toy's face into a raisin.

"I'm sure it would, but let's not try, OK?"

"But I need his leg cut off," the boy explained.

"Why?" I asked looking at the mangled thing. "Isn't he hurt enough already?"

"No!" the boy cried. "He stepped on a lamb mime! He lost his leg."

I took the figure from his hand and pulled a pair of tile snips from my back pocket. "Can't be too careful with all those lamb mimes around. Where do you want him cut?"

The boy touched his left knee next to a square adhesive stain from where a Band-Aid had been. "Right there."

I took the snips and pinched away the little man's soft plastic leg. "How's that?" I said, handing him back his soldier.

The boy touched his finger to the cut and smiled.

Joe hollered from the house, and I ran up the stairs with the cut tile.

The wall behind the bathtub was done. The tiles were staggered like bricks, looking a bit strange without any grout in the joints. Around the tub, Joe had nailed up wood trim for the tiles to rest on so they didn't slip down while the adhesive set. We were now putting on the round-edged bull-nose pieces for the trim near the top of the wall. I handed Joe the piece and he inspected it and nodded. Then he handed me a stack of other tiles he had pre-measured for the other wall.

When I got downstairs, the little boy was waiting for me with a green basket full of mutilated action figures. "These guys were hurt, too," he said, raising the basket.

I took a man with no arms out of the basket by his leg and sighed. "Shouldn't you be in school or something?"

"I'm too little for school!" he said, offended. "I go next year."

I looked at the mutilated toy. "Couldn't you just *play* with them?"

"I'm having a war." He jerked a thumb over his shoulder at his sandbox. Then he turned to see if he was pointing to the right place. "These guys are all hurt."

"Just let me do my work first, OK?"

The boy smiled at me, exposing a row of tiny baby teeth.

For the rest of the day, I cut glazed tile and action figures. The boy waited patiently as I worked the wet saw, twisting his little fingers into his ears every time I hit the green on button (later I thought, it probably wasn't too smart to have him standing so close). His eyes bugged in admiration at the destructive power of the spinning blade as it plowed through the tile. When I was done with the piece Joe wanted, the boy would show me where the next soldier needed to be amputated. He never showed me where he wanted them cut by pointing to the action figure; he'd draw a finger across his own arm or leg, making a slicing sound with his mouth. "Right about there," he'd say.

After about seven hours, the job was done. Joe came out of the house, wearing chalk-stained knees pads and hair speckled with globs of tile adhesive. The boy ran up to him, and Joe hoisted him up onto his shoulder. The boy sat perched like a parrot on a pirate's shoulder.

"All done," Joe said and pointed to the man on the lawn tractor. "He takes over from here." Joe took the boy from off his shoulder and gave him a playful pat on the bottom and the boy ran away, laughing.

Joe sat down on the driveway and picked white adhesive out of his hair. I sat down next to him. The pavement was hot and burned through my jeans.

"I don't want you to come back tomorrow," Joe said.

"I got better, though."

"Yes, you did. But on the boat, I can't take any chances."

"I'll be better on the boat," I said.

Joe was quiet for a minute, thinking it over. Then he stood and unplugged the wet saw. "No." The word popped from his mouth like a belch.

I stood up and followed him as he took the saw from the sawhorses and emptied out the water. "I can do *better*," I pleaded.

"No," he said again over his shoulder. "You lied on the phone. You said you had experience when obviously you don't. I'm not risking anything on the boat."

"You won't be risking anything. I'll work harder. Just give me another chance."

Joe spun around and folded his arms. He was going to give me a chance to speak, and it suddenly occurred to me what might make him change his mind.

"Take me out on the boat tomorrow—if you don't like my work, you don't have to pay me what you said you'd pay me today." I knew Joe wouldn't say no to a chance to save money.

He thought for a second. "You said you can swim on the phone—can you?"

"Yes," I said. "I've had lessons."

Joe pursed his lips. The sun slipped behind a tiny cloud for a second. "One more chance," he said. Then he pointed a finger at me and repeated it again slowly, letting each word sink into my head like bricks in mud. "One. . .more. . . chance."

Since I had arrived in Ocean City, I'd slept less than eight hours total. I could never sleep because I was worrying about money and work and the cops. The unused mustiness of the guest bed also kept me awake. As soon as I'd drift off to sleep, my eyes would pop open and, for a second, I wouldn't know where I was.

Driving home from Joe's, the lack of sleep caught up with me. It spread through my body like venom and I felt dehydrated and weak. The trees on the side of the road looked like a brown-green liquid creek turned up on its side. I tested how long I could keep my eyes shut before being pressed down into a dream. My head felt as if it was filled with sand, tiny grains pouring into my ears, darkening my vision. Several times, I jerked awake just before my forehead hit the steering wheel.

I have no idea how I made it back to the apartment without killing somebody. I trudged up the stairs; the sound of my footsteps sounded distant and out of sequence. When I reached Leah's door, I forgot who lived here for a second, and my arm and hand had forgotten how to knock. I almost fell over before something woke me.

"We need to talk." The voice was behind me. It was Fritz. He sat at a small table on the deck, smoking a cigarette and drinking a glass of pineapple juice. He wore a new-looking white sweatshirt with a hood. The sleeves came down almost over his hands.

I sat down on an aluminum and canvas lawn chair in front of him and rested my head on the glass top of the table. Wind chimes and pinwheels hanging above me on the deck clinked and fluttered in a warm breeze.

"Joe tells me you never showed up," Fritz said and ground his cigarette into the black bottom of the ashtray.

"I'm Pete," I said with my head on the table. "My name is

Pete now." I didn't know if I was speaking this or thinking it.

Fritz reached forward and touched my face. The smell of nicotine on his fingers was comforting. "You look sick," he said.

"I'm just tired." My breath spread fog on the glass. "I need to sleep."

"Why didn't you go to Joe's?"

"I did. He thinks I'm Pete."

Fritz lightly slapped me a few times on my temple. "Come on—wake up. Here, drink some of this." He handed me his glass.

As soon as the yellow liquid touched my tongue, the cool feeling of alcohol slid down my throat and stung like poison. I choked, trying to spit out as much as I could. I held my hands to my chest and counted the seconds until the burning went away. It was Caribbean rum, and there was more of it in the glass than pineapple juice. As I hacked and gagged, my head cleared up.

"Better?" Fritz said, eyebrows raised.

A man and a woman in their early thirties came onto our landing and continued to the apartment above us. The man came up first. He nodded hello to us, and I waved to him. The woman came up next. She looked at Fritz and tripped on the last step to our level. She smiled at him and laughed to herself; her face glowing red from embarrassment. Her husband looked down at her and frowned. As they continued up the steps, the woman kept sneaking peeks at Fritz, and he pretended not to notice.

"Why does Joe think your name is Pete?" Fritz asked.

"It just happened that way." I rubbed my face and looked at all the wind chimes on the decks across the street. It seemed as if every balcony was littered with either drying bathing suits or some kind of wind chime. Some were bamboo. Some were metal. Others looked like spiral staircases that twirled in the breeze. "Look," I said, "it'll be all right. The real Pete is in Florida. I'll be gone by the time Joe finds out, and you have nothing to worry about, because if I screw up, he can't hold anything over your head. He's got no idea I even know you."

"But you're going to ruin everything," Fritz said. "I have plans for you."

"I thank you for your help—I really do. But I have my own plans for myself. Besides, Leah and I will never be anything more than what we are right now."

Fritz lit two cigarettes and gave me one. I pinched it between my fingers and let it burn itself out. "You have no idea how happy you two could make each other." He looked off towards the ocean and blew a stream of smoke from his lips.

"Leah's not even interested," I said. "You're trying to force two people to fall in love—it doesn't work like that. I live in Baltimore, and Leah still loves Ron."

"But Leah talks only about *you*." Fritz said. "Do you really think she'd let someone she didn't like live with her?"

"She's only doing that because I distract her from thinking about Ron."

Fritz combed his hair with his fingers. "Are all you Baltimorons this way? Leah is using the Ron thing as an excuse!"

"Fritz!" I held up my hands to tell him I quit. "Even if Leah *is* over Ron and really *does* like me, I'm just not interested. OK? I'm gone in a week. That's it."

Fritz was quiet. So quiet that I could hear the soft crackle of tobacco when he dragged on his cigarette. I watched him closely. He didn't want to look at me.

"I'm sorry," I said after a minute. "She's friendly and pretty and fun, but I'm just the wrong guy."

"I guess you want someone who's mean and ugly and dull," he said and flicked his cigarette off the balcony. ". . .Someone more like you."

I WAS RESTING IN BED, when Fritz burst into the room and pulled the covers off me.

"Get your shoes on," he said. "I can't find Leah."

While I was doing up my laces he plopped down on the bed in front of me.

"Last night, did Leah say anything about skipping work or going anywhere?"

"No. Why?"

"She told me this morning that she'd be home around five. It's after seven now."

"Call the Sunset. Maybe she's working late."

He stood up and walked out into the hallway. I followed him. "I did," he shouted. "They told me she never came in today."

Fritz and I went outside. The sky shone copper at the horizon which bled into a turquoise evening sky. A few stars were scattered above us, winking like tiny shards of glass. My body shuddered from lack of sleep.

Fritz ordered me to take the bus north as far as I could, then take the bus south as far as I could. "Get out once in a while and look for her. I'm going to walk the beach and boardwalk."

"Should we call the police?" I said, and Fritz closed his eyes as if the thought was too painful for him to even consider.

I got on the southbound bus first. I looked out the window the whole time, cupping my hands around my eyes because of the glare. I rode all the way down to the bus station. The driver parked and told me I had to get off. Then I rode the northbound bus, getting off every tenth block to walk. I wanted to call out her name like a lost dog, but there were too many people around. I went into shops and fast food places looking for her. I went down side streets and alleyways. I even went into the Food Lion (whose window I had washed) and went up and down every aisle.

Around midnight, I gave up. I sat near the back of the bus and drifted off to sleep. The bus jerked to a stop outside a professional building around 120th Street. The hiss of the brakes slapped me awake. I watched a girl come on the bus carrying her shoes in her hands. She sat in the first seat, which faced to the side, not the front.

It was Leah. It took me a second to recognize her. The fluorescent lights overhead make her skin look blue. Her work uniform was a mess, stained with sand, and most of the buttons weren't snapped together.

I got up and sat in the seat behind her.

"Your uncle is worried," I said softly. I watched her profile, not sure if she was going to swing around and punch me or collapse into tears.

Leah just nodded. The purple-black circles under her eyes made her look dead.

"I was worried, too," I added. I reached forward and touched her shoulder, but she shrugged my hand away.

I sat back and saw that the driver was watching us. After a few blocks, I sat up again and said, "Please tell me."

"No."

"Please, Leah. I told you what was wrong with me."

She turned and faced me. "I can't."

I sighed. "Leah—you're starting to scare me. Please tell me what's wrong. It can't be just breaking up with Ron. There's more to it. *Tell* me."

"I *can't*," she said again. Her face was tensed, ready to cry. "Why?"

She looked up to keep the welled-up tears from falling down her face and laughed, embarrassed. "If I tell you—" she paused, trying to find a way to say it—"you'll leave." She hid her face with her hand, not because she was crying, but because she was shy about saying it.

I didn't know what to say; I just sat there dumbfounded. What Leah just said was the nicest thing anybody had ever said to me. I started to tell her I was leaving anyway, but the words locked in my throat. For the first time since I had been here, I didn't want to leave. RHP and cops and money steamed off and away from my body like vapors rising off melting ice. For a minute, I couldn't even see Steve's or Terry's or Conrad's face. They didn't matter now. The only thing that mattered was *why* Leah was so upset. And how I could help her.

I reached forward and touched her shoulder again. This time she held my hand there with the side of her face and closed her eyes. Her cheek was cold. She turned her face and kissed the back of my hand. Then she sat up and looked as if she regretted doing it. She stared straight out at her reflection on the other side of the bus, but I kept my hand there anyway. I wanted her to kiss it again.

"Stop worrying about me," she said after a minute. Her

eyes were closed and she looked very calm. "You'll be gone soon enough."

When we got back, Leah went straight to her room and changed into her boxers and tank top for bed. Fritz was passed out on the couch. A half-empty bottle of rum lay by his side. I was too tired to be mad at him.

I slapped his shoulder. "Leah's home."

His eyes cracked open slowly. "I looked as much as I could," he mumbled. "I came back here in case she showed up." His eyes rolled back into his head and he belched in my face. The sugary smell of rum and the sharp smell of bile punched my senses.

I undid the laces of Fritz's boots and pulled them off. He mumbled that he was sorry while I pulled the gray wool blanket from the rocker over him. Then he mumbled something else which I couldn't understand. Before I left him, I touched a finger to his hair—it was waxy, just as I expected.

Leah stayed in her room and wouldn't come to the door when I knocked. I stood out in the hallway, listening to her pace in her room for a half hour, then went to bed.

JOE HAD TOLD ME to be at his place by six. Since Doug was sick, he needed to do some work before we could go out on the boat. He said that going out at six would be a chance for me to sleep in.

I lay in bed and thought about the boat, how hard I would work and how proud I would make him. I could almost feel the bed swaying on waves. The echo of a bow cutting through water sloshed around in my head. I was halfway carried into a dream. The blackness of the room closed around me.

Then the sound of wood striking wood woke me. It was the door.

I lay still, not breathing, and listened in the dark. My eyes were wide open. I heard someone walk across the room to my bed. At first I thought it was Fritz trying to find his bed, but I knew it wasn't him. I could sense that it was Leah. It was just like the first night I was here and she watched me while I pretended to sleep. I knew the way she breathed and shifted her weight from leg to leg. The covers were pulled from me and cold air swept over my body.

Leah climbed on top of me and pulled the covers over us. Her skin felt warm, and the slight stubble on her legs scratched my knees. Leah leaned forward and paused for a second. I knew what she was worried about: crossing that line would either unite us or ruin everything. She had gone too far to go back now. Our faces were inches apart. I could feel her breathe out through her nose, and I couldn't move. It was as if I had a wolf sitting on my chest, and I wasn't sure if it was going to nudge me with its wet nose or bite the front of my face off. After a few seconds, she knew what to do.

Leah leaned closer and kissed me.

Our teeth struck as our mouths met. Her breath was sour and chalky, but I didn't mind. I put my hand on her back and felt the thin grooves in her tank top. The warmth of her skin bled through the cotton fabric. I kept my eyes open, staring wide-eyed into the red and purple specks that flowed like water in the blackness of the room.

Leah rolled over with her back to me, and I slid myself closer to the wall, where the sheets were still cool. Leah reached around and grabbed my right arm and draped it over herself like a blanket. My hand rested under her chin, and she held onto it with both hands. I could feel her breath like trickling grains of sand on my fingers. We never said a word. I just lay there, feeling her heartbeat in her throat. I closed my eyes and felt our breathing fall into the same rhythm.

Then we slept soundly and dissolved into our separate dreams.

eleven

I HAD ONLY SEEN JOE ONCE the whole morning. When I pulled onto his drive, he was spreading manure in a field of alfalfa on a rusty Ford 9N tractor. The sun was just rising, and dirty silver-blue fog covered the furrows in the field. A single light mounted next to the tractor's steering wheel and covered in a steel grid burned through the morning mist. I could barely make out Joe's face as he bobbed up and down on the metal seat of the tractor. Smoke from his cigar curled in the air above his head and mixed with the diesel clouds that coughed from the exhaust on the flattop motor. When I had pulled around the back of the house, Doug was sitting by the side barn door, picking sleep out of his eyes. I got out of my car, and he told me what we'd be doing all morning.

Today was the first time I had ever been inside the barn. About twelve dim lights in dusty cages hung from wires from the ceiling, which lit the main floor of the barn, but everything on the walls hid in shadows. A walk-in freezer was in the corner facing the side door; its steel door glowed. Next to the large freezer was an ice box. Doug opened it and showed me a shark he had caught. The shark was the size of a loaf of French bread and covered with bubbles of frozen condensation. I walked over and pressed my fingertip to one of the shark's teeth. When I drew my finger back, I noticed a tiny white line on the first pad of my index finger. I squeezed the skin around the line and a cherry dot of blood welled up out of it. I hadn't even felt the tooth cut me.

In the middle of the barn was a yellow-orange CAT bulldozer with a back hoe attachment. The machine was covered in clumps of dried clay, but the teeth on the back hoe had been worn a bright silver. Under the CAT's engine block was a tiny pool of oil, which had been covered with a layer of kitty litter. Behind the bulldozer was a forage harvester and a flail chopper, their long necks stretching up in the air like two dinosaurs trying to eat leaves out of tall trees.

I walked over to the wall, which was lined with tools hanging from steel spikes. My boots made a loud sweeping sound on the dirty concrete floor. Joe had axes, post diggers, pruning shears, shovels, and rakes all along the wall. Many of the tools looked to have been salvaged from the trash—shovels with rusty heads and new handles and old ax handles with new silver heads. On the other wall, behind human-sized spools of chicken wire and chain-link fencing, were gaff hooks, ring nets, fishing poles, and about a dozen STIHL chain saws of different blade lengths. The white fuel tanks on the chain saws were stained with bits of sawdust sticking to the spilled traces of gasoline. Next to the chain saws was an old nickel slot machine; on top of that was a forge for making tools, constructed of a truck's brake drum, a metal funnel, and a seven-inch piece of pipe. The stickers on the slot machine's dials had been removed, so you wouldn't know if you hit the jackpot unless nickels started pouring into the steel pan below. Doug told me that the machine still worked and was filled with nickels. He demonstrated by putting a nickel in and pulling the lever (but no money came out). I put a nickel in, pulled down on the black ball of the lever and watched the blank dials spinning, then halting to three consecutive stops— *shink*, *shink*, *shink*. The machine made a rumbling noise and a single nickel rattled down into the pan. I gave the coin to Doug. He put it in the machine and lost it.

I spent the morning in a walk-in freezer, tying bull snouts onto a trotline. My finger joints had become stiff from the cold. The walls were fuzzed with ice and lined with aluminum shelves, stacked with white plastic bags of beef, chicken, deer meat, and bait. The smell of fish-oil and blood tunneled into my sinuses and congealed like egg yolk behind my eyes. Doug had set out the bait for me: a clear plastic bag of bull snouts, a bucket of whole herrings, a bucket of chicken necks, and another bucket that he filled with blue fish heads and flounder heads. Each line I tied was over a half mile long. My fingertips were stained with blood and yellowish oil from the fish; my bare arms were flaked with gills. When I had finished a line, I'd give it to Doug, and he stored it in a white bucket, filled with a greenish pool of salty brine mix.

I sat on a galvanized bucket with the trotline draped across my lap. Doug stood behind me at a chopping block, hacking off flounder heads with a rusty cleaver. Sometime around eight he started whistling *When Johnny Comes Marching Home Again*. Then I joined in, and we couldn't stop. The tune became a noise as familiar to me as the whirling of the freezer's motor and the guillotine chop of Doug's cleaver. Whistling it became as instinctive as breathing. My lips changed the pitch of the song without my brain knowing it.

Doug walked over and dumped the fish heads from his cutting board into a white bucket in front of me. Blood and oil streamed down the board in red and yellow trails and worked itself into the gashes in the board. Doug wiped the blood away with the side of his hand and sat in front of me on a wooden crate with rusted nails. He took the line from my lap and tested to see how tightly I had been tying the bait.

He stopped whistling. "Tighter," he said, jerking the knot a couple of times. "Make sure the bait can't go anywhere."

"I will," I told him. I stopped whistling, too, and it made me dizzy, like I had just stepped off a merry-go-round.

Doug stood up, cleaver in hand, and went out of the freezer. Warm air blew in and made the frozen meat crackle in its plastic bags. He came back in, carrying a blue plastic grocery bag and shut the heavy steel door behind him. He set the bag on the floor and sat back down on the crate. He dumped the bag on the wooden floor. It had been filled with frozen eels. He chopped them up right there on the floor, and I wondered why he wasn't using the chopping block behind me.

I set the last trotline down and picked away the flecks of gills that had clustered between my stiff fingers. Doug looked like he wanted to say something as he hacked the eels into finger length black sticks. He breathed in, ready to speak, then he let the air deflate out his nose in a loud whistle.

"You OK?" I said, flipping bits of chicken necks from my lap back into the bucket.

Doug set his cleaver down and pursed his chapped lips. "I think Joe's mad at me," he said. "When he's mad, he changes jobs for the day. I was supposed to be doing something."

"I was supposed to go out on the boat," I said.

"Yeah, I know. He told me this morning that he wanted you to bait extra lines."

"Extra lines?"

Doug nodded. "Yeah, we've got others ready to go." He jerked his chin at a couple of buckets at the rear of the freezer.

"Does he change jobs like this a lot?"

"Sometimes." Doug picked up the cleaver and stuck his little finger in the hole on the square blade. "You never really know what you'll be doing when you come here. One time I thought I was going to help him install ceiling fans in a restaurant, but instead he had me snap the ends off about a million string beans." He smiled, and I handed over the finished trotline. Doug stood up and put it with the others, then said, as if he were thinking out loud, "Why would Joe be mad at me?"

"Well," I said, "I don't think he believes you swallowed a pack of catsup." Then I added, "I don't think I believe it either."

Doug's face went pale. His freckles looked as dark as rust. "Did he *say* he didn't believe me?"

"No, not really. But I sensed that he thought you were lying."

"Well," Doug said, folding his arms, "why don't *you* believe me?"

I stood up and stretched; my spine cracked as I arched my back. "Because if you swallowed an entire pack of catsup, you'd probably die—or be so sick you'd wish you were dead. The wrapper would get stuck in your digestive tract somewhere."

Doug leaned against the door and rubbed his hands through his bristly hair. "Joe asked me why I was sick, and that was the first thing I thought of," he said.

"So you didn't swallow anything?"

"No," he admitted. "I called Joe up and said that my stomach hurt. He asked me why, and it just slipped out."

"Should have just said you ate some bad food or something, Doug."

"Oh boy." He collapsed onto the crate with a thump.

"So why'd you lie, anyway?"

He looked up at me. "Promise not to say anything to Joe?"

I shrugged. "Sure."

"I went to visit Greg in jail yesterday."

"You had to *lie* to do that?"

"Sure. Joe wants me to keep away from him from now on."

"Didn't Greg used to work for Joe?"

"Yeah, but after the arrest, things are different."

I sat back down on the bucket and hugged myself. The cold was becoming too much for me. My burned earlobes felt as if they could be plucked from my head as easily as tulip petals. The sharp freezer air raked at my throat. A million ice splinters were piercing my lungs.

Doug noticed my shaking. "How do your feet feel?"

"I don't know." I looked down at my boots and tried to move my toes. "I can't feel them."

Doug stood up and brushed fish gills and blood off the front of his jeans. "Let's check the pots." He opened the clunky door, and we walked out of the barn.

I stood in the driveway and felt the hot sun calm my trembling. Doug told me to knead my hands together no matter how much it hurt, to get the circulation going again. I looked at my hands; my fingers were bone-white and felt as if they would shatter if I tried to bend them. Doug went into the house and came out with two golden apples and a gallon milk jug filled with iced tea. He said we could take a ten-minute break before checking the crab pots. We sat on the porch, eating the apples and passing the jug back and forth to each other. The tea was sweet and flavored with lime slices that had been pushed through the lip of the jug.

After a few minutes, I felt better. "So what's your friend in jail for?"

"Well," Doug said, swallowing a mouthful of apple, "he was accused of rape. But he didn't do it."

"Who accused him?" I found it difficult to eat the apple; every time I tried to take a bite, I could smell the dead fish and bull snouts on my fingers.

Doug had eaten his apple down to the core. He picked the stem out, then bit the core in half, crunching on the seeds. "His girlfriend set him up." After he swallowed, he put the other half of the core in his mouth.

"Why?" I tried to take another bite, but I almost gagged from the smell of my hand. So I just tossed the apple from hand to hand, as if it were a baseball.

"Well, Greg and Karen fight all the time. I saw her spit in his face. And when they get to drinking, they get violent. She hit him in the knee with some crab tongs once."

"Jesus."

Doug nodded. "All they do is fight. Greg was over her place a few days ago, and the two of them had been drinking. Greg told me that he said something sarcastic to her, and Karen blew up at him. She's always saying that he treats her like she's stupid." Then Doug nudged at me and added, "Because she *is* stupid."

I smiled.

"Anyway, they fought for a bit, called each other names, threw things, then she stomped off to bed. Greg said he stayed up for a couple more hours to cool off, watching TV." Doug stopped talking and looked at the apple in my hand. "You don't want it?"

I shook my head and handed it over. Doug popped it in his mouth, took a bite, and kept talking.

"OK, Greg goes up to her room a few hours later, and all the lights are off. He climbs in bed, and Karen starts acting all nice and sweet. Well, pretty soon, you know, they start . . . " Doug started to blush. "Anyway, after they do their business—

or whatever you want to call it—Greg falls asleep. When he wakes up, three cops are on top of him on the bed, putting handcuffs on him. And Karen's gone."

"What happened?"

"Well, Greg goes down to the police station, and Karen is there with a fat lip and a swollen eye. She told the cops that he raped her." A helpless look washed over Doug's face. "But he *didn't*. He wouldn't do anything like that."

"How did her face get busted up?"

"That's what we don't know. Greg thinks she did it to herself before he came to bed. She's the kind of nut that can do something like that. It was dark when he went into the room, so he never saw her face. Even when he opened the door, he said she was turned away from him. She could've hit herself while he was watching TV, right?"

"I guess." I wasn't sure what to say. "I suppose it's possible."

Doug looked at me and forced a smile. I could tell he missed his friend. I could also tell he saw me as Greg's replacement—and that made him miserable.

After Doug and I had stored the three trotlines in the brine mix, we rode a golf cart down to the water to empty the crab pots. I sat in the passenger's seat and propped my feet up. The plastic roof of the cart blocked out the sun, and the warm wind loosened my joints as we whipped down the dirt road. The path to the water was about a mile long and hugged the side of the cornfield. Doug drove as fast as the cart could take us. He aimed for bumps and chuckholes in the road, trying to get the cart to go airborne. He hit one dip so hard that he momentarily lost control of the wheel, and drove us into the cornfield for about twenty feet. I closed my eyes and gritted my teeth as the green blades slashed around us.

The ground near the docks was paved with oyster shells, bleached in the sun. Doug slammed on the brakes, and we skidded for six feet as we came to the first dock. I stepped out of the cart, still picking leaves and bits of stalk out of my hair.

There were three docks. Joe's snub-bowed crabbing boat was on the right, rocking gently in the water. The stern and bow lines made the sound of grinding teeth as they tightened. Across the water, a large tamarack tree had fallen into the river. The current rippled around its branches, trying to pluck off its cones. A blue heron stood on the back of a tree with a triumphant look on its face, as if it had just pecked the tree down itself.

Doug grabbed a couple of empty bushel baskets, and we walked to the first dock. The dark planks were deeply grooved and splintery. At the end of the dock were two wooden pillars, capped with tambourine-shaped pieces of tin, dotted with rust around their side from where they had been nailed. On each pillar, two nylon ropes led to the pineapple-size cork buoys in the water; the red paint on the buoys was flaking like the mud at the bottom of a dried-out puddle. Below, the pillars drank up the green water and were pimpled with barnacles.

Doug told me to pull up the first pot. He placed an empty crate on the dock and stood behind me with his arms folded. The rope was slippery with algae. As I pulled the pot up, I could see clouds of mud boiling in the green water. The pot was a large square cage, constructed out of galvanized chicken wire. Crabs fluttered inside it, spraying water into my face. At the bottom of the trap was a wire cylinder filled with rotted fish heads. A vinyl red ribbon was tied above the bait box, to attract the crabs. I opened the top chamber and paused.

"How do I get them in the basket?"

"Shake them out."

I hugged the clunky trap in my arms and shook it until I heard the hard-shelled bodies of the crabs fall from the top chamber and clack into the bushel basket. A few crabs hung onto the rings of the chicken wire, but Doug slapped the flat of his hand on the pot until they shook free. One crab missed the basket and landed on the dock. He reared up on his hind flippers and showed me the white of his abdomen. His blue claws were up in the air and open like armed traps. Then it scuttled towards me.

I shouted and dropped the cage. It bounced on the dock and splashed into the water.

"Don't let it get away!" Doug shouted.

I backed away from the funny animal, and it came towards me, threatening me with his claws.

"Pick him up!" Doug laughed.

"How?" I bent down and hesitated. When my hand was about a foot away, the crab came at me some more. I didn't know what to do, so I punted the thing into the water.

Doug watched the bubbles where the crab landed. "What'd you do that for?"

"It was going to bite me."

"Just pick them up by their butts, then they can't bite you." Doug reached into the basket and held a large crab by its back flippers. The crab spread its legs out like a spider. "Here," Doug said, "you try."

He handed me the crab, and I held it by its other hind leg. The thing kept its limbs tensed, but it couldn't get to me.

I pulled the pot I had dropped back up onto the dock, and Doug undid the rubber hooks on the bait box and pulled out the decomposed fish heads with his bare hands. He chucked them into the bushes. Then he put in new bait and told me to throw the pot back into the water.

"Make sure the bait is on the bottom," he said. "Don't let it tip over."

There were ribbed steel bars on the bottom to keep it anchored, but Doug said sometimes it could tip over when you put it back in the water. If the pot is on its side then the crabs can't get in. I lowered the box back down, then went to the next pot.

DOUG HADN'T BEEN LYING when he had told me that Joe had changed jobs on him. But his new job wasn't helping me bait the trotline; it was to observe me all day and report my performance back to Joe.

I was sitting in the kitchen, pressing my thumb into grains of sugar that were sprayed across the table, then licking the sweetness. Doug was talking to Joe in the dining room. When Joe had finished working in the field, he collected us out of the barn; he told me to wait in the kitchen, and he told Doug to come with him. Then they disappeared into the dining room, and I had spent the last fifteen minutes listening to the soft grumble of their voices.

Sitting there reminded me of a biology class I had during my first year in college. After our exams, our professor never handed back our graded work during class. Instead, we made appointments with him during his office hours, and he'd go over the errors with us, then give us our grades face to face. We lined the hall outside his office, sitting with our arms hugging our knees. The professor would have the exiting student send in the next person in line. The students leaving his office either looked giddy or shaken, as if they had just been told how and when they were going to die.

A month before the semester was over, our teacher's sixteen-year-old daughter was hit by a car and killed. When he returned to school, he announced that he was a Christian. We had just taken an exam on *The Origin of Species* by Darwin before his daughter was killed. He came back a week and a half later, and I had my meeting with him, to go over the exam. I wasn't sure how well I had done on the test; I remembered knowing that he could probably tell I hadn't studied. When I sat down in front of his desk, he held my exam up with his thumb and forefinger. He wore a college ring with an amber stone. Then, in one fluid motion, he ripped the paper right down the middle.

"This exam does not count," he said blankly, staring at my chest. "Don't believe in Darwinism any more. Please send in the next student."

We didn't study anything else after that. Instead, we took nature walks and watched films on birds and reptiles. Then our teacher resigned at the end of the semester.

Doug came into the kitchen and told me Joe was ready to see me.

"What did you say?" I asked.

Doug slapped me on the arm. "You're fine."

When I first went into the dining room, I didn't see Joe. The room was filled with dusty light. Then I heard a noise like rustling paper come from inside the wall next to the chimney. I walked over, the soft Persian carpet muffling my footsteps. Then a flimsy door in the wall sprang open. Joe was sitting in a tiny room, behind a paper-covered desk. He wore black-rimmed reading glasses with a missing stem, pulled down to the tip of his nose.

I bowed my head as I stepped into what looked like an office. There were no windows. The walls were the color of eggnog, sectioned with crossbeams that held the ceiling up. The tiny space was filled with the smell of paper and cigars and ink.

Joe wrote in a notebook and held up a finger to tell me to be patient.

I felt cramped in the little room. The endless stacks of paper seemed to draw the breath from my body. Waist-high bookcases surrounded the walls, filled with manuals and documents that didn't seem to be in any order. The edges of the paper were turning yellow. Across the room was a little workbench for making bullets. He had boxes of shells, orange medicine bottles filled with buckshot, and hard-bristled brushes for cleaning guns. Bolted to the bench was a press for making shotgun shells. It had rotating chambers of gunpowder, buckshot, primers, which were pumped into the empty shells by a large red, rubber-gripped lever.

On top of the bookcases were a few stuffed birds and about fifty pictures of a woman with dark brown hair. The frames of the photos were brass, and the glass was dulled from dust and the smoky air in the room. I looked at one of the pictures; Joe and the woman were sitting on the hood of a Mercedes station wagon. I remembered the car as one that was now crumpled in on itself next to the barn. The woman wore no make-up and had her hair pulled back into a ponytail. She had one arm around Joe and was smiling without showing any teeth. Joe was laughing as if the person taking the picture had just told him a joke that the woman didn't get (or didn't understand until after the film had been exposed). I looked at other pictures of the woman: there was one of her holding a large catfish the size of my arm, one with her red-eyed at night at some barbecue, and a bunch more of her posed with Joe. In every picture, I noticed that she was always wearing the same smile, as if she had practiced it once in the mirror and trained herself to smile that way every time her picture was being taken.

Joe set his pencil down and took off his reading glasses. He rubbed his eyes hard with the backs of his knuckles. Black lines of grime traced his fingernails. "I've been talking with Doug," he said.

I nodded and shifted the weight on my legs. Joe might have offered me a chair, if the room had the capacity for one. With all the space he had in this house, I wondered why he had chosen to make his office in this tiny room with no daylight or ventilation.

Joe leaned back in his wooden swivel chair; the wood cracked like bone. "He likes you very much."

I stayed quiet.

"Personally, I'm not thrilled with you. *But*," he said, putting emphasis on the word so I wouldn't interrupt, "I think you're starting to show promise."

I wondered if Doug had mentioned my kicking the crab into the water.

Joe leaned forward and picked up his pencil. "You be here tomorrow at three in the morning. Bring food. And be ready to work."

"Yes, sir."

"You have a warm coat?" he asked, eyebrows raised.

I shook my head. "No, sir."

"Well, I'll try and find you something tonight."

"Thank you, sir."

With that Joe told me I could go. Before I walked out of the tiny office, I caught sight of another picture: two teenage boys bundled in thick hunting coats in a snow-covered field. The boys' faces looked raw from the cold. I squinted at the picture and recognized one of the boys as Joe. He was smiling, with his arm around the other boy. The other boy was Fritz, who stared into the camera eye as if he were looking down the barrel of a gun.

I WAS NERVOUS about going back to the apartment. I wasn't sure I would know how to act around Leah.

When I opened the front door, Fritz was setting the table.

Leah stood behind the counter, chopping up a head of lettuce. She didn't look up when I came through the door.

Fritz nodded to me and sat down at the head of the table. He looked like he was holding in a laugh. I ignored him and looked back at Leah. She had her back to me and was pretending to inspect something on the refrigerator door. She wore a short-sleeved powder blue shirt and jeans with a pocket that was falling off.

I didn't say anything to them. I walked to the hallway, keeping my eyes on Leah. As I walked closer to her, she made sure to keep her back to me. It was slap-in-the-face rejection, and it made it feel as if I had ants crawling all over the inner walls of my stomach. Weak-kneed, I went to get my bag and take a shower.

I went into the guest room. The thickness of Fritz's cigarette smoke was like walking through a spider-web. I sat down on the bed and looked around the floor for my bag. I couldn't find it. I got up and checked under the bed. It wasn't there, either. I sat for a few seconds and wondered where I could have put it.

I walked down the hallway and cracked open Leah's door. My duffel bag was on top of her made bed. I walked into the room and unzipped the top of the bag. It was empty. Then I heard Leah behind me.

"I put everything in my dresser," she said. When I turned around, I only caught sight of her shadow shrinking away back to the kitchen.

Dinner was served on the children's place mats from Denny's. After the meal, Fritz traced the path on a labyrinth maze with the butt of his cigarette. I washed the dishes, while Leah sipped on a cup of strawberry tea.

Fritz crumpled the place mat up and flipped it onto the table. "Why are these here?" he asked as if the they bothered him. "Why are crayons all over the place?"

"My grandmother baby-sits during the summer."

"Have I ever met your mom's mother?"

Leah blew the steam away on her tea and shook her head. "You may have. I can't remember."

I came back to the table. I stood behind Leah, drying my hands in a blue checkered dish towel. During the meal, we had relaxed around each other. She initiated things by reaching under the table and squeezing my knee. When I looked up at her, she smiled at me and chewed her food.

"I can't believe you have to leave here at two in the morning," Leah complained to me. "That means you'll have to go to sleep in an hour."

I shrugged. "Guess so."

Fritz stamped out his cigarette and leaned back in his chair. "You like working there?" he asked. "Better than RHP, isn't it?"

"Anything's better than RHP."

"You getting along with Joe?"

I thought for a second. I wasn't sure how to answer that. "I think Joe is a hard person to get along with."

Fritz groaned. "You don't have to tell me. I've known the guy since high school." He pointed a finger at Leah. "He used to pal around with your dad. The two of them used to skip school to go Jimmy Potting every May."

Leah rolled her eyes, and made a little laugh through her nose.

"You didn't know your father did shit like that, did you?"

"So you know Joe through Mike?" I asked, sitting down next to Leah. She turned in her chair and propped her feet up on my knees.

Fritz shook his head and took another cigarette out of the breast pocket of his western shirt, clinked open a silver lighter, and lit it. "I was about sixteen when I started hanging around Joe. He was like twenty-one, I think. When Mike would go over to Joe's place, I used to tag along."

"Do you guys still talk much?" Leah asked. She finished her tea and slid the cup halfway across the table.

"No," Fritz said, staring thoughtfully at the smoke from his cigarette, "not too much." He looked at me and winked. "Joe's a difficult person to get along with."

"How's Joe so rich?" Leah and Fritz gave me weird looks. "I don't get it. He does a little fishing, a little farming, yet he

lives in that old mansion and has every boy in the county wanting to work for him. I just don't get it."

Fritz took a deep drag on his cigarette and blew the smoke
out his nose. "He's rich because he's a very useful man. When
people need a tree cut down or their driveway plowed or their
living room remodeled, they know to go to him. It's a well-
known fact that Joe knows how to do just about anything—
and do it *well*."

"But that doesn't make him *that* rich," I said.

"He owns land, too," Fritz said.

"Where?"

"Oh, places around Salisbury, Easton, and Centerville. He
owns a shit-load of condos down here, too. Hell, look around,"
he said, raising his hands as if he were praying, "he owns this
place."

"He owns *this* building?" Leah asked worriedly, pressing
her finger on the tabletop.

"Sure does. He even does all the repairs himself. Your
grandma calls him whenever her toilet backs up or her floor
squeaks." Fritz yawned and scratched the back of his neck.
"We used to have so much fun at that big old house of his."

"Joe doesn't seem like a fun guy," I said.

Fritz shook head. "Oh, no—Joe can surprise you. Years
ago, that house used to be filled with people. We'd go fishing or
hunting or swimming—anything. Every summer, we'd be at
Joe's. When I was a teenager, it was just the place to be."

"Well why don't you two talk much anymore?" Leah asked.

"Because his wife died," Fritz said plainly.

The face of the woman in the photographs sparked before
my eyes. I could suddenly see her moving around the house
before dust covered everything. I could picture her walking in
the grass before it had grown too high, and driving one of the
cars that decomposed next to the barn. "How did she die?" I
asked.

Fritz lowered his head. "Susan drowned."

Leah and I were quiet for a minute.

"You know that pond next to the house?" Fritz asked. "She
was on her way to feed the turtles, riding a three-wheeler." A

smile warmed Fritz's face; his eyes were foggy with nostalgia. "That was her favorite thing to do, feed those diamondback terrapins they had. She fed them worms and snails, and on one of their birthdays, she'd let them eat this purple flower with orange spots on it—don't know its name. Susan used to always clip the edge of that pond too close; she'd like to lean over the three-wheeler and see if she could spot any snails or things for the turtles. Joe used to tell her to get off the bike when she did that. But she never listened. Well, in May, about fifteen years ago, Susan was on her way to feed the terrapins, when she stopped on the three-wheeler to see if she could see any snails at the edge of the water. She must have been too close to the edge of the pond, because her bike tipped over. It pinned her under the water, and she died right there."

Leah bit down on her lip.

Fritz held his hands up as a way to say, "what can you do?"

"What was her name?" I asked.

"Susan Ann Colvin," Fritz answered.

I said the name to myself over and over. Each time the name sparked through the darkness of my mind, it became clearer why Joe was so quiet. Why he busied himself with work. And why he preferred the rooms in the house that had no light.

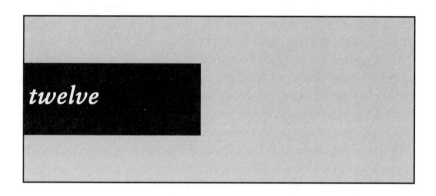

twelve

AT TWO IN THE MORNING, the buses on Coastal Highway were
filled with drunks, kicked out after last call. A bus stopped on
88ᵗʰ Street with a hiss that cut through the quiet air. I could see
the passengers' faces as I put the key in my car door, heads
pressed against glass, looking ghostly from the blue lights inside the bus. One man, with snot in his moustache, was passed
out in one of the back seats; his head was tipped back, making
his Adam apple look as if someone had speared the back of his
neck and the blade was protruding. When the bus's door closed
and jolted forward, the man's head rolled to the side and
thumped on the window, one eye open and one closed.

Standing there, I felt as if we were in different time zones.
Sleep gripped him and held him down, while sleep fell from me
like the dead skin being shed from a snake.

BECAUSE OF WHAT FRITZ had told me about Joe's wife drowning
in the pond, I found myself wanting to pity him. As I drove to
his farm, I tried to shake all notions of feeling sorry for him out
of my head. Gushing seemed a sure way to piss Joe off. Instead,
I decided to not speak at all today unless I was answering a
question, as I was sure Joe would have preferred.

When I parked my car behind his house, Joe was standing
on the porch, twirling a white enamel mug with blue specks on

his finger, as if it were a revolver. In his other hand, hooked on one finger, was the warm coat he said he'd try to find for me.

Joe drove us down to the docks in his truck, and I went through the dozen pockets of the thick blue coat he had lent me. In one of the inside pockets I found about seven empty shotgun shells. They were a dark green and ribbed; the brass ends were knobs of rust. In another pocket I found a crushed pack of cigarettes filled with used Maryland lottery scratch-off cards, dating back to the early seventies. All the pockets had large flaps that went over them, to keep out rain and dirt. The coat had a waterproof, rubbery feel and smelled of sweat and gasoline. The inside lining was tattered wool, and the left sleeve's seam was coming undone at the shoulder.

When we reached the boat, Joe had me load the boat with the empty bushel baskets and a large red cooler of ice in which we could keep our lunches and any fish we'd catch. The baskets were made of thin wood that reminded me of balsa. Joe undid the lines, then went into the cockpit to turn on the engine. The boat started with a loud rumble that scrambled up my legs. Joe revved the engine, and I gripped the side of the boat as it jerked forward.

Then we puttered out on the calm water.

Everything was dark. I couldn't see my way on the boat. The only lights came from a searchlight at the stern and two red and green lights on the top of the cockpit. Joe stood behind the wheel, wearing a green baseball cap, a strip of red flannel tied around his waist, and a long sleeve white shirt, rolled up over his thick forearms. He had his white mug next to him, but he hadn't filled it with anything yet. Above his head was a CB radio; its curly wire hung in a loop in front of his face. A few times Joe grabbed it and said things into it that I barely heard or understood. Then he'd release the long button on its side with his thumb, and a static-muffled voice would talk back to him.

A few blue-gray clouds made up the sky, a giant dome constructed of round stones. The moon was just a chalk-white sliver and shone down on the water, giving it the look of mercury. I stood near the stern and watched the mansions on the shore, my muscles feeling like bags of sand from sleepiness. The houses on the edge of the water looked deserted. The moon glowed off their windows in white streaks outlined in blue. In one yard, I could see the silhouette of a man smoking a cigarette. He was walking a large black lab on a leash. The dog squatted next to a tiny tree, and the man yawned while scratching his head with both hands; the cherry of his cigarette zigzagged in the darkness. The dog walked away from the tree and rolled in the wet grass. When the animal stood, its hide shone like a seal's. The man stood there for a moment and watched us. He took a deep drag on his cigarette; the cherry illuminated his entire face in an orange glow.

I was a little nervous about working on the boat; it was something that I knew nothing about, and I wanted to do a good job. When I was helping Joe tile, I might have done poorly, but at least I knew a *little* because I had seen my father cut tile before (although he always used a manual cutter with a tiny round blade). My father knew very little about boats and fishing. The only time he ever mentioned water to me was when he was telling me about sea burials. "Fish eat out your insides and live in your chest cavity," he had told me from his La-Z-Boy. I had made an ugly face, and my father went on. "It's usually the little fish that do it. They live in your ribs to hide from the bigger fish who'll eat them."

Wind picked up on the bay. It moaned in my ears, and I shuddered. This was a cold that I had never felt before. The wind was damp and strong, not dulled by buildings or trees. I rubbed my hands together and felt uneasy. I was making myself crazy worrying about being able to do a good job. It felt as if my performance was out of my control—my hands would do things my brain didn't tell them to, or I'd trip over my own feet, spilling a bushel of crabs in the water.

The houses on the shore seemed to shrink back into the darkness. The narrow river we were on began to open up. I felt as if we were heading for a black hole. I hadn't prepared myself for how far out on the Chesapeake we would go; I thought we were going to anchor in the river somewhere near Joe's house. We had been puttering along for a good while. I didn't know when Joe was going to stop. I looked back to the shore. The houses were tiny specks now. I felt a little dizzy, so I sat in a corner near the stern. My hands trembled as I heard the waves lap on the side of the boat. The inboard motor shook through my body, and I shut my eyes.

I had never felt less in control of my life. Till now, everything had been planned in some way. Conrad had told me to go west; he was taking care of the money at RHP. Fritz had ordered me to Ocean City; he got me work. But now, Fritz and Conrad couldn't help me. I was floating out on black water to nowhere, not sure when we'd stop. I couldn't see a destination or a crossroads, or the direction which would lead me home.

I opened my eyes and looked out over the side of the boat. The shore was gone. There was nothing. The water shimmered in the dull moonlight. The only light came from above Joe's head in the cockpit. It seemed so bright that it could have been seen from outer space. I stuffed the front of my face down in the warm coat and breathed in my sweat and the coat's old smell. The odors fused together, like clear water turning murky after a single drop of India ink is added to it. My muscles and joints relaxed. The blood in my brain turned muddy as I was carried on a thunderclap of the boat's engine into a dream.

Joe woke me out of a nightmare by toeing me with his boot. It was still dark; the moon highlighted the side of his face and neck in white bands.

"Get up," he said and walked across the boat to the tiller stick (which he had made himself out of a two-by-four and plastic-coated wire).

I'd had a dream that I had been mauled by a train.

I was in a forest near a shallow brook; the train tracks were woven between the trees. I entered the dream right after I had been hit, and I lay with my head in somebody's lap. An olive-green wool blanket covered me up to my neck. The person I was resting on was combing their fingers through my hair and comforting me. Leah was sitting on a tree stump about a foot away. She was crying. I tried to tell her that I was OK, but I couldn't speak.

Suddenly, more people came over to look at me. I didn't recognize any of them. One man knelt next to me and asked me what religion I was, and if I wanted a priest to come and pray with me. I tried to ask why that was necessary, but my mouth felt as if it was filled with dirt. Every time I tried to speak, tiny grains fell down the back of my throat and made me cough.

The man told me to not speak. I managed to ask him why, then he reached forward and pulled the blanket off me like a magician revealing a trick. At my waist, my body had been spun around, tapered above my hip like an hourglass. The front of my thighs and knees were flat on the ground. My boots had been either removed, or I had been knocked out of them. I tried to get up, but the person who was patting my hair held me down. I craned my head up and saw my bare heels sticking up in the air and out to the sides. Thick lines of blood trailed down the pale flesh on the bottoms of my feet. Blood collected in the wrinkles of my skin. My clothes were filthy with grime and coal. In every ragged tear of clothing, I could see blood and flakes of dead skin.

I let my head fall back into the person's lap. I looked up at the strange shapes of sunlight shining through the gaps between the leaves in the trees. The sky was a golden color with lime-green clouds. The leaves vibrated. The person behind me wiped a line of sweat off my brow before it went into my eye. I rolled my head back to look at whoever it was. Their face was upside down, and it took me a few seconds to recognize it. It was Leah's ex-boyfriend, Ron. When I went to speak, he leaned forward and kissed me on the forehead. That's when Joe woke me up.

I stood up and walked over to Joe, the dream's memory dropping off of me like chunks of melting ice. The boat was illuminated by the kind of bright light bulb in a yellow cage that mechanics use when they're under the hoods of cars. Joe had it hooked on the side of the catch bin. When I glanced at it, I was blinded for a few seconds, like an operator at RHP dealing with the sun. Green spots, outlined in brown, swirled in front of my eyes.

"Pick up that anchor," Joe said.

I blinked my eyes back into focus and grabbed an anchor that was tied to a trotline by a chain. The anchor was made out of an old propane tank for gas grills. When I lifted it, it felt like it had been filled halfway with concrete. I stumbled a bit with it because I still hadn't learned how to stand on a boat. I was always on the brink of teetering over into the water.

"When I tell you, throw that in," Joe said. "Keep your hands free after you release it. If that line grabs you," he said, then paused, "then you're no good to me." A few seconds later he said, "Now," and waved like a captain ordering a cannon to be fired.

I heaved the thing in the water; the trotline uncoiled after it, bait smacking on the side of the boat. Joe's buoys—bright orange empty laundry detergent bottles—flipped into the water next. Joe took the other end of the line, where there was a three-foot long rusty chain, and tied it to another anchor—a part of an old engine block, spray-painted orange.

"Get ready," he said, as we watched the line unravel to nothing on the deck.

I picked up the other anchor, and Joe told me to wait.

"When I say, chuck it in. This is the important one. If you throw it too soon, the bait won't be settled on the bottom. If you throw it too late, you could snap the line. It has to be perfect." After a few seconds, he told me to release it, and I pitched it in, unable to see where the engine block crashed through the dark water.

Joe and I threw out three more trotlines, then waited for the crabs to take the bait. Joe went into the cockpit and brought out his thermos and the mug he had been spinning on his finger earlier. He held the mug out to me, and I accepted it. Then he filled it with some steaming coffee.

"Drink that," he said, as a command. Then he filled the lid of his thermos with the rest of the coffee and went into the cockpit and sat on a little built-in stool.

I looked down at the hot liquid and smiled. So far this was the only thing Joe had done for me that suggested that he might end up liking me after all. I hated coffee, but I drank it because I appreciated the kind gesture—and I wasn't sure if Joe would ever offer me another.

About an hour later, the sun rose slowly, but it was still dark. Joe handed me a dip net that he had made himself—it was an old rake handle with a net made of chicken wire and the lip from an old bucket. He stood behind me and grabbed me by my shoulders, positioning me where he wanted as if he were setting up a mannequin for display. I just went limp in his arms and let him move me wherever he wanted to. He walked back to the tiller stick with a gaff hook in his hand. There was another throttle that he had set up next to the stern cleat. Its metal handle was dotted with rust.

"I'll hook this line, and you grab the crabs as they come up. If you miss one, holler and I'll try and grab it. When you get it, put the crab in there." He pointed his chin at the catch bin in the center of the boat, where the mechanic's light was hooked.

"Got it," I said, nodding. I readied the dip net as if it were a jousting pole, and Joe aimed the searchlight on the water.

"Now get ready—they have good eyesight. They'll drop off before they hit the surface."

I nodded my head again.

Joe aimed the light on the first buoy and readied his gaff hook, steering the tiller with his other hand. As we came to the line, he downshifted the motor to just above idle. He hooked the line and draped it across a pipe-like roller that jutted from the side of the boat. The ends of the white plastic roller were smeared from its rusty washers.

I watched the line as it came up out of the greenish-yellow water and continued over the roller. A couple of pieces of bait came up with no crabs. On the third piece, I saw the white belly of a crab come into focus through the murky water. I stabbed the net into the water and scooped him up. As I pulled him in, the crab tumbled out of the net back into the water.

"Do it fast," Joe said. "They'll get away from you."

A few more pieces of bait passed by. Then another crab was on the line. I scooped him up and slammed him so hard in the catch bin that I heard his shell crack. A few more pieces of bait then another crab; I scooped him out of the water so fast that I threw him over the other side of the boat.

"*Relax*," Joe said. "Don't try so hard. Pretend the crab is a lacrosse ball."

"I've never played lacrosse before," I said.

"Just keep them in the boat."

I didn't get the hang of trotlining until the first line was almost finished. I started to keep the dip net deeper in the water, letting the crabs drop off into the chicken wire net, instead of trying to pull them off the bait. I also learned how to catch the crabs after they cartwheeled out of the net by holding it up higher; that way I had more time to catch them if they jumped out.

The sun was up by the time the catch bin was full. I took off the coat, and the sun burned my skin. Lines of sweat wandered down from my armpits and tickled my side. My upper lip was salty from perspiration. A few other trotliners were out in the water. They all waved to Joe, and he nodded back.

You could map the foot traffic from the cockpit to the rear throttle. The powder blue paint on the floor of the boat had been worn to the bare wood, which was stained dark from sea spray and fish blood.

Joe pulled me over to the catch bin. "Time for culling," he said. He pointed to a five inch notch that had been cut out of the lip of the wooden bin. "Keeper size is five inches. Measure them point to point. If they can fit in here," he said, tapping the notch, "throw them back." He gave me a thick leather glove and a pair of crab tongs to use to grab them.

"Right," I said.

"Throw the sooks back, too."

"What's a sook?"

"A female crab." He explained how to tell them apart by the shape of the crab's abdomen.

The leather glove had a missing little finger, so I had to squeeze my first two fingers together. My hand cramped after only a few seconds. I measured the crabs by the length of their lateral spines and sorted them by size. I had several bushel baskets for five- and six-inch crabs; only two for seven- and eight-inch ones; and one for crabs bigger than that (which Joe had said would be rare). The crabs clambered over each other, claws raised. Water beaded off their blue-green shells. The crabs reminded me of the cartoon trucks on the map of America in the RHP new employee video.

With the sun up and vibrating off the green Chesapeake water, I felt more relaxed. I had also finally figured out how to walk on the boat: I shouldn't have been locking my knees. Now I walked as if my legs were two strings of spaghetti. It was good to see the other watermen; I didn't feel so far away from land. I also felt as if I were closer to Leah. When I woke this morning, I had to slide out from under her arm. I had dressed on the floor and watched her from the street lights that glowed in the room. She lay on her side, facing me, under a white sheet and a thick beige blanket. She was breathing in deeply through her open mouth, which caused her to snore a little.

I stopped thinking about the culling and wondered what we would do tonight.

Suddenly, I felt a sharp pain between my fingers. I looked down and saw a tiny crab (under the five inch keeper size) gripping the webbing between my first two fingers on my left hand. I shouted and dropped the crab tongs with a loud clang. I tried to shake the thing off, but its grip was like a pair of pliers. The little crab was so strong that I was impressed. I grabbed it with my gloved hand and tried to pull it off.

"Don't do that," Joe said. He walked over with a pocket-knife in his hand. He put the handle in the crab's other claw, and it let go and swung from the ivory handle of Joe's knife. He flipped the thing into the water.

I looked down at the place where the crab had bitten me. I wasn't bleeding, but the skin was red and looked like a piece of gum with teeth indentations. I thanked him, then went back to culling.

NOON. For lunch I ate some leftovers from dinner last night. Leah had made me a turkey sandwich with jellied cranberries mixed into the meat. Joe sat in the cockpit with his back to me, eating something that I couldn't see. Occasionally, he turned his head, and I saw him chewing something with a little mayonnaise in the corner of his mouth. Then he turned back around so all I saw was his huge back.

There was an odd tension between us. We hadn't spoken more than twenty words to each other the whole day. After I learned how to toss the anchors and scoop the crabs, there was no need for talk. Besides, Joe always had a look on his face as if he were figuring things out in his head, as if he were constantly thinking of ways to fix machines or cut back on expenses. His brow was always creased in thought, so I never wanted to interrupt him.

I finished my lunch and put the plastic bag in a pocket of the coat that was lying near the stern. Then I put the lid on the empty catch bin and stacked the crabs according to size. They scratched around groggily in the thin wooden baskets. I closed the last basket and fastened a wire loop around the tabs on the lid.

Joe hollered to me from the cockpit. "You see a point in making another run?" He didn't turn around when he said this.

At first, I thought he wanted my opinion. But then I realized it was a test. He wanted to know if I thought it would be *productive* to use fuel and bait and my wages on another run.

"No," I answered. "We didn't even get a bushel that last time. Let's save the bait for tomorrow."

I looked for a reaction out of him, but he didn't move. Then I added, "I think I'd be of better use—money-wise—doing something on the farm right now."

Joe didn't turn around, but he nodded. "Very good."

FRITZ AND I WERE SITTING on an empty lifeguard's stand with our backs to the ocean, so we could watch the sunset. Fritz sat on the right arm of the stand, and I on the left—our toes met in the center of the white-planked bottom of the seat. Above the condos, the skyline was a violent mixture of pink and orange and red, outlined in thin gray clouds The sky looked like a sea of flames turned upside down.

Leah was working until the Sunset closed, so it was just Fritz and me. The wind was dead, but he wore a heavy jeans jacket with wool around the collar. Fritz had started talking about Leah a few minutes ago, but the sky distracted him. Now he remembered what he wanted to say to me.

"I think I need to know what your plans are," he said.

I kept watching the bright sky as it melted behind the buildings. I didn't say anything. Fritz watched me; his stare felt like a bee sting behind my ear.

"You're not settled," he said.

I swallowed and glanced at him.

"You're in your mid-twenties and you don't know what to do with yourself."

"What do you want me to say?"

"Say whatever you like."

"Can I say I have to go back to Baltimore?"

Fritz nodded. "Just don't tell me you have to go back because you *want* to."

I sighed and looked out over the ocean. I had known this conversation was going to happen, but I just didn't think it would happen so soon. "I *do* like Leah," I said. "I just don't know how it can work."

"Don't go back," he said, pausing a whole second between the words.

"Fritz, I have to go back," I said.

"Right. Go home, get your stuff, then find a place near Dewey Beach. Leah will be back there at the end of the summer. My brother will give you a job. Joe could probably even give you a deal on an apartment he owns up there."

I laughed at how simple Fritz made it sound. "I might not be able to come back."

"The police?"

"Right."

Fritz gave me a paternal look. "With all the drugs and violence in Baltimore, do you really think the police give half a shit about you?"

I got a little embarrassed. "I think I have a right to worry."

"Did you pay the money back?"

"Yes."

Fritz held up his hands. "What are you worried about? No shit company like RHP is going to hire a lawyer and waste their time pressing charges for a couple hundred dollars. They got their money back. They've probably even forgotten your name. Now quit wasting your goddamn life and work for my brother."

"You think working at a bar is doing something with my life?" He tried to answer, but I cut him off. "You don't give a shit about what happens to me as long as I stay with Leah."

"I want to help you, you dumb little bastard."

"*Don't!*" I shouted. "Don't pretend like you're helping me— I know all you want is for Leah to stay away from this Ron guy. I'm just a damn good obstacle."

"I just want you two to make each other happy," he mumbled ineffectively.

I laughed in his face. "Oh you do? Then why can't Leah pack up *her* things and come back with *me*? Have Leah change *her* life. Make *her* start all over again."

Fritz fished a cigarette out of his jacket pocket and stuck it in his lips, but didn't light it. "She can't," he sighed. "She can't leave. Not now."

I snorted a laugh. "Not so easy is it?"

Fritz lit the cigarette and took a long drag. "But you're not settled anywhere. You may think you are, but you're not."

"What do mean?"

"Well," he said, smoke streaming through his lips, "when's the last time you took your dad to the movies?"

"He's dead."

"What about your mom?"

"We don't talk much."

"Brothers? Sisters?" He looked up to make sure we made eye contact. "Name me at least two friends that visit you on a regular basis."

I was quiet. I wanted to say Lisa and Conrad, but I didn't bother.

Fritz leaned forward and cupped both his hands on my kneecaps, cigarette jutting from his fingers like a smokestack. "Remember the night we went to that cemetery?"

I shook my head.

"I asked you, who would miss you while you were here, and you said there was nobody." After a second he added, "Now you *have* somebody."

I wasn't sure if I wanted to punch Fritz in the face or jump in the ocean.

"Listen to me—it's not too late. You're not settled."

"But what does that *mean*?" I blurted out and pushed his hands off my knees. "You keep saying that, but I don't know what the hell you're talking about!"

"I'm saying you still have a chance to move here and make Leah very happy. You still can start your life."

"I have started a life—and it's in Baltimore."

"What life? You got your dumb ass fired from RHP. You don't have any friends. I'm trying to bring you into my family. Leah likes you; my brother likes you. *I* like you."

"But why do you *care*?" I barked at him. "Why are you *doing* all this?"

"Because none of those people can fucking *stand me*!" Fritz's face was flushed in anger, eyes wild. After a second, he calmed down. "I'm trying to help Leah. If I help her, they might accept me again."

A quiet fell on us. The waves seemed to stop. The hiss of sand being blown by warm wind calmed. Fritz took his cigarette and dropped it off the lifeguard stand. I watched it hit the sand, and the cherry disappeared. Then he pulled off his jacket and rolled up his right sleeve.

"See this?" he said, slapping the tattoo of the little girl I had seen back at the diner. "This is my daughter, Sandy."

Without thinking, I reached forward and ran my finger on the blue-black lines of the tattoo. Around the edges of the girl's hair, the skin was puffed out and scarred. The tattoo seemed to have been placed a little off center on his forearm.

"My wife was two months' pregnant when I went away to prison." Fritz looked at the tattoo and sighed. "I was still in jail when she was born."

"What were you in jail for?"

"Well, it was a bunch of things: drinking in public, some theft, bar fights, and I got caught once stealing a tire off the back of a jeep. I got probation for that stuff. But I actually went to jail for not showing up for court on a DWI. Then they locked me up.

"One day, while I was in jail, there's a letter from my wife: 'I had the baby. Her name is Sandy.' That's all. She didn't even send me a picture. When I got out of jail, the kid was one, I think." A smile cut across Fritz's face. "About ten days later, I got myself arrested and sent back to jail."

"For what?"

Fritz waved me off. "It doesn't matter. Point is, I was glad to be going back."

"Why?"

"Well, it was like this family was forced in my face. At home, I had a kid who shit all the time, screamed all night, and cost a damn fortune. My wife didn't help. She was a goddamn coke-head. Most of the time I had her *and* the baby to clean up. My wife would fall asleep in her vomit and the baby would be off somewhere in the apartment chewing on electric cords or drinking peroxide. So when I went back to jail, I was happy—didn't have to deal with any of that crap anymore. I was a damn nine-teen-year-old kid—I didn't want a wife; I didn't want to pay for a million shots this baby needed, and I sure as hell didn't want the *baby* in the first place. While I was in jail, I could just forget about everything. My wife wrote me a few times, but I never opened the letters, just threw them away. My cellmate, this fat banker named Bill, used to bitch about how I never read any of the letters—*his* wife never wrote him. Bill used to get them out of the trash and read them himself."

"Where did your wife and kid live this whole time?" I asked.

"Up in Dewey," he said, then continued. "While I was in jail, my brother helped out; he bought clothes, diapers, formula, whatever he could. Goddamn." Fritz laughed in disbelief, as if he just realized that the story he was telling was about himself. "Hell, my wife wasn't making any money. She didn't have a job. I think she and the kid were living at her mother's house, in the basement. She used to leave the baby in dirty diapers all day while she drank herself to sleep. My wife's mother used to light about a million candles and listen to the radio at full volume, because of the smell of the kid's shit and the screaming were too much."

Wind picked up and spread a few strands of greasy hair

across Fritz's face, but he didn't bother pushing them away. His voice became a little strained. With each new word, it seemed as if he were going to break down and cry.

"Well, one day," he went on, sniffing and wiping his eyes, "I get a letter from my wife's sister. Immediately, I throw this thing away; I thought I knew what it said. I was fed up with her sister's bitching as much as I was with my wife's. Anyway, as usual, Bill gets the letter out of the trash and he reads it to himself, then tells me I ought to look at it. I told him to just read it to me. He read it quietly to himself first, then all he says is, 'Your wife is dead.'"

"How did she die?"

"She was found in the woods behind a bar. Autopsy said she had a shit-load of alcohol in her system, but they think the cold was what killed her. It was February when this happened, and they think she'd been out there for a couple of days, unconscious. The police checked for bruises or strangle marks that might suggest that she was forced out there, but they didn't find anything. They said she probably just wandered off to throw up, then passed out.

"In the letter, Bill read that my wife's sister wanted to know what to do with the baby. She said she wasn't going to take care of it; my wife's mother didn't want it. They told me that they would watch her until I got out of jail. Bill read this all to me, so it made the whole mess that much worse. Imagine finding out that your wife is dead and that you have a child that nobody wants from some fat bastard in his underwear.

"My wife's sister included a picture of Sandy in the letter. On the back she wrote: THIS IS NOT MY RESPONSIBILITY."

"What did you do when you got out of jail?"

Fritz looked out over the water for a long while. The sky was turning dark. The yellow lights in the condos behind us came on one by one. Fritz looked as if he was finished talking. He had managed to smother his urge to cry and seemed normal now. I didn't think he wanted to go on.

"You don't have to tell me any more." I was unsure whether or not I was supposed to put my arm around him, so I didn't.

"I'm telling you things that Leah doesn't even know, all right?

Can I trust you not to say any of this to her before I get a chance to tell her?"

I shook my head and closed my eyes, suddenly not wanting to hear the rest.

"See this?" he said finally, pointing to the tattoo.

I nodded. "Yes."

"No. Really *look*." He ran his finger along the side of the tattoo.

I followed his finger with my eyes, but I couldn't see what he wanted to show me. At the dark border of the little girl's hair, I couldn't see anything. Fritz twisted his arm so the light could hit the tattoo better. Then I saw it, coming into focus like some mirage. A long pink scar that went from the base of his wrist to the crook in his elbow, a narrow furrow under his skin. The crooked scar seemed to weave in and out of the dark edges off all his other tattoos. "What is that?" I asked—but I knew.

"When I got out of prison, I took a bus back home. But I never went to see my kid. I was waiting at the station and thinking of what the hell I was going to do. I watched some mechanic fixing a video game machine, and I just stared at him like I was in a trance. I just remember thinking, *I am not a father, I am not a father*, over and over. I just sat there completely scared shitless and watching this guy fix an old video game. When the mechanic got up and went to his truck, I knew what I was going to do. I went over and opened his toolbox and stole a utility knife. Then I went into the bathroom and locked the door. I took off my belt and wrapped it around my arm to get the vein to pop out. Then I took the knife and slid the blade up my arm, splitting the vein. The blood was really watery, I remember. It was kind of cold too—I had always thought blood was hot. When I took the belt off my arm, the blood gushed out like a fountain."

"Jesus," I said. "Did you leave a note?"

"No. Didn't want to. I didn't really have anything to say."

"You were just going to die on the men's room floor of a bus station?"

He shrugged. "If you're going to die, you're going to die. I didn't care where."

"Did somebody find you and call an ambulance?"

He shook his head and frowned. "I don't know. When I woke up, I was in the nuthouse. Mike had found out what I did and had me committed."

"They didn't think you were mentally competent?"

Fritz rubbed the back of his neck and groaned. "Jesus, they *knew* I wasn't mentally competent."

"What did they do about your arm?"

Fritz smiled. "It's funny. My doctor told me that it's actually very hard to die from a slit wrist. I always thought it was a sure way to go. Funny."

"How long were you in a mental institution?"

"Long enough for my arm to heal. When I got out, they set me up with a job as a janitor at an elementary school in Rehoboth. That's where I met Shelly." Fritz lit himself another cigarette. "She used to teach a little group of stupid kids in the corner of the library."

"She wasn't a counselor?"

He shook his head. "Not at this school. She just taught the slow kids. I remember she had a jar of cinnamon jawbreakers on her desk, and she'd give it to the kids when they got a right answer—like giving fish to a seal after it plays a song on a bunch of bicycle horns."

"Did you guys start dating then?"

"God no. It was common knowledge around the school that she was going through a hell of a divorce at the time. She was the last thing in the world I needed then. I thought she was pretty all right, but I was still on probation, my kid was being adopted, I was depressed all the time, and I had this big honking scar on my arm that I was really self-conscious about. I always wore a long-sleeved undershirt under my uniform, to hide it from the administration and teachers."

I figured that was why he always wore long sleeves around Leah. She might have seen the scar under the camouflage of tattoos.

"On top of everything," he said, "my shrink was still watching me like a hawk; he wouldn't have approved of me dating so soon."

"You were seeing a psychiatrist this whole time?"

An ashamed look drained the blood from his face. "I still see a therapist."

"Oh," I said, feeling stupid.

"After a few years, Shelly's divorce and custody crap was all settled, and I was ready to ask her out on a date. I told my doctor I was going to get a tattoo to try to hide the scar on my arm. I wanted to talk to Shelly at this point, but this scar had suicide attempt written all over it. My doctor told me the tattoo was a great idea."

"Really?"

"Well, he thought I meant one of those cosmetic tattoos. You know, the kind people with sun spots or skin grafts get to cover up the pale skin."

"Well, what did your doctor say when you showed up with a portrait of your daughter?"

Fritz laughed and couldn't stop. "He told me I was out of my goddamn mind." Fritz took a drag from his cigarette with a sheepish grin. "We had some talking to do after that. He thought there was some real profound reason I got it, but I just liked the picture; she's cute."

"Why'd you get all the other tattoos?"

He held the cigarette between his lips and gave the coming night a worried look, as if he expected rain. "These others are pretty recent. Shelly wanted me to get more so my arms would match. She said I looked lopsided."

"When did you guys start dating?"

"Three years ago. I was mopping the floor outside the library almost at the end of the day; her class had five minutes left before the kids went back to homeroom. I was waiting out there so I could go in and ask her if she wanted to get a drink or something. I remember waiting really long after the final bell rang and everybody had left the building. I finally got sick of waiting, so I went in to see what she was doing.

"When I opened the door, there were no kids. She was sitting behind her desk, crying."

"She got fired, didn't she?"

"Yeah," he said, wondering how I knew. "She did. I went

over and introduced myself and asked her out."

"And she said yes?"

"She said no. Told me she was going back to live in Maryland with her family. I told her I didn't care; I wanted to date her anyway. So I drove to her mother's house every weekend. I couldn't move up there because I was still on probation. And she couldn't stay here because she needed her family's help supporting her daughter, now that she was out of a job.

"So in order to see her, I met this guy down here who worked for a trucking company that handled distribution for a warehouse in West Virginia. He told me that I'd have to drive loads back and forth from this place in West Virginia about twice a week. I could see Shelly on the way."

I looked over at him and sighed. "And you want me to do the same thing with Leah. Drive down here once a week."

"No. I want you to *live* here."

The sound of the waves and the traffic beyond the sand dunes filled the space between us. Fritz's story made what I had to say much harder. I looked up at him and took a deep breath. "No."

Fritz lunged forward and jumped off the lifeguard stand. He hit the sand hard and rolled to his side, then got up and headed for the sand dunes.

I climbed down and shouted after him. "Wait!"

He didn't stop. The sky had become so dark I could barely see his figure.

"Why should I stay if neither of you is telling me the truth?"

I saw him pause and turn. His body was dissolving into the darkness.

"There's something wrong with her, isn't there?"

"You could say that."

I could barely hear him over the exploding waves.

"Tell me!" I shouted. "You owe me that much."

"I don't have the right. This will have to be between you and her."

Nerves were thundering under my skin. I wasn't sure if my legs would be strong enough to carry me over the dunes. I plopped down in the sand.

Fritz stepped over a snow fence and stopped on top of a steep dune. His figure was silhouetted against the blue night sky. It looked as if he'd sprouted from the sand along with all the spiky tall grass.

"Just *tell* me." My voice sounded pinched off in the air.

He turned and yelled, "You'll find out soon enough." Then he disappeared out of sight behind the dark dunes.

thirteen

A SPONGE CRAB came up on the trotline, yellow-orange bubbles
exposed at the abdomen. Joe told me to throw it back.

It was noon, and we had twelve bushels of crabs. I had
done a better job on the boat today. I moved more decidedly
and confidently. At one point, Joe said to me, "You got your
own stance now." But I couldn't tell if that was a compliment
or not.

After we wound the three trotlines up on the boat, Joe told
me we had to catch some more bait. He went into the cockpit
and handed me a cork-handled fishing pole. There was a cap
on the bottom of the handle that you could unscrew, and inside
were extra fishing lines and a scaling knife. The blade was
crusted with silver gills and dried blood.

Joe baited our hooks with three kernels of yellow corn from
a can he kept in the cooler. We cast our lines, standing on opposite sides of the boat from one another. I watched my white-
topped bobber rise on the tiny crests of water. Blades of sunlight bounced up from the pale-blue paint on the floor of the
boat, blinding me whenever I looked at my feet. My skin had
gotten darker; the hairs on my arms were sun-bleached. Joe
had given me some sun block earlier in the day. My skin was
slick and smelled of coconuts. Joe didn't bother to wear lotion
anymore. The skin on the back of his neck was like worn leather,

with deep cracks crisscrossing each other.

Joe reeled his line in and cast it back out, buzzing as it re-coiled. The sinker hit the water with a plop.

When I had gotten ready to leave for Joe's this morning, Leah still hadn't returned from work. Fritz had gone, too. When I went back to the condo after we had talked on the beach, he'd left for the night. In a way, I had been glad he was gone—we would have been too uncomfortable around each other. I had thought I wanted to know more about Fritz, but after he told me, I was sorry to know it.

It was strange going to sleep all alone in that condo. I went to bed in Leah's room around eight at night. I had to put a blanket over the curtains because the sun was still up. I lay in bed with my eyes closed, listening for the sound of the front door opening, hoping it would be either Leah or Fritz. When I woke up, I wandered around the house and realized that I was still alone. I went into the living room and waited for Leah to get home from the Sunset so we could talk. I told myself that I had to know what was wrong with her if I was going to move down here. I waited as long as I could.

It felt good to be at Joe's today; the hard work gave me a chance to forget about everything for awhile. I speared the dip net in the water all morning, and all the worry over what could be wrong with Leah drained away.

About two hundred yards away, a large yacht raced past us, rising on the waves and crashing hard onto the water. The sun flashed off its large, black-tinted windows. Gold horns and spinning antennas cluttered the top of the wheelhouse. A man sat on the bow, eating a pear. He had dark curly hair and wore a pair of sunglasses with orange lenses. He waved his pear to us as he thundered past. Above the froth of jetted water from the boat's propellers, the name of the boat was written in upper-case gold letters: GOTTERWAYAGAIN. It took me a few seconds to make sense of the name.

Something tugged on my line. I saw my bobber dart under the green-brown water. I jerked the line to get the hook stuck in the fish's mouth.

"I got something."

"Reel it in," Joe said with his back to me. He was pissing off the side of the boat.

As I reeled it in, I could feel the fish struggling under the surface. My silver line zigzagged through the choppy water. Joe came over with the net. The fish wasn't strong; I brought it up easily. It kicked and convulsed as it dangled from my line, splashing us with water. Joe scooped the fish in the net and dumped it on the deck. I leaned forward and squinted at it. The fish had a fat, stubby body and swollen, bug eyes. Its skin was a mint-green and olive color and looked to be covered in bacon fat.

"What the hell is it?" I said, with my face scrunched up.

"Toadfish," Joe said.

"What's a toadfish?"

"An ugly fish that looks like a toad. Throw it back. They don't make good bait."

"Why not?"

Joe looked at me. "Would *you* eat it?"

The ugly fish flopped around on the boat and left a dab of slime every place it touched. I picked it up, and got a nauseating chill the second my fingers touched its wet, muck-covered skin. I dug my fingers into its ribcage, and it slithered out of my hands and slapped on the deck, hard. My palms were covered with a greasy film that made a web between my fingers.

Joe handed me what looked like a funny handgun. There was a trigger on its handle, and a long, skinny barrel with a claw at the end. "Use this to get the hook out."

I took the tool, squeezed the trigger and three wire fingers of the claw opened.

"These fish survive on oysters," Joe said. "They crush the shells in their mouths. He could take off all your fingers."

I stuck the tool down the fish's gaping mouth, grimacing as I looked at a row of its tiny round teeth. When I felt the metal claw clink on the hook down the fish's throat, it bit down and flopped around on the deck. I grasped the hook and pulled it out; blood leaked from the fish's mouth. Then I threw it back. I went over to the cooler and picked up two handfuls of ice and rubbed them in my palms until I could feel the slick residue of slime wash away.

Before we headed in, I caught five more toadfish. I wondered if I was just catching the same one over and over. Joe caught a bunch of blue snappers and a couple of softshell crabs, which he would later use in his eel traps.

Back at the house, I loaded the crabs into the freezer, then followed Joe inside.

Doug sat on a wicker-bottomed stool in the kitchen, talking on a cream-colored wall phone, shaking his head. There was a burnt piece of toast in his hand and the room smelled of charred bread.

Joe was sitting across from me at the kitchen table with his hands folded. He had that look as if he was doing mathematics in his head. A pot of chicken soup was on the stove. I looked down at my arms; sunburn was setting in.

"That's because you're not pushing the grout in diagonally," Doug said into the phone. "Don't push it in straight up and down—it won't build up in the joints."

Doug was talking to the man whose bathroom Joe and I had tiled. He had told Joe that he could do the grouting himself, but he'd called Doug because he was making a mess of the project. Doug had good control of the situation for someone sixteen. He knew exactly what was wrong with the man's job without having to look at it.

"Don't soak the sponge! Just get it damp." Doug rolled his eyes. "Before the grout dries, lightly go over the tiles. You'll have to do this a bunch of times."

Joe took the tiny notebook from his T-shirt pocket. He wrote something in it with a little golf pencil with a dentist's name and phone number printed on it. "Doug," Joe said, looking straight ahead, "ask him if he has all the supplies there."

Doug asked him, then cupped his hand over the mouthpiece. "Yeah, he says he's got everything."

Joe flipped to a blank page and wrote something else down, then ripped the paper from the notebook. He folded it in half and set it on the table. "Why don't you get over there and finish the job," Joe said and glanced over at Doug.

He sighed and nodded, then said to the guy on the phone, "How about I just come over and do it for you?" Doug listened for a second then hung up the phone without saying goodbye.

Joe reached forward and tapped the piece of paper he had placed on the table. "When you're done, charge him this."

Doug took the paper and put it in his back pocket without reading it.

"Take my truck. If you need to buy anything, have him pay for it."

Doug shook his head and walked out.

"You're not going with him?" I asked, looking out the door to the truck.

Joe went back to staring at the wall with the focused scowl on his face. He didn't respond for a few seconds. "He knows what he's doing," he said distantly.

The soup on the stove was boiling; the lid rattled on the pot. The salty smell of chicken wafted in the room.

"Pour two bowls of that, then sit back down," Joe said.

I wasn't sure the second bowl was for me. I spooned the soup with a tin ladle and set both bowls in front of him. Joe slid one over to me.

We ate in silence. The soup was scalding and burned my tongue raw. The only sound in the room was the clinking of spoons on bowls and slurping of salty chicken broth, while the steam curled like dragon-tails into the light coming through the cobwebbed windows. The chicken and vegetables all came from the farm. The carrots and celery and potatoes were in huge clumps. The pieces of chicken were walnut-sized. I wondered if Joe would ever make me catch a chicken and lop its head off.

Joe set his spoon down in the bowl and wiped his mouth with the back of his arm. He still looked distracted, as if he were trying to hear a conversation in faraway room. "I got things worked out." His rumbling voice startled me. "I'd like for Doug to do the carpentry and farm work. And I want you on the boat and here, doing the housework."

"Is my work on the boat good?" I asked cautiously.

"No," he said. "But I think you might *become* good."

"Oh."

"How does that sound? You will fish with me, and when I'm doing something else, you will clean the house and cook."

"Well, we've never talked about money."

"I'll pay you after you've been here a week. Then you can decide if the money is fair."

"You can't give me a rough estimate of what I'll be making?"

Joe pursed lips and nodded as if it were a fair question. "I pay what I feel people are worth." He pointed to the door. "Doug is very valuable, so I pay him a lot; I want to keep him here." Then he pointed to me. "You, on the other hand, are not very valuable—not now, that is. If I were to tell you your worth as of today, you probably wouldn't want to hear it. I'm hoping by the end of a week's time, you can increase your worth. The more valuable you make yourself, the more I'll pay to keep you here."

"I understand."

"Good. Now, dust the dining room." He stood up and put both bowls in the sink and walked through the dining room to his little office. "Rags and polish are in the closet by the stairs." He stuck his finger in what looked like a black knot in the wood and pulled the flimsy door open. I could smell the gunpowder fanning across the room. Joe ducked his head as he climbed into the wall and closed the door behind him, which wobbled as it shut. After he was inside, I couldn't see the outline of the door or any hinges. It was as if the house had just swallowed him whole.

It took me two hours to dust the room. My nose burned and my eyes watered as I polished the old furniture to a glossy shine. At one point, Joe came out of his little office and looked around with a distant smile on his face. It looked as if this was the first time he had ever seen the room and was overwhelmed with the thought that he actually owned all these expensive antiques. Then he told me to go boil him some water for coffee.

Doug came back an hour later, covered in white grout stains, holding a black bottle of Spanish champagne.

"They wanted you to have this," Doug held up the bottle up by its neck.

Joe was sitting at the table behind a steaming mug. "Put it with the rest," he said, nodding towards the pantry.

Doug opened the pantry door and stood on his toes to put the champagne on the top shelf. It was the only glossy bottle up there, the others were very dusty. Now I understood where they came from.

When Doug came out he looked me over, then looked at himself like he wasn't sure which one of us looked worse. I was covered in gray patches of dust, and spider-webs clung to my hair.

"Money," Joe said, walking over to Doug. He stood with his back to the dining room and held out his hand.

Doug reached in his pocket and gave him a pink check with flowers all over it.

Joe put the check in his notebook, then looked to me and said, "You're free to go. Be back the same time tomorrow." Then he looked into the dining room where the sun glowed in the curtains and the china was winking in the cabinets. "It's working," he said with a broad smile on his face.

Before I went back to Leah's, I called Conrad to see if the charges against me had been dropped. I was at a crab house just outside Ocean City. Dark clouds circled above me and the air was filled with the mustiness of coming rain.

Conrad's roommate answered the phone on the first ring. He was the only person in the house who answered the phone politely. The only problem was that he always had to talk to you, had to know who you were, what you wanted, and why. There was still a lot of Pentagon in him, and it made me uncomfortable.

"Ocean City?" he asked. "What are you getting into down there?"

"Nothing," I said. "Is Conrad in?"

"Afraid not." I couldn't see him, but I could tell he was smiling.

"Do you know when he'll be back?"

"Not really," he said. "So, still hiding from a lawsuit?"

I stayed quiet. The static on the phone filled the space around me.

"You *are* the one who has the police knocking on his door,

aren't you?"

"Did Conrad tell you that?"

"I know everything," he said. "Not much happens here that I don't know about—or anywhere else, for that matter."

I wanted to hang up, but he excused himself.

"I hate to be rude, but I'm going to let you go."

"Sure."

"Listen," he said, "if you ever need anything, you'll come to me, yes?"

"I guess."

"Good," he said. "I may not be in the game anymore, but I still know people. Remember: with me, your problems are only a phone call away from being over."

THE SECOND I SAW RON standing in Leah's apartment, I felt something spark behind my eyes like a vein in my brain had burst. Worry sent ice needles through my body. I accepted the fact that I was probably going to be beaten up.

Leah was sitting on the edge of the coffee table with her head in her hands, fingers clawing her cheekbones. Ron stood above her with my duffel bag in his fist.

"You've been staying here?" Ron asked me, adjusting the weight of my bag in his hand. His voice didn't have any anger in it.

I looked at Leah. She was exhausted from crying.

"Well, I've packed your shit, so you can piss off." He threw the bag at my feet.

"What's going on?" I said, my voice sounding weaker than I wanted.

"Tell him," Ron said to Leah. "Why don't you tell your little boyfriend here what's going on."

Leah didn't blink. She shook her head on the heels of her palm. Her eyes looked like balls of glass.

"He doesn't know, does he?" he asked her, looking at me.

"Know what?"

Ron shook his head. He was wearing his work uniform, but the bow tie was off and his shirt was untucked. Seeing Ron and Leah together was strange—Ron looked much too old for her. He stood with his hands on his hips and waited for Leah to say something, but she just stared at the wall next to me unseeing.

"Let me ask you something." Ron folded his arms and started tapping the floor with one foot. He looked excited, as if he had rehearsed this a thousand times. "You know she's not house-sitting, but do you really know *why* Leah is down here?"

"No." I was looking for a weapon. All I could find were crayons.

"You never bothered to tell him?" He glared at the back of her head.

Leah cleared her throat. "I was going to."

"Leah?" I said. "Tell me now. What's wrong?"

"She came down here," Ron said, disgusted, "to get an abortion."

Leah closed her eyes when he said it. She had the face I'd have expected if someone were pressing a burning matchstick to her skin. Two white tears rolled down her cheeks. I wanted her to say something, but she was frozen.

"You're pregnant?"

"I was going to tell you," she said. "I wanted to wait for the right time."

"I got her a job down here," Ron complained, "and I was even going to pay for everything. But she *changes* her mind!"

"Why did you change your mind?"

Leah went to say something, and Ron interrupted her. "She did it so I would marry her. She set the whole thing up."

Anger twisted her face. "I'm not aborting this child!" she shouted at the ceiling. "I just can't do it." She craned her head around: "And I don't want to marry *you*!"

"We've talked about adoption," Ron said. "You don't have to abort it. We just can't raise it."

At that moment, I didn't care if Ron was going to hurt me. I looked down at Leah. "You're working things out with him?"

"Yes," Ron answered for her, "we're working things out. So you can leave now."

I faced Leah again. "You want me to go?"

She closed her eyes and covered her ears. I could tell that

she was wishing that when she opened her eyes again and removed her hands from her ears, she would be back in Dewey
Beach, where none of this had ever happened.

"*Go!*" Ron barked at me, stepping closer. "You got your
shit—now go!"

I ignored him and knelt next to Leah. She smiled when I
looked at her. "It's OK," I said.

She gave me a helpless look and said, "I don't *want* an abortion."

Ron stepped forward and pulled me away from her. Then
he looked down at Leah. "*Think,*" he pleaded. "We can't af-
ford a baby right now. I love you, but I'm not ready to be some
kid's father."

This whole mess was too much for me. I was suffocating in
the room. I looked back down to Leah. "I want to say goodbye
to Fritz before I go. Where is he now?"

"Oh, her no-good uncle?" Ron said. "He's gone."

"He left?" I asked her.

She nodded. "Sometime last night."

"Did he leave a note?"

She shook her head. "He came to my work and told me to
call him when you've made your decision." She looked up at
me. "You've just made it, haven't you?"

"I'm sorry."

Ron stamped off towards the kitchen, huffing.

I grabbed Leah's hands. "Just tell Fritz that I went back to
Baltimore and got arrested after all. Tell him I couldn't make it
back."

"Why?" She was looking at me in disbelief. "Why should I
bother? Why can't I just tell him you ran off because you don't
want to be with a pregnant girl?"

I shook my head, not wanting to argue with her. "I don't
want him to think he failed. Just tell him I couldn't come back.
It'll make him feel better."

"Don't leave—I don't want *him,*" she whispered, jerking
her head at Ron.

I looked down at the carpet. "I'm sorry. I can't handle this."

Ron picked up the phone and rested it on his shoulder. "I

swear to God!" he shouted. "I've been being really nice about all this, but if you're not gone in ten seconds, I'm calling her father and telling him the whole thing." He reached over and punched six numbers on the phone. "I'm sure he wouldn't want to hear that you had that damn uncle of yours here with you— not to mention *this* guy."

Leah covered her face in her hands and sniffed. Her ears burned red.

"Your shit's packed, pal," Ron yelled to me. "Just piss off and you won't blow everything for her."

I stood up and shouted at him. "You'll be in more trouble than me, idiot. *I'm* not the asshole who got her pregnant!"

Ron glared at me. He reached over and punched four more numbers.

I looked down at Leah. Her back was rising and falling in jerky movements from crying. I wanted to tell her I was sorry again.

"It's ringing!" Ron shouted.

"Stop!" I yelled at him. "Hang up!"

I heard a soft click in the phone, and his eyes popped open. "Yes," he said into the mouthpiece, glaring at me, "is Mike Greene there?"

"OK!" I snatched my bag from the floor. "I'm gone. I'll leave you two alone. You'll never see me again. Just don't get her in trouble."

Ron pulled the phone away from his ear. I heard a tiny voice say hello on the other end of the phone, and he hung up on him.

I turned, without looking at Leah, and opened the door. I glanced back at Ron, and he waved me off like he was shooing a fly. I stepped onto the balcony and let the door shut behind me.

The air was thick and humid. I was shuddering and couldn't sort out what had just happened. It felt like I had seawater crashing inside my skull.

I got in my car and pulled onto Coastal Highway, with no idea where to go.

RAIN SIZZLED on the roof of my car. About a mile away from Joe's, I had parked behind a little vegetable stand. I lay in the back seat, with the coat Joe had lent me draped over me like a blanket. With the rain came an eerie cold; it swept across the eastern shore, making steam vapors rise up off the mud.

When I had parked my car, I went through my duffel bag to see if everything was in there. It wasn't. Everything I had worn up until today was missing from the bag. I didn't have to worry about my money being taken. I kept that on me at all times.

I promised myself I wouldn't sleep tonight. I had no way of waking before three in the morning to go to work. I watched the droplets of rain clinging to my rear window. Once in a while, I'd look at my watch and count the hours I had left until I'd have to be on the boat. With each passing hour, sleep's grip tightened around my chest.

I reached behind my head and rolled down my window to breathe the cold air. The sky was black and the rain was like cold pins dotting my face.

I wished I had a way to contact Fritz. It hurt that he hadn't said goodbye to me, and that our last words to each other were shouted across a windy beach. It seemed strange that he didn't even stick around to find out if I was going to stay with Leah or not. But I guessed that he'd done as much as he could do, and he would find out eventually that I was leaving. I was sure that he would have understood. I didn't want a family forced in my face either. Leah had made up her mind to have the child. I didn't see any chance of staying with her. I wasn't doing a good job taking care of myself. How could Fritz expect me to take care of this girl and her child?

I was also furious at Fritz. I felt as if I had been set up. He'd meant to find some pushover for Leah that would go through the pregnancy with her. She would leave this asshole Ron, there would be a new baby in the family, and Fritz would look like a hero.

At quarter of three in the morning, I got out of my car and stretched. The concrete all around me was cracked and decayed; muddy puddles vibrated from the rain. Hunger sapped my energy, so I rummaged around in the vegetable stand for some leftover food. All I could find were some plastic bags and a receipt book that was soggy from the moist air; the edges of the writing on the top page fanned out in blurred trails of blue-purple ink. The walls of the stand were corrugated tin and painted the same beige color as RHP. The wood framing was so rotten that I could sink my thumb into it. Around the back of the stand was a faucet with a turned-up lip for holding the handles of pails. The outside walls were streaked with lines of moss, dark green at the bottom and lime-colored and spear-like at the top. I rinsed my hair out under the cold water until my scalp went numb. Then I brushed my teeth. I cupped my hands under the water and took a drink from it. Now there was grit whenever I bit down and I was spitting constantly. Across the street was a brown-shingled house with a wrap-around, screened-in porch. Flowers hung in white wicker baskets above the front steps. Two lights in honey-colored globes shone inside, where there was a weight bench and a barbell loaded with gold plates. On the end of the porch closest to me, there was a gutted piano that someone might have been refinishing. A big piece of wood with intricate flowers patterns carved into it leaned against the gray screened wall. It had CHAS. M. STIEFF—BALTIMORE printed on it in gothic gold lettering, which glowed against the dark-stained wood. Shadows on the far end of the porch made it hard to see much else.

I pulled a clean T-shirt from my car. The rain was so light now that I didn't bother getting back inside to change. The shirt smelled of detergent and Fritz's cigarettes, and while I was pulling it over my head I saw something move on the porch—slow and quiet.

I hadn't noticed, but at the far end of the porch, where there was little light, a man had been watching me. He stepped forward out of the darkness, and I could see his white cotton undershirt glow from the light overhead.

I smoothed out the wrinkles on my shirt and waited for him to yell at me. I spat rust onto the ground.

The old man stepped forward into the dim yellow light, and I winced when I saw that he was only in his underwear. His legs were pale sticks, knobby and fleshy at the knees; the hairs on his thighs were white and wiry. There were shadows around his sunken eyes, his hair was like dead weeds and his mouth was half-open—he looked like a zombie. I returned his stare and waited for him to do something. He stepped forward again, his bare feet swishing on the floorboards of the porch. I wondered if he was going to tell me I was trespassing, or accuse me of stealing things from the stand.

At that moment, I thought about apologizing before he could say anything to me—calling out and saying that I was sorry and that I was leaving. But the man stepped closer. Now I could see his entire face. His skin was red and wrinkled with white stubble like sand above his dry lips.

That's when I realized that the man was asleep. He was sleepwalking, and somehow had wandered out onto his porch. His eyes were closed and his bottom lip glistened with drool.

I got in my car and started the engine, hoping I wouldn't wake the man up. My mother told me once to never wake a sleepwalker, because they might get startled and hurt themselves. Grains of rust still crunched in my mouth. I kept the headlights off and pulled out onto the road, my car filled with the graveyard smell of mud and worms and rain.

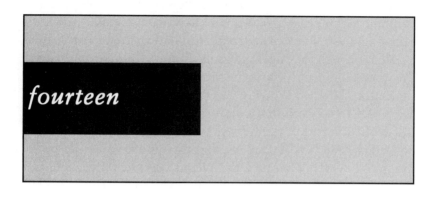

fourteen

A WEEK BEFORE I MOVED OUT OF MY MOTHER'S HOUSE, my father's aunt died. She was a ninety-year-old woman who always smelled of baby powder and was half out of her mind. She usually called Shawn "Brian," and she didn't have any idea who the hell I was half of the time. She was a proper old woman who gave piano lessons out of her house. Whenever I saw her, she wore a white silk blouse with a frilly collar that covered her neck and a ruby brooch at her throat. She was my father's mother's sister—the half of my family that didn't have to work for a living.

After her funeral, my family (the rich half) had a barbecue at the house of some cousin of mine. Most of them got drunk. They used the funeral as an excuse to get loaded—so did I. I remember sitting on a well cover away from everybody, drinking Sprite and vodka, when a woman came up with a green tin box in her hand. I had never seen her before. She appeared to be charge of distributing my great aunt's things.

"I don't think I can give this to your mother myself," the woman said, handing me the box. "I don't think I could compose myself. But I think she would like to see it."

The box was a rectangular cookie tin with a picture of an old English castle on it done in the same green ink as dollar bills, with a nutritional facts label stuck on its side.

"What is this?" I asked her.

"That's for your mother," the woman told me, lowering her eyes. Then she walked off and got in the passenger seat of a car and just sat there, waiting for the driver.

I took the tin and went around the side of the house, so she couldn't see me. I opened it and saw that it was filled with about a hundred letters my great aunt had written to my father. I leafed through the pages and noticed something strange about them: not one letter was over three sentences long. I read one that said: "DEAR LEO, THE BOY NEXT DOOR, THE ONE WHO EATS—" and that's all it said. On the last letter of the last word she had written, there was a tiny black dot, as if she paused, remembering that my dad was gone, while the paper drank the ink from her pen. Each letter was like that. Some had a couple of lines: DEAR LEO, ARE YOU CAREFUL WITH THOSE ELECTRIC SAWS YOU USE? I JUST SAW SOME-THING ON THE EVENING NEWS ABOUT A MAN IN— and others were only one word: DEAR (with an ugly black dot on one end of each R). Yet she kept every letter.

When I gave the box of letters to my mother after the bar-becue, she spread them on the kitchen table and read every one, laughing as she followed the strange path of my aunt's memory.

I didn't understand the point of those letters until I was on the boat today, still tasting the rust in my mouth from last night; a few times I spat into my palm just to look at the specks of rust floating in the bubbles of my spit. I had been culling crabs, when I wondered if I should pick up dinner for Leah tonight. Then I remembered and shook my head. I felt a pang of sad-ness, but shrugged it off and sorted faster.

I pushed myself to work as hard as I could, even though I got no sleep last night. If I had sat on the stern and rested even once, I would have fallen asleep. And when I didn't occupy my mind with work, thoughts of Leah raked across my brain.

Once we docked, Joe was surprised when I asked if I could tag along with him while he sold his crabs in town. I couldn't stand the idea of driving around in my car to find a place to sleep. He squinted at the ground, trying to think of a reason why I couldn't, but I jumped into the truck before he could say anything.

Joe and I drove fourteen bushels of crabs to a restaurant in a nearby town called Groves Burton. It was a narrow little strip of shops and cafés that sat right on the water. Joe confessed that he hated this little town. "All the farmers do," he said. "Last year, when there was that drought, the town manager made all the farmers cut back on our use of water, but she filled a dried-out pond on a golf course near by."

We drove down the bumpy main street slowly, and I looked out the window. Yuppies wearing sunglasses drank coffee outside the cafés, sitting in black-painted iron patio furniture. The shops going down the main street had tables sitting outside of them covered with discounted merchandise; the owners of the stores stood in their doorways looking at us drive by. Above the shops were small apartments. A man leaned out his window and called down to a store owner two floors below. A fat woman was planting a cactus with a red ball on the tip in a window-box above a store that sold hunting equipment. I made eye contact with her as we drove down the main street on the rough pavement. I thought the crabs were going to shatter in their bushel baskets.

"Think they'll pay to fix this road?"

"It *is* fixed," Joe said. "It used to be blacktop, but she had it ripped up. Said she wanted this place to look more like Europe, so they paved the road with bricks."

"Why's it so bumpy?"

"She wanted cobblestones, but they were too expensive. So she had the road crew put the bricks in crooked so it would *feel* like cobblestones."

We came to about the end of the block, where the road dead-ended in front of a small park with a large white gazebo and a brick oven for roasting pigs and lambs.

The restaurant was near the end of the block across from an Odd-Fellows hall. The front window had a white crab painted on the glass. A fisherman sat on a park bench outside the Odd-Fellows', drinking a can of beer out of a brown paper bag.

We drove past the restaurant then down a long alleyway that opened up behind the row of buildings to a large loading area. Two cars were up on cinder-blocks behind a black dumpster with silver locks on all its doors. All down the alley were rusty trash cans with flies buzzing around them.

The restaurant's receiving area was on the second floor, above a small cellar covering. The cinder-block walls were painted an ugly mud color. A mustard–yellow refrigerator with no handles was humming under the steps. Steam billowed out of the door from the kitchen. Two teenage boys were sharing a cigarette on the steps. I recognized them both from the day I had applied at Joe's. The boy on the left was the kid who told me about Doug and Greg being his main helpers. When I got out of the truck, they looked at me with a mixture of sadness and animosity.

Up some rickety stairs to the third floor there was a windowless barber shop. Next to the spinning, red and white cylinder in its glass tube there was a sign on the door made out of driftwood: GONE FOR THE DAY.

A fat guy came through the steam of the kitchen, looked down to count the bushels of crabs and yelled at the two boys to help. After looking uneasily at the sky, he reached just far enough beyond the green awning to get gold sunlight on his fingertips, then quickly retrieved them as if he were some vampire testing how far he could step out into the daylight before bursting into flames.

Joe told me later that this man was named Lewis and that he had four brothers that had all died of some kind of cancer. Joe said that Lewis wouldn't go outside unless he wore a hat, scarf, sunglasses, long sleeves, gloves, and his skin had to be slathered with sun block so thick it looked like a layer of margarine.

"Let those boys carry that for you," Lewis called down to us. Then he looked up at the sun, eyes filled with hatred. "We'll talk inside."

Joe told me to help the kids and come in when I was done. The boys went under the balcony of the kitchen and swung open the iron cellar doors that must have weighed sixty pounds each. They used two crowbars to open the doors, and the hinges screamed. A cool cloud of air blew in my face. In the cellar, a pen had been constructed, about three feet deep and fifteen feet around, filled with ice. One boy buried half the bushels of crabs in the ice, using a fireplace shovel that was mounted to the inside of the cellar door. I didn't help; the boys didn't let me. They ignored me and lugged the crabs around, mumbling obscenities under their breath about how it wasn't fair that I was working for Joe. I just watched the pipes overhead dripping onto the ice and the dirt floor.

When the boys were done, they opened the mustard yellow refrigerator that was under the steps. It was completely filled with bottles of beer with no label. The boys each stole a bottle and leaned their backs against the closed cellar doors, feeling the coolness through the thick metal. I walked away without saying a word.

The restaurant kitchen was busy with short-order cooks and dishwashers. The air was blurry from steam and reeked of bleach; my eyes burned. It was so hot I couldn't breathe. The floor must not have been level, because in one corner of the room, spilled water from the aluminum sink had collected two inches deep. I went through a set of double doors to the dining area, where air conditioning slapped my face. The sweat on my body turned icy, and my shirt clung to my back.

Joe and Lewis were standing behind a gray marble counter that had catsup and mustard bottles and a coffee machine on it. The dining area was nice. It was a seafood place, better than the one Leah and I had been to on our one and only date. All the tables had cloth napkins folded into seashell shapes on the plates and piano music on the speakers in the ceiling. There were maybe fifteen people eating lunch, sipping their soups and drinking wine. A waiter wearing black pants and a dark-blue dress shirt was reciting the specials to a man who looked like he wanted to be left alone.

I walked over to where Joe was signing some invoices for the crabs with a silver Cross pen. There were about twelve pages. Lewis watched Joe write his name over and over with a fistful of cash in his left hand. Lewis seemed to be as cautious about his bookkeeping as he was about his skin.

"Crabs are all off the truck," I said to Joe.

Lewis introduced himself to me, and I instantly felt sorry for him. When I shook his hand, I couldn't feel any bones under his fleshy palm. The smell of sun block beat off him like a too-strong after-shave. Lewis was pale; I could see all the blue veins in his arms. I could even see the squiggly veins in his eyelids when he looked down to see what Joe was writing. Lewis was like a frame of cottage cheese and Vienna sausages in a gray translucent wrapper.

I heard dishes clanging together and shouting behind me. Lewis's albino face showed terror. I turned and saw a woman with a man's haircut coming towards us. Joe didn't flinch.

"No good!" the woman boomed, with a thick German accent. She wore a black T-shirt, black dress slacks, and a row of pearls at the neck. Bread crumbs speckled the space between her tiny breasts. She had a cloth napkin in her bloodless fist.

Joe looked up at her and sighed.

The woman shouted something in German, then translated as best she could. "You pay money back now!" The woman looked at me and narrowed her tiny eyes. She had the face of a mole; her forehead and nose were covered with freckles. When Joe didn't respond, she threw her napkin to the ground.

Lewis started to back his way closer to the wall.

Joe stayed quiet and folded his arms. The woman's face came to his sternum. I heard more shouting. A man stomped over from the restroom—the German woman's husband, I guessed. His outfit and haircut were the same but he spoke better English.

"That deck was not worth shit!" he said.

The people at the tables were all staring at us. Lewis looked like he wanted to jump out into the sun-soaked street and die.

"You give me my money back," the German man demanded. He was the same height as me but twice as thick. His arms were heavily muscled and he had a boxer's flat nose. I thought he could have been a career military man.

Joe remained calm. He looked at the man and said, "No," then went back to signing his name over and over on Lewis's invoices and a disclaimer from the department of health (that had a logo of a thumbprint shaped like a heart).

The woman's face went ugly with rage. "Not worth shit!" She stepped forward and slapped the marble counter. The force was strong enough to make the coffee burble in the pots.

I wondered when Lewis was going to step in and tell everybody to calm down, but he was looking at the wall as if none of this was happening.

"I told you," Joe said, "that your house couldn't hold the weight of a deck, but you told me to build it anyway."

"But you are the professional," the man said.

"You told me to build it anyway, so I did. That's the end of it."

The woman spat out a sentence in German and stepped forward, her face red with anger. She jabbed Joe three times on his chest—three soft thuds. Everybody went quiet. Lewis and I tripped over each other, trying to get behind the counter. The woman didn't budge; she kept her ugly face cocked straight up to meet Joe's eyes. Because Joe's back was to me, I couldn't see if he was glaring at the woman or just coolly glancing at her. I looked at the man and wondered if he was going to do anything. The couple were so hot-headed I was sure he was going to take a cheap shot at Joe. Joe was huge, but he didn't look like a fighter. The military guy could have jabbed him in the throat and jumped on top of him before Joe even knew what was happening.

But the man didn't budge. He was staring at Joe's hand with a strange look on his face, as if he had a muscle cramp but was trying his best to not let it show. He reached forward and grabbed his wife by the waist and tried to pull her back. She looked down at his hands and tried to swat them away, shouting at him in German. The man looked at Lewis and me and smiled. His eyes shot back to something in Joe's hand. Lewis and I leaned forward and tried to see what the man was worried about.

In his right fist, Joe had bent the steel pen into a L shape, using only his thumb. A black bubble oozed from the nib. From what I could see of Joe, his arm never tensed, trying to bend it, nor did his neck and ears glow red from the effort. Calmly and easily, he bent the expensive pen as if it were a stem of warm solder.

The woman never saw him do this; she was too busy cussing in German. Her husband pulled her back, kicking and punching. Now she seemed more angry at her husband than she was at Joe. They squabbled in German all the way out of the restaurant (and never paid their bill).

Joe turned around to us and set the pen on the counter. The bubble of ink left a black smudge on the marble. "Sorry," he said, as if he had only been interrupted by a phone call.

Lewis and I looked at the pen in silence. Lewis scooted it off the counter into a trash can with a laminated menu. It hit the tin can with a hollow boom.

Joe snapped his finger at me and pointed to the kitchen. "Let's go."

Lewis didn't say goodbye. He stared at the pen at the bottom of the trash can in a frightened daze, as if it, too, might somehow give him cancer.

WHEN WE GOT BACK TO THE FARM, Doug was parking a large lawn mower in the barn. I could smell the cut grass and gasoline from the road, carried across the apple orchard by a warm breeze. Doug drove the riding mower into the barn and killed the engine. A moment later, I heard the huge hangar doors close with a boom. Doug walked over to us; he nodded to Joe and gave me a strange look.

"Get all the grass?" Joe asked, walking to the house. I didn't think he really wanted a answer—it was just Joe's way of saying hello.

Doug watched Joe step onto the porch and disappear inside the house. Then he looked back at me; in his stare there was a hint of disappointment mixed with anger.

"What's wrong with you?"

Doug looked up at the house and narrowed his eyes. "Not here," he said. "Let's go for a ride."

We got in the golf cart, and Doug drove me to a part of the farm I had never seen before. He drove parallel to the vegetable fields for almost a mile. A few times I asked Doug what was bothering him, but he said he didn't want Joe to hear. As we bumped along the rocky trail, I coughed a few times to relieve the tension.

He parked the cart near an old tree that was rotted from the inside. Moss covered the ground with such soft padding that I wanted to lie down. Fifty feet away, partially hidden behind tall dead weeds, I saw a fenced-in area. I walked over to it and Doug followed, kicking divots of moss out of the ground while making exploding sounds with his mouth. The chain-link fence was nailed to old posts that were eaten almost to nothing by fire ants. On the far end of the space, there were a dozen wooden boxes on the ground that looked like little dog houses. The boxes were made from plywood which had become warped and rotted over the years. Wet straw spilled out of the holes in the boxes onto the damp, muddied ground. In the center was a child's swimming pool turned upside down; mud was caked all over its side, kicked up from the hard rain last night. The little pool had a bunch of cartoon drawings of a crocodile wearing a tank-top, shorts, sunglasses, and a little bird on its snout dressed like a lifeguard.

"What is all this?" I asked.

"This was where Joe raised his turtles." He leaned against the chain-link fence; it gave way with a sharp crack, but he caught his balance in time. "He doesn't do that anymore."

"So what do you want to talk about?" I asked.

"A guy came here today—"

"Police?" I interrupted.

"No," Doug said, frowning, "this man said his name was Pete. He said he was supposed to be here a week ago. Said he was going to Florida, but he couldn't make it. *You* were also supposed to go to Florida. And *your* name is Pete. Does this sound strange at all?"

"Has this guy talked to Joe?"

"No, just me," Doug said. He looked down at his hands and cleared his throat. "I think either you or this other guy isn't being honest with Joe."

"Me," I said without hesitating. "He's the real Pete."

"Your name's not Pete?" He looked disappointed in me. Doug reached down and picked up a shovel handle by the fence that had been chewed to death by the turtles. He stabbed the moss with it.

"Joe just thought I was this other guy, and I went along with it to get the job."

"Well what's your name, then?"

"Tom," I said. "Listen, are you going to tell Joe about this?"

Doug shook his head. "I wanted to get your side of the story first. I knew something was wrong, so I told the guy I'd call him tonight when I knew if Joe was still hiring or not."

"What are you going to tell him?"

"I'll just say he hired somebody else." Doug stabbed the shovel handle in the ground again and pried up a chunk of moss, mumbling to himself. The dirt on the bottom of the divot was soft and bright. He sighed as if he wanted to say something. Finally he dropped the shovel handle and put his hands in his pockets. "I thought we were pals," he said quietly.

"We are."

"Well, why didn't you tell me?" Doug took a few steps away from me and kicked a toadstool off a tree. "I told you about the time I went to see Greg in jail."

"I wasn't sure if you would tell Joe or not."

"I'm not going to tell, but I think you should."

I walked over to him and shrugged. "I don't see the point," I said. "I'm leaving in about a week."

Dog snapped his head over at me. "You're *leaving*?"

"I live in Baltimore, Doug. I need to go back."

"I thought you were here for good."

"Well," I patted his shoulder, "you also thought my name was Pete."

After that, Doug and I hiked a little further back in the woods. We came to the north wall. It was made of steel-gray stones and laced with vines of poison ivy; the leaves had a sheen like vinyl. The wall was a little taller than me. I stood on a root at the base of a pin oak and saw the shark fins of green and brown pieces of glass imbedded into the top of the wall, to keep out intruders. They jutted from a thick layer of concrete that had been darkened a nice lime color from the dampness. All of the glass on the wall came from bottles of cola and beer. In some places, Joe had stuck the lip of the bottle down into the concrete and let the broken bottom stick up like some kind of deadly flower in bloom. The leaf-shaped pieces of glass spread beautiful amber and sea-green colors on the leafed and mossy ground.

A few hours later, as the sun was coming down, Doug drove us back. It was still light out. The moon loomed patiently up in the sky, as thin as a bitten-off fingernail.

JOE WAS STANDING NEXT TO HIS TRUCK with a shotgun in his hands when Doug and I parked the little cart next to the Gulf fuel pump.

Joe frowned at me. "You're still here?"

I nodded. "Doug was just showing me around."

Doug announced that he was leaving and went to the barn to get his moped.

I waved to him as he walked away, but I didn't want to look him in the eye. I was afraid that he was going to give me some kind of your-secret-is-safe-with-me wink or nod that Joe might pick up on. Instead, I just fixed my eyes on the gun in Joe's hands. He kept the barrel pointed to the ground. I could see shells protruding from his shirt pocket.

"You a hunter?" Joe asked me.

"No," I said. "My brother goes bow hunting for deer every November, though."

"I use a bow on wild turkeys."

I shrugged. "I've never even shot a gun before."

"Want to try?"

"Here?"

"I've got blackbirds in my tree." He pointed to the huge oak tree next to the house. "I come out here at least once a day to scare them off." Joe stepped forward and handed me the gun.

It was heavy and smelled of oil. I held it uneasily in my hands. All I could think of was that kid in Conrad's old house who had tried to blow his head off.

"It's not loaded," Joe said, smiling at my trembling hands.

I looked down at the shotgun. It was a Remington

Wingmaster. The steel was polished blue and had a glossy honey-colored walnut stock with a checkered fore-end.

Joe gave me a single twelve-gauge shell and showed me how to chamber it.

He tapped a button on the side of the trigger guard. "This is your safety. Press it when you're ready to shoot." Joe stepped behind me. "Keep that stock tight against your shoulder, so the recoil don't hurt too much."

I raised the barrel to the dome of leaves in the oak, and hit the safety. I could hear the blackbirds squabbling like a swarm of giant wasps

"Just pull the trigger," Joe said.

I fired the gun. The recoil punched into my shoulder and almost spun me around. Blackbirds darkened the sky. I could hear the sound of the gun reverberating off the trees in the distance, mixed in with the confused screaming of the birds.

Joe stepped around me and gently pushed the barrel towards the ground.

The birds fanned out over the cornfield and disappeared from sight. Joe and I stayed quiet, listening to their jabbering vanish into the air.

I handed the gun back and put my hands in my pockets. "Have you eaten?" I asked. The smell of gunpowder burned into my nose.

"No. Was just about to go inside and fix myself something."

"Do you mind if I stay around and cook it?" I asked. "I'm supposed to do the housework, right?"

"Don't you need to be getting home?"

I knew that was Joe's way of telling me he wanted me to go, but I didn't want to go sleep in my car. "I've got no plans," I said.

Joe rolled his eyes slightly. "Fine, then." He motioned to the house with a wave of his arm.

Inside, Joe watched the six o'clock news on the tiny television above the refrigerator while I prepared his meal. He wanted chicken breasts with honey and sweet potatoes. To drink, he had a glass of ice water that he got from the tap.

When the chicken began to sizzle on the iron skillet, the

smell filled the room. My stomach groaned from hunger.

"Make yourself something while you're at it," Joe said, staring at the fuzzy images on the television. Then added, "No sense dirtying all those dishes just for me."

The news report was about a murder on Boston Street in Baltimore. The scene of the crime was in viewing distance of RHP. The sight of the reporter standing in front of shitty buildings that I used to see everyday made acid burp into my throat. A dopey-faced witness said that the killing happened because two cousins were fighting over a car they owned together. One of the cousins was killed with a golf putter out on the sidewalk in front of the car. Joe stood up and shut off the TV.

I set Joe's plate on the table and refilled his glass. Joe cut his sweet potato open and curls of steam rose out. He smeared butter on it and picked up a piece with his fork, gently blowing on it before putting it in his mouth.

The house was silent. I could only hear the sound of Joe's chewing and the crickets outside, pulsing in the same rhythm. The food on my plate was too hot to eat, so I pushed it back and forth with my butter knife. Sitting there, I thought of my apartment in Baltimore—all the mail collecting in my box, the food expiring in my refrigerator, and that ugly phone that might have been stuck ringing the whole time I'd been down here, and now would be a melted pile of goo on my kitchen table.

"Don't let it get cold," Joe said, looking down at the table as he chewed.

"Do you ever get lonely in this big old house?" I asked—immediately wishing I hadn't.

Joe looked up at the ceiling then at the floor and sucked some chicken that was stuck between his teeth. He seemed to be giving the question some thought. "I guess not," he said after a moment. He took another bite of chicken and went back to staring at the wall, jaw muscles like knots when he bit down.

I couldn't think of anything else to say, so I shoveled the cooled-off food in my mouth so fast I'm surprised I didn't choke.

Joe set his knife and fork down on the plate and yawned. "Don't see much sense in you driving home if you just have to be back here at three," Joe said, staring at the melting balls of ice in his water. "I got some rooms upstairs if you want to stay."

"I could sleep here?"

Joe nodded. "I don't use the third floor anymore. You could stay up there."

"What's up on the third floor?"

"Just guest rooms. You can take your pick." Joe slid his plate across the table and stood up, groaning. "Wash up, then go grab yourself a room."

"Yes, sir." I still had most of my food on my plate. I planned on sitting there and finishing it.

"I'll come get you at three." With that, Joe walked out of the room. I heard him go down the hall to the parlor, floorboards moaning under his weight. I heard him open the parlor door, then the sliding door closing behind him with a loud crack.

THE HALLWAY ON THE THIRD FLOOR was a box shape with an opening in the center for the staircase and white doors every ten feet. On the east and west ends of the hallway, there were giant windows with the glass painted black. It was only eight at night, but up here, it looked like midnight. The doors were all painted white and the carpet was a bright red. I stood with my sweaty hands on the dusty rails and looked down to the intricate pattern in the Persian rug on the bottom floor.

Before I climbed the stairs with my duffel bag to pick a room, I stopped outside the parlor door. The sweet smell of cherry tobacco pipe smoke bled from the crack at the bottom of the door. I could hear old country music playing on a record player. The singer's twanging voice was accompanied with the pops and static from the record. I thought about saying goodnight to Joe, but decided just to go to bed.

I opened all the doors on the third floor and peeked inside. Some were guest rooms, and others were filled with old furniture, draped in white sheets.

In the furthest corner away from the top of the stairs, I settled in a small room with a large window over the bed. The doorknob was black, with dots of white paint spilled onto it. I cracked open the door, and breathed in the staleness of the room.

Through the window sunset was spreading a spiderweb of

shadows onto the floor. The white walls glowed soft pink from the sky. An old hospital bed with clear plastic wheels was in the center of the room on a rectangular rug with a floral pattern on it. The rails had been painted white, with a few chips showing the black iron underneath. The bed was stripped down to the bare, blue-striped mattress. Gray wool blankets and white sheets were folded neatly and placed at the foot of the bed, with a pale green pillow without a pillowcase on top. Facing the bed, on the opposite end of the room was a dresser with an oval swivel mirror on top. The glass was glazed a dirty pond-water color from smoke and age. All the drawers in the dresser had black key holes in them. The wood coughed as I yanked open a drawer, which was all full of old tennis shoes.

I looked around the room and noticed blocks of bright paint on the walls, where paintings had been taken down—but the nails still remained.

The room connected to a tiny bathroom the size of most people's closets. All the silver fixtures on the sink and tub were bubbled over with hard-water stains. The mirror on the medicine cabinet was cracked; silver-green lines distorted my reflection. I opened the cabinet door and reeled back from the medicine stench of decaying ointments and hair treatments crammed inside. All three thin shelves in the cabinet were stuffed with bottles of cologne of different colors, tin cans of salve, balms, shaving cream, shaving powder, and several orange cans of pomade with a handsome man on the lid with a baron's moustache and a tuxedo. I picked up one of the cans and opened it. A trench had been circled out in the center of the yellowish wax. Stray hairs were glued to the silver bottom of the can. I set it back with the others then noticed a shaving set exactly like the one I had given to Conrad for his birthday. It had the same fake-marble handle and ceramic mug for shaving lather. At the bottom of the mug was a dried out and cracked shaving disk. It still smelled of limes.

The hospital bed was soft but creaked as if I were lying on a million crickets who were all crying out for help. The light was a naked bulb with a long yellow string that was tied to the foot of the bed. I reached up and pulled the string, but the room stayed bright. Shadows of leaves on the tree outside shivered on the blue-gray walls.

I cracked the window open above the bed and felt cool breezes sweep across my face. The sound of the trees outside reminded me of the ocean from Leah's room. I didn't bother putting sheets on the mattress; I just lay with my arms tucked under my head and my eyes open. I watched the warm colors of sunset project onto the ceiling and thought of how much I missed Leah.

My feelings were confused about her and her pregnancy. I wanted to shrug it off, but couldn't. I might have felt differently if the child wasn't Ron's. I really wanted to be with Leah, but every time I would think of moving here, a picture of her giving birth burned in my mind. I fantasized about showing up at the condo and telling her I was moving to Dewey Beach, then, in a white flash, I'd see her all sweaty and red-faced with a bunch of doctors between her legs, telling her to breathe and push. And I'd be in the corner, wondering why the hell I was there. I added up what I thought diapers and doctor bills and toys and clothes might cost, and that made me nauseous.

I groaned to the ceiling and rolled over on my side. I wanted to call Leah, but I didn't know the number at the condo; I didn't even know Fritz's number. Leah didn't have a way of getting in touch with me. I was sure she couldn't ask her father for Joe's number.

I pounded my fist on the mattress. God! I thought, why do you even want her to call you? She's *pregnant*.

It would have been so easy and painless to walk away—go back to Baltimore and forget Leah and Fritz. If I did, I wouldn't have to worry about supporting her child; I wouldn't have to worry about her health during the delivery. I could save myself a hell of a lot of pain and worry. So how come I just couldn't do it?

fifteen

I HAD CAUGHT A LITTLE ROCKFISH ON THE BOAT. It had a green back, a silver belly, and black bars on its side. I didn't want to throw the fish back because it was the only thing I had caught that wasn't a crab or a toadfish. Joe shrugged and told me to chuck it in the cooler with his normal-sized fish. We headed in with fourteen bushels.

Doug was on the center dock when we got back, fastening zinc anodes to the crab pots; the fat silver sticks helped keep rust from ruining the chicken wire.

I carried the crabs from the boat to Joe's truck.

"Check the eel traps," Joe said, handing me a pair of long steel tongs.

Most of the eel traps were empty. Some were filled with strings of weeds. I pulled up the last one, and as the water drained out, I jumped back and landed hard on the dock when I saw what was inside. Splinters slid into my palms. There was a two-foot copperhead snake curled up in the center of the trap. Its eyes were glazed over a pearl color and its black forked tongue hung out.

"What's the matter?" Joe hollered.

"There's a snake in the trap."

Doug stretched his neck to see. "It's probably dead," he said. "Swam in and drowned."

I looked at Joe and shook my head. "I'm not touching it."

"Kick the trap and see if it moves," Joe said, irritated. "It's probably been in there for hours. It's harmless."

I nudged the wire cage with the toe of my boot. The snake's lifeless head rolled to the side and plopped to the floor of the cage. I kicked it again. The snake was motionless. "It's dead," I said.

Joe held up his hands then let them flop to his side. "Then pull it out of there and let's go." Doug was trying not to laugh.

I picked up the trap, slowly opening it by unscrewing the center. I couldn't believe how heavy the snake was. Suddenly, the copperhead writhed and twisted. The sound of its spine striking the aluminum frame of the trap made a cracking sound. I dropped the cage on the dock, and the snake stopped moving. It lay half out of the trap, looking like a brown deflated bicycle inner-tube.

Joe came over and looked at the snake. "It's *dead*," he said. "Just grab it and chuck it into the bushes."

"They can still bite you."

Joe sighed. He bent down and yanked the snake out of the cage. Its scales ripped on the pointy ends of the trap's throat. The snake wiggled mindlessly in Joe's hand. "It's just nerves," he said, then flipped it into the brush.

When we got back to the house, Doug opened the cooler to drain out the melted ice. He saw my little fish and laughed. "What's he doing in there?"

Joe was writing in his little notebook. Without looking he jabbed a thumb over at me.

"It's my first fish."

Doug reached into the cooler and held it up by its fin. The fish had been dead for some time. "It's not legal to keep them this small."

I shrugged. "I just didn't want to throw him back."

Doug closed the cooler lid and walked over to me. "I got an idea," he said. He walked past me to my car and put a finger to the top of my antenna. He opened the fish's puckered lips with his fingernails, then fitted the ball on my car's antenna in its open mouth. Joe stopped writing and watched him. Then Doug pushed the fish down on the antenna so the fin was sticking straight up in the air.

"What the hell are you doing?" I asked, looking at the impaled rockfish on my car.

"Stay there," Doug said, running to the house. "I think this will work." He came back out with a Polaroid camera. Joe just watched us without speaking. "Move back about ten feet," Doug instructed me.

I stepped back until he told me to stop. Joe folded his arms, frowning.

"Now," Doug said, squinting through the viewfinder of the camera, "raise your left arm straight out in the air." I did, then Doug told me to move a step to my right. "Hold it," he said. "Now, lower your left hand about two inches." I did, then he said, "Too far. Bring it back up just a smidgen."

My shoulder started to hurt. I looked at Joe; he was hiding a smile by holding his tiny notebook over his mouth. "Is he having me do something stupid?" I asked, and Joe held up his hands.

"Now," Doug said slowly, eye jammed shut, "make a fist and hold perfectly still."

"Hurry, Doug. My shoulder's hurting."

"Don't move," Doug said and clicked the button twice. The camera made a whining sound and two green pieces of paper ejected from its front, one after the other. Doug fanned the exposed pieces of film in the air and handed one to Joe; a smile cracked his face. He tucked the picture in his shirt pocket behind his little notebook.

I came over and Doug handed me the second picture. "Congratulations," he said.

In the photo, my eyes were red and my face was smeared with dirt. But the little rockfish looked three feet long as it appeared to dangle from my fist.

THAT NIGHT I made hamburgers for dinner. The lettuce and tomatoes came from the farm, but the bread had been bought from a store. The meat, however, was from a nearby slaughterhouse, run by a friend of Joe's; this was the same place Joe acquired his bull snouts. Joe gave the guy strawberries, apples, tomatoes, and permission to fish on his property. In return, Joe was given free meat.

Joe ate in his office, and I ate in my room, while rummaging in my duffel bag to see if I would have enough to wear for my remaining time here. I placed the wrinkled clothes on the bed and saw the paperback memoir by Bradford Waltz at the bottom of my bag; I had forgotten about it.

I crept out of my room, hoping I could slip the book back on the parlor shelf before Joe noticed it was gone. When I got to the bottom of the stairs, I heard the soft country music being played on the record player in the parlor. Sweet pipe smoke filtered into the hallway. I breathed out and knocked on the sliding door.

The record player screeched off. There was a moment of silence. "Yes?" Joe's deep voice boomed.

I didn't know what to say, so I just knocked again like an idiot.

I heard a groan and the pounding of feet on the floor as he came across the room. The sliding door opened in a rush.

"Everything all right?" Joe asked, squinting down the hall past me.

I nodded. "Yes."

He narrowed his eyes. "Then what do you want?"

"I was just wondering what you were doing."

Joe's face went a little soft. "Relaxing," he said. He stepped aside and held out an arm to one of the leather chairs. "Come in."

I stepped into the room, and he closed the door behind me.

The walls glowed warmly from the lamps. His pipe let out a thin line of smoke from where it lay on its side in an ashtray next to Joe's chair. The ashtray was black marble on a thin, three-foot gold stand with tripod legs. Orange specks of tobacco glowed in the black-charred bowl of the pipe. A brown bottle of beer with no label was on the floor next to Joe's chair.

"I saw a bottle like that in the refrigerator under Lewis's receiving area."

"I sell them to him," Joe said, sitting down in his chair.

I stayed standing. I walked over to the bookcases with my hands behind my back. "You brew your own beer?"

"I make my own jam, too," Joe said.

"I noticed in your pantry that you make a lot of things."

Joe shook his bottle to see how much was left at the bottom. The liquid made a low sloshing sound and foamed like peroxide in an infection. "You want to try one?"

"Sure," I said.

Joe raised his eyebrows, surprised. "Really?" He stood up and went to the door. "I've been working on something new. You can tell me if it's any good."

When Joe stepped out of the room, I took the thin paperback from where I had it stashed in the back of my pants and looked to where I thought I had taken the book from the shelf. I wedged it next to a thick hardback with a mint-green spine and brown lettering. Its title was *The Ghost Ships of New England*. I pulled it from the shelf. The dust jacket was torn and brittle. The cover had an ink drawing of a skipjack being pummeled by violent waves. The book was a collection of stories of sightings of ghost ships and accounts of ghosts seen on yachts and fishing boats. There was no single author to the volume— only an editor: Dr. George W. Regal.

Joe came in the room with four beers clutched in one fist. He handed me two, then saw the book in my hand. He looked a little embarrassed.

"I can't believe you have this," I said.

Joe sat down in his chair with an awkward smile twisted on his face. "It was a gift."

"Have you read it?"

"Bits and pieces."

I sat down in the other chair. The leather was cold on my back. I flipped through the pages, and the dustiness of the book fanned across my face. "Are there any good stories in here?"

"You like ghost stories?" Joe seemed genuinely interested.

"A lot," I said. I sat the book down on my knees and picked up my beer. Joe raised his eyebrows as I put it to my lips.

"Tell me what you think," he said.

I took a swallow, expecting the bitterness of home-brewed

beer to stab my jaw muscles, but it was smooth with a slight aftertaste of cherries or blackberries. I rubbed my tongue against the roof of my mouth to taste more of it.

"Well?" Joe said.

"This is good," I said, surprised. I almost added that he should think about selling it, but then I realized that he already was.

"You like it?" Joe said, nodding. "I keep peeled cherry pits in the brew."

I took another drink and sat back in the chair. My stomach was tingling warm. After I finished the beer, I felt very relaxed. I melted into the leather backrest. The glass-eyed animals on the walls stared at me in the warm glow of the room. The smell of pipe smoke seeped into my bones.

"I got a ghost story," Joe said. "This is something that happened to me back in the mid-eighties."

"A *real* ghost story?" I asked.

"Swear to God," Joe said.

"Tell me."

Joe repositioned his weight in his chair. He leaned forward, resting his elbows on his knees. "I was alone on a camping trip up in the woods near Kingsville sometime in November. One night something woke me up around two in the morning—some kind of a noise. It was really soft, and sounded far away; it was so distant that I could only hear if I held my breath. At first, I thought it was the trees rubbing against each other in the wind. But this sound was too—I don't know—uniform.

"So I get out of my tent, and I shine my flashlight through the trees. I thought it also could have been a screech owl, so I waved the light upward, thinking I could scare it off. I even shouted at this thing. But the sound just kept on. I'd scream my head off until my throat was going to rip, but when I ran out of breath and my ears stopped ringing, the sound was still there.

"I wasn't scared at this point; I was more curious than anything. I sat down in my folding chair and listened real careful. If I moved and rustled the leaves under the chair even in the slightest, I couldn't hear it. I just stayed perfectly still and listened to this noise in the pitch black. After a while, I started nodding my head to the sound without knowing it. The sound started to make sense; I could even hum it: do, re, mi, fa, so, la, ti, do." Joe's gravelly voice sang the scales, while he conducted himself with a finger in the air. "The scales played over and over. Now I listened even closer. I wanted to figure out if it was a person singing it, or if it was a person playing an instrument. I thought it could have been someone playing the violin. But whoever was playing it wasn't very good. I can't really describe it. The notes didn't change smoothly; it was real awkward and jerky. And, even though they played all night, they never got better. There was no difference between the scales. This went on for hours, and the pitch never changed. It was like a stuck record."

"Weren't you scared hearing this music in the middle of the woods?" I asked.

"Well," Joe said, "you know how you can hear trains blowing their horns on a clear night from miles away? Well, I thought this was the same thing. I mean, I was real far out in the woods, but I figured that maybe the sound was coming from somebody's house a few miles away. Maybe they left a window open or something, and the sound was being carried by the wind." Joe took a long swig of beer.

I had finished my second drink during his story.

"Now, I didn't get scared," he said, "until I got home and read my paper." Joe leaned back in the chair and crossed his legs. "There was an article about a little boy who was found dead in the woods in Harford county. Kingsville—where I was camping—is just south of the Harford county line. The kid was found in a trash bag near an abandoned crematorium that was once used to incinerate roadkill. The article said that the boy had been missing for months and that they had a suspect in custody—found some of the guy's dead skin under the boy's fingernails. A little further along in the article, they described the boy, and *that* was the part that scared me. It said that he had a twin brother; he had a painting of a dinosaur in display in some bank nearby; he was the catcher for his baseball team. But what really struck me was something they quoted from the little boy's mom. She said that right before he went missing, he had broken his arm. The mom said that he was real upset over it because that meant he couldn't be in his school's fall assembly. The mom said he had been practicing for weeks. The little boy was in the school's orchestra." Joe leaned over towards me. "His instrument was the violin." Joe rested back in his chair and stared, blank-faced at the snarling bear's head above his door. "That's the noise I heard in those woods. It was the little boy practicing his scales on the violin."

The room fell quiet. I wanted another beer.

"Man," Joe said, rubbing his arms, "when I read that article, it felt like someone was tickling my neck with a feather. I didn't want to be alone for the rest of the day. I went out to the barn and watched Charlie—this kid who was working for me at the time—replace the ring gear on the flywheel on my tractor." Joe tipped the brown bottle back, and I watched fat bubbles rise as he drank.

Joe and I stayed up for a few more hours telling ghost stories. I told him about the stories that my dad had told me (as many as I could remember), and Joe told me some other stories of his own. He said he once saw an old man hunched over with his eyes closed on a dinghy with no paddles in the middle of the Chesapeake. When Joe went into the cockpit to radio for help, he looked back out the side window to describe the man . . . but he was gone.

I laughed at the story and slouched in my chair. There was a comfortable quiet between us. Joe reached over and put the needle to his scratchy record. Then he picked up his pipe and stuck it in his mouth, puffing on it like exhaust out of a big truck. The song on the record was about a circus clown who went to jail, but he was the only person who had the keys to the elephant cage. I had no idea who was singing it. His twanging voice quivered over the words: "I'll be fired Monday morning, 'cause the circus will be boring. Where are the el-e-phants?"

At that moment, I felt very comfortable inside myself. It was as if my life had split in two different directions when my dad died—like two pieces of me split and wandered their separate ways. Now, I could almost feel the wayward ghosts settling back down inside my body as I rested on the warm leather of Joe's chair. The numbness of sleep curled around my bones.

The singer's voice on the record sounded as if it were playing down the end of a long hallway—echoing and sad. I felt as if I was finally back on the right road again. What lay over the horizon, I had no idea.

THAT MORNING Joe let me sleep until six, because we weren't going out on the boat. Instead, he wanted me to sharpen all his axes, knives, and fishhooks that were in the barn. He gave me a little diamond-stone in a brown leather pouch. For the chain saw teeth, I used a whetstone that was shaped like a pencil to get into the concave blades.

A small beige Datsun truck came down the driveway and skidded to a stop on the pebbles. Dust blew away from its wheels like smoke and trailed into the cornfield. I had been sharpening a sickle outside, perched on a tractor wheel (I'd started inside, but the light was so bad I'd cut myself). I stopped sharpening the blade and stayed quiet among the weeds and rusted junk.

The driver's door groaned open, and a guy who appeared to be my age got out of the rust-speckled truck. The guy was wearing faded blue jeans and a pink T-shirt with a marlin smashing through the crest of a wave on the back. The leather over the steel toes in his boots had been worn away; the steel cups were as bright as the top of the T-rails on a railroad track. He wore a baseball cap with dark sweat stains around the bill. Brown curly hair stuck out the back. His arms and face were deeply tanned.

I sat still, so he wouldn't see me. He hopped up on the porch and went inside without knocking. Then I knew who he was and why he came. Joe was in his office, doing paperwork. Doug was at a woman's house fixing her gas stove.

The guy was in the house for about an hour. Then I watched him and Joe come out and shake hands on the driveway. I watched them from the side door of the barn. The guy walked away with his hands in his pockets—he didn't take his truck. Joe came into the barn and walked up to me.

"So that was Greg?" I said.

Joe nodded and rocked on the balls of his feet.

"And he wants his job back?"

Joe pursed his lips. "It's more complicated than that." He looked up at the ceiling of the barn and made an uncomfortable face. He motioned towards the open sliding doors. The sunshine looked like a huge block of white. "Let's talk."

We went over to some empty milk crates with carpet samples tied to them for cushions and sat down. A single jet trail slashed the afternoon sky, looking like a long line of chalk going down a blackboard. The wind kicked up dust off the fields.

"Apparently, Greg's case was dismissed," Joe said. "That girlfriend of his never showed up in court."

I stayed quiet, nodding to the ground. I looked at all the old nails and screws and spark plugs ground into the dirt by truck and tractor tires.

"Now I have a decision to make."

I held my breath.

Joe arched his back and stared at the bright sky. "Greg is a better fisherman than you, he can fix things, he's smart on his feet, and he's one of the best carpenters I have ever met. *But,*" Joe said, snapping his head back to me, "I wouldn't piss on him if he was on fire."

I looked up and met his stare.

"No matter what he's got Doug believing, I know he raped that girl. She just didn't show up in court because she was probably scared that he'd kill her when he got out of jail. I don't want a rapist around here." Joe cleared his throat, momentarily losing track of what he wanted to say. "I get the impression that you're a wanderer. But I'd like to keep you here full-time."

"I don't live in the area, though."

Joe held up a finger to tell me he wasn't finished talking. "*If* you stay, and you do all the cooking and cleaning—and, of course, the work on the boat—the third floor of the house will be yours. We can convert it into an apartment."

"So I'll be an indentured servant?"

"No," Joe said. "Indentures aren't paid. You will get a weekly paycheck."

I scratched the back of my neck. "So far, I'm mediocre on the boat, so-so at cooking, and terrible at building," I counted the things off on my fingers, "but you want to hire me full-time and even give me a place to live? I don't get it. Why are you doing this? You said yourself I'm not valuable."

Joe made a face like that was the one question he didn't want to have to answer. "Listen—it's not for you and it's not for me. I'm doing this for Doug."

"Doug?"

Joe nodded. "He's a sixteen-year-old dropout who's been working for me since he was twelve. I've watched this kid grow up. He started here as an apple and tomato picker; now he's a better mechanic than me. This is all he knows how to do. Ask him to read Shakespeare, and he's shitting his pants; ask him to replace your transmission, and he'll do it blindfolded. The boy has more potential than I will ever know." Joe paused and stared at the dead weeds at the edge of the cornfield. "I want to see the boy succeed."

I looked down at my feet, not sure if I should say something.

"The last thing in the world that kid needs is someone like Greg to look up to. Doug listens to every damn word that comes out of that shit's mouth." Joe looked over at me. "He tells me he likes you, so I think you'll be a good influence on him. And *that* makes you valuable."

"But what about being valuable at trotlining or hanging drywall?"

"If you stay, I'll teach you—just as I did with Doug, Greg, and every other boy who has ever worked for me. I'll *make* you a valuable worker." Joe reached forward and clasped his paw on my shoulder. He squeezed hard. "Now what do you say?"

I breathed out. "I'll have to make a phone call. There's still something I'm dealing with that needs to be sorted out."

I walked to Groves Burton and used a pay phone next to an ice-cream shop. Yellow jackets swarmed around the spilled milk on the sticky sidewalk. It was hard for me to hold the phone because my hands were sore and stained yellow from iodine. Before I had left, Joe noticed the nicks on my hands from sharpening the tools. He dragged me inside by my arm and poured iodine into the cuts. The sting of the liquid needled straight to the bone. I tried to jerk my hand away, but every time I struggled, Joe just tightened his grip. He could have kept squeezing until my arm broke, so I quit and let him clean out the cuts. I left the house fanning my hands in the air as if I were trying to take flight.

I set the receiver against my ear and dialed the number with my knuckle; it burned to open my fingers all the way.

On the third ring, my mom answered the phone.

"Hi, mom—it's Tom."

There was a pause on the line, as if she were expecting me to call only if there was bad news. "Hello, Tommy," she said uncertainly. There was a game show on television in the background. I could hear shouting and bells and sirens. Then I told my mom all about Leah.

She breathed out heavily into the mouthpiece. It was like wind going right into my ear. "Oh, Tommy," she said, "you didn't get this girl pregnant, did you?"

"No," I said. "Somebody else did. I just wanted to ask you about it."

"Ask me what, Tommy?" she said in a miserable voice. "Oh, God."

"I just want advice."

My mom laughed. "Then I'd tell you to get as far away from this girl as you possibly can."

I sighed. "I don't think I can do that."

"*Please*," she begged, "don't make this your problem. You have no idea what you're getting yourself into."

"I'm just asking," I said. "I want to be with this girl, but I'm sure if it works out, the baby thing will be an issue."

"'The baby thing'," she repeated. "You're calling a pregnancy 'the baby thing.' That alone tells me you're not mature enough to handle this. You can't even *talk* about it like an adult." My mom sounded exhausted discussing this, as if every sentence she spoke was sapping years of her life.

"OK," I said. "The *pregnancy*. If I stay with this girl, what do I do about that?"

My mom didn't answer. I could hear her breathing.

"Mom."

"What?"

"Can you talk to me, please?"

She sniffed. "Has she talked about adoption?"

"No." I didn't mention abortion; if I had, my mother would have died right there on the phone with me. "She says she wants to keep the baby."

"And you want to keep her as a girlfriend, is that it?"

I paused. I hated talking about stuff like this. "I think so, mom. I mean, I haven't seen her for two days . . . and, I don't know."

"How do you feel like when she's not around?"

"Like shit."

My mom made a noise at the cuss word. "Where would you and this girl even *live*? You can't expect her to put up with that little room of yours in the city."

"I've found a job down here as a fisherman. My boss has agreed to give me a floor of his house."

"I didn't know you fished."

"I just started."

"Isn't that dangerous work?"

"Not at all. I really like it. I want to move down here to be closer to Leah."

My mom said Leah's name quietly a few times, testing it on her lips. Then she remembered that she was pissed. "You just don't know what you're getting yourself into," she snapped. "You have to baby-proof your whole *life*—put plugs in electric sockets, lock doors, put up cages. Oh, God. For the first three years of a baby's life, everything they do is geared around trying to hurt themselves. You have to watch them every second. You blink and they're off kissing broken glass or licking dirt off the floor." I could tell she was pinching the space between her eyes as she talked, suppressing a headache. "And the *money*," she cried. "Children cost a fortune. Did you know that Shawn was born with infected lungs? We had him for two days and we spent over two thousand dollars on doctors and medicine. Two days. Two thousand dollars. Poof! And it only got more expensive from there."

I made an impatient noise.

"Well, I'm *sorry*, Tommy," she said. "If you expected to call me and get my blessing, then you're dead wrong. You are not married to this girl, and this is not even your child. I find so much wrong with what you're doing I don't even know where to begin. I will not sit back and watch my son make the stupidest mistake of his life."

"I know it's stupid," I said. "But that's just how it is. If I want Leah, I guess the baby just comes along with the package. I'm not talking about being this kid's *father*—I'm just talking about being there for my girlfriend. I just wanted to call you and hear a little goddamn support. I know I'm doing something stupid. But that's the way it is, and now I just have to deal with it. Lucky me!" I shouted. People walking on the street stopped and looked at me. A shirtless man in a wheelchair, wearing a fluorescent green painter's hat with a cigarette company's logo on it, rolled past and laughed at me.

My mom was quiet again for a long time. The static sounded like rustling leaves in my ears. "Honey," she sighed. "I know that we aren't close. I know we don't talk. But if this girl and her baby drive us further apart, I don't think I could take it."

I stayed quiet, feeling the shame of being a terrible son.

"If you do this, Tommy, promise me you won't get yourself committed too deeply. Help this girl out and love her, just don't make this something you can't get out of." My mom sounded so sad to say this. "I will try to help out. But only *after* I have met this girl and approve of her."

I wasn't sure what to say. "I don't know if it will even work out. If it doesn't, then I'll get out of it. But if it does, I'll do whatever I can, I guess."

There was quiet on the phone. "Just be careful, Tom," she said, sounding defeated. "Oh, God, please be careful."

Joe was sitting in his office when I got back, rummaging through the shoe box of bullets I had put on the refrigerator my first day here. Doug still hadn't come back from the woman's house.

I knocked on the door jamb. I startled Joe; he dropped a brass bullet on his desk. It rolled across his red leather blotter, across some invoices, and rattled on the hardwood floor to my feet. I reached down and picked it up. Its tip had been painted black, and the primer was red, with LC 52 printed in a circular pattern around it. I tested the point of the bullet against my thumb.

Joe lowered his reading glasses to the tip of his nose but didn't say anything. The clock on his wall was ticking loudly.

I nodded and smiled. "I'm staying."

Joe leaned back in his chair, wood creaking. "Good to know."

I went to leave the room and something on the bookcase caught my eye. Leaning against the picture of Joe and Fritz was the Polaroid of me and the rockfish on my car antenna. Fritz and I had the same expression on our faces.

THE BOAT WAS SOAKED BY MID-MORNING, sprayed by strong winds that cut off the waves. I steered the tiller at the rear of the boat, watching a school of fish shimmering near the surface.

Joe was tying the chain of the trotline to the propane tank anchor. Dirty water pooled at his feet, then drained out of the scuppers as the boat tipped to the side. Joe wore a hunter green raincoat to keep his notebook dry. His jeans were dark and wet.

The sky was a dirty blue-gray blanket of clouds.

Joe had been teaching me new things on the boat today. He showed me the inboard Volvo motor, and he had me do most of the steering as he scooped up the crabs. Then he had me steer and scoop the crabs in the dip net all by myself. He said he wanted me to get as much practice as possible, because one day I might have to go out on my own.

Joe came forward and took control of the stick. "OK," he said, "get the anchor ready."

I waddled over to the propane tank. The boat was rocking on the waves.

"Last run," Joe said. "I got some things back at the house I want to show you." He blinked the water out of his eyes.

I nodded and picked up the anchor. I hoisted it on my shoulder and waited for Joe's command.

After dinner, Joe was going to come upstairs and see how we could make the upstairs more like an apartment. We were eventually going to knock out a couple of walls and make the smaller rooms into a nice living room with a small partition for a kitchen. I was going to use the same room I had been staying in as a bedroom. This weekend I was going back to Baltimore to get my stuff and visit my mother. Joe also told me I could use any of the furniture in storage while I lived with him. Tomorrow, Doug and I were going to go through the stuff after work and pick out things. But before I did anything, I was going to drive to Ocean City and ask Leah to stay with me for the summer. I didn't care if Ron was there. I was ready, no matter what he might do to me. I had called Lewis last night and he'd agreed to give her a job for the summer. When I hung up the phone, I thought of how funny it was that this had all started because Leah was supposed to find *me* work—and now I was setting her up with a job.

Joe called out to me, and I readied the anchor.

I looked down and watched my reflection in the shimmering green water as the boat raced along. Water sprayed me again, carried on the back of a moaning wind. I smiled as I looked down at my blurry face reflected on the surface of the water. I was finally where I wanted to be.

Joe told me to throw it in.

Then I fucked everything up.

THE TRUCK JOUNCED OVER A CHUCK-HOLE, and I hissed through my clenched teeth. The towel wrapped around my left hand was dripping blood. It pooled on the floor-mat of Joe's truck and mixed with the dirt and bits of leaves in the crevice of the seat. My pants and shirt were splattered with blood, which was drying to the color of chocolate.

Joe reached over and felt my forehead. "You're cold," he said.

I felt bile bubble in the back of my throat. I spat something orange and yellow in my lap. Joe didn't notice. The nerves in my hand popped like static on an old radio. I trembled because of the loss of blood.

"Hospital's only two more miles," Joe said.

We walked into the emergency room, and Joe led me to a seat on a long row of chairs built together with purple vinyl cushions. I sat down and heard magazines rumple under me and something warm burned on my back. There were about ten other people in the room, faces drained from worry. Joe walked up to a desk and talked to a nurse with tight curly hair, wearing eye glasses with a silver beaded chain hooked on the stems. She handed him a clipboard with a pen attached to it with a piece of yellow string.

"They need you to fill this out," Joe said, frowning at me curiously. He looked at all the seats around me. "What are you doing?" he asked.

I looked around. I wasn't sitting in a chair; I was on an end table next to a chair. I crumpled the lampshade of the cream-colored lamp behind me and smothered a stack of news magazines.

Joe moved me to a seat and sat down next to me with the clipboard in his lap. He took his reading glasses out of his pocket. "What's your full name."

"Thomas Leonard Banner," I said without thinking.

Joe started to write then paused.

"I lied," I slurred. The bleeding left me weak and jittery; I was too exhausted to continue lying. "My name is Tom."

"Wait," he said, squinting up in the air with his mouth half open, "*you're* the guy Fritz Greene called me about?"

"Yes."

"Why the hell did you tell me your name was Pete?" Joe shook his head and coughed a little laugh. "I wondered why you never showed up."

I sighed at my stupidity. "When I first met you, the first thing you asked me was if I was Pete. Before I could answer, you said that you thought Pete was supposed to be in Florida, so I just. . . I figured I'd be gone by the time you figured it out, and I thought you had already made up your mind to hire this Pete guy."

"I didn't hire you because your name was Pete," Joe said, annoyed.

I rolled my head over to him. "Why did you hire me?"

"Because of your *age*," Joe said. "You were probably the only person there who could legally drive a car. I didn't want to get a bunch of kids, and I'd finally got rid of Greg. I wanted to start over. I was hoping that you could help me get my place looking the way it used to. I needed somebody older, somebody I could depend on."

"Are you mad?" I asked.

Joe frowned. "I'm confused. Does Doug know?"

"Yes. The real Pete showed up while we were selling crabs to Lewis."

Joe held up his hands like he didn't even want to talk about it anymore. "Fritz told me you were strange," he said. Then he helped me fill out my form, reading off a list of things I might be allergic to or diseases I may have had or were common in my family. The only one I said yes to was cancer.

After the form was filled out, we waited. Joe sat next to me and stared at the wall.

In my head, I watched what I had done wrong a million times. It played like a movie behind my eyes. I was holding the anchor on my shoulder. When Joe told me to throw it, I tried to push it forward, but my left hand slipped on the water beaded on it. The chain on the anchor looped around my left wrist and ripped forward as the anchor hit the water. My wrist hit the side of the boat, and I felt a crack shoot up my arm. The nylon trotline sliced the back of my hand open as it recoiled into the water. This all happened in a second. I pulled my hand back and held it to my stomach, wrapping it in the tail of my shirt so I couldn't see it. I knelt down in the water. The shock dulled the pain. I tried to get my brain to go blank. I could only hear the waves lapping on the side of the boat. Every time I tensed a muscle, I could feel the sharp broken edges of bone in my wrist scrape against each other.

Joe stopped steering and was staring at me. "What did you do," he asked, wide-eyed. He pushed the throttle forward and killed the engine.

I didn't answer. I peeked down at my hand. Before the blood welled up out of the ragged flesh between my first knuckle and down my wrist, I could see the bone; it made me nauseous to see how white it was. I clamped my hand down on the cut, and a pain shot through my wrist like a spike of ice. I gritted my teeth and growled, body trembling as if I was being shaken by something invisible. It felt like I had a congested river of needles at the bend of my wrist, trying to rip their way out of my skin. The blood pooled out from between my fingers, cold and slick like oil. I was shaking so bad my teeth chattered.

Joe saw the bottlecaps of blood on my clothes and knelt next to me. "Let me see," he said. When I didn't move, he shouted, "I have to see it!"

I unhinged my hand from the cut. Joe's face turned pale.

He put two of his fingers in the bloodied palm of the injured hand. "Squeeze my fingers," he said.

When I tried to bend my fingers, pain like a white flash of lighting bolted up my arm, through my shoulder, and fizzed on the back of my neck. My hand was bent in an impossible angle. It looked like something dead that needed to be severed from my body. I could see the twisted, cracked bone spiking almost out of the skin.

"Your wrist is bad," Joe told me, as if I couldn't see it.

I belched. "I'm going to throw up."

Joe stood up out of the dirty water and sloshed over to the cockpit. A wave tipped the boat and spilled me to my side. The gray water felt good on my face and neck. I wanted to open my mouth and drink it. Joe came back with a pea-green metal toolbox. He sat it down in the water and opened the lid. Inside the box was a bright orange flare gun and three red twelve-gauge aerial flares kept in a wax tube. The was also a bright orange warning flag folded into a plastic pouch that had BOATING DISTRESS FLAG printed on the outside of it.

"Hold out your hand," Joe said.

He dropped three aspirin in my red-stained hand. I tried to throw them back in my mouth, but they had already started to dissolve in the blood on my hand. So I licked them off my palm and chewed them like candy. They tasted bitter and made my nausea worse.

Joe sat down next to me in the inch-deep water and flipped

through a green book with a plastic cover. On the cover was a white circle with a red cross in it. Under that, in thick black letters was THE AMERICAN NATIONAL RED CROSS. I glanced at the pages as Joe flipped through them, tonguing the bitter chips of aspirin from between my teeth. Joe flipped past colored pages of deadly snakes (a copperhead was pictured, but they called it Agkistrodon mokeson), poisonous plants, and poisonous berries. As Joe looked for the section on broken bones, I looked at the drawings on the pages as he flipped through them; there was one of a woman sticking her fingers down a baby's throat to pull out an obstruction, another of someone compressing the femoral artery by squeezing their butt, and other pictures of people making slings out of belts and blankets and tablecloths.

Thunder rumbled above us. Joe took out a brown bottle of peroxide and told me to show him the cut. He doused it with the smelly liquid, but it didn't sting or foam much—the cut was too new. Then Joe bandaged it, looking at the picture in the First Aid book as if he were a chef consulting a recipe card.

After an hour of waiting in the emergency room, I told Joe he should just go home. I felt guilty enough that a trotline was now at the bottom of the Chesapeake being looted by crabs. I didn't want to waste Joe's entire day by making him sit in a room next to me and stare at the wall.

When Joe left, I slouched back and watched the people in the waiting room. There was a couple in the corner wearing matching tan overcoats, with a look on their faces beyond worry or shock. The man's face was a yellow-white color. The woman's make-up had run down her cheeks and dried in gray trails. There was a man directly across me on the other side of the room. He had a cotton ball taped over his eye, and he calmly watched a soap opera on a TV that was mounted to the wall. He had dots of blood on his shirt.

Something caught my eye. I looked to my left, and a little girl was staring at me. She looked to be about three years old, with fine straw-colored hair. She held a white washcloth to her mouth; it was wrapped around a sandwich bag filled with ice. When I looked at her, she smiled at me with only her eyes. I lifted my good hand and waved to her; the blood on my hand had turned yellow on my fingernails and a raspberry color in the mosaic cracks in my skin. The little girl's mom was talking to another woman about how her husband was right now stalking her neighborhood with a rifle looking for the Doberman that almost bit her daughter's lip off.

"So when I'm done here," the mother said tiredly, "I guess I'll be picking up my husband from jail." She reached over and petted her daughter's hair. The little girl rested her head against the wall, and we had ourselves staring contests, to pass the time.

A nurse came out of two metal doors about a half hour later and called my name. She took me to a small room and asked me to sit on a bench that was covered with tissue paper. Then I waited in there for another hour.

A short Indian man came in wearing a white lab coat and a tie with ducks all over it. He wore thick glasses that made his eyes look huge. He looked at my chart for a long time before he spoke. He kept seven pens in his lab coat pocket and a checkbook with gold triangles capped on its edges.

"Let's see what we've got here." he said, snapping on a rubber glove. He unraveled the bandage. The blood had glued the fabric to my skin, but the cut had clotted. "How did you do this to yourself?" His accent was so thick I had a hard time understanding him.

"Fishing," I said.

He shook his head and sighed. I could smell whiskey on his breath.

I looked away from the cut and the mangled knots of protruding bone.

"I can set this bone—no problem," he said. "We'll take some X-rays and get you into a cast. But first we'll have to get this nasty laceration cleaned out. Did you already try to clean it?"

"My boss dumped some peroxide on it."

The doctor nodded. He had such dark stubble on his face that I thought that it must be painful for him to shave. "I know your wrist looks bad, you're lucky it broke as clean as it did. You have a pretty nasty crack in your radius with some deep bruises, but it should heal with no problems. This cut, on the other hand, concerns me. I really want to keep it from getting infected. We're looking at about ten to a dozen staples." He petted my arm and smiled at me; his rubber gloves were cold on my skin. "Expect a pretty prominent scar."

A nurse came into the room with a stainless steel tray covered with a paper towel. She set it on a little table behind the doctor that had tongue depressors and Q-tips on it in glass jars. The doctor took the paper towel off the tray and looked at the tools.

"So," he said, "do you fish for a living?"

"Yes," I said.

"Been doing it long?" he asked distantly, lost in the glittery shine of tools straight out of the autoclave.

"Not long," I said, "only a week."

He picked up needle and stuck it into a rubber cap of an upside down little bottle. "Well," he said, drawing back on the plunger, filling the syringe with clear liquid, "maybe you should consider another line of work."

I put my duffel bag in the back seat of my car. My head was fuzzy from painkillers. I still wasn't used to the cast on my arm; it felt too tight.

Joe came out onto the porch with his shotgun. "You can do other things here while that wrist heals up, you know."

I shook my head. "I just think its time for me to head back."

"You won't change your mind?" Joe cradled the gun in his huge arms. He looked down at the beige cast that covered my forearm.

I shook my head again. "Sorry."

I had had time to think at the hospital. The Indian doctor gave me a shot of something to numb my hand, while he cleaned the cut. Then he gave me another shot in my upper arm that felt like a bee sting. I lay back on the tissue-covered bench with my eyes closed while the doctor stapled the gash on the back of my hand closed. The stapler was made of a cheap light-blue plastic that made a loud snap every time it pinched the skin together. All I felt was a slight tugging.

I lay there and thought: if I had been wearing a watch, I

might have been pulled overboard and dragged to the bottom of the Chesapeake. Hell, I had thought, even if I had been fine today, how long would it be before I cut a thumb off with a table-saw or ax or chain saw? How long before I fell off a ladder and broke both my legs? I had only worked for Joe for a week—and I had already broken my wrist and got twelve staples in my hand. There were reasons Joe's hands were scarred and rough. I wondered if I was strong enough to wear those scars myself. Jesus, I had thought, how long would it be until I found my stupid self at the bottom of that filthy green pond, pinned under machinery like Joe's wife, watching the shimmering shape of the sun blacken as green water filled my lungs.

Before I had left the hospital, the doctor told me I'd have to see another doctor in Baltimore in a week, to cut the cast off and thoroughly clean the cut. Then I would wear a brace that looked like a bowling glove for at least three months. He said I had to clean the cut by putting A+D ointment on a Q-tip and stick it down the cast.

Joe stepped forward and patted my shoulder. "If you change your mind," he said, "call me. I'll have a spot for you."

I wanted to tell him not to bother, but I just thanked him.

There was an awkward silence between us. Joe looked down at his gun, then at the blackbird-infested oak tree. I opened my car door and got in.

"You'll tell Doug?" I asked.

Joe nodded. "I'll tell him."

"I'm sorry," I said again.

With that, Joe just offered a quick smile and walked away. That was all there was to our goodbye; we didn't shake hands or wish each other well.

I started the car and headed out the driveway, wet pebbles crunching under my wheels. The furrows in the fields glistened from the rain, and the beaded leaves in the apple trees bowed their heads under the weight.

When I reached the end of the drive, I stopped my car and looked at the tiny shape of the house in my rear view mirror. Fog vapors bled off the slick black rooftop. The windows were as dark as mirrors. All the colors of the trees and grass were darkened from the rain. I let it all burn into my eyes for the last time.

As I turned onto the road, the shotgun echoed off the trees. Blackbirds peppered the sky.

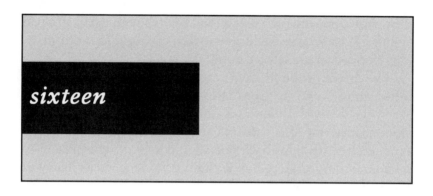

sixteen

I LAY IN BED, staring at the ceiling until my eyes were so dry that it hurt to blink. My apartment was warm and musty from being closed up. Sunlight glowed through my caged windows and cast grayish bars on the floor. Cars outside sounded their horns in jolting shouts. Stabbing pains in the bend of my wrist kept me awake half the night, but I never bothered taking a pill. This morning, the gash burned and I could feel the pressure of the staples pinching the raw skin.

I had made up my mind: now that it was clear I wasn't cut out for the work my father had done, I was going to go back to RHP to beg for a job. I didn't care where they put me. I would settle for being a shipper or a driver. It didn't matter. If Steve still wanted to have me arrested, so be it. I was going to RHP no matter what, and the only way I was leaving was with a job or in handcuffs.

The sound of crunching metal and smashing glass thundered in the street. I thought the building was collapsing. A man screamed. Car horns howled.

I crawled out of bed and went to the window. Sunlight bounced off the wet street. Cars were backed up for as far as I could see. A black Lincoln had rear-ended the car in front of it. The driver sat in the car, holding his nose. The other car's trunk had popped open, and red shards of the brake lights winked in the sun. The driver of the hit car was in the middle of the street, screaming at the man in the Lincoln. I realized the screaming man was my gun-selling upstairs neighbor. I figured he had been hit trying to do one of his U-turns to park his car. He wore a clear plastic poncho over his clothes, even though it had stopped raining. The two wrecked cars blocked the right lane of traffic. Cars flooded to the left lane, and got stuck.

The driver of the Lincoln staggered out of his car. He had coffee stains down the front of his white dress shirt. I couldn't hear what he was saying, but he talked a lot with his hands. Blood trailed out of his nostrils and stained his lips. He took a handkerchief from his back pocket and held it to his nose. My neighbor stomped up to him with his fists clenched as if he was going to throw a punch.

Cars in the left lane started moving, flattening the busted pieces of brake lights. A cop car sounded its siren in two high-pitched yelps. The spinning red and blue lights could barely be seen because of the afternoon brightness. My neighbor's face dropped when he saw them. He ran back to his car and slammed the trunk closed, but the latch had been broken; it popped back open again. He pushed it down again and again, looking back at the cop car.

I squinted and saw a Quaker-patterned quilt, covering a large rectangular box in the trunk. My neighbor growled as he slammed the lid shut. But it just yawned open each time.

I knew why he didn't want the cops to see what was under the quilt: it was a wooden box filled with rifles. Many a time I had seen him running to the building, carrying those boxes.

My neighbor eventually sat on his trunk to keep the lid shut. He scratched the back of his neck and shook his head, chanting something to himself through clenched teeth. He looked over and saw me watching him. His face had gone pale and blood-less. A chubby black cop came up to him and motioned for him to get down. My neighbor kept his eyes on me the whole time. The officer shouted something with his hands on his hips. Then my neighbor saluted me and hopped off his trunk.

HUMIDITY fogged RHP's windows.

Steve wore sunglasses behind his desk. He was sorting through invoices and talking to himself. The moisture from his hair dripped down onto his shoulders, darkening the light-blue fabric. I knocked on his cubicle entrance. He looked up at me, and his face dropped.

I sat down in front of him. The sun made his ears glow red. Steve didn't seem to know what to say. He cleared his throat and fidgeted with his tie. Water dripped down from his hair and dotted his blotter.

"Can we talk?" I asked.

He nodded uneasily, shifting his weight in the chair. He looked at my hand and frowned. "How'd that happen?"

"Broke it fishing."

"How long ago?"

I didn't answer. "I know I'm not in a good place with you, but I've come to ask a favor."

Steve looked down at his desk and picked at his fingernails.

"I'd like another chance."

Steve shook his head, not looking up. "Impossible."

"I'm not asking for my old job back. I'll take anything."

"The head office can't employ an employee who has been terminated from the company before."

"I know," I said. "But I think I deserve another chance."

Steve looked up and straightened his sunglasses; I could see my disheveled image reflected in the black lenses. "The head office—"

"I'm not talking to the goddamn head office," I snapped. "I'm talking to *you*. I'm asking for your help."

He held up his hands. "You were fired for stealing."

I rolled my eyes. "I didn't know I was paid that money," I sighed. A few tele-operators stopped typing and tried to eavesdrop. The room became quiet. "Why do they care anymore?"

Steve snorted a little laugh. "Because they lost money."

"But I gave it back!" Steve gave me a look like he didn't know what I was talking about. I leaned close and put my hands on the desk. "You *know* I did."

The puzzled expression didn't leave Steve's face.

"Stop," I said, laughing. I bounced my fist off the top of the desk. "Whatever you're doing, just stop."

"What am I doing?" Steve gave me a cute smile.

I gritted my teeth, thinking how Joe would have just reached across the desk and snapped Steve in half, like Lewis's pen. "Listen," I said, "I gave you the goddamn two hundred dollars."

Steve took off his sunglasses and rested them on a stack of fax paper. "It was reported as eighty."

"You told Terry it was two hundred."

"Terry?" His face was scrunched up. "I haven't seen him since you left. His parents made him quit after one of you shippers put a mousetrap in his forklift."

"Terry quit?"

Steve sat back in his chair and made a tired face. "The only person around here I could stand," he mumbled.

"What happened to my money?"

Steve sighed, annoyed. "*What* money?"

I stood up. "You *know* what money!" I said through my teeth. "What did you do with it?"

Steve stood up, too, and rested his palms flat on his desk. His wet hair fell in his face. He met my stare. "You never gave me any money."

"Conrad told me he gave it to you."

"Conrad?" Steve laughed. "Why are you listening to *him*?"

"What do you mean?"

Steve leaned close, his face bitter and ugly. "Who do you think reported you to the head office?"

I fell silent. The air around me buzzed as if an explosion had just gone off. I sat down, blinking like I had just been snapped out of a daydream. "Bullshit," I mumbled. I wanted to call Steve a goddamn liar and slap his face, but I just slumped back in the chair. I stared at Steve's desk until my vision blurred. "Is Conrad here?"

"You can't have a confrontation here," Steve said. He picked up a stack of papers, banged them on the desk, then set them back down.

I snapped my head up. "I want to hear his side."

"I think you should just go home before you get yourself in trouble."

"I have to know if it's true. I'm not just going to take *your* word for it."

Steve looked exasperated by the whole thing. He rubbed his hands through his wet hair and closed his eyes. "You're trespassing on private property. You cannot go on the dock if you are not an employee of this company."

"Call him out here, then. Let's all three talk it out."

"I think I'm done talking about this."

I stood and shoved the chair back. The tele-operators had all turned in their seats to watch me. Steve reached for my arm, but I pulled it away. I marched to the dock, then I ran, slamming the metal doors out of my way.

Steve picked up the telephone and waved it in the air. "Stop!" he shouted. "I'm calling the police!"

The dock was busy with shippers scurrying around with boxes. The steel rafters dripped humidity onto the concrete floor. I ran over to my old desk. Conrad's calendar had been taken off the wall; his green flannel shirt was draped across the back of my chair. The big pile of boxes in the middle of the floor hadn't been broken down enough to be ready for the afternoon trucks.

A new guy, whom I had never met, walked by with tube packages of maps or posters in his arms.

"Where's Conrad?" I asked him.

He nodded at one of the open doors. "Box run," he said.

When I ran outside, the sun stabbed my eyes. The sick smell of low tide was strong in the air. The harbor water was a glimmering mirror of light.

Conrad was walking back towards the dock, pushing a little hand truck and whistling. His bald head was sunburned and he hadn't shaved for a few days. He stopped when he saw me. A few seconds passed and neither of us moved. He squinted from the sun and smiled cautiously. When I didn't smile back, he dropped the cart and ran.

I tore after him, feet slipping on the slick pavement for the first few steps. My wrist hurt from the jolt of sprinting. Heat splashed all around me.

We ran parallel to the water into the yards of other docks. Puddles were scattered around the ground. Conrad reached a chain-link fence with coils of razor-wire on top. He slithered into a gap in the honeycomb of metal. His shirt tangled on the sharp wire. I caught up to him and grabbed his sweaty arm, but he jerked free and kept running. I slid through the hole and followed him.

Years of heavy drinking and laziness must have taken its toll on Conrad. I caught up to him after only a hundred yards. My calves burned; adrenaline numbed the pain in my wrist. I was a step behind him. I could hear his heavy, pained breathing. The after-shave I had once bought him muddled with the sweat under his arms.

I reached a hand out for his shoulder, and as my fingertips touched his warm shoulder, I had a thought, a pang of reality: I had no idea what I was going to do with Conrad, once I caught him. I wasn't sure if I wanted to hurt him or just get an explanation. My face went blank.

And in that second of uncertainty, I heard the sweeping of feet on the wet sandy ground. There was a flash of sun and something exploded in my back and chest. I was on the ground. I couldn't breathe—my chest felt hollow. I put my arms over my face and curled into a ball, smelling sweat and mud. Sounds of grunting and ripping cloth scraped over my ears. I was pulled to my feet by my shirt and flung back to the ground, hard. My bones clacked on the pavement. I didn't know what was going on—my ears were buzzing.

The ground was skillet-hot. I tried to stand, but my legs wouldn't hold my weight. I fell on my knees and looked for Conrad, but I could only see the crystal reflections of sun off the black harbor water. I felt something grab my hair. My head rammed down into the ground again and again. The sound of my forehead bouncing off the concrete made a low thud. I could feel my brain scrape around in my skull in flinty sparks of pain. I felt like I was being scrubbed under the axles of a large truck.

It took a while, but I realized Conrad was beating the shit out of me.

I grabbed him around the waist and held on. I was on my knees. I buried my face in his crotch and breathed in sweat and laundry detergent.

Then I was flung off. I exploded into a large rainbow-slicked puddle, filled with oil and rain and mud. The gray water burned my eyes like acid. I choked a mouthful of it, tasting gasoline and dirty water. The warm water felt good on my body. I wiped my face. There were bits of something hard in my forehead; my shattered skull?

Conrad raged towards me. His face was boiling red, knuckles bloody. With a flailing arc of his right arm, he swatted me over the ear. White flashes raked across my brain like spikes. Then Conrad hit me so hard in the face my eyeballs felt like they had cracked like hard-boiled eggs in the sockets. I fell back into the dirty puddle. I saw strange green and white patterns in the darkness behind my eyes. Conrad knelt on my chest, pinning me in the foul water. His punches bounced my head off the concrete bottom of the puddle. The sound of his knuckles sinking into my face and the sloshing of water were like cannonball explosions. I thought my cheekbone had caved in.

I sprang forward out of the water and wrapped my arms around him again, blinking gray-black water and blood out of my eyes. Conrad threw me off him again, and my body landed on my wrist. I felt a staple rip out of the skin. Razor edges of broken bone sparked against each other. I gritted my teeth and growled from the pain. My eyes popped open. Gnats swarmed around my face in figure-eights. Then they faded into nothing like tiny ghosts—I was seeing stars.

Conrad grabbed me again, but I scrambled behind him and held on. My head somehow ended up under his shirt; my face was pressed against his kidneys. His back was drenched with sweat, stinging the cuts on my forehead and around my eye. Everything was hot like steam. I couldn't breathe. There was a doughy fold of fat right at my mouth. Conrad tried to shake me free, but I knew if he could shake me off again, he would kill me. So I put the roll of flesh in my mouth and bit down as hard as I could. I heard the skin pop as my front teeth met in the center.

Conrad's body spasmed from the pain. He lurched forward and tried to run. I let my body go limp from where my jaw clamped onto the skin over his kidneys. Conrad screamed and clawed my face. But I wouldn't let go. He thumbed me in the eye, and I just ripped my head back and forth like a dog mutilating a chew toy. Conrad fell to his knees and begged me to let go. He had his fingers dug around my jaw, trying to pry my teeth apart. My spit ran down his hand as it dug into my face. I kept my eyes closed and tasted the salt of his skin.

I felt hands on me. Voices shouted. Someone pinched my nose so I couldn't breathe. More shouting.

I let go, and both Conrad and I fell to the ground. I opened my eyes. Conrad rolled on the pavement, holding his back. His eyes were jammed shut and his teeth bared, but he couldn't make a sound. A cop stood over him. A cop stood over me. Two police cars were behind us, blue and red lights flashing and driver doors open.

A young cop with round glasses and a friendly face helped me to my feet. He wore a black shirt and gray pants with a black stripe going down each leg. He led me by my arm to his car. His gun belt's leather creaked as we walked. He opened the back door and sat me down with my feet on the street.

"You OK?" he asked, looking from my forehead to my eyes. "Anything broken?"

I was dazed. "My wrist is broken," I said and held up the muddied cast. I read the cop's silver name badge: D. TRISTAN. He looked to be about my age. His skin was pale and his cheeks were flushed with blood.

Tristan went into his trunk and got out a white metal First Aid kit, then came back and knelt in front of me, putting on a pair of powdery rubber gloves. He reached forward and pulled down the skin under my right eye with one finger. Then he took out a key flashlight and moved it slowly side to side. "Try to follow this light." I turned my whole head to see it, and he added, "Just your eyes." He put the flashlight away and took out a pair of black-handled tweezers. "This might hurt," he said, "but just hold still so we can get it over with."

I kept quiet and let him pick out the hard things that were

embedded into my forehead. I could feel my face swelling faster by the second. My entire body stung and pulsed as if it had been scrubbed with sandpaper. I looked at the tweezers as he pulled them away—he was picking out bits of broken glass.

More cops showed up. A black guy got out of his car and walked up to Tristan. He said hello, then leaned close to my face and laughed. He had a gap in his front teeth and smelled of cigarettes. Tristan gave him an impatient look. The black officer shrugged, then walked back to the rest of the cops.

"Your boss gave us a call," Tristan said. "I was only expecting to see a shouting match."

I smiled and thought: only now did Steve have a reason to call the police on you.

Conrad was handcuffed and put in another car. They had taken his shirt off to look at the wound I had made. My bite looked like a purplish-red football on his back. The extra cops stood around and talked to each other.

"Am I being arrested?" I asked.

Tristan nodded. "Sorry." He dabbed my face with cotton balls dipped in witch hazel. Then he dragged a scratchy, dry towel down my face a couple times. "Once this bleeding stops, you'll be OK." He wiped my face again then stuck a few Band-Aids to my forehead. "You can go to the hospital, if you want."

"I'm fine," I said, but I wasn't. If I'd said I was hurt, it might have led to more questions that I didn't think I had the energy to answer.

Tristan asked me to stand and put my hands on the trunk of his car. He read me my rights and bound my hands together with a white plastic drawstring—handcuffs wouldn't have fit over my cast.

The car Conrad was in drove off. I watched his head bob up and down in the back seat as the car splashed through rain-filled potholes.

Tristan sat me in the back of his squad car; there were no door handles. The spinning lights on the roof sounded like two large marbles rumbling against each other. The CB next to his steering wheel beeped and fizzed with static. Tristan got in the front seat and cleared his throat before starting the engine.

I looked back at RHP. The tele-operators were all watching from the windows. Steve stood outside on the dock among the shippers, his arms folded. He shook his head and slumped his shoulders. I thought he was upset that he had to call the cops on us.

The first of the afternoon trucks pulled into the parking lot. The driver was the man that had thrown a soggy banana at me. He looked like he was in a hurry—as if he had once again promised his wife that he'd pick up their kid from school. I remembered the pile of boxes in the middle of the shipping area; it still hadn't been broken down for the trucks. Now I understood why Steve looked upset.

I WAS TAKEN around the back of the station to a small office. The floors were streaked with black marks from rubber-soled combat boots. A dripping air conditioner rattled above the steel door. Tristan handcuffed my good wrist to a lead pipe that was cemented to the wall next to his desk. I sat on a wooden chair that had warped veneer on the backrest; it crackled when I sat back. There was a row of lockers behind the desk, on top of which were black cans of mace. One officer had his dry-cleaned uniform covered in plastic hanging on one of the locker doors. Behind me was a little room where they took mug shots. And in front of me and to the right was a cage door that led to the cells.

Tristan was filling out a piece of paper that had PRISONER'S ARREST RECORD printed across the top. It had spaces for my height, weight, complexion, eye color, and any scars or tattoos I may have had. I thought of what the Indian doctor at the hospital had told me about having a prominent scar on the back of my hand—I wondered if I should have mentioned it. For my address and name and date of birth, Tristan used my license that he had taken back at RHP. I noticed on the bottom of the paper there was a place for behavior; it had three boxes: cooperative, uncooperative, and agitated. I was checked off as being a cooperative prisoner. I felt oddly proud of myself.

Tristan set his pen on the desk and stood. He undid my cuffs, then had me empty everything out of my pockets. I set a couple of dollar bills and my car keys on the desk, and he listed them on the back of the arrest record. Then he put everything into a plastic sandwich bag.

"Let's get you printed and your picture taken." Tristan led me to the small photo room. There was a veneered counter to the left with silver trim around the edges. A pad of black ink for fingerprinting prisoners was recessed into the top. There was an empty gun cage on the wall and a sign that had a cartoon drawing of a camera with arms and legs and a huge smile—it said something about juveniles not having to be photographed.

It was hard for both of us to move around in the room, especially because Tristan had to keep hold of my arm. The full yellow light above us flickered and buzzed.

Tristan set a white card with green lettering on the table. He started with my right hand, rolling each finger in the ink then doing the same on the space on the card. It hurt the way he had to twist my wrist to get the print to go on evenly.

"Can I do the left hand?" I asked. "It still hurts."

He nodded. "Just roll your fingers—don't smudge it."

I did each finger, and Tristan watched me closely, holding his tongue between his front teeth, hoping I wouldn't mess up.

I had to put four fingers on each hand simultaneously at the bottom of the card. My fingers were greasy from the ink. I looked around the cramped room and noticed that black finger smudges were everywhere—on the walls, on the tin paper towel dispenser, there were even a few hand-prints on the ceiling.

There wasn't a sink in the room, so I had to wash my hands with some liquid soap that was mounted under the desk. It was a gallon tub that had a drawing of an orange slice on the label and smelled like orange taffy. Tristan helped me get the ink off my hands, because I couldn't really knead my hands together to work up a lather. I wiped the soap off with a brown paper towel. My hands were stained gray-orange.

For my picture, I stood behind a sign that was attached to a pole that slid up and down, to adjust to your height. The sign had black dials with white numbers. Tristan rolled the dials so it matched the number on my arrest card: 27513, with the date written under that in marker on a piece of notebook paper.

He took one picture of me facing front, then two profile shots. The exposed pictures came out of the back of the camera. He slid back a latch and a black piece of paper came out. He sat all three pictures on the desk and let them develop.

"You get a phone call now," he said. "You can use the one on my desk, just make sure you call collect even if it's local."

"There's nobody to call," I said, testing the stickiness of the orange soap on my hands by pinching my fingers together.

"You got no relatives to call, no friends?"

"I do," I said. "But I don't want them to see me here."

He shrugged, letting it show on his face that he thought it was a bad decision, and walked me out of the photo room. Then Tristan told me I had a choice of either taking off my shoes while I was in my cell or I could just take out my laces. "I'd just take off my laces," he said in a hush. "Some guys defecate on the floors—and we don't bother cleaning it too well."

He led me through the cage door to the first cell on the right. I had to shuffle my feet as I walked or my boots would have fallen off. Tristan carried a single fat key on a large metal loop. All the cells were to the right. The wall facing the cells was made of glazed brick, with a mint-green rotary phone on a mismatched beige cord mounted all the way at the ceiling. Tristan swung open the heavy door, which moaned on its hinges. He held a hand out, and I stepped inside.

I turned around and watched the iron door seal shut with a soft thud. "What happens to me now?"

"You can either make bail, which is five hundred dollars, or the commissioner will decide what to do with you."

"When's he come in?"

"Could be hours; could be days." He tapped on the bars and raised an eyebrow. "Let me know if you need a phone call." He turned the key in the lock, then tugged the door a couple of times to make sure it was secure. His round glasses slipped down and he pushed them back up with one finger. "I'll be at my desk," he said and walked off. The cage door clanged shut behind him.

The bunks in my cell were two concrete slabs fitted to the beige cinder-block walls. I stood there and wiggled my toes in my loose boots. There were no lights in the cell. People had scratched initials and obscenities into the paint on the walls with their fingernails. An aluminum toilet with a tiny sink attached sat so close to the bottom bunk that you had to step over it to reach the wall. The urine in the toilet was the color of cider. The smell got into my hair and snaked into my pores. There was a button to flush it on the wall under a bolted-shut fuse box. I pressed the button, and the toilet made a low gurgling sound, then the piss bubbled, like someone blowing a straw into chocolate milk. Then it settled again. I sat as far away from the toilet as possible, with my face turned to the painted-black iron bars, smelling the coffee from the office.

I could tell there were other prisoners in the cells that went down the hallway, but nobody talked. A few times I heard feet swishing on the concrete floors and a few throat-clearing coughs, to break up the silence. I wondered if my neighbor was here.

I rested my back against the wall. I wanted to sleep, but I was in too much pain. My mouth felt wrecked. I rubbed my tongue along my teeth and gums, to feel the damage. My bottom front teeth were loose; I could wiggle them back and forth with my tongue, as if they were only hanging on by threads of nerves. The insides of my cheeks had stopped bleeding on the drive over, but I could still taste the steely blood in my saliva. Where my teeth cut into the insides of my mouth every time Conrad punched me, ragged meaty chunks of skin dangled. I picked them off with my fingers, tasting the oily ink and bitter soap. The bleeding started again. I stood up and spat into the steel sink, a glob of white bubbles streaked with red. I found it hard to spit without having a line of drool run down my chin. Then I noticed there was a tooth stuck in the drain. It had been broken in half, yellow on the outside, white along the break. The roots were stained with a layer of gums.

I sat back near the door and told myself to just spit on the floor from now on. My face was so swollen it hurt to open my mouth. I sat there and felt my cheeks balloon up. Coming into the barracks, Tristan had given me a wet paper towel that had been frozen. I had held it to my face until it melted and he took it away.

The thick smell of urine had started to get to me. It fused with the candy-orange smell of my hands into an indescribably bad odor. I stuck my face as far as I could through the bars, like a kid trying to get his head through the banisters in his house. The bars cast bands of shadows onto my arms. I looked straight ahead to the glazed tan wall of the hallway, and tried to forget where I was.

After a few minutes, I heard a voice in the cell next to me.

"Who's over there?" he whispered.

I didn't answer. I knew it was Conrad.

"Tom?" he asked. "Are you there? I got to talk to you." He waited for me to say something. When I didn't, he let the air out of his lungs in a sigh. "Can I please explain? I did everything I did for a reason. Just let me tell you."

"No," I said.

"*Please*," he cried. "My wife was going to leave me." I didn't respond, but he kept talking, anyway. "She called me about a month ago and told me that she wouldn't be there after I got released from the house." He paused, waiting for me to say something. "Do you hear me?" he hissed. "My goddamn wife was leaving me!"

"Good," I said. "About time she came around."

"I know you don't mean that."

"I don't?"

"You have a right to be pissed. But . . ." He began to say something else, but he stopped himself.

I listened to him start and restart a bunch of sentences, looking for the right way to say what he had to say. I just stared at the shadows on my arms.

"I had to prove to her that I was making changes," he said finally. "I had to show her that I wasn't going to be a shipper for the rest of my life. The night she said she was leaving me, I lied and told her I had been promoted. I didn't know what else to do." He was crying already. I wanted him to just shut up so I could get some sleep. "She seemed so happy that I couldn't tell her the truth. Goddamnit, I can't lose my *kids*!" He blubbered for a bit, sucking in air in sharp gasps. He was crying so hard it sounded like he was laughing. "I turned you in so I could get your job." Someone down the hall told him to shut up.

"How did you know I was paid extra on that check? Terry said all that stuff is kept in Glen Burnie."

He sniffed. It sounded like mud being sucked through a tube. "I hired my roommate."

"The Pentagon guy?"

Conrad made a dog-like whimpering noise as a way of saying yes. "As long as I signed him in and out on the house's log, so he could stay out as late as he wanted, he agreed to help."

"How did he get my records?"

"I don't know," he blubbered. "He just made a phone call."

I remembered what his roommate had said to me when I called from Ocean City, about my problems only being a phone call away from being solved. I now knew what he meant—he was offering his help to stop Conrad.

"He got me your file, your time sheets, and a list of the amounts of all your paychecks."

Thinking of the furtive ex-Pentagon guy stealing my information made my palms sweat. I felt queasy knowing that a man who had taught people how to fake their deaths had access to my financial information. I could picture him meeting some old colleague in a restaurant and slipping manila folders to each other under a table.

"I searched through the pages all night," Conrad went on. "And I found that Thanksgiving you were paid but didn't work. Then I showed it to Steve, and he started the paper trail on you."

"How long ago did you show him?"

"About a week before we were hiding up on the roof. I wanted you to go down to talk to him about the shippers doing the clean-up, hoping you'd piss him off enough that he'd bring it up. But you didn't go down, so you kind of pissed away my plans. So I talked to him again on Monday morning."

"Didn't Steve want to know where you got these checks?"

"I tried to make it sound like I was fed up with you. I told Steve that when you got paid for the Thanksgiving you didn't work, you waved the check in our faces, bragging that you ripped off the company." He sniffed again, but he was all cried out. "I said that I stole the check from you and copied it. Did my best to make it seem like I was looking out for the company."

"So did I even have to pay the money back?"

"No," he said. "They took the eighty dollars on the chin."

"But you said it was over two hundred."

Conrad laughed sheepishly. "That was how much Terry's doctor bill was. Originally, I just wanted to get you fired, and you wouldn't have to pay a dime. But Terry was going to sue me for putting the trap on his seat. So I came up with the extra money at the last minute, to pay his doctor's bill."

My mouth hung open. I thought of that fold of skin on his back that I had bitten, and wished that I had ripped it off. Any chance of me forgiving Conrad blew away like sand. Everything that was wrong with his life he brought on himself. He put Terry in the hospital for a laugh; he wanted my job, so he got me fired. And when he got caught by Terry's family, he thought nothing of ripping me off to pay the doctor.

"I needed the goddamn money—I'm sorry. What did you want me to do?"

I laughed at him.

"And I'm sorry I had to rough you up. You shouldn't have came after me like that."

"You were hitting me like you hated me."

"I don't *hate* you," he said. "I just got caught up with everything—my wife, the house, bills. I didn't see you anymore. All I saw was every shitty thing about my life that's all gone wrong, rolled into one person. I took it out on you, and I'm sorry." Conrad sounded so insincere I could picture him rolling his eyes as he said this. "It was just a fight. Don't take it so personally."

"So," I said, not wanting to talk about the fight anymore, because it was most personal thing I had ever experienced, "after all this, did your wife even take you back?"

Conrad paused. "No. She left for Ohio two days ago. Took the kids with her."

I laughed.

Conrad shook his cell door, a soft rattling sound. "Don't

laugh, asshole!"

I couldn't help it. I opened my mouth and exploded, feeling the swollen skin of my face stretch, and the cuts in my mouth bleed again.

Conrad kicked the bars. "Don't *laugh*!" he barked, and the guy down at the end of the hallway told him to shut up again.

"You lost your wife and kids, and you're still stuck at RHP," I said. "Enough to drive a man to drink."

"You can shut your goddamn mouth!"

"You'll be needing those Polaroids of your wife, Connie. That's all that's left." I rested my forehead on the cold steel bars and let my laughing splutter out. "Knowing that she dumped your stupid ass makes this whole mess worth while."

I wasn't sure if I was truly mad at Conrad, or just thought I was supposed to be. But I knew I had to let him know that our friendship had dissolved right there in our separate cells. I did this by telling him that he should kill himself. I told him he should just be a drunk, because it's the only thing that he could do well. I told him any mean-spirited thing I could that I knew would hurt any chances of us ever forgiving each other. And I didn't mean a thing I was saying. The words seemed to float just beyond the bars, close enough for me to see their ugliness, but far enough out of my reach that I couldn't take them back.

Conrad never said another word to me. He just let me go on and on. The person at the end of the hall now told me to shut up. But I just kept on. I felt like a madman setting fire to a photo album—plastic pages turning with the heat, flashing pictures of Conrad on the dock and in my apartment. Images of Conrad twisted in the air like glowing embers outlined in sparks and fire. With every mean thing I said, the fire seemed to spread, making things between us beyond repair. As his image bubbled over in brown and black spots, his face faded from my memory, along with my anger. All that was left was exhaustion.

I woke to the sound of the cage door in the hallway whining on its hinges. Shoes clicked on the ground, then came to a halt. I looked to my wrist to see what time it was, but I didn't wear a watch now that I had a cast over my arm.

The silhouette of a man stood in front of my cell. He put a key in the door and popped the lock. The door swung open, and he stood to one side.

"Time to go," he said, voice deep and coarse. I could smell cigarette smoke on him.

I could only see through bruised, swollen slits. Everything was dark and blurry. My whole face had gone stiff and sore while I had slept. I went to speak and winced under the pain in my mouth. "Are you the commissioner?" My loose front teeth clicked together when I closed my mouth, and my eyes jammed shut from the pain.

The man tapped his foot. "Someone posted your bond," he said.

I wanted to ask who, but it hurt too much to talk. I stood up and took a step forward, and my foot slipped out of my boot.

The man breathed out impatiently. I saw that it was the black cop that had laughed in my face when Tristan was bandaging me. When I stepped into the light, he bugged his eyes and laughed at me again. His face was still a blur. I felt like a mole stepping out into the sun.

He took me into the office and set the plastic bag with my keys, wallet, and money on the desk. I had to sign and date the back of the arrest record, stating that I had received all my property. I squinted around the room with my puffy eyes. Three teenagers sat on a bench by the door, handcuffed and shackled. When I squinted at them, one boy mumbled, "Jesus," under his breath.

I wanted a mirror to see how bad my face looked, but I doubted this cop would give me one. I wondered if Tristan was still here. I saw a flash go off in the mug shot room. Then I heard him tell someone to face right and to stop laughing.

The cop checked the box marked BOND on the HOW RELEASED part of the arrest record. His pen made sharp scratching sound on the paper.

"What happened to the guy who was in the cell next to me?" I asked, face throbbing as my lips made out the words.

The cop didn't answer. He was writing on the card with my

fingerprints on it.

"Did someone bail him out?"

The cop still didn't answer. He set a stainless steel clipboard with a yellow piece of paper on it. "Sign this," he said making an X at the bottom of the page. I signed it, and he gave me the pink copy.

"Well, is he still here?" I asked.

The cop sighed and started shuffling papers. "Clocked out ten minutes ago. This is *my* time. You can leave now."

"Can you even tell me who bailed me out?"

He glared at the top of his desk. "If you would *read* the form I gave you."

I folded the paper and put in my back pocket, then walked to the door before he said another word. When I got to the door, I groped for the knob like a blind man, bracing myself for the bright sun. But when I stepped outside, the sky was black. Sensor lights glowed yellow in the humidity of the parking lot like giant dandelions. The windows of the office buildings around me were dark. Everything appeared as if I were looking through a film of wax. The headlights of the cars on the street spread pearl-colored washes on the pavement.

I took the pink form out of my pocket and tried to read it. Tristan hadn't charged me for fighting or assault. Instead, he gave me a two-hundred-dollar citation for trespassing on the property of the shipping yard next to RHP. The ticket said I could go to court in Towson or just pay the fine. I scanned the paper for the name of the person who had posted my bail. In a box for release information, there were two spaces—one for a last name and one for the first name. In the first space, the name GREENE was written. I got excited, thinking it might have been Fritz. Then I read the name in the next blank, and I rubbed my eyes, thinking I was reading it wrong. The first name of the person who had bailed me out was SANDY. The tattoo of the girl on Fritz's arm flashed in my mind.

I squinted at the parking lot. Cars and pavement were muddled. I couldn't see where the tops of the building ended and the sky began. How would she even know who I am? I wondered. What does she want with *me*?

I heard a car door creak open then shut. I tried to focus my eyes, but everything was blurry-edged, as in a dream. I saw a little white truck parked under a steel street light. It was a rusty Datsun, just like the one Greg had driven to Joe's.

Leah walked over and stopped about ten feet away from me. Her glance went from my face to my dirty cast to my face again. "What have you been *doing* to yourself?" She stepped forward and touched my cheek. "Your *face*." She hugged me.

I didn't hug back. My arms hung at my sides.

Leah let me go. She looked down at the smudges of dirt on her shirt, rubbed off from my filthy clothes. She had on a white tank top with green trim around the neck and a pair of jeans. Her feet were bare. She brushed the dirt off her shirt then wiped her hands on the front of her pants. Wind scattered her hair in her face.

"I don't know what's going on," I said.

Leah rubbed her goose-bumped arms and looked at her feet. "I told my dad everything," she said, nodding to the ground. "I told him I was staying at my grandmother's; told him about the baby. I even told him I tried to have an abortion."

"Was he mad?"

She shook her head. "He was mad that I didn't tell him. But he said there was no point in being angry with me for getting pregnant." She looked back up; her eyes were bloodshot and tired. "I moved back home. Mom and Dad will help me raise the baby."

"What about Ron?"

Leah smiled without showing any teeth, but her eyes remained sad. I could tell that he was gone.

I went to say I was sorry, but she cut me off.

"I really *tried* to have an abortion," she said. "I'm not doing this for attention or because I'm stupid. I've been in the waiting room a dozen times, trying to move out of the chair when the doctor was ready. I even got undressed one time and let a nurse examine me. But I could never do it." She looked up at the sky and stretched her neck. "That night you found me on the bus—I had been in the parking lot of an abortion clinic all day. I sat on the curb and prayed for the guts to just go through with it."

We stayed quiet for a long time. Leah didn't look as if she was going to cry, but I could tell talking about this was wearing on her.

"How did you find me?"

"My dad took me to Joe's. I figured we still had things to talk about."

"No, how did you find me *here*?" I asked, pointing to the space on the ground between us.

"Joe said he'd lend me a truck." She frowned, suddenly distracted. "He's strange, isn't he?"

I nodded.

"He said that if I didn't come back with you and all your things, I had to pay him fifty dollars for gas and wear on the truck."

A smile muscled its way onto my puffy face.

"He seems to like you," she said. "He told me he misses you."

"No, he didn't," I said.

"Well, no. Not exactly. But I could tell."

I looked up at the dark sky and couldn't get rid of my smile. "He still wants me?"

Leah nodded and stepped forward. I could smell the cleanness of her hair. She was standing only a couple of inches away from me, so close I could feel the warmth of her body. "We all miss you," she said. "Uncle Fritz has been going nuts looking for you. He's the one who gave me directions to that RHP place. He said I might be able to get your address or phone number off somebody. But when I got there, some lady told me you were arrested for fighting. I called my uncle when I learned how much bail was, and he wired the money to a grocery store for me. He told me on the phone that if I couldn't get you to come back, he was going to come for you."

I held up the pink release form. "It says that Sandy Greene bailed me out."

"Yeah, that's me. But I've always gone by my middle name: Leah."

Leah backed away. "I wish it didn't have to be like this, but

I'm sorry. I know this isn't your problem. Still, I think . . ." Her voice trailed off into a murmur. It was as if she had been practicing what she wanted to say to me the whole ride up from Dewey, but now that the words left her mouth, it didn't feel right.

I stepped forward and rested my broken hand on her shoulder. She faced the ground, and tucked a few stray stands of hair behind her ear. Leah stepped forward and buried her face in my dirty, sweat-damp shirt. Her breath burned through the fabric. I put my chin on the top of her head. Her hair was soft and tickled my face in the wind. "Can you drive us somewhere?" I asked.

She nodded, breathing in my sweat and the dried dust from the puddle.

The salty air sealed my eyes shut. "My mom wants to meet you."

seventeen

FRITZ carried a four foot section of wall to the window. The edges of the two-by-fours jutting between the two slabs of sheet rock were ragged and blond. Fritz staggered as he pitched the awkward wreckage out. I listened as it crashed onto the grass, then started the reciprocating saw again. The blade gnashed through the studs and sheet rock. My eyeglasses fogged, and a yellow spray of sawdust prickled my lips. When the screaming motor whined down, Fritz took the piece of wall and heaved it out the window. It made me nervous when he did this, because he never looked outside to see if anybody was standing below. I set the saw on the plywood floor, and Joe came up behind me and looked at the open space where the wall had been.

The air was thick with dust and heat. Chips of wood and spare nails lay on the ground like confetti. My hands were cramped from using the saw, and the vibration of the motor still rattled through my bones, like an echo. Fritz wiped the sweat off his brow with the back of his forearm and rested, hands on hips, before going back to work.

It was now late August, and the apartment on the third floor of Joe's house was halfway complete. We had just knocked out a wall to make two of the smaller rooms into one big living room. All the stowed-away junk Joe had kept in here was now piled in the hallway, but the old smell of polish and mouse crap lingered. The room I had been sleeping in was to remain the same, although Leah and Mrs. Hartly were now giving it a coat of antique-white paint.

Joe walked over to where the wall we had just removed connected to the perpendicular wall. He rubbed his hand down the rough and ugly six inch gap. "Got to fill this with some drywall," he said, his voice bouncing in the empty room.

I heard an airplane's engine outside, cutting through the sky a mile above us. It drifted past over the trees, and we all kept still as its drilling motor was replaced with quiet. Only then did I feel exhausted. I rubbed the grit and sweat that had collected on my neck and wiped my hand on the back of my pant leg. It was three in the afternoon, and the sun had baked the house like pottery in a kiln.

We had opened all the windows, but every breeze that came in was miserable, like hot breath in our faces. Joe didn't have any air conditioning—didn't believe in it. He said he only liked the cool breeze of a window fan. If we wanted artificial cold, he had said, we could go bait trotlines.

I looked at Fritz, sweating and red-faced in his long-sleeved western shirt, and I wanted to throw him into the walk-in freezer, just to see if he'd bleed steam like an overheated engine. Fritz's hair hung in his face in sweaty blades. All day, as he cut drywall across the hall in what was to become my kitchen, his hair would flop in his face, he'd push it back, then it would fall again.

Although Fritz had cut all the drywall, I had to tack it to the walls. Joe didn't care that my wrist was still in a brace. He said that I was showing a lot of promise, but my hanging of drywall was shoddy at best.

"This way," he'd said, arms folded, "when you mess up, you're the only person who has to see it. It'll be a good incentive for you to get your act together."

Joe had been hard on me all summer. After returning from trotlining, he would give me lessons in the barn, teaching me how to cut dovetails for drawers with a router, how to make tenon shoulder joints with a table saw, and how to measure for pitch and run and rise. When I wasn't being taught how to use power tools, he had me read a volume of *Audel's Carpenters and Builders Guide* every week. On the boat, as I scooped crabs from the trotline, he'd quiz me.

"Black walnut, Tom?" he'd call out over the burping Volvo motor.

I'd say, "Used for interior finish and cabinet work."

Then Joe would change the questioning. "I was thinking of making a cofferdam to build another pier. . ."

"You'd want to use red spruce." Then when we'd get back, he'd make me build a cofferdam—or a stool or a bench or hip joints for rafters.

I didn't mind the work. It was interesting, and everyday I felt myself becoming more useful. In July, Joe even trusted me enough to go alone to a woman's house in Groves Burton, to build shelving in her walk-in closet. The woman's husband watched me the whole time and asked me questions about the tools I was using. He was friendly but unnerving. When he didn't have a question, he'd shake his head and say, "Bet I could do this if I had them fancy tools," just to break the silence. He even said this when I was using a hammer.

Joe stretched his back and yawned. "That's all for today."

At the mention of quitting, Fritz collapsed, arms flopping to his sides as if he were some machine that had just been unplugged.

I went to the bedroom to check on Leah. From the hallway, I could hear Mike and Doug in the bathroom, giggling as they told each other jokes. They were replacing the pipes under the sink with PVC and copper.

"What do you name a girl with one leg shorter than the other?" Mike said.

"What?" Doug asked, already laughing.

"Eileen!" Mike burst forth, and on they jabbered like the blackbirds outside in the oak tree.

I opened the bedroom door. The smell of latex paint was sour and dizzying. Leah and Shelly (who wouldn't speak to me unless I called her by her first name) were sitting on the bed eating purplish stalks of rhubarb. There was a little saucer set between them with an ant hill-sized mound of sugar on it. Leah and I had furnished this room with some of the things Joe had

in storage. I'd thrown almost all of my furniture from Baltimore away—everything except the clunky phone that had once
caught fire. I now kept it on a dinner plate on a gum wood
night table next to the bed. The plate was to protect the surface
of the table in case the phone ever caught fire again.

Leah held up her arms. Her fingertips were dabbed white.
"Like it?"

I looked around the room. The walls were glistening wet
with paint. All the furniture had been scooted to the middle of
the room. Joe had lent us a cheval dresser, a golden oak bed,
and a washstand with a bevel-edged mirror. Joe said Leah and
I could use these things for as long as we lived with him.

The only piece of furniture that Joe hadn't loaned us was a
bookcase, which I had made out of some cull stock of Norway
pine. When I had finished building it and staining it, I rubbed it
with steel wool, then stained it again. Joe came into the barn
after I had put on the second coat and said, "You better not be
finished." He folded his arms and nodded at me. "You're a
professional now. Professionals use no less than three coats of
varnish."

This was the best compliment Joe had given me, because it
didn't involve me showing promise or improving or progress-
ing.

The bookcase looked empty, though. A few of my borrowed
builder's guides were piled on the bottom shelf, and Leah kept
a plant on it that was already dying. There were only two books
on it that I owned. On the top shelf, I kept a copy of Bradford
Waltz's memoir and a copy of *They Are Still Among Us*. I had
bought the memoir off of Joe for two dollars. But I had found
George Regal's book in a junk store in Groves Burton. A man
had a table set up outside his shop, piled with milk crates filled
with Billy Fury and Herman's Hermits records, the damp smell
of basements and silverfish sunk deep into the sleeves. He had
a velvet-lined suitcase filled with individually wrapped Doc
Savage adventure novels, priced at ten to fifteen dollars a piece.
Next to that was a grapefruit box with books that cost a nickel.
I weeded through the junk on this table while I was waiting for
Leah to get off work from Lewis's; she was a crab steamer and

usually came home watery-eyed and smelling peppery. At the bottom of the grapefruit box, I found Dr. Regal's book. The pages were tan-brown at the edges, and the binding glue had dried up. But George Regal's superior half-smile was still clear on the front cover.

I didn't buy the book to read it. I just liked having it around. The sight of the aged and crumple-edged paperback sent me back to the spot on the floor next to my father's La-Z-boy. Sometimes, I'd pick it up and fan the pages across my face, just to breathe in its age and mustiness.

Fritz came in the room and sat on the floor in front of Shelly. She wrapped an arm around his neck and stuck a stick of rhubarb in his mouth.

Leah was wearing a paint-blotted bandanna over her hair. She held up a bitter stalk of rhubarb by the white end, but I shook my head. "Shouldn't you get started on dinner?" she asked. Fritz and Shelly looked over and agreed. Then they added that Leah should go help me.

I plopped down on the bed between Leah and Shelly. "I'll go in a minute."

"What are we having, anyway?" Fritz said.

There was a ham thawing on the chopping block in the kitchen, but before I could answer, Doug burst into the room. "They're here!" he said. "A truck just pulled onto the driveway." Mike came up behind him with his hands in a white towel.

Leah and I ran downstairs, and Mike and Doug followed behind us. Shelly and Fritz stayed put. As I was halfway down the stairs, I heard my door shut.

I stepped onto the porch and watched my brother's Dodge pick-up come to a stop on the dusty driveway. The ladders and tools in the bed shifted and clanged.

Strawberries were in bloom and lay in green bands in the fields. Leah stepped next to me and put a hand on the small of my back. Mike and Doug stayed further back on the porch, where there was shade.

The doors on my brother's truck had SHAWN BANNER—PRIVATE CONTRACTING in three-inch white vinyl letters. His windows were tinted as dark as mirrors. Leah walked down the steps, took off her bandanna, and stuffed it into the back pocket of her jeans. Then she combed her hair with her fingers and straightened her shirt.

My mother stepped out and staggered a bit until her cramped legs could support her weight. She tilted her head back to take in all of Joe's house, then had to put a hand on the hood to keep from falling back. Her hair was pulled back into a ponytail, streaked with a ribbon of gray. My mom put on a straw hat and shut the door. Leah ran over and gave her a kiss, but I stayed on the porch and waited for Shawn to step out.

After dinner, I wanted to take him out on the boat for some late night fishing. By this time I was catching catfish and blue snappers; toadfish didn't bother with me anymore. All day I'd hummed with nervous energy, waiting to take my brother on the boat to show off what I had learned. I daydreamed that Shawn would be clumsy with his fishing gear, then quiet with embarrassment after I'd shown him how to fix his lines. I imagined taking him into the barn while I made up the brine solution for the week. I'd even give him the honor of dropping the egg in the salty mix to see if it would stay afloat.

The driver side door opened. I hopped off the porch, no longer able to act calm, and Lisa stepped out of the truck. She shut the door, lips pressed tightly together, and tried not to look me in the eye. I walked over to her, unable to keep the disappointment from showing on my face. I dragged my feet through the gravelly pavement as I approached her.

Lisa shook her head before I could say anything. "He has a lot of work to do this weekend," she said soberly.

I pointed to the ladders and toolboxes in the pick-up. "But you've got his truck!"

"I'm sorry," she said, with a twinge of sadness and disgust drawing out the words. She stepped forward and grabbed my brace. "This about to come off?"

"In a week." I wanted to call Shawn's house just to catch him at home, with his television buzzing in the background.

Lisa scratched me softly under my chin. "Have we ever needed your brother to have fun?" she asked.

I nodded, then walked around the back of the truck to take

their bags.

Just as Leah and I were ready to go downstairs to eat that evening, I found Doug in my bathroom looking for cologne.

"I don't wear any," I told him.

"Well, do you have anything that smells nice?" he asked, briefly considering a can of shaving cream he had in his hand.

"What do you want to smell nice for?" I took the can from him and placed it back in the medicine cabinet.

"I just want to smell good." He toed an elbow joint of PVC on the floor that he'd install tomorrow. "*You're* wearing a dress shirt," he said. "Why do *you* have to look nice?"

"Because I'm having dinner with my mother."

"Well, if everybody downstairs is going to look nice, I don't want to stand out."

"Just tuck your shirt in and chew with your mouth closed," I said, but Doug didn't move. To look at him you'd think he was being asked to go downstairs without any pants. Really, he wanted the cologne to impress Lisa.

All day Doug had stumbled behind her as if he were being dragged by a foot of invisible wire. When I had driven Lisa and my mother around the farm on the golf cart, Doug insisted on coming along. He kept to himself the whole ride, but when we stopped and walked around, Doug stole glances at Lisa and laughed at everything she said, even when she was being serious.

When we were heading back to the house, I let my mother drive the little cart. She and Lisa sat up front, Doug and I in the back. When we rounded a curve along the cornfield, a strong wind blew Lisa's hair back in Doug's face. I looked over and saw him, grinning at the smell, eyes closed.

Doug looked at his face in the mirror and sighed.

"Doug," I said, snapping him back to reality, "she's thirty-seven."

At first he looked as if he were going to pretend like he didn't know what I was talking about, but instead he said, "I know it," then slumped his shoulders and walked out of the room. "Come on," he mumbled, "let's go eat."

Shelly, Fritz, and Doug sat at the dining room table with their backs to the stuffed marlin over the fireplace. Mike, Lisa, my mother, and Leah were crammed together on the other side. Joe and I sat at the heads of the table.

The windows were open, and fans were creating a constant breeze through the room. It had been in the upper nineties today, and the heat still lingered in the walls and rafters as night approached.

My mother had baked a ham with slices of pineapple and dots of cherries on its checked-grooved skin. I boiled a dozen ears of silver corn and made some scallop stew. Fritz sliced the ham and had everybody hold out their plates. Then we passed around the corn, potatoes, biscuits, and a little silver dish of cinnamon to be sprinkled on the pink ovals of meat. Mike, Lisa, Shelly, and my mother drank chilled red wine with orange slices floating in the red liquid. Fritz, Joe, and I drank the home-brewed beer. Doug and Leah had ginger ale.

The sound of talking and silver against china was like the whirring of a motor. The chandelier above the table spread strange shapes on the whiskey-colored walls.

Shelly was talking to my mother with half a new potato sprinkled with paprika stuck on her fork. She pointed the white ball at Leah and me. "I was the one who talked Fritz into getting these two together," she said, then looked back at him while he was talking to Doug (who was staring at Lisa and not paying attention) about how he used to collect robots when he was younger. "Can you believe Fritz wanted to set her up with a teen-aged mechanic he works with?"

Leah shook her head, cheeks glowing from embarrassment.

"I saw this boy only once—and he's the first person I've ever met who had fouler language than Fritz." She almost took a bite of the potato, then paused. "He even cussed when he was shaking my hand as we were introduced."

Leah smiled at my mother. "Shelly keeps my uncle grounded," she explained. "If it wasn't for her, God knows where that man would be now."

"Oh, he means well," Shelly said. "But half the things he does make sense only in his mind. He even wanted to set you up with some guy from my diner who's on parole." Shelly leaned over and patted Leah on the knee. "We had almost given up on trying to find you somebody until Tommy came along."

After that, my mom and Shelly exchanged stories about me as a kid. Leah listened and squeezed my knee when I tried to get them to stop. Then I looked around and listened to pieces of conversations. Mike and Lisa were talking about how long it had taken her to get here, and what routes she had driven. Doug and Fritz were going on and on about robots—but now they were talking about real-life robots the police use to dispose of bombs. Fritz was doing all the talking. Doug just nodded, eyes fixed on my brother's wife.

Lisa wore a sleeveless green T-shirt and white shorts. Her hair was curled and held back with a white headband. "So," she said, nodding to Mike and Fritz, "Tom tells me you two are brothers."

Mike looked down at his plate, and Fritz nodded weakly.

Lisa turned to Mike, who was examining his ham. "And you're Leah's father?"

He nodded quickly, then said, "Tom tells me your husband's a private contractor," with no real purpose or interest.

All week I had noticed that Fritz and Mike barely spoke to each other if Leah was in the room. If she was gone, they were chatty and friendly, but the second she appeared again, their conversation diminished to nods and grunts. Then one of them would walk out. Tonight, when we were all jammed together at the dinner table, Mike and Fritz had a hard time even looking at each other. It was as if there was a strange balance to their relationship with Leah, which secrecy kept stable. The funny thing was that everybody knew the truth. Leah had found out long ago that she had been adopted by Mike and his wife (who had refused our invitation because Fritz was going to be here). She knew that Fritz was her real father, and they, I was sure, suspected that this was something she had figured out. But not talking about it seemed to keep them happy. And they pressed on.

I sat back in my chair and folded my arms, listening to the voices muddle together in the warm glow of the room. Mike relaxed and listened to Lisa go on about my brother's business; Doug even mustered enough courage to join the conversation. Shelly and Fritz were picking food off each other's plates, shiny-faced from alcohol. And my mother and Leah made plans to pick strawberries tomorrow morning while I was on the boat.

But I noticed one voice missing from the conversation. I looked across the table at Joe. The candles in the centerpiece blurred his face. He was sitting back in his chair, arms folded just like mine, looking from person to person without saying a word. I watched him over the blurring flame of the candles. The talk became a low hum in the air. Joe looked up at the ceiling and nodded his head as if someone were whispering plans into his ear. Then his eyes scanned down the walls and onto the carpet. His expression was bright as he looked at all the polished wood and the luster of his antiques. The marlin had been dusted and its indigo hide shone like vinyl. The decoy ducks on his fireplace mantle were in perfect formation. While looking at the table a drunkard's careless smile cracked his leathery face. Now that the dead-skin layer of dust and junk had been peeled, the rooms were full of light, and Joe's house had come alive with laughing voices. It had all come together for him.

ABOUT THE TIME I HAD PLANNED to take my brother out on the boat, I was sitting alone on the dock. The heat of the boards numbed the backs of my legs as I stared at the silvery surface of the water, listening to the trees hiss in the wind. The water lapped against the wall of cattails and grass around the dock, and bats fluttered above me so dark I couldn't make out their shapes.

I heard the soft putter of an engine. I turned and saw a set of headlights needle through the blackness. The Datsun came down the path and stopped twenty feet away from the dock. Dust swarmed in the long bars of the headlights, and the smell of oil and gasoline gathered in the air. The engine died in a raspy cough, and Leah stepped out, wearing a pair of jeans shorts and a white tank top, a pink beach towel slung over her left arm.

Leah and I came to the docks a lot on hot nights, to cool off in the water. Then we'd drive back with the windows down, feeling the rushing wind dry our skin.

"I've been looking for you," Leah said, bare feet sweeping on the dock. I felt the vibration of her steps clamber up my back. "Having a think?"

I nodded, then turned back to the oil-black water and stayed quiet. The night was filled with noise. Cicadas screamed in the trees around us, crickets sang to each other in bedspring chorus, and the dock lines on the crabbing boat cracked as they tightened.

Leah sat down next to me and hooked her arm under mine. I smiled at her, then looked down at my knees.

She nudged me with her hip. "You need to start telling me what's on your mind," she said. I didn't say anything, then she nudged me again.

"Why'd my brother have to not show up?" I slashed the air as if I were swatting a fly. "If there was one person I wanted to see this weekend, it was him."

"You never mention your brother, though. I didn't think you two were close."

"We're not," I said. "I was thinking we might *become* close."

Leah rubbed my arm. "I'm sorry."

"Goddamnit," I said, then plopped my head down on the heels of my palms. "We're not kids anymore—you'd think he'd give half a shit about me by now."

"Honey," Leah began, trying to calm me down, but I cut her off.

"I'm finally at a point in my life where I think me and my brother can get along. I mean, we both do contracting, he likes fishing, and we're *related*, for Christ's sake." I shook my head. "I just wanted to impress him finally."

Leah scooted forward and pitched herself into the water. Water flicked up into my face and shimmering rings marked where her body entered. A second later, she resurfaced and pushed her hair back out of her eyes. "Keep me company," she said.

"I don't feel like it," I said.

She blinked water out of her eyes. "I want to talk to you," she said, voice wavering from the effort of treading water. "Get in."

I climbed off the side of the dock and let myself fall into the water. Millions of bubbles like carbonation came into being down below and closed in on me. I swam forward and met Leah. I couldn't touch the muddy bottom. The gentle current of the water moved around us.

"I wouldn't try so hard to impress your brother," she said. "There's other people in the world who need you."

"I know," I said, feeling guilty.

"No. You don't." Leah tipped in the water and floated on her back, blinking up at the darkness.

"Who, then?"

Leah looked over, dipping in the mercury-like water. "His name is Robert Leonard Banner," she said. "You'll meet him in January."

I smiled and rocked backward so I too was facing the sky. The moon was like a white pebble dropped into a pool of tar. Its light shone grizzly on the treetops.

The water rushed around my ears and cut off all sound. I could only hear the pulsing of blood in my skull. Heat lightning sparked miles above me, purple-orange flashes behind a dirty veil of clouds.

Leah floated next to me, holding my hand. She stayed quiet, and I thought of all the people in Joe's house. I pictured them in the parlor. Joe would be sipping his beer, deep in thought in some corner. The lilting talk of Shelly, Lisa, and my mother murmured over the scratchy music of the record player, laughter from Doug and Mike and Fritz cracked any silence that thickened the atmosphere in the room. They would all talk with each other until sleep clamped down on them like a dizzying fog. Then in the morning they would greet each other as if they weren't strangers. I pictured them around the kitchen table, sleepy-eyed and anxious, wondering when Joe and I would return from work. For this, I couldn't stop smiling.

A cool wind picked up off the shore. The current rippled, then hooked around my arms and legs, dragging me away. My fingers pulled out of Leah's grip and my skin prickled from the cold. I looked over and saw her saying something to me, hand outstretched. But I could no longer hear. The water welled around my temples and around my face. My body felt heavy. I closed my eyes and breathed in the cool air. Then I let myself relax into the warm black water.